"LOOK OUT!" Keir shouted . . .

Something arced down from above, trailing fire like a comet. Keir slung Maris down onto the porch as the fire exploded in a parked car, blowing glass in every direction. A torrent of flame belched from the car windows. Maris flung her arms up over her face as heat and smoke blasted across her skin.

"He's on the roof!" someone shouted. "Shoot him!"

Maris tried to see through the smoke, but then a sun burst into life on the pavement between the cars, blossoming into a vast, incandescent billow of flame. As the explosion rolled up the steps toward her, she wrenched the door open. Something hit her between the shoulder blades, sending her sprawling. Then she saw Keir slide past her, the back of his leather jacket scorched and smoking. She scrambled after him, yanking him out of a pool of sparks and bits of flaming upholstery.

Keir sat up and put his arms around her, holding her so tightly it hurt. They clung together, silent and still. Through the open doorway, she could see that the night had turned into a flickering orange hell.

"He's getting away," she said through chattering teeth.

"Maybe not," Keir said. And he held her tightly. . . .

SHADOW VENGEANCE
WENDY HALEY

ZEBRA BOOKS
KENSINGTON PUBLISHING CORP.

To all my friends at Russell Memorial Library,
who have been there from the beginning.
And special thanks to Dr. James Cochran,
for being so generous with his medical expertise.

ZEBRA BOOKS

are published by

Kensington Publishing Corp.
475 Park Avenue South
New York, NY 10016

First Printing: March, 1993

Printed in the United States of America

One

The newspaper rustled softly as he turned the pages. Anger rolled through him. Reading the Sunday paper used to be one of his favorite pastimes. Now it just added to the slow burn that was his stomach these days. The world had turned to shit. People didn't like their government, their country or their neighbors.

He flipped through the pages to find the continuation of a front-page story, something about a county sheriff who'd been caught picking up a prostitute on a Houston street. The press was ripping the man to shreds.

He found the continuation. Folding the paper in half, then in half again, he began to read. A moment later he whistled. The sheriff was in deep doo-doo, that was for sure—caught in the act of getting a blow job from a transvestite prostitute.

Well, he thought, that was one career dead and gone. Maybe that might have gone over in California or something, but not down here in Texas. Folks here were conservative about that old demon s-e-x. Especially the kinky kind. Hell, old Joe-Bob the sheriff would have had more social standing if he'd been caught strangling his mother.

Something farther down the page caught his attention. This was the Personals section, one he scorned. Just a bunch of nuts trying desperately to meet other nuts, date, fall in love and marry, thence to make one another miserable for the rest of their lives. The ad that had caught his attention was double-sized, standing out sharply among the ranks of uniform rectangles that filled the page.

And it said. . . . It said. . . . His brain went numb for a moment. Then feeling flooded back in, washing through him like acid. He read the ad again, moving his finger along the lines as though to imprint them on his flesh, then once more, trying to comprehend the scope of the disaster.

He pushed the paper away and stood up, pacing the length of the room with quick, agitated steps. If only he could make himself believe it was a coincidence. But there weren't any coincidences that good. And if someone else happened to see it. . . . The past came flooding in, crowding into his mind in a jagged jigsaw puzzle of images. Blood and pain, flavored with the tang of fear that had never lost its savor.

He pressed the heels of his hands against his eyes. "I can't *deal* with this!"

Damn it, this wasn't fair! The room suddenly seemed too small, the air thick and smothering. For a moment, he thought he might be having a heart attack. He sat down again, putting his head between his knees, and after a moment the feeling passed.

His self-confidence seeped back in. He'd had a lot of time to make contacts. He'd done a lot of favors for people over the years. Useful people, people with skills he could use, people who could move around freely where he couldn't. It was time to call in some of those favors.

There were debts to pay. Big ones.

Two

The phone started to ring as Maris staggered into the kitchen, juggling her purse, a stack of mail, and two heavy bags of groceries.

"Hang on," she muttered, dumping her load on the table and snatching up the phone. She was just in time to hear a click as the caller hung up. "Damn!"

Suppressing a groan, she pried her boots off and let them fall. The worn linoleum floor was cold under her stockinged feet as she padded from table to refrigerator and back again. The freezer, she noted, needed defrosting.

She shouldn't be so annoyed about it. After all, this old house had some advantages: it was near the new highway, a straight, twenty-minute shot to the medical center, and rent was cheap. Cheap counted for a lot these days.

The thought of money pulled her over to the table. She began sorting the mail into two stacks. Accounts payable, accounts receivable. The first stack was a couple of inches high; the second contained one envelope.

7

"Good news first," she said, ripping it open. "Hey, they sold the dragon pin I left over at the Gold Earring! Two hundred smackeroos. Let's see . . . minus the ten percent consignment fee, then figuring in time to design and make it, cost of materials, we come out with a profit of . . . ah, approximately eighty-two dollars. That comes out to about fifty cents an hour. Wow, we're getting better and better."

"Mom?" Cyndi called. "Can you come here for a minute?"

"I'm coming, hon." Maris thrust the check into her pocket as she walked toward the living room. It would be nice to be able to share some good news with her daughter.

She found Cyndi lying on the sofa, her back propped against a stack of pillows. The child had discarded the knitted hat she wore in public, and the smooth dome of her head gleamed in the bluish light from the TV.

"Mom, will you put a movie on for me?"

"Wouldn't you rather play Battleship?"

Cyndi shook her head. "I'm kind of tired."

A knot formed in Maris's stomach. Today had been one of Cyndi's bad days. Right now, bad days were the exception. But a year from now, they'd be the rule. "What would you like to see?"

"*E.T.,* I guess."

"Again?" Maris stroked the smooth curve of her daughter's head. "You know, you look a bit like a space alien yourself."

That got a hint of a giggle. "How about you fix me up with some glow-in-the-dark antennae? That would really flip people out."

Maris slid the movie into the VCR, then sat down on the edge of the sofa. Gently, she tucked the folds of the big, flowered afghan around Cyndi's body. Leukemia had been hell—the tests, the fear, the chemotherapy and radiation treatments, the metamorphosis of a ten-year-old child into a cancer patient.

And none of it had worked. God, the prospects had been so hopeful! Ninety-five percent of children with leukemia went into complete remission after chemotherapy. Great odds, but they meant nothing to those who happened to fall in that other five percent. Like Cyndi. Then came new, stronger drugs in new, stronger combinations, but they didn't work, either. Now the only hope was a bone marrow transplant. Since the likeliest donors were Cyndi's close relatives, Maris had instantly volunteered. But she wasn't compatible.

And that was when Mom told me I was adopted. Maris Durant no longer existed. This new woman had no name, no past. The only thing she knew about herself was that she'd been born somewhere around Houston, Texas, thirty-four years ago.

Maris sighed. She wasn't sure she *wanted* to know more. And as a person who valued privacy, she shrank from pushing herself upon a woman who probably wanted to be left alone. But the best hope of finding a donor lay in her immediate biological family. It was Cyndi's only chance, and Maris was willing to turn the earth itself inside out to give it to her.

"Mom?"

Instantly, Maris's attention refocused. "Yes, hon?"

"You look so sad."

"That wasn't sad; that was indigestion from the pizza," Maris said. "And it's all your fault, anyway."

Cyndi giggled again, louder this time. "My fault?"

"Yeah. You're the one who wanted a pizza with

9

everything on it. I'm not positive all that stuff was even edible." *Reality check,* Maris told herself. *Don't overdo the jolliness; it's worse than the tears.* Forcing a smile she didn't feel, she pulled the check out of her pocket and snapped it open. "Look what I got today."

"Hey, they sold the dragon pin! Two hundred dollars—way to go, Mom!"

"Thanks, hon." Maris got to her feet. "I think this calls for a celebration. How about I get us some ice cream and we'll snuggle under the covers and watch TV, just like old times? I've got your favorite."

"Rocky Road? Ooooh, yeah." Cyndi scratched the side of her head, her nails leaving faint red marks on the pale skin. "I think my hair's starting to grow back. Dr. Polk said it would. Do you think it'll be blond again?"

"Maybe. But if it isn't, would you rather be a redhead or brunette?"

Cyndi shrugged. "Any kind of hair will be great. Remember how you used to put it in french braids?"

"Yeah. It was almost down to your waist." The memory was powerfully visceral, so real that Maris could almost feel that fine, golden hair in her hands. Quickly, before the tightness in her throat turned into tears, she turned and hurried back to the kitchen.

As she was spooning Rocky Road out into a pair of bowls, she heard the clatter of a lawn mower outside. Mr. Simonedes. In this semi-rural neighborhood of two- and three-acre lots, the old man used his riding lawn mower to get around to his neighbors. She liked Arthur Simonedes; he was one of the few people she knew who didn't greet her with "and how is Cyndi doing today?"

"Hello, Mr. Simonedes," she said as she opened the door.

"You knew it was me?"

"Who else would ride his lawn mower when there are six inches of snow on the ground?"

The old man laughed, setting his fat jowls and belly shaking. "Better than walking, no?"

"Better than walking, yes," she said. "Won't you come in?"

"No, no. My wife is holding supper for me. But the mailman—what are we going to do with this new fellow, eh?—delivered this to my house instead of yours." He held out a manila envelope.

It was from the *Houston Chronicle*. Maris took it from the old man, her hand shaking noticeably. "Thank you, Mr. Simonedes."

"You need anything, you call," he said.

"I will. Thanks." She retreated into the house, hardly hearing the lawn mower's roar as it chugged back down the driveway.

Tearing the envelope open, she upended it over the table. A single letter fell out. It stared at her like a pale, rectangular eye. Her past might be in that envelope—her past, and Cyndi's future. Life or death, hope or more disappointment in one small envelope.

Three weeks ago, she had placed an ad in the Personals section of every Texas newspaper she could find. It said, "Looking for information about a woman who gave a baby girl up for adoption in May of 1958. Very urgent health reasons. Please help." There had been four replies before this one: three requests for money and one almost incoherent missive from a woman who thought Maris might be the reincarnation of her dead aunt.

Maris tried not to hope too much. She tried to

make herself believe that she was prepared for disappointment. But she wasn't. Cyndi's life might lie here in her hand.

With a sudden, impatient movement, she ripped it open. "Be there," she muttered, taking a single, folded sheet of paper out of the envelope. "Come on, be there!"

The note consisted of two typewritten sentences that said, "I know who you are. You weren't wanted then, and you aren't wanted now."

Maris gasped, staggered by the cruelty of it. Deliberate, malicious cruelty.

"I know who you are. You weren't wanted then, and you aren't wanted now." The words seemed to burn themselves into her heart.

"Damn you! Damn you, damn you to hell!" The tears started then. She sank to her knees, beating her fist against her chest in a futile attempt to stop the pain inside. "I can't let her go, I can't!" she whispered. "God, if you're up there, listen to me. Help me. Give me what I need to save her!"

Suddenly she felt her daughter's thin arms come around her from behind. Momentary shame washed through her at the thought that her sick child had to comfort *her*. She bowed her head, her short, straight hair falling in a light brown curtain across her vision.

"It'll be all right, Mom," Cyndi murmured, her arms tightening around Maris's waist. "You'll see."

Maris covered those wasted limbs with her hands, holding on for dear life. Hers and Cyndi's.

Sleep eluded Maris that night, as it did many nights. She needed rest to handle the stress, but stress made it impossible to sleep. It was a cycle that drained her physically and emotionally, but one she couldn't seem to break.

"I might as well get some work done," she muttered, pushing the covers aside.

She padded barefoot to the big desk at the far end of the room. This had been her late husband's desk, the only legacy Paul had had from his grandfather. She ran her hand along the top, feeling the familiar gouges where Paul had carved his name when he was twelve. The memory of his face and voice was vivid, almost as real to her as the wood under her hand. Almost.

"I miss you," she murmured, switching on the desk lamp. "I wish I had you with me on this one, Paul. It's a toughie."

She sat down in the big leather chair that still seemed to remember Paul's contours. He'd been tall, a full six inches over her five-ten height. The chair had been built for him, and although it had never quite been comfortable for her, she had no desire to replace it.

I wonder if she is tall. Maris grimaced, annoyed that she'd let that thought slip through. She shouldn't care. She didn't care. After all, she was looking for a donor, not a mother.

Her gaze went to the bills that were stacked neatly on the desk. Thank God insurance picked up most of the medical bills, but even twenty percent was a staggering amount of money. Money she didn't have.

Maris pushed the subject from her mind. She was getting good at doing that; after all, there was simply nothing she could do about it. She didn't have that kind of money and wasn't likely to get it. Designing custom jewelry, while it had the advantage of letting her stay home with Cyndi, was hardly making her

13

rich. But with only a high school diploma and three years of secretarial experience to offer, a "real" job would pay less than what she was making now. Besides the fact that no new boss was likely to tolerate the amount of time she spent running to the doctor, the truth was she just didn't want to leave Cyndi. Dr. Polk had said they had a year, two at most, and by God, Maris wasn't going to miss any of it.

With a sigh, she leaned her head against the back of the chair and looked at the bookcases that held the makings of her livelihood: gold and silver wire, molds and tools, neat ranks of cases holding beads and feathers and semi-precious stones. She was good at what she did. Her jewelry was unique and clever, and she had persuaded a number of ladies' apparel stores to handle it on consignment. Her designs were becoming increasingly popular. But not nearly fast enough.

She reached for the drawing of her latest creation, a necklace that echoed the bold, primitive grace of Celtic jewelry. This one was going to hit well; she could feel it. But something was just a little off. Perhaps if she made it just a tad slimmer there, just where the clasp joined . . . yes, that was it! She began to sketch, her pencil moving across the paper with swift surety.

A few minutes later, something tugged at her awareness, pulling her out of her creative well. The acrid smell of smoke stung her nose, and she swung around to face the door.

"Cyndi?" she called softly.

Smoke oozed beneath the closed door. A thin mist of it crawled along the ceiling toward her. Terror pulled her to her feet and got her moving. Vaguely, she heard the chair topple to the floor behind her.

She flung the door open and ran out into the hall—and straight into a wall of smoke. It closed around her in a thick, choking blanket, stealing her breath and sight and sending her to her knees.

The air was purer here near the floor, and her brain began to work again. *Don't panic. If you panic, you're dead, and Cyndi's dead.* Every moment counted; this old house was going to go up like pile of tinder. Maris felt behind her with her feet, nodding when she found the open doorway to her room. She knew where she was. Cyndi's room was about twenty feet down the hall.

Twenty feet, that was all. Holding the end of her pajama top over her mouth and nose, Maris began crawling down the hallway. There was no up or down or direction, only smoke. It was so thick now that she couldn't see the floor beneath her knees. There wasn't much time. She moved forward as quickly as she could, keeping her right shoulder against the wall for orientation.

Maris lurched as her shoulder bumped against a ridge. The doorjamb! Reaching up blindly, she felt along the door for the knob.

"Mom?" Cyndi's voice was faint through the closed door.

"I'm coming! Stay where you are!" Maris shouted. She breathed in reflexively, then coughed it back out.

Maris found the knob. She turned it, nearly falling into the room, then hastily closed the door again. The air in here was almost pure, and she drew it into her starved lungs with great, gasping breaths. Her eyes were still watering, blinded from the smoke.

"Mom, are you okay?" Cyndi asked. "That smoke—the house is on fire, isn't it?"

Maris managed to focus her eyes at last. Cyndi

was standing beside the bed, her arms wrapped tightly around her body as though she were literally holding herself together.

The sight pulled Maris to her feet. "Put your robe and slippers on, sweetheart. We're getting out of here."

"Can we get downstairs?"

"We'd never make it," Maris said. "There's too much smoke. And I think the fire's down there."

She grabbed a pillow and jammed it under the door. Then, as calmly as though she had all the time in the world, she went to the window. She wanted to run. She probably would have panicked completely if it weren't for Cyndi.

Maris heaved at the window. It moved upward a fraction of an inch, then stuck. *Nothing in this damned house ever works, not even the smoke alarms!* The floor beneath her bare feet felt warm, and she could hear the fire roaring downstairs. Time was running out fast. Terror rose in her throat, thick and bile-tasting. She forced it away.

"Cyndi," she called over her shoulder. "Do you remember that escape ladder I bought a couple of months ago?"

"Y-yes."

"It's under your bed. Get it out for me, will you?"

As Cyndi rushed to obey, Maris braced her feet and tried to force the window upward again. She might as well have tried to lift the house for all the good it did.

"Damn it!" she gasped.

She snatched up a nearby chair and swung it against the window with all her strength. The glass shattered, and cold, clean winter air swept into the room.

16

"Here, Mom." Cyndi thrust the ladder into her hands.

Maris set the hooks in place over the windowsill and let the ladder roll down along the side of the house. It had looked sturdy enough when she'd bought it. Now, however, when she had to trust her and Cyndi's lives upon it, it seemed a mere spiderweb construction of chain and flimsy plastic rungs. *Thank God it's only a two-story house!*

She held her hand out to Cyndi. "Come on, honey. Let's go. I'm going to carry you —"

"I can climb down myself, really I can."

Maris shook her head, even as she admired her daughter's guts. But guts weren't going to get her down that ladder in one piece; strength was. And strength was the one thing Cyndi didn't have. "Sorry, hon, but I've got to carry you."

She backed out of the window and lowered herself until her feet were on one of the ridged plastic rungs. The ladder shifted sickeningly for a moment, then steadied. Gripping the chain with one hand, she reached out to Cyndi with the other. "Come on, carefully now."

Cyndi climbed down until she was poised upon the rung above Maris's. "I'm scared I'll make you fall," she said.

"I'm not going to fall." Maris turned Cyndi to face her. "Put your arms around my neck and your legs around my waist and hold on tight. Don't move, or you'll throw me off balance."

Once the child was in position, Maris began to move downward, feeling carefully with her bare feet to make sure she was steady on one rung before leaving another. She had to angle her body backward to keep Cyndi from banging against the wood siding,

17

and the strain sent jags of pain shooting through her arms and shoulders. She lost track of time, lost track of everything but keeping her grip on the rungs. Finally she had to stop for breath. Daring a glance downward, she saw that she was poised a few feet above the kitchen window.

"We're almost there," she panted. "Can you hang on?" When she felt Cyndi nod against her chest, she gathered what was left of her strength and moved to the next rung.

Just as she began to grope with her foot for yet another, the window exploded outward. Maris found herself hurtling through the air, surrounded by shattered glass and bits of burning wood. Then something slammed into her back, and the world went black.

Three

"Mom? Mom, please wake up!"

Maris followed that voice upward through shrouding layers of awareness. The darkness lessened, gray instead of black, and then she opened her eyes. She found herself lying in the flowerbed on the far side of the driveway. Cyndi moved into her field of view, a dark silhouette against the orange glare of the fire.

"Mom, please talk to me."

"Are you all right?" Maris croaked.

"Of course I'm all right! You were underneath me when we fell!" Sobbing, Cyndi clutched Maris's hand to her chest. "You didn't wake up for the longest time! I was so scared!"

"It's okay now," Maris said, reaching up with her other hand to wipe the tears from the child's face. Other than a couple of scratches and a bruise on her chin, Cyndi seemed unhurt. They'd made it. They were alive.

"Just lie still," Cyndi said.

"Honey, I can't stay here. The snow's melting under me, and I'm getting wet." Now that some of the shock was wearing off, Maris was beginning to register the condition of her body, most of which was hideously uncomfortable. She ached from head to foot, and it hurt every time she took a breath. Slowly, she levered herself to a sitting position.

The house was completely aflame now, fire spouting from every window. The heat had melted the snow around the house, and the wet asphalt of the driveway was a river of orange light. A loud, grinding roar came from the house, the death cry of wood stressed beyond its strength. Then the roof fell in. A column of flame belched high and triumphant above the ruin. Sparks showered down, hissing into the snow.

"We've got to move," Maris said. Waving Cyndi off, she rose slowly and shakily to her feet. God, it hurt! She managed to hobble to the shelter of the big maple tree in the side yard.

A flutter of movement out in the street caught her attention. Then a shape materialized out of the smoke-filled darkness—Mr. Simonedes on his lawn mower. It was a sight Maris would never forget: the old man in his plaid bathrobe, slippers on his feet, riding his steed hell-for-leather up the driveway.

If she didn't hurt so much, she might have laughed. Instead, she leaned her good side against the tree and waited for her rescuer to arrive.

The old man parked the mower and hurried toward her, leaving dark footprints in the disintegrating snow. "Maris! Cyndi! Thank God you got out," he gasped. His hands fluttered like startled butterflies. "What should I do for you?"

"Did you call the fire department?"

"Yes, yes, Mrs. Simonedes called the 911."

As though on cue, sirens sounded in the distance. They grew rapidly louder and closer, and a moment later a police car came screaming down the street. A fire engine followed, attended by a flock of vehicles. Red and blue lights flashed like fireflies in the darkness. *Too little, too late,* Maris thought.

The policeman reached them first. Although he hid it well, Maris saw his involuntary double-take when he noticed Cyndi's bald head. "Is there anyone else in the house?" he asked.

Maris shook her head. "We're the only ones who live . . . lived there."

"Your names, please."

"I'm Maris Durant, this is my daughter Cyndi, and this is Mr. Simonedes, my nearest neighbor."

The policeman's gaze lingered for a moment on the lawn mower. "Just try to relax, Mrs. Durant. The ambulance will be here in a moment. We'll get you to a hospital as soon as we can."

"I'd like my daughter to go to Tremont Hospital, Officer," Maris said. "The doctors there are familiar with her medical history. I can't—" she broke off, realizing that both Cyndi and the policeman were staring at her as though she'd completely lost her mind. "What's the matter?"

"Mom, he isn't talking about *me* going to the hospital," Cyndi said. "He's talking about you."

"Me?" Maris asked in astonishment.

"Look at yourself, Mom."

Maris looked down at the front of her pajamas. Dark patches marked the beige flannel, and the knees were completely torn out of the bottoms. She touched the largest of the dark spots. Her fingers came away red. Shocked, she looked up at the others.

21

"You've got a big cut on your head, and there's blood all over your face and in your hair," Cyndi said. "Why do you think I was crying?"

"But it doesn't hurt," Maris said, knowing it was a stupid thing to say. It did hurt. It hurt like hell. She felt dizzy all of a sudden, which was stupid, too.

"Look out!" Mr. Simonedes yelled. "She's going to faint!"

A moment later she was surrounded by uniforms, and felt herself being lowered onto a stretcher. Lying down didn't seem to help the dizziness, but one thought remained perfectly clear. "I want my daughter," she said. "To the nearest E.M.T."

He nodded. A moment later Cyndi appeared beside the stretcher, taking Maris's hand in a grip that hurt. Someone had given the child a baseball cap with "St. Louis Cardinals" embroidered on it.

A stranger's kindness, Maris thought. *So rare in these cynical times, so very precious.* Her throat ached with emotion.

"It's going to be all right, Mom," Cyndi said.

"Of course it's going to be all right," Maris retorted. "We got out, didn't we?" Moisture trickled down her cheek. She wiped it away and was surprised to find that it wasn't blood, as she expected, but tears.

One of the paramedics bent to insert an IV in her arm, then looked over at Cyndi. "You ride up front with the driver, sweetheart."

Maris felt the stretcher being lifted, and pain, and then she found herself in the white and stainless interior of the ambulance.

A paramedic leaned over her, his dark hair ha-

22

loed with gold from the light behind him. His eyes were brown and gentle. "I want to check those ribs, Miss Durant—"

"Mrs. I'm not—Ah!" Pain lanced through her as he touched her, making her gasp, and the gasp made it hurt even more. Then it was over. "Wow," she said on the exhalation.

"Hurts?"

"Yeah. Are they broken?"

"A couple might be. We'll have to look at an X ray to be sure." He cocked his head to one side. "Your daughter said you cushioned her fall when the window blew out."

She nodded. "I kept a five-gallon can of kerosene in the pantry. For the heaters. Stupid to keep it—Ouch!"

"Can you remember how far you were from the ground when you fell?"

"Ah, we were just above the top of the window."

"About eight feet from the ground?"

"I think so."

He blew his breath out sharply. "You carried her that far down that ladder?"

"My daughter has leukemia," Maris said, as though that explained everything.

"I see," he said, as though it had.

The ambulance began to move. As it swung out into the street, it hit the pothole just beyond the driveway. Maris gasped as the vehicle lurched, bouncing her painfully. Her consciousness pulsed on and off in rhythm with the whirling lights. Then, for the second time that night, the world went dark.

* * *

Maris poked at the pile of reconstituted eggs on the tray in front of her. Hospital food. "God, I hate this stuff," she snarled. "I want out of here."

"It's only been one day," Cyndi said.

"It's been thirty-six hours and twenty minutes."

Cyndi curled up in the chair beside the bed, tucking her feet under her like a sleepy cat. "Quit complaining. The nurse said the doctor might let you go home this afternoon if you check out okay."

Home? What home? Maris laid her fork down, no longer interested in even pretending to eat the awful stuff they called scrambled eggs. Everything they owned had gone up in flames last night; clothing, furniture, her livelihood. Her wedding pictures. The only possession she still had left was her eight-year-old Regal.

And our lives, she reminded herself. *The most precious thing of all.* "I called Grandma to tell her we're all right. She sends her love."

"Was she upset?"

"Not very." Actually, Maris hadn't told her mother more than that there had been a fire at the house, and that she and Cyndi were fine. Ava Guthrie was in a nursing home, confined to a wheelchair by arthritis, and Maris hadn't wanted to frighten her. Later, when things were sorted out a little better, she could be told the whole story.

Maris forced herself to smile. "Grandma told me about a place called the Steadham Motel that rents rooms by the week. We can stay there until I can find us another place. It's less than a mile from the nursing home. We might even be able to walk there to visit her."

"Sounds great."

Silence fell; they both knew Cyndi wasn't going to be able to walk that far, even on her good days. Then Maris sighed and reached to tug the brim of the Cardinal's baseball cap. "I like the hat."

"He was really nice." Cyndi reached up to adjust the bill. "He knew I felt funny in front of all those men, so he gave me this. I'm going to wear it forever. Or at least until my hair grows out."

Someone knocked at the door. Maris eased upward in the bed and called, "Come in." Maybe it was the doctor, come to release her from reconstituted eggs and Jell-O.

The visitor was tall and thin, somewhere in his late thirties, judging by the sprinkling of gray at his temples. In Maris's opinion, he didn't look much like a doctor; he was too eager, and his smile was sharp enough to slice bread.

"Hi," he said. "I'm Carl Hansson. How are you feeling, Mrs. Durant?"

Maris was confused enough to answer. "Pretty good, considering."

"Considering that you have a concussion and two badly bruised ribs, and that they pulled about a pound of glass slivers out of your skin?"

"You're no doctor," Maris said. "Who are you, and what are you doing here?"

"Don't get upset, Mrs. Durant." He raised his hands. "I'm from the *Post/Dispatch*."

Maris reached for the call button.

"My brother Mike was one of the paramedics who brought you in," Hansson said, his words tumbling out in a rush. "He told me about Cyndi having leukemia and how you lost everything in

25

that fire. That's his hat your daughter is wearing."

Maris held her finger poised over the button, but didn't push. Not yet. His brother's act of kindness bought him a hearing. "And?" she prompted.

"I'd like to do a story on you and your little girl."

Ordinarily, that would have been enough for Maris to stop listening. But she looked past the brash smile to his eyes, and they were the same gentle brown eyes that had looked down at her in the ambulance. His brother's eyes. She took her finger away from the call button. "Sit down, Mr. Hansson. Tell me what kind of story you want to write about us."

"Human interest." He framed an imaginary picture with his hands. "Widow and child lose everything in fire—"

"That's what I was afraid of," Maris said. "No."

"You wouldn't believe the amount of community support an article like this can rally."

"I'm not interested in charity," Maris said.

"I didn't say you were."

"And I don't want pity. Yours or your readers'."

He met her gaze steadily. "Mrs. Durant, we're not talking pity here. I came because my brother told me about a lady who carried her daughter down the side of a burning house. That's heroism—"

"It's being a mother," Maris said in automatic denial. "And hardly newsworthy."

"People like heroes," he continued, as though she hadn't spoken. "So do I. Come on, Mrs. Durant. It's a great story, full of poignancy and drama."

Maris grimaced. "Make them weep, huh?"

26

"Absolutely."

"You'll write it with or without my approval."

"Again, absolutely," he said. "But I *want* your approval. I want to give *you* to my readers. I want them to feel your pain and fear, sheer gut reaction. That's where the power comes to move people."

Maris wanted to refuse. Every cell in her body shrank from the prospect of putting Cyndi and herself in the public eye. But Cyndi needed a bone marrow transplant. If the newspaper story prompted even one person to come forward for testing, that was one more chance of finding a donor. Maris closed her eyes for a moment, gathering her courage, then looked at Hansson.

"I'll give you your story," she said.

"Great—"

"But it's not the story you think it is."

His smile faded. "It isn't?"

Maris turned to her daughter. "Cyndi, take off the hat."

Cyndi obeyed. Her bare scalp gleamed in the fluorescent light, every curve, every bump starkly revealed. Maris sighed. Even after all this time, the sight never failed to make her chest knot with pain. To give Hansson credit, he didn't flinch. Maybe he was the right person to tell Cyndi's story.

"There's your hero," Maris said, pointing to her daughter. "She doesn't need new clothes or new toys. She needs a bone marrow transplant."

Hansson pulled a small tape recorder out of his pocket and turned it on. "Would you repeat that, Mrs. Durant?"

Maris hesitated for a moment, intimidated by the thought of laying her heart out for all the world to see. Her most private feelings there in black and white. "Cyndi, maybe you ought to leave for a while. It might upset you to hear some of this."

"I want to stay."

Maris nodded. Cyndi had incredible courage, and had borne much more than this. Besides, this was her story, and her life. No one had a better right to be here.

"Mrs. Durant?" Hansson prompted.

She looked away from the machine and into his compassionate dark eyes. She'd talk to the man, not the machine, and not the faceless multitude who would soon be peering into her life. When she finally began to speak, her voice was steady.

He wanted guts, he wanted pain and power, so she gave them to him. She gave him chemotherapy, she gave him the despair she'd felt when treatment failed, and then she gave him the frustration of not being able to find the person who might save her daughter's life. And through it all, she didn't cry.

But *he* did.

It was Cyndi who comforted him; Maris was curled in around her emotions, too shattered herself to offer him anything.

"I thought I'd been a reporter long enough to be immune to that," he said afterward. "Man, oh, man, you pack a punch, lady." He sighed, then shook himself like a wet puppy. "I need to take some pictures. Let's try it without the hat, Cyndi."

He went through several rolls of film, posing Maris and Cyndi together, then Cyndi alone, with and without the hat. By the time he finished, Maris had regained her composure.

As he put his camera back into his briefcase, she

28

asked, "Well, Mr. Hansson? Did you get the story you wanted?"

"Yeah. And a little more to boot." He snapped the briefcase closed. "I'll be in touch."

Four

"That can't *all* be for me," Maris protested, staring at the box the deliveryman was holding. It was stacked to the top with envelopes. Letters.

"Are you Maris Durant?" he asked.

"Yes, but—"

"These are all addressed to Maris Durant, care of the *Post/Dispatch*. Mr. Hansson sent them over. Where would you like me to put them?"

Numb with surprise, Maris pointed to the table near the tiny kitchenette.

The deliveryman plopped the box down on the table, cracked his knuckles loudly, then came back to Maris. "Here. Mr. Hansson said to give you this," he said, thrusting an envelope into her hands.

He hurried back to his truck and drove away. Maris stood looking after him for a moment, then closed the door against the noise of the traffic.

"What is it, Mom?" Cyndi asked.

"It's from Mr. Hansson," Maris said. She pulled his letter out of the envelope and read it aloud. "Hi, girls. Just wanted you to know that our story was picked up by the *Associated Press*. It went all over the country. This box of mail is only the beginning; get ready to do a lot of reading. Hansson."

"What a sweetheart," Cyndi said.

"A sweetheart would have read the mail for us."

"Come on, Mom."

There was a tremble in her voice, and Maris knew it wasn't from emotion. This was one of Cyndi's bad days. She was pale and drawn, and had been too tired to get out of bed this morning. Living in this motel room didn't help much.

Forcing a smile took some doing, but Maris managed it. "How about we read some of those letters together?" she asked.

"Sure."

Maris took a double handful of envelopes out of the box and carried them to the bed. "This is incredible. It's only been a week since Mr. Hansson's story hit the paper."

Cyndi picked one off the stack and opened it. "Hey, there's money in this one. Five dollars. The letter's from a farmer in Illinois. He says he'd like to send more, but he's got four kids . . . well, you get the picture. People really are nice, aren't they?"

"Most of them." Maris was glad for the man's kindness, but wished he hadn't sent the money. With a half-formed plan to send it back, she asked, "Is there a return address?"

"No. Come on, Mom. Let's open the rest!" Cyndi dragged a handful of envelopes closer and began tearing them open.

Just like Christmas morning, Maris thought. She hadn't seen that much color in her daughter's face in a long, long time. It was worth the loss of privacy, worth anything.

It took them almost two hours to get halfway through the box. They collected a hundred and seventy-six dollars and fourteen cents, the fourteen cents having come from a six-year-old boy in Louisiana.

Finally, Cyndi fell asleep mid-letter, completely exhausted. Maris couldn't stop. She read letters from old people, from children, from churches and garden-clubs. There was such an outpouring of goodwill that she was overwhelmed by it.

Then she came to an envelope addressed in bold, block letters. A Houston postmark. Maris shuddered; she'd recognize that writing anywhere. She knew she shouldn't open it.

Slowly, she slid her fingernail beneath the flap to loosen it. The letter was brief and cruel. It said, "Bitch. You're not wanted, and you're not welcome. You or your daughter."

She crumpled it in her fist, sickened by it. After the outpouring of compassion from the other letters, it was devastating. "Bitch" it had said. "Bitch." Had it been written by the woman who had given birth to an unwanted girl-child all those years ago? Maybe. Probably. Who else would know? Who else would care?

Maris tried to imagine that woman. To her discomfort, her mind conjured someone very much like herself; a tall woman, broad-shouldered and slim, with a determined jaw and long, clever hands. She looked down at her own hands, trying to imagine them printing the word "bitch" in bold, black letters and sending it to the mother of a dying child.

"I feel sorry for you, whoever you are," she whispered.

With a shudder, she tossed the note into the

trash can. Then she reached into the box for another handful of letters. Reading them would go a long way in renewing her faith in humanity.

But she couldn't forget that ugly letter or dismiss the person who had written it. Even amid the outpouring of sympathy and support from all across the country, the taint of that cruelty sat in her mind like a fat, black spider, ready to bite at any moment.

"You're stupid to let one lousy jerk outweigh all these other nice caring people," she muttered under her breath.

It *was* stupid. But it was also true. And why? Because it was personal. That letter pointed to her and said, "You, Maris Durant, aren't wanted, were never wanted, and your daughter can die because I don't give a damn." It mattered because she wished she could think her mother had given her away because she'd been young and afraid, unable to support herself or a child. She wished she could think there had been love. And that was the dumbest thing of all.

The phone rang, startling in the quiet room. Maris jumped up hastily to answer it before it rang again. "Hello?"

"May I speak to Maris Durant, please?"

It was a nice voice, Maris thought. No, it was a great voice, deep and vibrant—Bing Crosby, Billy Idol and Elvis all rolled into one package. "I'm Maris Durant."

"My name is Keir Andreis. Carl Hansson gave me your number. And please don't get upset with him for doing so. We've known each other for a number of years, so he figured I was safe."

33

"What can I do for you, Mr. Andreis?" Maris asked.

"I saw the story about you and your daughter here in the Austin *American-Statesman*. I'd like to help."

Maris shook her head. He was going to offer her money, and she didn't want to hear it. "Please don't think I'm ungrateful, Mr. Andreis, but I can't accept any money. I know you're trying to be kind, but —"

"Pride gets in the way."

"I'd prefer to call it dignity," she said with as much of it as she could muster. "Besides —"

"Besides," he cut in with that rich, wonderful voice, "money isn't going to buy what your daughter needs, is it?"

Her breath went out sharply. "You don't pull any punches, do you?"

"Neither do you," he said. "Mrs. Durant, I didn't call to offer money. I know how little money means when it can't buy health. You see, my brother died of bone cancer twenty years ago."

Maris drew a deep breath. "Oh, I see."

"I'm campaign manager for Texas Senator John Hauck," he said. "I think I can do something for you."

"This isn't politics."

"No, but it's people. And the more who allow themselves to be tested, the more likely you are to find a donor. You're a public figure now, Mrs. Durant. We just make you more of one. We'll educate the public about leukemia and bone marrow transplants."

"I don't know," Maris said, instinctively rejecting

34

the picture he was painting. "Letting Hansson run the story was one thing, but this. . . . Even if I could do that, what makes you think the newspapers would be interested?"

He chuckled. "I wouldn't worry about that. I'm a pro at managing the media. And if I can get people to the polls, I bet I can get them to a doctor to be tested as donors. And if we happen to flush out your birth mother in the process, so much the better."

"It sounds so manipulative."

"You bet it's manipulative. And you can't care. For your daughter's sake, you can't allow yourself to think about it."

"Is that what you did for your brother?"

"No. He had bone cancer, and there was nothing anyone could do to stop it. But if there'd been any chance of saving him, any chance at all, I would have taken it. There were times when I think I'd have ripped someone's heart out to give to him if it would have helped."

Her throat ached with tears. *He knows! He really knows.* "It isn't right to feel that way."

"Maybe not, although it's a hell of a big gray area. But I *did* feel that way, and so do you. So would anyone else who stood in our shoes for five minutes."

Maris was both repelled and fascinated by the conversation. This unknown man had pushed aside all the normal codes of converse and was treading with brutal honesty across things she would never have considered discussing with a stranger.

"You don't have to worry about staying in a hotel," he said. "Senator Hauck's mother, Sophie, has

35

offered the use of her home. It's convenient to Houston, yet far enough away to put you out of the rat race."

"What rat race?"

"The publicity rat race. At Gavilan Farms, you'll be insulated from the worst of it."

"That's very kind, but I couldn't impose."

"The house is too big for any guest to be an imposition," he said. A teasing note came into his voice. "You and Cyndi would really like it there. Unless, of course, you've become attached to your present living quarters."

"You know," Maris said through her teeth, "that I'm standing in a motel room right now, don't you?"

"I *did* have to go through the switchboard."

She sighed. "If I decide to do this, why can't I do it from here?"

"Because you were found in Houston, and that's the best place to begin searching for your birth mother. I'm planning to offer a reward to her, or to anyone else in your family who comes forward for testing. What people won't do for humanitarian reasons, they'll do for money."

"Oh, ye of little faith," she murmured.

"I heard that."

"Go on, Mr. Andreis."

"Why don't you call me Keir? Surely we've insulted each other enough to be on a first name basis."

"Okay," she said. There was a long, expectant silence, so she added, "Keir."

"You need to be in Houston to interview the people who come in answer to the reward."

"People?"

"People. Maybe a lot of people. You're the only one who can cull them. Do you know anything specific about how you were found? Something only the woman who gave you up would know?"

"I didn't ask any details. It was such a shock, you know—learning that I wasn't who I thought I was. But there must be something. I could ask my mom."

"Does that mean you've decided to come?"

Maris closed her eyes, trying to discover why she was so reluctant. It was the perfect solution to her problems, and although it was charity, it was a brand she could easily digest. But she felt as though she were about to step onto a roller coaster and wasn't going to be able to get off until the ride was over. God, she hated to have her picture plastered across the papers again! This time she would be the focus, not Cyndi's illness. *Face it, Maris. You're afraid.*

She sighed. "Tell Mrs. Hauck I'll take her up on her offer."

"Good. I'll make arrangements for Cyndi to be seen by Dr. Guaymus at M.D. Anderson Hospital. You've probably heard of him; he's the foremost expert on pediatric leukemia in the country."

"He's the best in the world," Maris said. "Are you sure you can get her in? I tried to get Cyndi into his program six months ago, and was turned down because there was no room. They put her on a waiting list."

"They've already agreed to take her."

"So someone else got bumped, then?"

"Give those over-active scruples a rest, Mrs.

37

Durant. No one got bumped. I merely talked them into expanding the program by one patient."

"Thank you."

"You're welcome," Keir said. "I can get you on a plane whenever you want."

Maris glanced at Cyndi. "Actually, if Cyndi's doctor says it's all right, I'd rather drive." Having her own transportation would give her a small measure of independence.

"Okay."

She was glad that he didn't push; maybe he understood a little of what this was costing her. But there was one thing she still needed to know. "Ordinarily I wouldn't be this blunt, but you've—"

"Tread on enough sacred ground to have set myself up for it?"

"Yes."

"Shoot, then," he said. "I can take it."

"You're going to great lengths to help us. I can't quite believe a twenty-year-old grief is the only reason."

There was a long silence. Then he said, "My brother was only a year younger than I. Gary and I were like twins, and it tore me to pieces when he got sick. Somehow, I hoped that if I tried hard enough, if I loved him enough, I could keep him with me. But he slipped through my fingers anyway."

"How old were you?" Maris whispered.

"Sixteen."

She wished she could see his face. "Oh, God. Go on."

"Do you know what bothered me most about my brother's cancer? My own helplessness. As time

38

went on, I thought I'd come to terms with it. It wasn't Cyndi's story that hit me so hard; it was yours. You see, I've stood in your shoes, Mrs. Durant. I've felt your pain. And as long as we're being so damned honest with each other, I'm going to tell you that I'm not doing this for you, or even for Cyndi. It's for me. This is payback. I couldn't help Gary, but I *can* help your daughter." His breathing was clearly audible; rapid, as though he'd been running. "Is that good enough?"

"Yes," Maris said. "It's good enough."

Maris parked the Regal in the lot beside Cypress Gardens Retirement Community. The curving concrete sidewalk had been scraped clear of snow, and salt crystals glittered like tiny gems on the steps. They crunched beneath her shoes as she walked.

The lobby could have graced the poshest of office buildings: sleek sofas and chairs with mauve, gray and blue upholstery, marble-topped tables and a stretch of gray carpeting. In the eight months she'd been coming here, she'd never been tempted to sit down.

"Hello, Mrs. Durant," the receptionist said.

"Hello, Phyllis." Maris signed her name in the register, then pushed through the double doors leading to the west wing. The tile underfoot was the same shade of gray as the carpeting in the lobby, but the walls here were painted a muted blue. Doors were spaced at about twenty-foot intervals along each side of the corridor. Many were open, letting a babble of TV noise out into the hallway.

Maris's wet tennis shoes squeaked on the tile as she walked. This wasn't a bad place, but, the "Community" title aside, it was a nursing home. She hadn't wanted her mother to come here. But Ava had insisted, not wanting her daughter burdened with the care of two sick people. A noble gesture, Maris thought, wishing she could appreciate it more.

The second-to-last door in the hallway was numbered 1016. Maris knocked softly. "Mom?"

"Come in, sweetheart."

Ava sat in her wheelchair. Arthritis had put her there two years ago. It had turned her hair white and had given her hands that looked as though they'd been melted and reformed in some demonic forge. She was seventy-eight, and looked a hundred. She'd deteriorated rapidly since Dad died four years ago; even the blue of her eyes had paled.

Some day soon, Maris thought as she leaned down to kiss the older woman's cheek, *I'm going to lose her, too.* "Hi, Mom."

"Hi. You're looking better every day. When will they take that bandage off your head?"

"I get the stitches out tomorrow. Good as new, except for a little missing hair." Maris knelt beside the wheelchair. "I know this is hard for you, but I've got to ask you some questions about how you found me."

Ava's gaze skittered away. "What exactly do you want to know?

"I'd like to know what kind of clothes I was wearing, what was wrapped around me, everything."

40

"I see. You're going to try to find *her.*"

"Mom, I have to. She might be a match for Cyndi. I might even have a half-brother or sister who might match."

"Are you going to Texas?"

"Yeah. A man down there got interested in Cyndi's case, and offered us the use of his house. He even got Cyndi into Dr. Guaymus's program."

"I thought it was full," Ava said.

Maris lifted one shoulder in a shrug. "Not to a state senator. Mom, this guy—the senator's campaign manager—has done everything but throw rose petals in our path. He even raised money for a reward. But that's going to bring the money-grubbers coming around in droves. That's why I need such specific information from you. I've got to try and separate the wheat from the chaff, so to speak."

"I should have told you years ago. But I was afraid you might want to find the woman." She looked away, focusing her gaze on the window. "I was afraid of losing you."

"Oh, Mom." Gently, Maris took the older woman's bird-claw of a hand in hers. "You couldn't lose me. You're the only mother I've ever known, and the only one I *want* to know. I just don't have a choice here."

"I know." Ava sighed. "It isn't a long story, really. I'll start at the beginning. Let's see . . . Tom and I had been childless through thirteen years of marriage. We'd resigned ourselves to it, decided to just enjoy each other. Well, when his father died, leaving him a bit of money, we decided to make a camping tour of the West."

41

"We swung down into Texas, ending up in a Houston trailer park. We were only going to stay the night before heading to San Antonio. But when Tom went out that night to buy a newspaper, he found a cardboard box underneath the trailer. And in the box was a newborn baby. You were wrapped in one of those striped Mexican blankets, and pinned to the blanket was a note saying 'Please take care of me.' "

"Are you sure I was born that day?"

"Honey, I used to be a nurse. You were only a few hours old, still had blood on you from being born."

So new, so very new. *Couldn't wait to get rid of me, could she?* "Go on, Mom. Tell me the rest."

"Well, Tom went around trying to find who you belonged to," Ava said. Her gaze was turned inward now, focused on the past. "You can imagine your father going around from one government agency to the next trying to get something done."

Maris rolled her eyes. Her father had been a blue-collar worker with a ninth-grade education. Anything stamped "Official" would have been both annoying and intimidating. He wouldn't have lasted long being bounced around the innards of a bureaucratic machine.

Ava touched her cheek, bringing her back to reality.

"No one did anything. No one even offered to look into it. The police, the politicians and the newspapers were all atwitter about the murder of some socialite. So we kept you."

Joy softened the lines of the old woman's face. Seeing it, Maris felt her own throat tighten. She

42

would always remember this. Years down the road, she would smile at the knowledge of being wanted so much.

"I knew he wouldn't find anything," Ava said. "All along, I knew you were meant for us. I was forty-four years old, and you were the answer to my prayers. We took you home with us and never looked back."

"But what did people say when you showed up with a baby?"

Ava smiled. "Well, we told people I'd been having some health problems — fortunately, I'd been putting on some weight — and was completely surprised when those problems turned out to be a baby girl."

"And they believed it?"

"Why not? You hear about things like that happening all the time," Ava said. "Some woman thinks she's got gas —"

"But she's in labor. I know, I've read those stories. I just never expected to be one."

The old woman's smile faded, and she leaned forward to look deeply into Maris's eyes. "Are you going to be all right with this? How will you feel if you find her?"

"I don't know," Maris answered to both questions. "I just don't know."

Five

"When are we going to get there?" Cyndi asked.

"About five minutes less than the last time you asked." Maris glanced in her rearview mirror to check the traffic, then eased into the left lane to pass a heavily loaded tractor-trailer truck.

As she accelerated to pass, the truck's tires sloshed a spray of muddy water across the windshield. "What a mess," she said, reaching to turn the wipers on. "And it's going to be even more of a mess if this stuff freezes overnight."

"I haven't seen a sign in miles and miles," Cyndi said. "Where exactly are we?"

"Somewhere between Springfield and Joplin, but I'm not sure exactly where." Maris checked her watch. It was nearly eleven; they'd been on the road more than three hours already. "How are you feeling, hon?"

"I feel great, Mom."

Maris glanced at her daughter. The red baseball cap had become a permanent part of her wardrobe. Beneath it, her hair was beginning to grow back. It was only peach fuzz now, but it gleamed gold in the sunlight. Maris couldn't wait for it to get long enough so that she could brush it. Chances were, however, Dr. Guaymus would start Cyndi on another round of chemotherapy before that happened.

"Are we going to stop for lunch, Mom?"

"I'd rather not," Maris said. "The next leg of the trip is going to be in the Ozark Mountains, and I'd rather tackle it in daylight." She pointed to the small cooler on the floor at Cyndi's feet. "There are some sandwiches and fruit in there."

"I saw you put some brownies in there."

"Sandwich and fruit before brownies."

Cyndi made a face, then bent to rummage through the cooler. Maris smiled. The excitement of the trip had been good for Cyndi. She'd pay later, when the rush faded, but right now she was more animated than Maris had seen her in a long time.

"Do you want a sandwich?" Cyndi asked.

"Thanks."

Maris accepted the sandwich, but then laid it on the seat beside her while she negotiated a curve. The landscape here was hilly, a sea of snow-covered rolls lapping at the base of the Ozark Mountains. Highway 44 was a stark black ribbon against the snow, the bright winter sun reflected in the rivulets of water streaming across the asphalt. There was little traffic here; Maris hadn't seen another vehicle since she'd passed the tractor-trailer.

"Want one?" Cyndi asked, holding up a twelve-ounce bottle of soda.

"Not yet. And if I were you, I'd watch how much I drank. What goes in is going to have to come out again, and there might not be a place to stop. I don't think you're going to want to go pee in the woods."

"No way." Like a man rationing water in the desert, Cyndi took a single swallow of soda, then recapped the bottle.

45

Maris grinned, but her smile faded as she glanced in the rearview mirror to see a blue pickup truck cresting the hill behind her. She was going nearly seventy, but the truck was overhauling her as though she were standing still. It moved up close on her bumper and stayed there. The windshield was streaked with mud, and she could see nothing of the driver but a blurred shape.

"Well, go around, why don't you?" she muttered. "The whole left lane is clear, idiot!"

But he stayed where he was, his grille hovering in the rearview mirror. Maris slowed down in the hope of annoying him into going around her. "Come *on,* will you?"

In between watching the road and watching the mirror, Maris registered a sign saying, "Humbert's Creek." Maybe there would be a gas station where she could pull off and get away from this fool. Then she saw a bridge up ahead.

The pickup truck pulled around her, his engine roaring. Maris heaved a sigh of relief. Suddenly he swerved back toward her, scraping along the Regal's left front fender. She fought to hold on to the steering wheel as the car plunged toward the shoulder of the road.

"Look out!" Cyndi shrieked.

The car bounced over the mound of hard-packed snow that bordered the road, then slithered sideways down the slope beyond. They were headed right for the swiftly moving water of the stream. *We're going in,* Maris thought. Time seemed strangely distorted, the world moving around her in slow motion as the car plowed through the brush.

Desperately, she dragged at the steering wheel, wrenching it hard to the right. The Regal's back end slewed around in a spray of snow and dirt, and for a moment Maris thought they were going to flip. But after a few teeth-jarring bounces, the car churned to a stop less than twenty feet from the water.

Maris killed the engine and flung her seat belt off. "Cyndi, are you all right?"

"I'm fine," Cyndi said. Then she began to cry.

Gathering the child into her arms, Maris silently blessed whoever had invented seat belts. She and Cyndi were shaken, but that was all.

A man's face appeared in the driver's-side window. "Hey! Are you all right?" he shouted.

Maris slid across the seat and opened the door, ready to give him hell for running her off the road. "What's wrong with—" she broke off abruptly as she saw a battered white van parked on the road above. *Oh,* she thought, *he's come to help.* She swung around to look at him, goggling at the sight of about an acre of red plaid flannel. The man was carrying at least three hundred pounds on a five-foot-eight frame, and was still breathing hard from climbing down here.

"Are either of you hurt?" he panted.

"No, we're okay. Thanks for coming down, Mr. . . ."

"Braun. Andrew Braun. And you're welcome."

"Maris Durant." She shook hands with him, wishing her own weren't trembling so badly.

"What happened?" he asked.

"Some guy in a pickup truck ran me off the road," she said, pointing to the long scrape on her fender. "Did you see him?"

"Just his taillights. Then I saw your car going down the hill, and didn't look for anything else."

Now that her shock was wearing off, outrage

kicked in. "I wish I'd been able to get his license number. He ought to be locked up. The creep didn't even stick around to see if he'd killed us or not!"

"He was probably drunk," Braun said. "There's been a lot of it, with the plant laying people off right after Christmas and all. At least you and the little girl weren't hurt."

"No thanks to him." Maris looked past the Regal to the creek's slate gray water. It looked deep and cold, and if they'd gone in . . . A shudder rippled down her spine. She and Cyndi had been living with a very real possibility of death for more than a year now. But this was today. Neither of them expected it to happen *today*.

Braun ran his hand down the left front fender. "He clipped you good." Dropping down to one knee with an effort, he bent and looked under the car. "Nothing's leaking. Does it still run?"

"It did a minute ago."

"Well, everything seems to be in good shape, except for that fender."

Maris smiled, seeing that the tire nearest him was flat. No matter; he'd come down here to help them, and she didn't give a flip whether he knew anything about cars or not. He was her rescuer, an oversized angel of mercy in a red plaid jacket. "What do you suggest?" she asked.

"I guess I could try driving it back up to the highway."

She turned to look up at the swath of flattened brush that marked the Regal's path down the hill. "I don't think so."

With a grunt of what might be effort, but which Maris thought was probably relief, he heaved himself to his feet. "There's a service station a couple

48

of miles down the road. I'll take you there."

"Thanks." She leaned down to peer into the cab. "Get your boots and gloves on, Cyndi. We're going to have to walk up to Mr. Braun's van."

In true angel-of-mercy style, Braun got them to the gas station and made sure the tow truck was available. A nice man, Maris thought. He probably needed money, but she knew better than to offer any.

"Well," he said, "I think you'll be all right now. If your car's not driveable, the station manager will take you to a motel about fifteen miles down the road.

Her throat was tight with suppressed emotion as she shook his hand. "Thanks."

"You're welcome," he said, then reached down to lay his hand on Cyndi's shoulder. "Good luck."

Maris put her arm around her daughter as she watched him drive away. "Well, there goes my angel."

"Angel?"

"My angel of mercy," Maris explained.

Cyndi giggled. "He said he was a salesman."

"Okay," Maris said. "So he's a part-time angel. But we were awfully lucky he showed up when he did. Now let's hope our luck holds and we get the car back on the road today."

Four hours and three hundred dollars later, they were able to resume their journey. There wasn't much daylight left; the sun was a brooding crimson ball hanging upon the rim of the mountains, and the trees had laid long, spider-leg shadows across the road.

"I can't believe the only damage was the fender, the tire and a crunched muffler," Maris said.

Cyndi grinned. "Maybe Mr. Braun really *was* an angel."

"If he was, we wouldn't have needed a tow truck to get the car up the hill." Maris couldn't help but chuckle, remembering her first sight of that vast red plaid jacket.

Her humor faded, however, when she glanced at her daughter. Even in the ruddy light Cyndi's face looked pinched and pale, and there were indigo shadows beneath her eyes.

Worry settled heavily in the pit of Maris's stomach. "We'll stop at that motel Mr. Braun told us about," she said.

"I'm fine, Mom."

"Well, *I'm* not. I want a shower and a meal, and then I want to get about twelve hours' sleep." Besides, she didn't want to face that drive through the mountains at night. Her mind conjured a vision of headlights plunging toward her, her car flying off the road into a dark abyss. No, she thought. Not at night.

East Texas was flat. Maris had grown tired of the monotonous landscape hours ago, and was relieved to see the Houston skyline ahead. It wasn't quite five o'clock, but already rush hour had hit on Interstate 45. Traffic on this side wasn't too bad, but the opposite side was packed with vehicles, all speeding along nose-to-rear-bumper as though they were racing in an incredibly overcrowded Indy 500.

"I'm glad we're going the opposite way," Cyndi said.

"Me, too." Maris peered up at a sign overhead. "There we go. The 610 Loop. We'll take that around the city and miss the worst of the traffic."

She soon learned the folly of that assumption.

Houston had grown beyond the Loop; instead of routing traffic around the city, 610 was just one segment of the highway system. Six lanes of bumper-to-bumper traffic going seventy miles an hour.

It didn't take long for Maris to realize that hesitation was interpreted as a sign of weakness, as was courtesy. And although she tried to keep a proper distance from the car ahead, it was impossible; the moment a space opened—whether it was car-sized or not—someone zoomed into it. After having been forced to slam on her brakes several times, she'd finally had enough. Adrenaline shot through her. She'd never been much of a fighter, but by God, she'd faced cancer, she'd faced death, and she wasn't about to let herself be intimidated by a little traffic.

"Okay," she muttered, tightening her grip on the steering wheel. She matched her speed to that of the rest of the traffic, riding the bumper of the car ahead. "Try and cut in now."

"Mom, you're as crazy as they are!"

" 'When in Rome, do as the Romans do,' " Maris quoted. She didn't dare look away from the road, even for an instant. "Honey, I've got to fight back; they'll run me right off the road if I don't."

"How do people live like this?"

"Survival of the fittest, I guess. Those who can't hack it go live in Iowa or something." A gray BMW sidled toward the miniscule space between the Regal and the car ahead, trying to intimidate her into dropping back. She gritted her teeth and maintained her speed. The BMW slid away, apparently without rancor, to muscle in on someone else.

"Ha!" she cried.

"Are you sure you didn't hit your head when we went off the road?" Cyndi asked.

51

"I'm sure, hon. I'm just tired of getting pushed around."

By more than just freeway traffic. Since Cyndi had gotten sick, both their lives had been run by the dictates of the illness. They had worked so hard, tried so hard, and it had been for nothing. Maris knew she was entering the last big battle to keep her daughter alive. If she had to be pushy, fine. If she had to read a million nasty letters, fine. And if she had to face a mother who hated her, who spit in her face, well, that was fine, too.

"What's the number of the road I'm supposed to watch for?" Cyndi asked. There was a note of resignation in her voice that made Maris smile.

"Highway 288. We take that for about twenty miles, then turn onto 655." Maris risked a glance at Cyndi, and saw that she was tracing their route with her finger. "After about ten miles, we'll hit South County Road and take that to Hauck. The estate is about four miles outside of town."

"Hauck . . . Hauck . . . oh, here it is," Cyndi said. "No wonder I couldn't find it; I thought it was spelled 'Hawk.' "

"I did, too. But it's H-a-u-c-k. A German name, I guess."

"They should have changed it to 'Hawk,' " Cyndi said. "It's neater. Hey, there's the sign for 288. You're going to have to change lanes soon."

"No problem."

Maris put her signal on and began drifting toward the lane to her right. A red Blazer accepted the challenge, skimming by her with scant inches to spare. But the next car was brand-new, and evidently the driver was not willing to risk it. He pulled up enough for her to slide in front of him. She waved thank-you and smiled when she got a grudging return wave.

Highway 288 was just as packed with traffic as the Loop, but the speed was only a crawl. Maris could see flashing blue lights up ahead.

"Looks like an accident," Cyndi said.

"Yeah. It's going to be slow going for a while."

"Slow going" turned out to be an understatement; it took Maris an hour and a half to drive the twenty miles to the exit for Highway 622, and another half hour to reach South County Road.

Once she did, however, it was like passing into another world. Darkness had fallen. The moon was full tonight, casting a bright, fairylike illumination over the world below. South County Road was a straight, dark arrow heading due west, bordered on both sides by barbed-wire-enclosed pasture. Off to the right, the pump of an oil well moved its steel arm up and down in a lazy cadence.

"Now *this* is Texas," Maris said with a sigh.

Cyndi leaned forward against the seat belt. "I can see lights up ahead."

"That'll be Hauck," Maris said. "Look, there's a sign. 'Hauck, Texas. Population 9,327.' "

It was a pleasant little city, mostly residential. A small business district straddled South County Street: a few two-story office buildings, several expensive-looking stores, a library, a police station and, surprising in a place this small, a slew of restaurants.

After passing straight through town, Maris turned north onto Aberdeen Road. Again, pastureland stretched off on both sides, separated from the street by a white rail fence, miles and miles of it. Maris shook her head, overwhelmed at the thought of painting it all.

"There's a road ahead on the left," Cyndi said.

Maris squinted at the sign. "Sylvan Lane. That's ours."

She turned left, passing a brace of "Private Road. No Trespassing" signs. Up ahead, a graceful, arching sign curved over the road. It said simply, "Gavilan." Above the letters was the painting of a swooping hawk, yellow-eyed and fierce.

She could almost feel the bird's vigilant gaze as she passed below the sign. A few hundred feet farther on, Italian cypresses lined the road, tall sentinels guarding their territory. Their shadows lay across the road in thick, dark lines.

The trees went on for a quarter of a mile, and coming out of them was like emerging from a tunnel. Beyond the trees was a vast stretch of manicured lawn, bordered at a distance by more white rail fence. Maris was surprised by the openness of the place. After the brooding, Gothic effect of the cypresses, she'd expected gates and fences, maybe even a few ravening guard dogs.

"Wow," Cyndi breathed. "Will you look at that!"

Six

"Wow," Maris echoed, slowing the car.

The house was breathtaking; it was as though some-one had taken a Spanish hacienda and blown it to enormous proportions. A two-story construction of stuccoed brick, the house had two wings stretching off from the massive central section. The windows on the second floor each opened onto a tiny balcony. Huge, old cottonwood trees stretched their branches over the red tile roof.

Maris couldn't put her finger on why she didn't find the house beautiful. Oh, it was big and imposing, and fairly screamed "money," but it seemed out of place, somehow out of step with the setting.

A concrete driveway looped away from the road, made a graceful curve in front of the house, then re-joined the road a hundred yards farther on. Maris turned onto the drive, thinking that the Regal must look like some ragged beggar-man come to plead for scraps at the kitchen door.

The moment she parked, a small, dark man came out of the house and ran down the steps toward her. The light picked out platinum strands in his dark hair, and she realized he was older than she'd thought at first, perhaps mid- to late-forties.

"Señora Durant?" His face was impassive, his black eyes incurious.

"Yes."

He opened her door. Taking Maris's hand in a firm, cool grip, he helped her from the car, then went around to do the same for Cyndi. "Welcome to Gavilan." Spoken in his Mexican accent, the Spanish name sounded like music.

"Is Gavilan a Spanish word?" Cyndi asked.

"Yes, señorita. It means 'sparrow hawk.' "

"Hawk, Hauck," Maris said. "Is it meant to be a play on words?"

"I do not know, señora." He held out his hand, palm up. "If you will give me your keys, I will see that your car is taken care of."

"My bags—"

"They will be taken care of."

Maris dropped her keys into his hand. "Would you—"

"Alejo, introduce me to our guests." The imperious voice brought them all around to look at the house.

An old woman stood in the doorway, her smooth cap of white hair seeming almost to glow in the bright afternoon sunlight. She was of medium height, but the immense dignity of her bearing made her seem taller. Her shape was blocky despite the expert tailoring of her burgundy dress, her legs and ankles thick despite the slim high-heels she wore. Her lips were pressed tightly together, accentuating the spoked lines around her mouth.

Maris's stomach lurched. *She doesn't want us here!*

Alejo came forward, sleek and obsequious. "I was just bringing the ladies in to you, señora," he said.

Almost, Maris expected him to bow. He turned to

56

her and Cyndi, urging them toward the house with a graceful sweep of his hand, and began the introductions in his beautiful, liquid accent.

The old woman silenced him with a gesture. "I am Sophie Hauck, the senator's mother. Welcome to Gavilan." The name, when she spoke it, didn't sound like music at all.

"Thank you for having us, Mrs. Hauck," Maris said.

"I hope you had a good trip down from Missouri."

Maris nodded, the artist in her fascinated by the strong lines of Sophie Hauck's face. Surely she'd gotten those jet-black eyes and that warm olive coloring from some Latin ancestor. Indeed, with that square chin and jutting prow of a nose, her face could have come straight off a Roman coin.

Alejo spoke rapidly in Spanish. Sophie replied, her Spanish sounding harsh and flat compared to his, then turned her attention back to her guests. "He says you have a fresh scrape on your fender. Did you have an accident on the way?"

"Just a slight one," Maris said. "Neither of us was hurt, so it turned out all right."

"I'm so glad. We'll see that it is fixed for you."

Maris spoke up quickly. "That's very kind of you, but I couldn't allow you to do that. If you could—"

"Nonsense," the old woman said. "Alejo, see to it."

"Si, señora."

"I'm sorry," Maris said, a shade too loudly. "But I can't allow you to do that. Really. But I would appreciate it if you could recommend a good body shop."

The spokes around Sophie's mouth deepened. It was obvious she wasn't used to being challenged. After a long, uncomfortable moment, she nodded. "As you wish. But I advise you to let Alejo make the arrangements; he knows the best places for car repairs."

57

"All right, Mrs. Hauck. Thank you."

"Come, I'll show you to your rooms," Sophie said. "I'm sure you would like to freshen up."

"We would," Maris said, turning back toward the car. "Just let me get my small case from the backseat."

"Alejo will bring it to your room."

Maris turned toward the car. "Cyndi's medication is in it. I like to keep it with me."

Before she'd taken two steps, however, Alejo had retrieved the case from the car and carried it into the house.

"Is this a real Spanish hacienda, Mrs. Hauck?" Cyndi asked.

"I'll tell you the history as we go, child." Sophie's black gaze moved over Cyndi, studying the areas of bare scalp that weren't covered by the baseball cap.

Maris had become expert at gauging strangers' reactions to Cyndi's appearance, but she got absolutely nothing from Sophie Hauck. The old woman was as opaque as stone; she might have been repulsed or compassionate, or anything in between.

"This way, please." Sophie said, leading the way into the house.

The foyer reached out like a welcoming hand. Mahogany paneling reflected the light with a burnished glow, and the wood's ruddy highlights were picked up by the Mexican tile on the floor. A staircase rose in a gentle curve, the wooden stairs fanning out into wedges at the turn. To the right was a drop-leaf table, flanked by two upholstered armchairs. A mirror reflected a painting of an autumn landscape that hung on the opposite wall. Everything looked very old and very expensive, even to Maris's untrained eye.

Sophie walked toward the stairway, her heels clicking on the polished terra-cotta tiles. Maris followed, her arm around Cyndi's waist.

The old woman glanced over her shoulder. "You asked if this was a real hacienda, Cyndi. It isn't. My husband's father, Garvin Hauck, grew up in California. Although he left at fifteen to make his fortune, he always missed his home. So, when he had this house built in 1922, he ordered the architect to follow the Spanish style. Actually, he went through three architects before finding one he liked: the first few objected to tearing down the plantation house that occupied the site. A bit of a pirate, Garvin was."

Maris imagined a sprawling plantation home in this setting, with rambling porches shaded by the cottonwood trees and tall, white columns reflecting the sun. *Yes, that's it. That* house belonged here, nestled into the landscape as though it had grown there quite naturally. "Why did he tear the old house down?" she asked.

"I asked him that once," Sophie said. "He told me 'because it was there. Another man's mark, another man's dream.' Garvin was never one to settle for anything other than what he wanted. A bit of a pirate, as I said."

Three hallways stretched off the landing at the top of the stairs; one headed straight toward the back of the house, one to the left, and the other to the right. Sophie turned left, her footsteps silent on the Oriental runner. "I thought you'd prefer privacy, so I put you in the west wing, away from the bustle."

Maris felt her brows go up. Other than Sophie and Alejo, she hadn't seen any people, let alone bustle. "Whatever is convenient for you, Mrs. Hauck."

"Call me Sophie, please."

"Sorry. Sophie." The name didn't feel right in Maris's mouth. Too familiar, somehow, with this woman.

Maybe she was being oversensitive, but she couldn't

help but notice that Sophie stayed far enough ahead that they couldn't catch up without breaking into a trot. Lady of the Manor. The old woman didn't have to go through so much trouble to establish the pecking order. *I already feel like a supplicant.* It bothered her. It bothered her a lot. But she'd take much more than this to find a donor for Cyndi. *How about you, Sophie Hauck? Will you take the trouble to go down and be tested?* Maris already knew the answer.

"I hope we get to a bathroom soon," Cyndi whispered. "I've got to go *bad*."

So did Maris. "We're almost there," she whispered back. "Just hang on."

"My eyeballs are floating," Cyndi hissed. "If I don't get to a bathroom soon, I'm going to wet my pants."

Maris's tension snapped. A giggle bubbled up, and she clapped her hand over her mouth to stifle it. Then Cyndi started, and that only made it worse. The old woman walked on, tailored, impeccable, oblivious to what was going on behind her.

"Here we are," Sophie said, opening a door on the right side of the hall.

Maris managed to get herself under control as she followed the old woman into the room. Everything seemed to come in twos, like Noah's Ark: two windows with blue draperies, identical-twin nightstands bearing identical-twin lamps, two matching Oriental rugs set in precise line with the walls, the fireplace flanked by two chairs with upholstery to match the drapes. Even the bed with its blue-and-white-flowered bedspread was reflected in the mirrored closet doors.

"I've given you adjoining rooms," Sophie said, pointing to a pair of doors in the far wall. "I hope you don't mind sharing a bathroom."

"I've got to go," Cyndi announced. "Really bad."

"The door on the right, dear," Sophie said.

The wrinkles around Sophie's mouth deepened as she watched the child disappear into the bathroom. With a dart of surprise, Maris realized this was the first time she'd seen the woman smile. She hadn't noticed the lack before; smiling just didn't seem necessary for Sophie Hauck. It was nice to know there was a sense of humor beneath that rather formidable dignity.

"I want to thank you for welcoming us into your home like this," Maris said. "It's very kind of you."

Sophie swung around to look at her, that momentary flash of warmth gone. "The senator is a very kind man."

Maris was taken aback. Not only because Sophie had assigned her own kindness to another person, but because of the fact that she hadn't said "John," or "my son," but "the senator."

The old woman smoothed the front of her dress. "We put a television in Cyndi's room, as well as a number of children's books."

"Thank you, Mrs. Hauck, but you didn't have to go to so much trouble—"

"Oh, it was the senator's idea." Emotion came into Sophie's dark eyes, a dash of motherly pride.

Maris opened her mouth, realized she was about to say "thank you" again, and pressed her lips together. She *was* grateful. But she also felt . . . beholden, her mother would have called it. Beholden to a woman who didn't smile when she did you a favor, who assigned all acts of kindness to a son she called "Senator."

"Alejo will be up with your bags in a moment," Sophie said, glancing at her watch. "It's almost eight o'clock. Have you eaten supper?"

"We stopped to eat in Dallas, so—"

"That was hours ago. I'll have something prepared.

61

I'm assuming you'd rather have it sent up here?"

No, but it's obvious you would. Aloud, Maris said, "That would be fine. Thank you."

"Good night, then." Sophie pivoted with ponderous grace and headed for the door. "I hope you and Cyndi will enjoy your stay here."

The door closed. With an explosive sigh, Maris sat down in the nearest chair and stretched her legs out in front of her. "Holy cow," she muttered. "Holy, holy cow!"

This wasn't turning out well at all. She'd felt funny enough about coming into a stranger's house like this, but Sophie made her feel downright uncomfortable. Charity with a capital "C." And she had to accept it, just as she had to accept the fact that she couldn't give Cyndi what she needed. But the Haucks could. The door to Dr. Guaymus's program had been closed to Maris Durant. The simple invocation of Senator Hauck's name, however, had opened that door.

Money and influence, influence and money.

As soon as Keir Andreis got here, she was not only going to have to accept charity, she was going to go begging. Publicly. Aggressively. *Got any spare bone marrow, mister? How about you, lady? Can you give us a few nice, healthy cells?*

The bathroom door opened a crack, and Maris saw Cyndi peering out at her.

"Is she gone?" the child whispered.

"She is. Come on out."

Instead, Cyndi opened the door wider and gestured urgently. "Come here, Mom. You've just got to see this bathroom. It's got a hot tub, gold-plated faucets and everything. They've even got two toilets! Is that too weird, or what?"

"Yeah" Maris agreed, feeling a hundred years old as she climbed to her feet, forming an explanation of a bidet for her ten-year-old daughter. "Too weird."

Even in her sleep, Maris knew the dream was starting. It was always the same.

She was aware of motion, her body moving with the smooth roll of a gentle sea-swell. The smell of the ocean was sharp and fishy in her nostrils. Paul stood in the bow of the little sailboat, his hands sure and skillful on the sailboat's lines. She was at the tiller. The wind was high; the boat's hull drove through the water like a spear, and she could feel the power vibrating in her palms. The sea was a vast sheet of purest azure, and the outline of an island hung low and green on the horizon.

She looked up at her husband and found him staring at her, a smile tugging at his mouth. He knew what she was feeling. Later, they'd make love, sex and the sea and the driving wind all mingled together. This was their second honeymoon: two lazy, wonderful weeks in the Virgin Islands. There were times when it seemed the whole world was encompassed in Paul's tawny eyes.

"If you keep looking at me like that, I'm going to have to drop anchor right here," he called.

"Do it," she replied, feeling the familiar, sweet heaviness between her thighs.

He took a step toward her. Suddenly the wind changed, and the boat heeled sharply. Off balance, he was thrown onto the mainsail, bringing the boat over onto its side. Maris hit the water hard. But her life jacket buoyed her, and she kicked up to the surface a moment later.

The mast was just to her left, the mainsail spread out over the water like a great wing. She looked around wildly, relaxing when she saw Paul on the opposite side of the mast, his arm thrown over the slender aluminum column.

"You okay?" he asked.

"Yeah. Are you?"

"I think so."

Maris was glad they'd picked the smaller of the two sailboats they'd been offered this morning. There would have been no way of righting the twenty-five-footer. This boat, however, should be a piece of cake. "The wind's picking up. We'd better get this girl back up."

"No can do," Paul said. "My foot's stuck in the line."

Quickly, Maris swam around the mast to him. "Give me your knife."

"It must have fallen out of my pocket when I hit the water."

Maris shucked her life jacket and handed it to him. Taking a deep breath, she moved hand-over-hand down his body to his feet. One of the lines was wrapped around his right ankle, pinning it against the mast. She couldn't loosen it at all.

Alarm tightened her chest. *Take it easy,* she told herself. *The boat is buoyant; it can stay afloat—and keep him afloat—for hours.*

She came back up to the surface. "I've got to cut it. Can you remember where the tool kit was?"

"I usually keep it . . . Never mind. I took it out when I fixed that line, remember? I was too damned lazy to put it away. It got dumped when we capsized."

"Shit." She ducked under the mast and swam to the boat. The radio didn't work, so she activated the automatic Mayday signal. She spent a few more minutes searching the storage compartments, but found nothing that was going to cut that rope.

When she returned to Paul, he thrust her life jacket at her. "Put it on," he said.

"Let me try to loosen the rope again."

"With what, your teeth?" he growled. "You got a Mayday out, right? Then, all we have to do is sit tight and wait for the cavalry to come. I want you to put this on, and then I want you to climb up on the hull. No need for both of us to be in the water."

She shook her head. Her teeth were chattering; part cold, mostly fright. "I want to stay with you."

"Damn it, I wish you'd do what you're told!"

"After twelve years of marriage, you ought to know better."

"Yeah."

Maris laid her palm against his cheek for a moment, then turned to scan the horizon. Nothing yet. The solitude that had seemed so wonderful a few minutes before was now frightening. It was terrible to be so alone and so helpless.

When she turned around again, she saw that Paul was straining to keep his mouth above the water. She could hear herself speak, but her voice sounded shrill and distant, like the cry of a seabird. "Paul, what's the matter?"

A wave slapped into his face, made him cough. "The boat's sinking."

"That can't be!" she cried. But it was. The mast was slipping beneath the surface, and it was taking Paul with it. Black terror rose into her throat.

Hurrying now, she unbuckled her life jacket and stuffed it under the mast in the hope of slowing its downward movement. Then she dove, not daring to pull her way down Paul's body lest she drag him beneath the surface. The line was still wrapped around his ankle, too tightly for her to jam her fingers beneath it. Damn! This wasn't going to happen. This *couldn't* happen. Not to them, not to Paul.

She tried tracing the line along the mast, but there was such a tangle of rigging that she ran out of air before she'd gone a yard. As she rose the surface, she saw that Paul's mouth was almost under water now, and waves were splashing into his face.

"I've tried everything I know," she cried. "Tell me what to do!"

He waited a moment, evidently timing the waves, then lifted his face enough to speak. His voice was soft and low. "I love you, Maris."

It was goodbye. Maris shook her head, not accepting it. She drew air into her lungs and dove again. Frantically, she tried to trace the line again. If she could release it from its point of origin, she could pull it through the tangle and release Paul. She ran out of air, went up to the surface, then came back down to try again. Twice more she went up. Each time Paul was a little lower in the water. She didn't dare go down again.

Swimming out to the end of the mast, she propped it on her shoulder and tried to heave it upward. She failed. Climbing out onto the boat's hull, she tried to counterbalance the mast with her weight. "Please, God," she prayed. "Please. Help me."

Paul's head slipped beneath the surface. She threw herself flat and grabbed the back of his life jacket, pulling him up with all her strength. She might as well have tried to lift the boat itself.

Not like this. Oh, God, not like this! She jumped back into the water and tried to support him with her own body. The top of his head was just beneath the surface, his hair fanning out in the water like dark seaweed.

"No!" she shrieked. "Paul!"

His movement slowed, then stopped. Air bubbled up, his life escaping into her hands.

Maris started to scream then. She was still screaming when a boat came. Too late. She felt hands on her, felt herself being pulled out of the water.

She fought to get out of the dream — clawed at the fabric of sea and sky in a bid to escape. For the rest was worse. In a moment, her rescuers would bring the corpse up, lay it on the deck beside her as though it were the catch of the day. And it would have Cyndi's face.

She did it. She broke free. Her eyes opened to darkness, but that was all right. Sweat chilled her body, and her chest heaved as though she really had gone through all that exertion. Maybe she had; the covers were tangled enough for it.

Slowly, she pushed herself to a sitting position. The dream hadn't come for several weeks now, and she'd hoped it was gone for good. Maybe it would stay with her forever. The thought was depressing. She wanted to let the past go. She wanted to get over it.

But she'd gone to the Virgin Islands with a husband she adored, and had come back with a coffin. How did a person get over something like that? How could she forget the feeling of Paul's life bubbling through her fingers, knowing he was dying right between her hands and not being able to stop it? That damn dream . . . it didn't take an expert to figure out why she kept having it over and over. Maybe if she could find a way to save him in the dream, she could put some of the guilt aside. Guilt for failing him, for not being strong enough or smart enough to free him from the line.

Guilt for being glad that she hadn't been the one to die.

And now she might lose Cyndi, too. It terrified her.

There was a limit to how much loss she could take. Sometimes she felt as though a great yawning darkness was lying just beyond her feet; one more step would take her into it, and she'd never get out.

Tears threatened, and she pressed the heels of her hands against her eyes, hard. *Let's face it, Maris. You're not only fighting for Cyndi, you're fighting for yourself.*

Seven

An insistent noise dragged Maris from a deep sleep. For a moment she was disoriented, then slowly returned to full awareness. Someone was knocking at the door. With a groan, she rolled over and peered at the clock on the nightstand. Seven forty-five. She'd gotten about four hours' sleep.

The knock came again, and then a woman called through the door. "Señora Durant?" Her English was accented, but less so than Alejo's. "Señora, are you awake?"

Now I am. Aloud, however, she called, "Yes, I'm awake."

"Señora Hauck asked if you and your daughter would like to join the family for breakfast."

Maris was abruptly conscious of a gnawing emptiness in her stomach. "When should we come down?" she asked, swinging her legs over the side of the bed. "And where should we go?"

"It is a bit complicated to get to the dining room from here. I'll come back up for you in thirty minutes."

"We'll be ready."

Maris went in to wake Cyndi. In the dimness of the room, it was hard to find her in the big bed. *So* little, so fragile, Maris thought. *And so precious.*

"Cyndi," Maris called. "Time to wake up."

"Is it morning, already?" she mumbled.

"It is." Maris went to open the drapes, letting a flood of morning light into the room. "Want some breakfast?"

"Yeah, I guess so."

"Then, come on, lazy," Maris tried to ignore the child's pallor, the shadows that stood out like bruises beneath her eyes.

At exactly eight-fifteen, the discreet knock came again. When Maris opened the door, she found herself looking down, way down. The woman who stood in the hallway was almost child-sized. She might have been sixty, or a little more. Her face was more Indian than Spanish, with broad, high cheekbones and an arching nose. Beautiful dark eyes were set like jewels amid nesting wrinkles.

"I am Dolores Munoz, the housekeeper," she said. "Are your rooms to your satisfaction?"

"Yes, thank you," Maris said, thinking of the rug she had pulled askew to relieve the stolid squareness of the room. "Everything is lovely, Mrs. . . . Señora Munoz."

The woman inclined her head, a regal gesture. "Good. If there is anything you need, please ask me or one of the maids. We want you to be comfortable here." She turned away with quick, birdlike grace. Her shoes made not the slightest sound on the carpeting.

Feeling gawky and huge in comparison, Maris linked arms with Cyndi and followed. "I hope the family didn't delay their breakfast for us," she said.

Mrs. Munoz glanced over her shoulder. "No, señora. They eat at eight-thirty every morning. The *patrón* is a punctual man."

"The *patrón?*" Maris repeated, startled by the note

70

of deep respect in the housekeeper's voice. It sounded so . . . medieval.

"Señor Ballard Hauck. The head of the family, señora."

Mrs. Munoz started down the stairway, her shoes making no noise even on the polished oak of the stairs. Maris felt — and sounded — like an elephant coming down after her. Even Cyndi, fragile as she was, made more noise than the housekeeper.

And where's Uncle Fester? Maris thought.

Mrs. Munoz led them through the foyer and then down a short hallway. Pausing before a set of double doors at the end, she waited for Maris and Cyndi to catch up.

"Enjoy your meal," she said, pushing the doors open and stepping back.

Sophie was alone in the room, reading a newspaper at an enormous oak trestle table that had seen plenty of hard use. The fact that it was set with fine sterling and Limoges china was even more startling. Maris registered it all in one astounded glance; this was absolutely the last thing she would have expected to find in the elegant Hauck home.

"Good morning," Sophie said, laying her newspaper aside. "Please come in; the others will be here in a moment. Maris, sit there across from me. Cyndi, to your mother's left, please."

Maris obeyed. Her back was to the door, and it made her feel strangely vulnerable. She glanced at Cyndi. The child was engrossed in reading something that had been carved into the wood so long ago that it had been almost obliterated by use.

"What does this say, Mrs. Hauck?" she asked.

"It says 'Jonas Lefevre' — or did, rather. I believe he worked for my husband's grandfather many years ago."

Cyndi traced the blurred outline with her fingertip. "Didn't he get in trouble for it? I'd be grounded forever if I did something like that to the furniture."

Sophie smiled. "I suppose he did. But it was—" The old woman broke off, rising to her feet with ponderous grace. "Good morning, Ballard."

Turning, Maris saw a man in a wheelchair. Long ago, he must have been a big, handsome fellow. But he was wasted now, his body seeming to drape from his wide shoulders like clothes on a hanger. Yellow-gray hair fringed his head. Once, his deep-set indigo eyes must have been piercing. Now they were empty.

Sophie bent to kiss his cheek. "Ballard, we have guests," she said. "This is Maris Durant and her daughter, Cyndi. They'll be staying with us while Cyndi gets some medical treatment."

There was no response in the old man's eyes, no awareness. Maris realized that Ballard Hauck, *Patrón,* had already checked out.

"Robyn, come meet our guests," Sophie said without looking away from her husband's face.

Maris turned farther, only now noticing the woman standing in the hallway behind the wheelchair. "I'm sorry, Robyn. I didn't see you back there. Hello."

"Hello." Robyn's voice was clear and high, like a young girl's. She was obviously past forty, but there was something unformed about her that belonged in a much younger person.

Maris watched her curiously—curiously because here was a woman who ought to be beautiful and wasn't. Robyn Hauck had her father's indigo eyes, which, with her thick, black hair and pale coloring, were stunning. But that vital something was missing, and she came off as mousy and diffident.

Robyn positioned the wheelchair at the head of the table, and Sophie opened a napkin and tucked it into

72

the front of the old man's shirt. He never looked right or left. It gave Maris a chill to see the two women fussing over a man who obviously didn't know what the hell was going on.

A door at the far end of the room swung open. Two Mexican women hurried in, carrying large, cloth-covered trays. The delicious aroma of bacon and eggs drifted through the room.

Maris checked her watch surreptitiously. Eight-thirty, on the nose.

Robyn fixed her father's plate. Scrambled eggs, bacon, sausage and toast were all mixed together and cut into tiny bits. Then she began feeding him. The old man's eyes never focused, but his mouth snapped at the food hungrily. Crumbs dribbled down onto the napkin.

"Coffee, Señora Durant?" a soft voice asked.

Maris turned with a start to see one of the maids standing beside her, coffeepot in hand. "Yes, please."

A few moments later she had a steaming, fragrant plateful of food in front of her. After glancing at Cyndi to make sure the child was eating, she started in on her own food.

"Good morning, everyone." The voice was male and deep, and Maris would have known it anywhere. Keir Andreis.

She swallowed hastily and turned to look at him. He didn't live up to the voice, but then, no one could. His hair was brown, thinning a bit at the top, his eyes a rich, warm brown. He wasn't particularly tall, particularly thin or heavy. A medium sort of man. Maris found his sharp-featured face more intelligent than handsome. Then he grinned, and she did a double-take. Maybe his face didn't compare to the voice, but that smile came close.

He strode toward Maris, his hand outstretched. "Nice to meet you in person, Maris. I tried to get here

73

before you went to bed last night, but the traffic between here and Austin was horrendous."

Maris shook his hand, studying him closely. This was the man who had completely reordered her life, and in a way she didn't think she liked. "You didn't have to rush."

"The senator owed me a day off, anyway." His gaze shifted to a point behind her, and she realized he was looking at Cyndi. The grin came back. "Hi, Cyndi," he said. "How're you doing?"

"Fine."

"How was your trip down from St. Louis?"

"Fine."

Maris sighed. The Haucks had put Cyndi into what Maris called Shy Mode. And Cyndi was a stubborn, determined child; no one was going to get more than one-word answers out of her until she came out of it.

"Do you like Texas so far?" Keir persisted.

"Uh-huh."

"What about your room? Do you like that?"

"Uh-huh."

Maris watched Keir's face, waiting for him to get annoyed. But there was only amusement in his eyes, and she relaxed.

But he was obviously not the sort of man who gave up easily. He crouched beside the child's chair, leaning one elbow on the table as he met her stubborn blue gaze. "Are you going to say anything besides 'fine' and 'uh-huh'?" he asked.

Cyndi shook her head. Suddenly she grinned at him, that heart-stopping, crooked smile that was so like her father's. Maris had to turn away from it.

"Sit down, Keir," Sophie ordered. "My husband likes to eat breakfast at a certain time."

Keir looked startled, but took the seat across from Maris.

Maris glanced from him to Ballard Hauck, who was staring vacantly as he dribbled bits of egg onto his chest. Ballard didn't look as though he knew what planet he was on, let alone what time it was. He must have been one hell of a tyrant to so dominate his family even now. But then maybe it wasn't him, she reflected, but them. Maybe they were holding on to routine so hard because it was all they had of him. *That* she could understand.

Sophie buttered a piece of toast. "Before the rest of you came in, I had just begun telling Maris and Cyndi the history of this table."

"Did you tell them about the spurs?" Robyn asked. "That's my favorite part."

Maris looked up, startled. "Spurs?"

"Look at the trestle below your feet," Sophie said.

Maris obeyed, finding a network of white scars on the dark oak of the trestle.

"Those marks were made by spurs worn by Ballard's grandfather, old Josiah Hauck."

"He wore spurs in the house?" Maris flushed, embarrassed by the impulsive question. It wasn't any of her business what Josiah Hauck did.

Sophie didn't seem to mind, however. "Josiah's wife died young, you see. He didn't remarry, preferring to raise his four sons himself. Without a woman to look after things, I'm afraid their living arrangements became rather . . . unorthodox."

Rather, Maris thought, but didn't say it. Glancing up at Keir, she saw that he was grinning at her as though he'd read her mind.

"This table was built by Josiah's father, Hubert. It's been in the family for more than a hundred years," Sophie continued, "and has graced the dining room of every Hauck dwelling, no matter how grand or humble."

Keir laughed. "Of course, the Haucks haven't been humble for a very long time."

"Not since 1901, when oil was discovered on Garvin's land," Sophie said.

Suddenly Ballard Hauck spoke, bringing them all around in surprise. "You, boy!" he growled.

"Me?" Keir asked.

But Ballard was staring straight at Cyndi, his eyes tracking her like a gunner' s range finder. "You, boy!"

The child shrank toward Maris. "Me?"

"Didn't I teach you better than to wear a hat at the table?" the old man asked.

Cyndi reached up to touch her baseball cap. "But—"

"Take it off."

Maris glanced around the table, seeing shock on every face. She didn't dare think about what hers looked like.

Keir was the first to regain his wits. "Mr. Hauck, why don't you finish your eggs before they get cold?"

"Take it off!" A line of spittle ran down Ballard's chin.

"This happens sometimes," Sophie said. In a low voice that had more command than apology in it, she added, "Humor him."

Maris pushed her chair back with a sharp scrape. "I think we'd better leave," she said. As she started to get to her feet, however, Cyndi grasped her hand.

"I don't mind, Mom. Really."

"I mind."

"Mom, don't."

Maris let her breath out in a long sigh, then nodded.

With her firm little chin held defiantly high, Cyndi pulled the baseball cap off and tucked it in her lap. Her head gleamed as though it had been polished. The beginning fuzz of new hair caught the light, and it made the near-nakedness of her scalp even more shocking.

Robyn gasped sharply. Although Sophie's face was impassive, her coffee cup rattled as she set it down into the saucer. And . . . Keir's eyes were dark with remembered pain. Maris knew he was seeing his brother again. She turned away from it; her own pain was more than enough to bear.

Cyndi hadn't looked away from Ballard Hauck. "Is that better, sir?" she asked.

The old man grunted. The focus of his eyes faltered, and he looked from Sophie to Robyn to Maris with obvious bewilderment.

"Ballard, it's time for breakfast," Sophie said. "Would you like some bacon and eggs? Romona cooked them especially for you."

He nodded. Sophie gestured to Robyn, who hurriedly picked up the spoon and resumed feeding her father.

"Have some more toast," Sophie offered a plate piled high with golden-brown triangles.

"No, thank you," Maris said. Her appetite was gone.

"We're supposed to have marvelous weather today," the old woman said, speaking quickly and with false brightness. "Sixty-four degrees has been predicted. I hope you and Cyndi brought some lightweight clothing."

Seeing the shine of tears in Sophie's eyes, Maris let go of her anger. For the first time, she felt as though she and the old woman might have some common ground. Maris knew she was oversensitive about Cyndi's baldness. It wasn't the lack of hair; it was the fact that there was never a time when she could look at her daughter and pretend she wasn't dying of cancer.

And Sophie had her husband, an autocratic, demanding . . . senile old man. Still running the household according to his dictates, still hurrying to meet his every need. The *patrón*. In essence, he was gone. But there was love in Sophie's eyes when she looked at what had once been her husband, and she was obviously not ready to give up on him.

"So, Maris," the old woman said. "What are your plans?"

"I thought I'd take a ride up to Houston and find a library. I want to start going through their old newspapers."

"Before you bury yourself in the stacks, I'd like to call Hugh Carideo at VNOR TV," Keir said. "He hosts a show geared to community doings, and has already expressed an interest in the donor search. I think it would be a great forum for us."

Dread closed Maris's throat, and she laid her fork down. "I didn't expect to have to go on television."

"Carl Hansson said you're a natural," Keir said. "You'll be great, don't worry. Before I'm finished with you, you'll be speaking to civic groups and at churches, women's auxiliaries and garden clubs."

Maris opened her mouth to tell him exactly what she thought about him taking her family's private misery and turning it into a three-ring circus.

Then Cyndi leaned forward. "You're going to be on TV?" she demanded, her face bright with excitement. "That's *great!*"

"Would you like to be on television with her?" Keir asked.

"Yes!" Cyndi turned back to Maris. "Can I, Mom? Can I?"

Realizing that her mouth was still open, Maris closed it. She reached out and lightly stroked her daughter's head, feeling the light peach fuzz of new hair against her palm. "Yes, hon, you can."

Cyndi swung around to Keir. "Are we going to do it today?"

"If I can arrange it with the station," he said.

There was so much confidence in his voice that Maris knew it was as good as done. Wave the magic Hauck name, and anything was possible. God, that sounded cynical! She ought to have more gratitude than this. Whatever their motivations, these people were making it possible for her to help Cyndi.

"How about it, Maris?" Keir asked. "Will you do it?"

Maris wished she could say no. But she no longer had any boundaries; she would lie, cheat, steal, sell her body on a street corner or her soul to the devil if that would buy Cyndi's life. She ought to be happy that all she had to do was be interviewed on television.

"Yes, I'll go," she said.

Sophie cleared her throat. "About these public speakings, Maris. The Haucks are public figures, or at least the senator is. People are curious. Since you're living in our house, you're going to be asked a great many questions about us."

"Yes?" A sick feeling came into Maris's stomach.

"I trust you will be discreet. Keir will teach you how to direct an interviewer away from unwelcome subjects."

Maris felt her cheeks grow hot. She hadn't been so bluntly insulted since . . . she couldn't remember when. "Then, I shouldn't mention the senator's kindness in arranging for us to stay here?"

"It isn't necessary to go quite that far. But" — Sophie's gaze shifted briefly to Ballard before returning to Maris — "every family has things they would rather not parade before the public view."

"You can rest assured that I won't be gossiping about the Haucks." Barely, Maris kept from snarling.

"Thank you."

What is she protecting? Maris thought, looking into the old man's vacant eyes. *This? Don't the Haucks get old and senile and drippy like the rest of the world?* She glanced at Sophie's straight-backed posture, the rigid set of her shoulders, the fear of having her family's weakness exposed. Maybe the Haucks had been aristocracy for so long, they had lost the substance beneath the glitter.

The old woman laid her napkin on the table. "Robyn, it's time we got your father settled."

Robyn got to her feet and went to her father. With the ease of long practice, she wiped his chin, removed his napkin-bib, then wheeled him out of the room.

"Have a nice day," Sophie said, then followed her out.

Maris shook her head in disbelief. There was still food on Robyn's plate.

Cyndi yawned. "I think I'll go upstairs and lie down."

Instantly alert, Maris pushed her chair back and stood up. "come on, squirt, I'll get you settled."

"After you do," Keir said, "Come back down and I'll take you on a tour of the garden."

Cyndi left the room. Maris hung back for a moment, leaning her hands on the table to bring her face closer to Keir's. "Are you going to coach me in the fine art of bringing the senator's name into every interview?"

"Is that what you think?"

"I don't know. You said you wanted to exorcise demons, but—"

"But this *is* an election year."

She blew out her breath in exasperation. At times it felt as though he were reading her thoughts. She hated it, hated it more because she couldn't seem to read him

80

the same way. "What do you want from us — really?"
She watched his expression close as he slid away from
her question.

"Today, I just want to take a lady with pretty gray
eyes out for a walk in the garden," he said, his tone
light.

"Sorry," she said. "I'd rather not."

Eight

"Okay, ladies, you can relax now," Hugh Carideo said. "You were great." Pulling a handkerchief out of his pocket, he mopped his round, sweat-streaming face.

Maris was shaking, had been throughout the interview. If Hugh hadn't been so sympathetic, she didn't think she'd have gotten through it. But he had, so she did; but now she didn't remember a thing she'd said.

"Did I make a fool of myself?" she asked.

"Mo-om!" Cyndi gasped in preteen horror.

A smile split Hugh's good-natured face. "You'd be surprised how many people ask that," he said. "No, Maris, you were not a fool. And, Cyndi, you were born for the camera, darlin'."

"I want to be an actress when I grow up."

Cyndi was always bubbling with plans for her future: astronaut, model, actress, ocean biologist — the list changed from week to week. *Please God,* Maris prayed, *let her grow up to be some of those things.*

Hugh pushed himself up from his chair. "Come on, let's take a look at the tape."

He led them to a room a short distance away. Keir was there, talking to a man who was fiddling expertly with a mind-boggling array of electronics equipment.

Keir glanced over his shoulder at them. "Wait 'til you see this," he said.

Hugh pointed to a TV screen on the opposite wall. A picture flickered to life there, and Maris realized this was the very beginning of the interview.

Do I really look like that? She smoothed the front of her skirt. Those were her eyes, her hair, her features, but the person on the TV couldn't be Maris Durant. That woman looked poised and self-assured, her face not showing a hint of the terror that had been inside her. She'd even remembered the obligatory expressions of gratitude toward the Hauck family, and Senator John Hauck in particular. Payment for Dr. Guaymus.

"Maris photographs like a dream," the technician said, pointing to Maris's TV persona. "Look at the way that skin picks up the light."

"What about me?" Cyndi asked.

Keir picked her up and carried her closer to the screen. "You were the star, sweetheart. Every kid in Houston is going to want a Cardinal's baseball cap."

The technician began fast-forwarding through the tape. Suddenly his finger stabbed down on a button. "Whoa, fellas, look at this."

Maris recognized the part of the interview when Hugh had asked her how she'd felt when the doctors had told her Cyndi's only hope was a bone marrow transplant. She was relieved to see that she'd been coherent and calm. Maybe she hadn't made too much of a fool of herself, after all.

Suddenly she saw a tear slide from the eye of the TV-Maris. It caught the light for a moment, a brief, brilliant gem beneath the spotlights.

"Wow, look at that," Hugh breathed. "I didn't even notice it at the time."

Neither had Maris, and the sight of it was like a punch in the guts. She'd thought she'd held everything inside. But that tear had revealed her pain more vividly than if she had sobbed it aloud, and was all the more powerful because it had been controlled. She felt as though she'd been stripped naked.

"What a shot!" Keir said. "We couldn't have gotten such impact if we'd rehearsed it a thousand times."

"Will you let me do another interview in a couple of weeks?" Hugh asked. "I want to follow Cyndi's story as it progresses, and I think the viewers will, too. Maybe we can get the senator on as well?"

"I think that could be arranged," Keir said. "Are you sure you're going to run this tonight?"

"Yeah, five o'clock. Even if I hadn't been juggling things around today, I would have slotted this to run. It's good and solid, a couple of minutes' editing, max. These Durant girls have it."

"Have what?" Cyndi asked, her face avid.

"Charisma, darlin'," Hugh said.

Keir set Cyndi back on her feet, but kept her hand tucked in his. "Thanks, Hugh."

"What do you mean by charisma?" Cyndi demanded.

"I mean," Hugh said, "that you're going to slay them, darlin'."

It was afternoon by the time they got back to Hauck, and raining. This was no gentle shower, but a downpour of such force that the raindrops seemed to bounce when they hit the pavement. Maris, watching the wipers slash water from the windshield, was glad Keir was driving.

"Look," Keir said in a low voice, jabbing his thumb toward the backseat. "The poor kid is exhausted. Too much excitement, I guess."

Maris swiveled around. Cyndi had fallen asleep, her head pillowed on Keir's jacket, her body swaying with the motion of the car. All morning, she'd been buoyed by the excitement of the interview. Now she was paying the price.

With a sigh, Maris turned back around. "Tell me it doesn't always rain like this," she said.

Keir's faint Texas accent became more pronounced, a perfect imitation of Hugh Carideo. "This is just a good, old-fashioned Houston gully-washer, darlin'. Nothin' to worry about."

"I liked Hugh a lot," Maris said. "Even if he did call every female darlin'. At least he didn't call me 'little darlin' like he did that secretary."

"Considering that he had to look up to you, that might have made him look kinda silly. He did call you a long-legged darlin' once, though."

"Only once."

"You've got a glare that would make a basilisk cringe, Ms. Durant. But you can't blame him for trying." Keir glanced down at her legs, waggling his eyebrows in mock lechery. Maris couldn't help but laugh.

"That's the first time I've heard you laugh," he said. "You should do it more often."

Sudden, unexpected tears stung her eyes, and she turned to look out the window. Paul would have said than. He always laughed easily. She was the intense one, the one who always felt wrongs too deeply.

As though reading her thoughts, Keir reached over, gripping her hand in a grip that didn't quite hurt, but which wasn't quite gentle, either. "You can't afford to lose your sense of humor, Maris. It can keep you sane."

I can't afford to lose my daughter, either. Keir's sympathy required too much from her, and right now she had nothing left to give. She let her hand lie unresponsive beneath his. After a moment, he let her go.

The sign marking the estate's entrance loomed up in the water-drenched dimness. Keir made the turn slowly, then sped up as he neared the drive to the house. The rain beat down with renewed viciousness, drumming loudly on the car roof.

"Better wake Cyndi," he said. "I'm going to park in front so we can make a dash for the door."

The moment he stopped the car, the rain started coming down even more heavily, torrents of it. Keir helped Cyndi climb over into the front seat, then turned to Maris.

"Run!" he said.

She flung the car door open and pelted toward the door, Cyndi a few feet behind her. It was only a few yards, but they got soaked, anyway. The instant they reached the porch, the rain stopped—suddenly, completely, as though someone had thrown a switch.

Keir was still in the car, looking as surprised as Maris felt. Then he grinned. Maris was sure she wouldn't have gotten quite so annoyed if he hadn't smiled. She glared at him as he got out of the car with elaborate lack of haste.

As he sauntered up the steps, the sun came out, gilding the water-covered pavement and bringing a rainbow to life in the distance.

"I ought to shove you off the porch," Maris snarled.

"Hey, am I responsible for the weather?" he asked, spreading his arms wide.

"You said to run!"

Cyndi took off her baseball cap and wrung it out, spattering the tops of Keir's polished dress shoes. Keir looked down at his feet, then up at her, then over at Maris. The three of them started laughing.

"I never thought I'd be glad not to have hair," Cyndi gasped, scrubbing at her head with the hem of her dress.

"That dress is wetter than you are." Keir took his tie off and pretended to buff her head with it.

Cyndi squealed and dodged. Keir stalked her, holding the tie out in front of him like a garrote. Suddenly he straightened.

"Hey, you're a blonde!" he said.

"Yup. Want to feel?"

He reached out and ran his hand over her scalp. Maris admired him for being so casual about it.

"Neat," he said. "Like one of those Ken dolls with the plush heads they used to have years and years ago. Remember those, Maris?"

"Unfortunately."

The door opened. Maris turned, expecting to see Alejo or Dolores, but the man who stood in the doorway was a stranger. He was tall and wide-shouldered, with just a hint of a roll around the middle. His facial skin was just beginning to sag around the jawline, and Maris guessed him to be in his early fifties. *This is definitely a Hauck,* Maris thought, studying his strong, jut-nosed face.

"John!" Keir exclaimed. "I didn't expect you until next week."

"I came down early. Couldn't wait to meet my guests," he said, reaching out to shake hands with Maris. "Welcome to Gavilan."

"Thank you, Senator," Maris said. His grip was warm and dry, his large hand totally engulfing hers. He was wearing black dress pants and a white shirt with the sleeves rolled up on his forearms. With those blue-gray eyes and perfectly coiffed salt-and-pepper hair, he looked like he'd stepped out of a menswear ad.

"My mother tells me that you and Cyndi were guests on Hugh Carideo's show. How did the interview go?"

"Pretty well," Maris said. "Considering that I was scared to death. At least I didn't babble."

"Having babbled on more than one occasion, I congratulate you on your poise." He smiled.

Maris smiled back, noting that his teeth were nearly as white as his dress shirt. She got the impression that his attention was totally focused on her. At this moment, there seemed to be nothing more important to him than Maris Durant. *Good technique,* a small, cynical corner of her mind murmured. She knew she was in the presence of The Politician.

Then he looked at Cyndi, and his focus shifted swiftly and completely. "Hello, Cyndi. How are you enjoying Texas so far?" His voice softened when he spoke to the child, hitting just the right note to make her relax.

"We're going to be on TV," Cyndi said. "At five o'clock."

"Then, I'll have to make sure I see it, won't I?" The senator checked his watch. "It's nearly a quarter to five. Why don't you two run upstairs and change while Mr. Andreis and I catch up on some business?

Then we'll all meet in the family room and watch your interview together."

He swept his arm wide, a courtly gesture ushering them into his home. Maris stepped past him, hesitating when she saw the pristine expanse of tile.

"Cyndi, take your shoes off," she said. "We don't want to track up Mrs. Munoz's floor."

"Don't worry about it," the senator said. "It'll be nostalgic for Mrs. Munoz; we kids were always tracking up the place."

Maris wasn't sure any woman would list a dirty floor under "nostalgia," but it was, after all, the senator's floor. "We'll be down in a few minutes," she said, herding Cyndi toward the stairs.

"What do you think of him?" Cyndi asked when they were out of earshot.

"The senator?" Maris cocked her head to one side. "I thought he was pretty nice. What do *you* think?"

"He seems okay. What do you think about Keir?"

"He seems okay."

After changing into dry clothes, they hurried back downstairs. It took them a couple of minutes to find the family room, finally tracking it by the faint rumble of men's voices.

The door was open, and Maris could see Keir and the senator sitting on opposite ends of a vast sofa, papers spread out on the cushions between them. Campaign strategy, she guessed. If Cyndi hadn't wanted to watch the interview so badly, Maris would have gone back upstairs. Instead, she knocked softly.

The senator looked up. "Come on in! Don't mind our mess, ladies. This isn't anything important."

His unconscious elegance made Maris feel out of place in blue jeans and a long-sleeved tee shirt. But Keir looked rumpled and very human, and the sight got her moving forward. The family room was long and narrow, spanning at least a fourth of the rear of the house, and she suspected it had once been two rooms. A wet bar at one end helped relieve some of the disproportionate length, but the space was still awkward. The sofa, two wing chairs and a roomy, upholstered rocking chair were grouped in front of the biggest TV Maris had ever seen.

The furniture, wood paneling and carpeting were in earth tones, beige and brown and russet. A man's room, a man's taste. Maris wouldn't have been surprised to find a moose head or a set of longhorns mounted above the fireplace. But someone had managed to slip in some touches of pale turquoise in the accessories, giving the room a nice Southwestern flavor.

It wasn't until Maris was halfway across the room that she saw Sophie sitting in one of the wing chairs, her large, square hands folded in her lap.

"Hello, my dears," Sophie said. "I hear your interview went well. I'm anxious to see it."

"Mr. Carideo made it easy for us," Maris said. Something hit her wrong about Sophie, but she couldn't quite. . . . Now she had it. Those idle hands. *My mother would have been sewing,* she thought. *Mom never just sat.*

"Hugh Carideo certainly didn't make it easy for *me,*" John said. "The last time he interviewed me, he raked me over the coals for my vote on certain legislation."

"Oh?" Maris asked. "What legislation?"

"He wanted to take food away from widows and orphans," said a man from behind Maris.

She turned to see yet another Hauck. There was no mistaking the jutting nose which Sophie had apparently bestowed on both her sons. Maris wondered how Robyn had escaped it.

"This is my brother, Garrick," John said. "Garrick, Maris and Cyndi Durant."

Garrick reached to shake hands. He might have been forty-five or so, his wide-shouldered Hauck frame tending toward fat. His smile was practiced. "Hello, ladies. I'm the black sheep, entrepreneur, Hauck-of-all-trades."

"What is it this week, Garrick?" his brother asked.

"Widgets, Senator. Widgets and boondoggles. The best you ever saw. Want to buy a gross?"

John's and Sophie's mouths were set in precisely the same grim lines of disapproval. The senator didn't have quite so many wrinkles, but the effect was the same. Maris glanced up at Garrick and saw malicious laughter dancing in his eyes. *Black sheep, indeed,* she thought.

"How about it, John?" he asked. "With all that money you save from not feeding the widows and orphans, you might be able to swing *two gross.* Pass 'em out to the good ole boys up there in the Senate."

"That isn't funny, Garrick," Sophie snapped.

"Don't pay any attention to him, Mother." John indicated the sofa, which Keir had just cleared of papers. "Come on, ladies. Sit down. There's plenty of room."

Cyndi rushed to sit beside Keir. Maris got the senator. Out of the corner of her eye, she saw Garrick take the chair opposite his mother. He was still smiling, but the humor in his eyes had turned bitter. Maris could almost taste the tension in the room. And although she knew asking her next question would only increase it, she couldn't let it go.

91

"Senator, exactly what does Hugh Carideo dislike about your politics?" she asked.

"He didn't approve of my vote on a few budget cuts last year, claimed social programs should be sacrosanct." His gaze wandered to his brother, the first time Maris had seen his intense concentration shaken. "But this is a very complex issue. I take the position that *everything* needs to be cut when you're looking at massive deficits. Bold measures must be taken, both on a state and national level if we're to dig ourselves out of this hole."

"But social programs are sometimes the only safety net for people," Maris protested.

He clasped his hands on his stomach. "I understand that. After all, I come from a working-class background."

"Working class!" Garrick gave a hoot of laughter. "What do you think about that statement, Maris?"

Maris thought John must be badly out of touch to think that he had much in common with the working class, but was saved from answering by Sophie.

"There's no need to be nasty, Garrick," the old woman said. "It's true that we have money, but that has never stopped John from sympathizing with those less fortunate." She turned and gave John a look of such simpering maternal pride that Maris nearly choked.

Garrick snarled something under his breath.

"Now, Maris," John said, tapping her shoulder to regain her attention. "You have to realize that no matter how I voted, I would have made *someone* mad. The Democrats, for instance, are always mad at me."

"That's because they know they can't beat you, darling," Sophie said.

Maris glanced at Keir, who was engaged in a whispered conversation with Cyndi. Again, she wondered at his motives for bringing them down here. It seemed the senator definitely needed a boost in the human-interest aspect of his image. And just like Carl Hansson had said, Cyndi's story had poignancy and drama. *So what?* whispered that cynical corner of her mind. *As long as Cyndi gets treatment, who cares?* She ought to believe that. Maybe if she worked hard at it, she might be able to.

"Hey, it's nearly five o'clock," John said, glancing at his watch. He aimed the remote control at the TV, and light bloomed on the huge screen.

"That's the biggest TV I *ever* saw," Cyndi said.

John chuckled. "My father is . . . was a football fan. He had a box for every Oilers game. When he became too sick to go out, we had this room done so he could continue to watch football."

Cyndi looked from the senator to his mother. "Does he—"

"Ssst!" Maris hissed.

"That's all right," John said. "The question is only natural under the circumstances." He leaned forward. "No, Cyndi, my father doesn't really watch all the games. Sometimes, however, he seems to enjoy what's going on, so we keep putting him in front of the TV."

Maris tried to imagine the old man sitting parked in front of the television, staring blankly at the screen. Did they sit here with him, watching him in case he responded? Probably. She glanced at Sophie out of the corner of her eye and saw that the old woman was still looking at John with obvious adoration.

She doesn't like Garrick much, though, Maris

93

thought. Black sheep, black sheep . . . how hard had he tried to win the love that seemed available only to the senator? Ballard had been a senator, too. Oh, boy! Freud would have had a field day with this one.

"Turn it louder, turn it louder!" Cyndi said.

Keir chuckled. "You're not excited or anything, are you?"

"Yes!" Cyndi all but bounced on the cushion. "Hey, can we borrow a blank tape? I want to keep this so I can show my friends at school when we get home."

"There's one in the VCR, all ready to go." Keir reached across Cyndi and Maris. "Here, John, let me have that remote. I think I'd better put Cyndi in charge."

The Hugh Carideo Show was just coming on, Hugh's broad, good-natured face floating like a helium balloon in the oversized screen. Then the camera panned to the studio where Hugh conducted his interviews.

Again Maris found herself watching a poised, articulate stranger with her face. The scene with the tear still bothered her, however; it was disturbing to know things could slip out without her knowing.

When the interview was nearly over, Hugh swung around in his swivel chair to face the camera and said, "So, folks, now you understand why it's so important for Maris to find her birth family. Senator John Hauck is offering a five thousand dollar reward for information that leads to finding Maris's birth mother." He swiveled to face Maris again. "Maris, darlin', give us the date of your birth."

The TV-Maris cleared her throat. "It's May 23, 1958."

Sophie rose from her chair, slowly, as though the

movement hurt. Her face was pasty, her eyes glazed with shock. She took a single, staggering step toward the sofa, then another.

"Mrs. Hauck, what's wrong?" Maris asked, sure the woman was having a stroke. "Grab her! She's going to fall!"

Garrick jumped to his feet, but the old woman held out her arm in a gesture that was imperious even in her agitation. "No," she rasped. "John."

The senator was up in an instant, supporting her with his arm around her shoulders. She leaned against him, her footsteps dragging as he led her from the room.

"What the hell?" Keir asked.

Maris looked at Garrick, who was still standing with his arm outstretched. His rejection had been complete and very cruel, made even more so by the fact that it had been done before strangers. Then he looked up at her, his eyes stark with pain.

"I'm sorry," she said. Sorry it happened, sorry she'd witnessed it.

He let out his breath in a long sigh. "I shouldn't give a damn. Not anymore."

There was nothing Maris could say. Garrick didn't speak again, and a moment later he turned and strode to the bar.

"What's going on," Keir demanded. "Is Mrs. Hauck ill?"

Garrick poured a hefty amount of Scotch into a glass and drained it with an ease that spoke of long practice. Then he poured another. "Mother?" He gave a harsh bark of a laugh. "She's fine. Physically, she's as strong as a horse. But as Daddy used to say, our dear mother is 'high-strung.' And just now she got a very nasty shock."

"It was something in the interview, wasn't it?" Maris asked.

"Yeah." Garrick gulped half the second drink. "You said you were born on May 23, 1958, right?"

"Right."

"That's a very special date to us. You see . . ." He took another big swallow of Scotch. "That's the day my sister Lee was murdered."

Nine

"Murdered?" Maris echoed.

"Yeah. May 23, 1958," Garrick said. "Shot by her lover, Drew Eniston. A cowboy from *way* on the wrong side of the tracks. He seduced her, then turned her against her family. Didn't even marry her. Can you see it? Lee Hauck, the prim little debutante, shacked up with him in a dump of an apartment? And then he killed her and their baby. God, Daddy hated that man."

Keir looked stunned. "John told me he had a sister who'd been killed years ago, but I had no idea it was so . . . so . . ."

"Lurid?" Garrick supplied.

"I'm not sure that was the word I would have used."

Garrick took another long pull of Scotch. "Why not? The newspapers loved it. You should have seen the headlines. I was only ten years old then, but I'll never forget some of the things they said."

Maris's mind floundered as she tried to assimilate it. *Lee Hauck died a violent death the day I was born.* Suddenly something else Garrick said penetrated. "There was a baby?"

97

"Was. After he killed my sister, Eniston dumped the baby in the river. Drowned it like a damned kitten." The brutal words were made even worse by Garrick's flat, emotionless tone.

"Oh, God!" Maris whispered. "Why did he do it?"

"No one knows," Garrick said.

"He never tried to explain why?"

He shook his head. "All he said was, 'Sure, I did it.' He said it to the press, the lawyers and the judge, then clammed up. Never tried to defend himself in any way. Then or since."

"What happened to him?" Keir asked.

"He got life in prison without a chance of parole," Garrick said. "It should have been the electric chair. Why they let him live after what he did to Lee, I'll never understand. When they read the sentencing, I thought Daddy was going to have a stroke."

In the appalled silence that fell, he tucked the bottle of Scotch under his arm. "Now, if you all will excuse me, I'm going to go up to my room and try to make reality just a little less real."

He left the room. Keir shook his head like a punch-drunk boxer, then trotted after him.

"Garrick, wait!" he called.

There was a rumble of low conversation, which grew more and more faint as the men moved away.

Maris held her breath until the sound of voices faded completely. Then she heaved a long sigh. "Wow."

"Did that man really do that, Mom? Did he really drown the baby?" Cyndi asked.

Putting her arm around the child's shoulders,

Maris drew her close. Cyndi was tough and level-headed, but there were some things no kid was tough enough for. Her own stomach was clenched into a knot at the thought of what had happened to Lee and her baby. "I wish you hadn't heard that, hon."

"Oh, Mom, there's worse stuff than that in the newspaper every day. Did he do it?"

"I guess he did, or they wouldn't have put him in prison," Maris said. Her mind was working frantically now, trying to reorder the world according to these new rules. How was she going to deal with Sophie? *Her daughter was killed the day I was born.* It was both a tie and a barrier between them.

She needed to get out of the house, if only for a while. The sight of the Haucks' smooth, public persona being stripped away was shocking, somehow, an intimacy she neither expected nor wanted. She didn't want to see their wounds; her own were enough to bear.

"Come on, squirt," she said, rising to her feet and drawing Cyndi up with her. "I need a break. Let's go somewhere and eat."

Cyndi nodded, apparently as eager as Maris to escape the confines of the house. "Where's the car?"

"I think they parked it off to the side of the house."

"Front door's closer."

"Let's go."

They made it to the foyer without meeting anyone, and Maris began to hope they might get away without having to explain themselves. But just as she reached for the doorknob, Alejo came hurrying into the foyer.

"Good evening, señora, señorita," he said. "There is something I can do for you?"

"We were just going out for a while," Maris said.

"Ah." His sleek, dark hair gleamed in the light as he glanced down at his watch. "Now? But you will miss dinner. Mrs. Hauck just sent me down to tell you that they will eat at six-thirty, as usual."

Even now they can't let go, Maris thought. *How sad.* "Please extend my regrets, but we've made other plans."

His expression didn't change, but there was surprise in his black eyes. He remained silent, apparently waiting for her to elaborate. Maris did not intend to. Maybe no one else in this house crossed the *patrón* — God knows why, the man wasn't aware of what went on around him — but she wasn't about to dance to that tune.

Alejo waited; Maris waited. Then he shrugged "I will bring the car around."

"We don't mind walking," Maris said.

"It is no trouble." Without waiting for a reply, he went out.

Maris let her breath out in a hiss of exasperation. But there was nothing to be done, nothing at all. "Come on, Cyndi, let's wait out on the porch."

A moment later, Alejo pulled up in a black Cadillac. Leaving the engine running, he slid out from beneath the wheel and trotted up the steps toward them.

"That's not my car," Maris said.

"No, señora. But I took your car in to the body shop this morning. While it is gone, Señora Hauck

100

put this car at your disposal. And please do not worry about inconveniencing anyone; this is a spare vehicle."

"Oh. Well, thank you," Maris said, astounded by the idea of someone having a spare Cadillac lying around.

She got in, and the soft leather interior of the car wrapped around her like a glove. It was a *nice* car.

"I could get used to this," Cyndi said.

"Better not. I don't make enough money to put gas in this thing, let alone buy one." Maris took a minute to familiarize herself with the controls, then put the car into gear and let it ease forward.

Keir rushed out of the house, waving his arms to flag them down as he ran down the steps toward them. Maris stopped the car. Cyndi fumbled a moment with the electric window, then got it down about the time Keir reached them.

"Where are you going?" he asked.

"We're going out to eat," Cyndi said. "After experiencing Ballard Breakfast this morning, we thought we'd try something a little different for supper."

He opened the door. "Shove over, sport. You're not leaving me here alone."

"Coward," Maris said.

"Look who's talking," he retorted, sliding into the seat. "Hurry up, before they send Dolores out here to bring us back."

Maris drove the Cadillac gingerly, terrified of being responsible for so expensive a car. Cattle stared at her from the pastureland on either side of the road, their broad, white faces giving them a faintly incredulous look.

"Get a grip, Mom. At this rate we'll starve before we get to town."

"Get a grip, yourself. I don't think I have enough insurance to pay for this thing if I wreck it."

Cyndi snorted. "Where are we going to eat?"

"I've been in Texas two whole days now, and I haven't had a single bite of Mexican food," Maris said. "Some chips and salsa, a nice, big burrito—"

"Yuck!" Cyndi wailed. "I'm going to barf!"

Maris ignored the stifled laugh that came from Keir's side of the car. "Okay, so what's your suggestion?"

"I saw a Burger Wonder on our way through town."

"Pedestrian swill!" Maris snarled.

This time Keir laughed out loud.

"You know, Mom, you sound just like Daddy," Cyndi said. "He always said that when I suggested fast food."

Memory flooded in, sharp and visceral, but it didn't hurt as much as Maris would have expected. "You're right, he did. That was one of those sayings we called his 'college-professor talk.'" She risked a glance at Keir, who was grinning like an ape. "You could at least suggest a compromise."

"I'll give it a shot," he said, taking a deep breath. "How about I take you to dinner at Pedrito's? They serve Mexican food *and* hamburgers."

"But I've got to watch her eat that stuff," Cyndi said. "I promise you, I'll puke."

"Have you ever tried fried ice cream?" he asked.

102

"Huh?"

"Apparently you haven't." His voice dropped an octave. "Oh, Cyndi, you haven't lived until you've tasted Pedrito's fried ice cream. It's the absolute best dessert on the face of the earth."

Cyndi was silent for a few moments, and Maris could almost hear the gears whirring in that ten-year-old mind. Finally Cyndi said, "Okay. I'll go to Pedrito's. But only if you promise to buy me some of that fried ice cream."

"Done!" Keir said. "Now, if your mother could speed up to say, thirty-five, we might get there before it gets crowded."

The food turned out to be all that Keir advertised. Especially the fried ice cream. Maris scraped her plate clean, wishing she had room for another helping.

"Anybody want anything else?" Keir asked. "Maris, some coffee?"

"I'm full up," she said. "All the way up."

"Where's the bathroom?" Cyndi asked.

Keir pointed toward the rear of the restaurant. "Back there by the telephones."

"Okay, let's go," Maris said.

"I'm fine, Mom. I was just teasing before about puking, really. I just have to go to the bathroom."

Maris, however, had seen too much of chemotherapy's effects to take it at face value. "Are you sure?"

"Mo-om, I'll be *fine!*"

Aware that Keir was watching her, Maris flushed. He probably thought she was some neurotic kind of mother, hovering over her child like. . . . She took a deep breath. Like Sophie and Robyn, hovering over an oblivious Ballard.

I won't. Cyndi's going to have her dignity. "Well, go on," she said, flapping her hands in dismissal.

But she couldn't keep from watching her daughter's small, spare figure as Cyndi wended her way through the tables. *So little time,* Maris thought. *And so much to lose.*

Keir reached across the table and touched her hand. "Maris, something's bothering you. Want to talk about it?"

"You mean something besides my daughter having leukemia?"

"Don't use that as a smokescreen, Maris. If you've got something on your mind, spill it."

"Tell me — what's Senator Hauck's record on public issues?"

Keir grimaced. "Fair to middling."

"Fair to poor?"

"Okay, fair to poor." The waitress came with the bill, and he paused to take his credit card out of his wallet and drop it into the tray. "Some people think the Haucks have been too rich for too long to ever be in touch with the so-called common man."

Maris, remembering the spare Cadillac, couldn't disagree with that assessment. "So instead of voting to feed the widows and orphans, he decided to bring Cyndi and me down here."

"No. I'm the one who asked him to do that. And you know my reasons."

Do I? But to say it would mean an argument, judging by the look on his face. So, instead, she

104

leaned her elbows on the table and asked, "Are you from Texas?"

"I was born and raised in Paris, Texas, went to Texas A & M, grad school at Harvard." He said it "Hahvahd," like a proper Bostonian. "I liked A & M."

"But not Harvard?"

He shrugged. "They helped me tame my Texas drawl."

"I didn't go to college," she said. "I've always wished I had."

"Why didn't you?"

It was her turn to shrug. "Wasn't expected, I guess. My dad was an autoworker. He was a great father, but a college education just wasn't on his list of necessities for a girl. It's not that he would have stopped me if I'd wanted to go. But I just never quite got around to pushing for it."

"You married a college professor."

"Hey, if you can't have it yourself, marry it."

His brows went up. "Do I detect bitterness there?"

"Yeah." Suddenly noticing that she had folded her napkin into a tiny square, she unfolded it and smoothed the wrinkles with the palm of her hand. "I'm disappointed in myself for not doing it."

"What about designing jewelry? Don't you enjoy it?"

"Yes, I do."

"From what Carl Hansson said, your designs are wonderful. If you can hang on during the tough starting-up times, you should have a nice, thriving business for yourself. What's wrong with that?"

"Nothing. I like working for myself. But it bothers me that I didn't get my education. Sure, I had a husband and a child, but that's no excuse for not going to school."

"Maybe," he said, "you don't really want a degree. You just feel you should have one."

She stared at him in surprise. Could that be true? She'd met so many other goals over the years, why not that one? Most of Paul's friends were college-educated, and there had been many times when she'd felt like the odd man out. But then she'd have to consider the flip side; if she had gotten her degree, she might *still* have been odd man out.

"Maris, what do you think about Lee Hauck?" Keir asked.

Startled out of her reverie, she looked up at him. A number of answers occurred to her, but she chose the most honest, if not necessarily the one that answered his question directly. "As soon as possible, I'm hitting the library."

"Research?"

"I just want to take a look at some old newspapers."

"Are you interested in your birth or in Lee Hauck's death?"

"I'm interested in May 23, 1958."

"And Lee Hauck."

She spread her hands, capitulating. "Okay, I admit it. I want to know more about the murder. Wouldn't you, if you were me? I was born the day she was killed, and now, all these years later, I'm living with her family. Isn't that a little too weird to ignore?"

"It probably doesn't have anything to do

106

with your birth family. A coincidence of dates."

"Maybe. But the date is all I've got."

He nodded. "With all the other things you've got on your mind, I wish you didn't have to go through searching for your birth mother. What if you don't like what you find?"

"I already don't like it. But I don't —" Seeing that Cyndi was coming back, she made a chopping gesture with her hand.

Keir nodded, indicating that he'd taken the hint. "Let me get my card," he said, waving to get the waiter's attention.

A few minutes later, they were headed toward the Cadillac. The night was mild and very humid. Although it wasn't raining, a film of moisture lay upon everything. The Cadillac looked like a sleek, black insect in the light from the restaurant.

"Keir, do you want to drive?" Maris asked.

"Not me, no, uh-uh. I ate so much I'm in a stupor."

"I'll do it," Cyndi offered.

"Get real," Maris said. "And get in the car."

Cyndi insisted that Keir sit in the middle, between her and Maris. "I want to sit by the window," she said.

Maris put the car in gear and eased out of the parking lot. "You just want to play with the buttons."

"You got it." The bill of the Cardinal's cap swiveled from side to side as Cyndi took in the sights of the little downtown, quizzing a sleepy Keir about everything she saw.

Maris remained silent, preferring to concentrate on her driving. There was a surprising amount of

107

traffic, considering the size of the town. When she finally commented on that, Keir laughed.

"Maris, Hauck is no ordinary small Texas town. Just about everybody who is anybody who doesn't want to live in the Houston rat-race lives here."

"Huh?" Maris said.

He laughed again. "Hauck probably has the highest percentage of millionaires of anywhere in Texas. Julian Barney, the baseball hero, retired here. We have an active federal judge and two retired ones. A whole slew of high-powered lawyers live here and commute to Houston, as well as some corporate bigwigs from the oil companies. We've got three quack doctors and three *real* good ones, and the local hospital, Hauck Community, is better equipped than those in cities five times this size. And of course, there are the Haucks. Almost better than the Kennedys, at least in East Texas."

"Where are the regular people?" Maris asked, stopping behind a line of cars waiting at a red light.

"Thataway." Keir pointed southeast. "Most of the 'regular' people work at the chemical plant about seventeen miles outside of town. Going into that end of Hauck is like passing into another country: pickup trucks, Lone Star beer and country-western nightspots."

The signal turned green. Traffic moved forward, but the light turned red again before Maris made it into the intersection. She drummed her fingers on the steering wheel. Nine-thousand-odd inhabitants in this town, and it seemed that every one of them had decided to come downtown tonight.

"I'll take you, if you want," Keir said.

Maris blinked. "Take me where?"

"To the 'regular' people's end of town. There's a place called Smokey Pete's where you can dance."

"Are you asking Mom for a *date?*" Cyndi asked. "Cool."

Maris expected him to deny it, to say he was only offering to show her the town. But he didn't. Alarm bells went off all through her mind.

"Well?" he prompted.

"I . . . don't know." And she didn't.

"Think about it," he said.

The light turned green again, giving Maris an excuse to let the conversation drop. This time she made it through the intersection, and a moment later turned onto Aberdeen Road. She was feeling confident enough with the Cadillac now to accelerate up to the 55-mile-per-hour speed limit.

"How about some fresh air?" Cyndi asked, reaching for the window button.

Moisture-laden air slashed into the car, snatching the baseball cap off Cyndi's head and flipping it into the backseat.

"Hey, my hat!" Cyndi released her seat belt and swiveled so that she was kneeling on the seat. "There it is, on the floor."

"Just a second, I'll get it for you." Keir started to unfasten his seat belt.

"No, that's okay," Cyndi said, straining over the back of the seat. "I can almost . . . got it!"

A car zoomed out of a side street right in front of the Cadillac. Maris saw no headlights, no turn signal, nothing; the car almost seemed to materialize out of the darkness.

"Hang on!" she cried, jamming her foot down on the brake.

The rear wheels locked up, sending the Cadillac skidding down the street on shrieking, smoking tires. Maris lifted her foot off the brake, hoping to unlock the rear wheels, then braked again. This time the pedal slammed all the way to the floor.

The Cadillac slid onto the shoulder of the road, where the rain-wet earth grabbed at the tires, slowing it down slightly. Gritting her teeth against the jolting, Maris struggled to keep the right wheels on the shoulder.

"That's it," Keir said, his voice low and calm. "Hold it there, Maris."

The Cadillac slowed even more. Finally, after what seemed an eternity, it bounced to a stop and stalled out. Maris turned her head to see Keir holding Cyndi in his arms, his legs braced against the dashboard of the car. They both looked shaken, but were obviously unhurt. Cyndi was clutching the Cardinal's baseball cap in both hands.

She wasn't wearing a seat belt, Maris thought. If Keir hadn't caught her, if he hadn't been quick enough or strong enough. . . . Her heart jagged in her chest.

"Cyndi . . ." Her voice was a squeak.

"I'm all right, Mom."

One by one, Maris pried her fingers from around the steering wheel. The moment her hands were free, Cyndi was in her arms, holding, being held, shedding a few tears of reaction. After a few moments, Maris opened her eyes and looked over at Keir.

She still didn't know him, and she still wasn't

sure what his real motives were for helping Cyndi. It was possible he was using them to help put John Hauck in the governor's mansion. Governor Hauck would no doubt be very grateful to his campaign manager.

Then again, he could be just what he portrayed himself to be: a nice guy doing good in his brother's memory. Maris gave a mental shrug. Knight in shining armor or savvy shark in political waters, he had saved Cyndi from being injured.

Maybe he *was* using them. After what he'd done tonight, Maris figured he was entitled.

"Thanks," she said.

"My pleasure." He smoothed his hair back with hands that shook just a bit. "By the way, you can take your foot off the brake now."

Startled, Maris looked down to see that she was still holding the brake pedal jammed to the floor. She lifted her foot, only then feeling the tingle-stab of returning circulation.

"Any sign of the bas—jerk who pulled out in front of us?"

"Nary a one," Maris said. "I think I may give up driving. Two accidents in one week is just too much."

Keir's eyes widened. "Twice?"

"We got run off the road on the way down here," Cyndi said. "Mom managed to steer out of that one, too."

"A drunk," Maris explained. "Apparently he was so bombed that he didn't know there was someone else on the road."

"I didn't see this guy coming at all," Keir said. "Did he have any lights on?"

111

Maris shook her head. "It was like he came out of nowhere."

"I'd like to get my hands on that—" Glancing at Cyndi, he swallowed whatever else he was going to say. "Well, we ought to be glad it turned out as well as it did."

"I think there's something wrong with my brakes," Maris said. "The second I touched the pedal, the rear wheels locked up on me."

Keir unsnapped his seat belt and leaned forward to rummage in the glove compartment. "I hope there's a flashlight in here somewhere," he muttered. "Ah, here it is. Maris, put the emergency flashers on, will you? I don't want some yahoo running over me in the dark."

He shucked his jacket and got out of the car, his face reflecting the yellow pulsing light of the flashers. Maris lost sight of him when he moved around to the back of the car. A few minutes later he came back, mud smeared diagonally across the front of his shirt.

"There's a split in the right rear brake line," he said. "Every time you stopped, a little fluid got pumped out. Did the brakes feel strange to you earlier?"

"Everything in this car feels strange," Maris said. "I'm used to driving a 1984 Regal, remember?"

"Yeah." He let out his breath in a long sigh. "You done good, Maris, steering through that. And we were lucky it happened where and when it did; if you'd had to brake in traffic, or say, on one of those soaring flyovers on the highway—"

"We get the picture," Maris said.

112

"I'm going to walk to that house over there and call the house," he said.

Maris felt sudden tension in her shoulders. "I'd rather not tell the Haucks how close I came to wrecking their car."

"They're not going to care about that," he protested. "If anything, they'll be upset that we were in danger."

"But it's embarrassing to me," she said. "Look, I borrowed their car, and since it was damaged while I was driving it, the responsibility of fixing it should be mine. The Haucks are going to go all gracious and refuse to let me pay, and then I'm going to feel, well—"

"Beholden?"

"Yeah. And that would be fine, if there were any hope of me being able to repay their favors."

"Ah. The Durant pride again."

I don't own much else. "Come on, Keir. A brake line is nothing; it'll take all of a half-hour for a garage to fix it."

"Maris, it's Saturday night. Almost nine o'clock on Saturday night. The garages are closed. Besides, every mechanic in town knows Alejo and his cars. No matter where you take it, he'd know about it within minutes."

"I can see that there are disadvantages to living in a small town," she said.

Grinning, Keir folded his arms over his chest. "Face it, Maris. There are no secrets in Hauck, Texas. Yours or anyone else's."

"Damn," she muttered.

113

Ten

The next morning, Maris went down to breakfast expecting to face questions about her near accident. But no one mentioned the Cadillac's brakes. No one mentioned Lee Hauck's death, for that matter. It was Hauck business as usual: Ballard gobbled and dripped as Robyn silently fed him, Sophie divided her adoration equally between her husband and John, while Garrick sulked.

"So, Keir," Garrick said, "what do you think my brother's chances are of being elected governor?"

"Pretty good, as it stands," Keir said.

Garrick's gaze drifted to John. "Today's *Chronicle* has a story about Tim McPherson, your Democratic opponent. He's billing himself 'a man of the people.' Says John is too rich and too privileged to understand the majority of his constituents."

"A man of the people?" Keir repeated. "Wow. That's an interesting claim from a guy who made three hundred thousand dollars last year."

"Maybe *I* should run," Garrick said. "I can bill myself as the 'poor Hauck.'"

"There are no poor Haucks," Sophie said. "Only shiftless ones."

That statement left a gaping hole in the conversation. Maris saw Robyn shoot Garrick a look of mingled anger and sympathy, then wipe Ballard's mouth with more than necessary vigor.

Keir sat for a moment, his fork suspended in midair, then cleared his throat. "We can handle McPherson. Monday, when we get back to Austin—"

"We'll be staying here for a while," John said. "A couple of weeks, at least."

"We will?" Keir looked completely surprised.

John nodded. "With McPherson shooting off his mouth here in Houston, I think we need to counter him before the idea gets entrenched in people's minds. You'll need to rent a place in town. Talk to Bob Harmon at the realtor's office; he'll find you something."

Maris noticed that Sophie was staring at Cyndi, or rather, Cyndi's baseball hat. After Ballard's reaction to it yesterday, wearing it had been a small act of defiance, one Maris endorsed. Sophie's gaze moved from the hat to Ballard and back again, an obvious hint. Cyndi ignored it. So did Maris.

"We missed you at dinner last night, Maris," Sophie said.

There was a thinly veiled disapproval in her voice that was both a challenge and a reproof. Maris chose to meet it head-on. "Cyndi, Keir and I went out to eat, Mrs. Hauck. I thought that under the circumstances, the family would rather be alone for a while."

Sophie's gaze faltered, and she visibly withdrew from the subject.

"Did you take her to Pedrito's, Keir?" John asked. "I did."

The senator patted his lips with his napkin. "Pedrito's is arguably the best Mexican food north of

115

the border, Maris. It was opened in the early 1950's by Pedro Durillo as a combination cafe/cantina. His son owns it now. But as long as Mama Durillo runs the kitchen, the food will be wonderful."

Ah, a real politician's politician, Maris thought. *Drown everything in words, talk and talk until the issue is completely obscured.* And judging from the look on Sophie's face, it was just what the old woman wanted. She wasn't going to deal with the issue of Maris's birth and Lee's death. Like Ballard's senility, she was simply going to ignore it. And expect the rest of the world to ignore it, too.

The meal ground to an end much too slowly for Maris. But finally, Robyn wheeled Ballard out. It was like a rubber band had snapped, releasing the rest of the family from some sort of social paralysis.

"Keir, meet me in the study," John said, rising to his feet. "We've got a bundle of work to do today."

"See you." Keir winked at Cyndi and Maris, then trotted out of the room.

With a courtly gesture, John extended his arm to Sophie. She accepted it, letting him help her to her feet, then leaned heavily on him as they left the room.

Garrick stared at them from beneath shaggy black brows, his blue eyes sullen. He'd probably spent his life trying to please his mother, and failing. Sophie could see only the senator. Now Maris could understand why Robyn had looked at him with mingled sympathy and anger; the first for his pain, the second because he wouldn't learn not to care.

"I'm going to go upstairs and watch TV in bed," Cyndi said.

Maris turned to study her daughter. Even her lips were pale. It was the price of all the excitement of the past few days. "Want me to come up with you?"

Cyndi shook her head. "If I need anything, I'll call."

Don't hover. Maris stroked her fingertips down the child's cheek. "Okay, hon. I'll be up later."

Once Cyndi left, Maris was alone with Garrick. She didn't want to be, possessed as she was by conflicting desires to comfort him and give him a good, swift kick in the rear. When she turned to him, however, she was surprised to find him staring at her intently, the brooding look gone from his face.

"What is it?" she asked.

He stared at her a moment longer, then stood up and crooked his finger at her. "Come with me."

He led her to an honest-to-goodness library, with floor-to-ceiling shelves of books and a scattering of deep, comfortable chairs just made to curl up in. Maris turned in a slow circle, staring. Out of all the Haucks' wealth, this was the only thing she truly envied.

"This is wonderful," she breathed.

Garrick lifted one eyebrow. "Old Garvin bought them when he bought the rest of the furnishings for the house. I think the decorator picked them out for him; he wouldn't have known Shakespeare from Dr. Seuss, or cared. The rest of us seem to have been cut from the same cloth. The only people who come in here regularly are the maids, and that only to dust."

Maris felt true outrage. It seemed she'd spent half her life in libraries, reading, reading, reading. Even college-professor Paul had been surprised by the amount of reading she did. And here there was a treasure trove of books that no one bothered to open!

"You ought to see the look on your face," Garrick said.

"It's hard for me to imagine having all this"—she spread her arms wide to encompass the room—"and not using it."

He shrugged. "Lee was the reader. She'd curl up in that chair by the fireplace and stick her nose in a book for hours."

"Did you bring me here to talk about Lee?"

"Uh-huh. You're stewing over this thing with the date, aren't you?"

"Wouldn't anyone?"

"I guess so. I just. . . . Look, I don't think you ought to talk about it to my mother. She's too fragile."

Sophie, fragile? Maris thought in astonishment.

Her face must have reflected that thought, for Garrick said, "Lee was her favorite. Not only hers, but everyone's. Lee was a sweet, generous person. A little flighty, maybe, a little too vulnerable as I look back on it. But back then she was the big sister who watched over us smaller kids, played with us, took us places. I loved her."

He paused for a moment, breathing hard. When he began speaking again, his voice was tight. "When Lee left home to live with Drew Eniston, it almost tore this family apart. Then she was murdered. Daddy was like a crazy man, and my mother withdrew from the world. For weeks, she spent her days sitting in a chair, staring off into space. We kids, especially me and Robyn, did everything we could to pull her out of it."

Turning away, he raked his hand through his hair. "But that's past history, as dead as Lee. I probably shouldn't have told you. But I wanted you to under-

118

stand why you shouldn't discuss Lee's death with my mother."

You're afraid you're going to lose her again, Maris thought. *But you probably never had her; Lee did, and John, but not you, and certainly not Robyn.* "I can hardly ignore it, considering the date," she said.

"I'm not asking you to ignore it. Just don't talk to my mother about it." Garrick strode to one of the bookcases and took down a cream-colored picture album. Bringing it to her, he thrust it into her hands. "Mother put everything in here. Just do me a favor, and don't tell anyone I let you see this."

"Why *are* you letting me see it?"

"Ten minutes in the public library, and you'll have all this anyway. But I want you to read it *here.* I want you to understand what it meant to this family."

She met his gaze levelly, then nodded. "Fair enough." He started to move away, but she called, "Garrick, wait."

He stopped, turned.

"Why do you bother?" she asked.

He didn't pretend to misunderstand. "Because I can't help myself." Turning on his heel, he left the room.

Maris sat down in the chair nearest the window, where a flood of golden morning sunlight poured into the room. Slowly, apprehensively, she opened the album.

Even though she knew what was inside, it was stunning. A whole book full, not of Lee Hauck's life, but her death. Page after page of newspaper clippings: Senator Hauck's Daughter Shot to Death; Socialite Slain, Lover Accused; and more of the

119

same. A week later, there was another furor. Those headlines read, Murdered Socialite's Infant Missing; Where Is Lee Hauck's Baby?

A shudder ran through Maris as she imagined Sophie cutting the articles out of the newspapers and pasting them in here. The gossip, the speculation, the swift and merciless inspection of the family's private life—it was all there, pasted neatly in place, with the date written below.

"Why, in God's name, did you do this to yourself?" Maris asked the empty room.

But even as she spoke, she knew the answer: Obsession. Sophie could no more let her daughter go than she could her husband. Had she always doted so on John, or had that rather frighteningly intense love been transferred from Ballard and Lee? And if something happened to John, would she then focus on Garrick or Robyn? Maris shuddered again.

The trumpet fare of headlines announced the next round of the Hauck murder case: Socialite's Lover Confesses; Drew Eniston Admits Killing Mother and Child; Grand Jury Indicts Eniston For Murder.

It was all there, as Garrick had said. The killing, the confession, the funeral. Everything public, the murder's notoriety increased by the family's stature. But there was one issue, however, that Sophie hadn't touched, and that was Drew Eniston. Other than the articles about his arrest and confession, his presence was glaringly absent. Maris was glad to know that even Sophie had limits.

The last page held Lee Hauck's high school portrait. Seeing her in person, so soon after reading those headlines, literally took Maris's breath away. What it must have cost Sophie, she couldn't even imagine.

120

It took her a moment before she was composed enough to study Lee Hauck's picture objectively. Lee had been a pretty girl, with regular features and masses of curly red-brown hair. She had her mother's black eyes, but hers were gentle and sensitive. Her mouth was tilted in a Madonna half-smile. The photo had been taken in 1957, a year before her death. She'd been nineteen years old the day she died.

"So young," Maris murmured. "So very young."

She flipped back to the beginning and started reading the articles themselves. They had a faintly Victorian-shocked tone to them; in the 1950's, living with a man and bearing his child was not taken as lightly as it was now.

There was one article she couldn't bring herself to read, and that was the one accompanying the picture of Lee's funeral. The photo itself was bad enough, with a much younger Sophie being supported by John on one side, Ballard on the other. Two young children, looking very confused and very frightened, stood off to one side. Garrick and Robyn.

Maris touched their faces gently. "Didn't anyone hold your hands?"

But it was the picture of the small white casket, wreathed in roses and baby's breath, that made her close the album. Too many of her own fears were raised by that photograph, too, too many.

A chill ran through her despite the warmth of the sunlight, and she tucked her legs up under her the way she used to when watching Hitchcock movies; get those feet off the ground lest something grab them in the dark.

"No wonder the Haucks are so weird sometimes," she muttered under her breath. "Such a terrible thing to happen."

But, terrible and interesting as it was, it didn't seem to have anything to do with the birth of an unwanted girl-child so many years ago. It was time she tended to her own problems, instead of peeping into the Haucks' old tragedy. Trying to make a connection between her birth and Lee Hauck's murder was only going to distract her; besides, there were probably several dozen babies born in the Houston area that day.

"So, that's that," she said, slapping her hands down on the arms of the chair.

Hearing the sound of a vehicle outside, she glanced out the window. A truck bearing the familiar purple and orange Federal Express logo went by, then pulled to a stop in front of the house.

Her vision shifted, focusing on her own reflection in the glass rather than the scene outside. "You look like hell," she told herself. "And you feel like hell, too. Go upstairs and take a nap or a hot bath."

The thought of the hot tub got her moving. As she entered the foyer on her way upstairs, she found Alejo jiggling a large box. Just like a kid trying to guess what was in his Christmas present, she thought.

"Good morning, Alejo," she said.

He turned around with what might have been a guilty start. But there was no guilt in his flat obsidian eyes, just polite deference.

"Good morning, señora," he said.

"Is the car all right?"

"*Si*. It was only the one hole, easily fixed. You will have no more trouble with the car; I checked it over very carefully."

"Then, it isn't necessary to bother Mrs. Hauck

with it, is it?"

"No."

Maris was surprised to see relief cross his face briefly. Did he think *he'd* be the one in trouble? Interesting. They stood assessing each other for a moment. Maris didn't know what he was looking for in her, but she certainly didn't get anything from him. His face was coolly composed, as readable as a stone.

Suddenly he held out the box to her. "This is for you, señora. It is from the St. Louis *Post/Dispatch*."

Tension knotted Maris's stomach. Had *she* written again?

"Where do you want me to put it?" he asked.

She held out her arms. "I'm on my way upstairs now. I'll take it with me."

"No, señora, it is heavy. I will take it to your room for you."

He turned and trotted up the stairs, leaving Maris to trail after him like an errant sheep. When she got to her room, he had already been and gone.

The box sat on the bed. Maris walked over and laid her hand on the cardboard. She would rather have touched a snake. Then she let her breath out with a hiss. "I'm not afraid of *you*," she said. "Call me anything you want, but I'm not afraid."

With a sharp motion, she ripped the tape off the box. Then she upended the carton, spilling a cascade of envelopes onto the bed. They made quite a pile.

"Okay, let's get it over with." She sat cross-legged on the bed and started going through the envelopes, looking for one addressed in bold, block letters.

She found it about halfway through the pile. The same white envelope, the same block printing. She didn't open it right away, but let it lie in her palm. Weighing it. The letter wasn't heavy, but the hate was.

With a sigh, she ran her nail under the flap and slid it open. "I told you not to come," the letter said. "You'll be sorry."

"I'm already sorry," she hissed through clenched teeth. "But I'm going to find you. Hate me all you want, but you're going to have to do it to my face."

She crumpled the note in her fist, wishing *she* were here now, wanting to look her in the eye and tell her how much she despised her for doing this.

"I don't want much," Maris said, furious that tears were beginning to flood her eyes. *Just my daughter's life. Just a chance, however slim, of saving her.* Why did this woman hate her so? What could this cost her, after all these years? "Damn. Damn, damn, damn!"

Maris sat for a while, pressing the heels of her hands against her eyes to keep the tears in. They leaked out, anyway, soaking the ball of paper in her hand.

The sound of Cyndi calling her pulled her back to reality. The note wasn't important. The hatred of the person who wrote it wasn't important. All that mattered was that child in the next room.

Maris stood up. Opening her hand, she let the sodden wad of paper drop to the floor.

"This is war," she said.

Eleven

Even at ten o'clock on Monday morning, the parking garage of M.D. Anderson Hospital was crowded. So crowded, in fact, that a car followed Maris and Cyndi as they walked to the borrowed Cadillac. The moment Maris backed out, the other car zoomed into her spot.

She took the turns carefully, remembering the near-disaster of the other night, but the Cadillac behaved itself perfectly. It looked like the day might even go well. The visit with Dr. Guaymus had gone smoothly, and she was comfortable putting her daughter in his hands.

"Well, hon, what did you think of Dr. Guaymus?" she asked.

"He' s okay."

"Just okay?" She glanced at Cyndi, stiffening when she saw tears on those pale cheeks. Pulling over to the side, she turned the ignition off and released her seat belt so that she could slide closer to Cyndi.

"What's the matter?" she asked.

"I'm going to lose my hair again," Cyndi sobbed.

Gently, Maris gathered her close and rocked her.

"Dr. Guaymus said you might not. Everyone reacts differently to different drugs—"

"Maybe I shouldn't do this at all."

Maris's breath went out in a gasp. "Cyndi—"

"I'm tired of being sick, Mom. I'm tired of being brave. I'm tired of needles and tests and drugs and throwing my guts up."

"You can't mean that," Maris said. Panic fluttered in her chest. "Dr. Guaymus—"

"Dr. Guaymus knows this chemo's not going to work. You saw his face. If we don't find a donor, forget it."

"He said a donor is our *best* hope. This chemotherapy just might work, you know."

"Oh, sure. He's going to try it out, just in case. But *I'm* the one who's got to take it." Cyndi broke down completely. "I want it to be over," she sobbed. "I just want it to be over!"

Maris held her tightly as her own tears started to flow. This was the first time Cyndi had faltered. Oh, she had cried, she'd been afraid of pain, she'd fought discomfort, but she'd never, ever considered giving up.

It was only now that Maris realized how much she'd come to rely on the child's courage and commitment to life. Somehow, without her knowing it had happened, leukemia had blurred the lines between them; child and adult, daughter and mother, patient and caregiver, shoring each other up equally. *Maybe,* Maris thought, *I've taken more than I've given.*

Listening to Cyndi cry, hearing the pain and fear in her voice, Maris was shaken. Shaken to the foundations of her soul.

I assumed I had the right to keep her. But did she?

Was she being selfish to expect Cyndi go through this torment over and over? Maybe. But as Keir would have said, it was a hell of a gray area. The real question was, Could she let her daughter go as long as there was a chance to save her?

And the answer was no.

What if there was no chance? What if a donor wasn't found, and the unknown birth mother remained a mystery? *Can you give Cyndi up then? Can you hold her hand and watch her slip away? Can you let her die in peace?*

Maris pushed that thought away. Until that time came, she wasn't going to think about it. Right now, there was a reason to fight. Taking Cyndi by the chin, she tilted the child's face upward.

"Cyndi, do you trust me?"

"S-sure I do, Mom."

"Then listen to me. I'm going to find you a donor, and we're going to win."

"But the chemo—"

"Shhh." Maris gently laid her finger over Cyndi's mouth. "The chemo is going to buy us time, Cyndi. Just be brave a little while longer."

The desire for hope bloomed in Cyndi's eyes. "It's so hard sometimes."

"I know, baby. But we've got to try."

"Do you really think we'll find a donor?"

I don't dare think otherwise. "Yes, I do."

Cyndi heaved a sigh, then nodded. Maris found a tissue, wiped her daughter's tears, then her own. Faith, she thought, was both a wonderful and terrible thing.

One day at a time. She had to take it one day at a time. And today, she had promised this child a donor. It was time she got started on it. "Do you feel up to going to the library?" she asked. "The research will go twice as fast if you help."

"I'm game," Cyndi said. "Are we going back to Hauck?"

Maris shook her head. "While you were getting your blood work done, I asked one of the nurses if there was a library around here. There is, and not too far away. She even drew me a map."

"Sounds good to me."

Maris framed Cyndi's face in her hands. "Are you sure you feel strong enough?"

"I'm fine, Mom. Can I use the microfiche?"

"Sure."

"Will you buy me a burger afterward?"

"Sure."

"A Burger Wonder burger?"

Maris grinned. "If there's one around."

"There's always one around," Cyndi retorted.

"You've got me there."

"Ha!" Cyndi settled back in her seat, her tears gone.

How resilient she is, Maris thought. Although the return to normalcy was reassuring, her own heart felt as though it had been beaten with a sledgehammer. Her hand shook as she started the car again.

She found the library easily. This particular branch of the Harris County Library was housed in a two-story modern structure, all angles and brown glass. As Maris parked in the lot surrounding it, she almost expected it to get up and walk away.

The inside of the library was much cozier than the outside suggested. Brown carpeting and pale blue walls gave it an airy, spacious look, and there were interesting nooks and crannies in which a person might curl up and read.

128

A desk sat near the entrance, manned by a blond woman whose massive shelf of a bosom hung far out over the desk top. Her hair, makeup and clothes were expertly put together, and she was gorgeous. A larger-than-life beauty. The nameplate in front of her said "Fancie Foster, librarian."

"Can I help you?" she asked in a deep Texas drawl.

Maris steered Cyndi toward the desk. "We'd like to look at newspapers from May, 1958. If you could direct us toward the microfiche—"

"Sure. Come with me, and I'll get ya'll set up." The librarian got to her feet with a vast swirl of russet fabric.

They followed her to a room just large enough to contain two work stations and chairs. The black faces of two microfiche readers stared blindly at the door.

"May we use both?" Maris asked. "We'll be happy to give one up if someone else needs it."

"Ya'll just help yourselves," the librarian said. "Now, the microfiche files are in the folders beside the machines." She flipped one of the folders open and indicated headings of various pages. "You can cross-reference things according to date or subject. Do you want Houston newspapers only?"

"Not necessarily," Maris said. "Although the event I'm researching happened in Houston. I'd like to take a look at any Texas paper from that date."

"Whew! I don't envy you that job. Let me give ya'll some advice; concentrate at first on the *Houston Chronicle* and papers from geographically close areas. Even then, you've got the *Chronicle,* the *Alvin Sun,* the *Hauck Gazette,* the *Galveston Daily News,* the *Pasadena Citizen* and three or four small community papers."

Maris sighed, for the first time getting a clear picture of the magnitude of the job. "Well, it's a start, anyway. Thank you, Miss Foster."

"Call me Fancie. I've been librarian here for twenty years, and everybody from the mayor to the kindergarten class calls me Fancie." With a smile, she patted a stray hair back into place. "I'll leave you to it. If you need any help, just give me a holler." She turned away, closing the door behind her.

"Which one do you want?" Maris asked.

"This one." Cyndi took the work station on the right. "Where do you want me to start?"

"Why don't you take the Hauck, Alvin and Galveston papers? Check the birth notices for each day, and write down the name of every girl."

"May 23, 1958."

"Right."

"Right in the middle of the Hauck murder."

Maris couldn't help but smile. "You sound like something out of Travis McGee."

"Goll-ee, Mom, you're the one who started me on Nancy Drew and the Hardy Boys."

"I can tell I'm not going to be able to get you to stick to local birth notices, huh?" Maris asked.

"Not on your life," Cyndi said, flicking her machine on.

"Okay, wallow in sensationalism to your heart's content. But don't — I repeat, don't — repeat any of this where Mrs. Hauck can hear you.

"Not even to liven up Ballard Breakfast?"

"Especially not to liven up Ballard Breakfast." Maris took the other work station and got started. It took her a couple of minutes to get used to the microfiche reader, but once she did, it was easy to access what she wanted.

130

She started with the *Houston Chronicle* dated May 15, 1958. A little early, perhaps, but she wanted to immerse herself in those times, get the feel of it so that she'd be able to tell if anything was off-kilter.

Open a newspaper in the nineties, and you saw violence. Guns in the schools, guns on the streets, drugs everywhere. Kids killing kids, husbands killing wives, taxes, the recession, the recession, the recession. Thirty-four years ago, it had been a different world. There was the hysteria of McCarthyism, of course, but that was directed outside. America itself seemed strangely innocent, unaware of the forces that would soon come to shake that naïveté: the Civil Rights Movement, the Vietnam War, the vast rebellion of the young. Mom and Pop and apple pie would never be the same.

Maris scanned each day's news, working her way forward chronologically. A lot of girls were born in the Houston area in May 1958. None seemed to be a very good prospect. The names of the proud mothers and fathers were listed in the notices: Mr. and Mrs. Herbert Davis; Mr. and Mrs. Hugh Tavelson; Mr. and Mrs. . . . All married, all eager to take their new daughter home.

"And that, Maris Durant," she muttered, "just doesn't apply to you. The only way you're going to show up is in the news section, or maybe the lost and found with the other abandoned puppies and kittens."

Finally, she got to May 23, 1958. That day, there was a dearth of news. A couple of fires, a few accidents and robberies, the usual. Buried way in the back was a brief article about a shooting in the Mexican section of town. No big deal, apparently, in 1950's Houston. But the next day, May 24, the dead

131

woman was identified as Lee Hauck, and that *was* news. All hell broke loose.

"Have you gotten to the murder yet?" Cyndi asked.

"Just. Terrible, isn't it?"

"That guy is so creepy—killing his woman and baby like that."

Maris looked over her shoulder at her daughter. "His woman?"

"Well, the newspapers said they weren't married. I can't exactly call her his wife, can I?"

"No, I guess you can't." Maris decided to drop the subject. This was another symptom of the nineties: children who lost their naivete early on. Hell, it was pretty hard for a kid to remain innocent of the world when there were pregnant eighth and ninth graders attending school.

With a shake of her head, she went back to her microfiche. She tried to ignore Lee Hauck's murder. Hard. But she got sucked in anyway. Her awareness of the world faded as she delved into the next newspaper, and the next.

Much of what was in the paper was gossip, innuendo and wild speculation. And there was Drew Eniston, the intense-looking young man from the wrong side of the tracks who was the center of it all. He looked like a hothead. From what the newspapers said, there was no love lost between him and Lee's family from the beginning. Not surprising; how many wealthy aristocrats would approve of their daughter seeing a fella who fixed cars for a living?

The Haucks claimed that Eniston was a brutally abusive monster who had forced Lee away from her loving family. Eniston's friends labeled him Lee Hauck's knight in shining armor, who protected an overly gentle and idealistic girl from the world. Somewhere in there was the truth, but Maris couldn't find it.

"What are you?" she muttered.

"Talking to yourself is the first sign of old age," Cyndi said.

"I wasn't talking to myself," Maris lied.

"Sure. Don't worry, Mom. If you get really bad, I'll just strap you in a wheelchair and set you in front of the TV."

"And make me watch football?"

Cyndi giggled. "Yeah. And for lunch, I'll mush up food from Burger Wonder and feed it to you with a spoon."

"You might as well push me off a cliff," Maris said, with a shudder that was only half-pretend.

She went back to the microfiche. Back to Drew Eniston. If the man had given a reason, any reason, for what he had done, she might have been able to understand him.

But he had refused to talk about Lee Hauck to anyone, including his court-appointed lawyer. Then, two weeks after his arrest, he suddenly confessed.

"I did it," Eniston had told the startled detectives. "I killed them both." Then he'd taken the policemen to the Buffalo Bayou and shown them where he'd thrown the infant into the water.

"Holy cow," Maris said. She could understand the man losing his temper and killing Lee. People murdered their lovers all the time. But what could provoke anyone to take a helpless infant out and drown it?

She peered at the photograph of the killer, trying to find an answer in his face. But he was only a thin, intense-looking young man, the sort you could see

133

on any street in any city. Maybe that was why he was so scary; he could be anyone. Your neighbor, your mailman, your husband. A shudder rippled up her spine.

Ten days after Lee's murder, Maris noticed a subtle change in the newspaper's treatment of it. The articles were less strident, less invasive. Flipping back, she saw that the reporter who had begun the story, one Adam Gregory, was no longer writing it. His replacement seemed to have been more sympathetic to the Haucks. And, apparently, more acceptable.

"Verrry interesting," Maris said.

"You're talking to yourself again," Cyndi said.

"So I am."

"Well, what?"

Maris shrugged. "I'm just getting a lesson in power and influence."

She returned her attention to the screen in front of her, scanning headlines to see if any blared the trumpet call of "Body of Hauck Infant Found." But there was nothing.

She flipped back to June 5, 1958, the day Drew Eniston broke his silence. There was a photo of him standing on the bank of the bayou, pointing down into the dark water with shackled hands. She shuddered.

There was nothing in the newspaper to indicate the infant's body had been found. But Drew had been convicted of two counts of murder. And then there was the picture of the tiny coffin in Sophie's photo album. So that meant they'd found the child's body, didn't it?

Didn't it?

"Holy shit," she breathed.

Feeling the kick-start of adrenaline in her veins,

Maris knew she was hooked. A missing baby. Probably a dead missing baby, but she wasn't going to be able to let it go. Paul had often teased her about this particular facet of her personality, calling it one-track, brick-wall stubbornness. "Maris, you're worse than a pit bull," he'd said.

It's the only missing baby I've got.

"Mom, I'm hungry," Cyndi said.

"Already?" Maris would rather have had a tooth pulled than walk away from this microfiche machine just now. Then she looked at her watch. "It's almost three o'clock! Why didn't you say something earlier?"

"You looked like you were having a good time. Like when you're in the middle of designing a piece of jewelry."

"I was kind of involved, wasn't I?"

"You could say that." Cyndi cocked her head to one side, a swift, birdlike gesture made even more so by the billed cap she wore. "You know, Keir's staying in town now; why don't we call him and ask him to come eat with us? So he won't be alone or anything."

Maris raised her eyebrows. "A purely humanitarian gesture."

"Sure."

"You like him, don't you?"

"Uh-huh. So do you."

"I think he's probably a very nice man," Maris hedged.

"He's a hunk. He likes you, too. You're crazy if you don't grab him."

Maris felt her mouth drop open. "Grab him?" She pushed her chair back and stood up. "I've got a couple of other calls to make first. I'll be, oh, fifteen or twenty minutes. Park yourself in

135

the Young Adults section while I use the phone."

She borrowed the librarian's phone, muttering, "Grab him," as she dialed the Haucks' number.

Robyn answered, her light voice making her sound like a teenager. "Oh, hello, Maris," she said. "Are you coming for supper?"

"No, I think we'll get something here in Houston."

"That sounds like fun."

The wistfulness in Robyn's voice caught Maris off-guard, and she responded to it impulsively. "Why don't you drive up and join us, then?"

"You mean, just jump in the car and come eat dinner in town?"

"Yes."

There was a long moment of silence. Maris could almost hear Robyn struggling with herself. Who was going to win, the Robyn who wanted to have dinner in town, or the Invisible Woman created by Sophie Hauck?

"I couldn't," Robyn said at last. "Not on such short notice. It would upset Mother."

Maris sighed. The Invisible Woman had won. Or rather, Sophie had won. "Some other time, then. Is Garrick there?"

"Yes, but he's outside somewhere."

"Then, I'll ask you," Maris said. "Was Lee's baby ever found?"

There was another long silence, then a click. For a moment Maris thought Robyn had hung up on her. Then the other woman said, "No, it wasn't. Maris—"

"Just one more question," Maris said. "Please."

"Maris, listen—"

"Do you know if it was a boy or a girl?"

"I . . . it—"

136

"We don't know." John's smooth voice came over the line, startling Maris.

"I didn't realize you were listening, Senator," she said. It was a pointed statement, as pointed as his eavesdropping.

He didn't rise to the bait. "Robyn, you can hang up now," he said.

"Just a second," Maris said. "Robyn and I happened to be talking."

But a sharp click showed that Robyn had already obeyed. Maris was left alone with her defiance and the senator. He didn't speak for a moment, but the silence was tense, the message clear.

"Talking about Lee's death is upsetting to my sister," he said.

"Why?" Maris countered. "It was thirty-four years ago, Senator. Robyn was a child when it happened."

"Then, let me rephrase my statement. Lee's death is a private family matter."

A week ago, Maris would have backed off. Not anymore. "I can hardly ignore it, considering the coincidence of dates," she said. "All I wanted to know was whether the baby was a boy or a girl."

"Look, it isn't that I'm unsympathetic to your need. But you have to understand that the scars left on this family by Lee's murder are still very deep and very raw. My mother, especially, has never quite recovered from it."

"I wasn't going to go to your mother," Maris said. "Look, Senator, all I want to know is whether Lee's baby was male or female."

He sighed. "I don't know. No one knows, except the man who killed her. But I *do* know that girl or boy, Lee's child is dead." Emotion trembled in his voice, real and sharp and strong. "That's the truth.

137

By his own admission, Eniston took that baby and dumped it into Buffalo Bayou."

An idea hit Maris like a sledgehammer, and she nearly dropped the phone. "Whatever you say, Senator."

"Good. I hope this settles the issue, once and for all."

"Me, too." Maris broke the connection, then dialed the number Keir had given her. "Please, be there, please!"

Fortunately, he was. "Hello?"

"Keir," she said without preamble, "I need to talk to Drew Eniston."

"Who the hell is that?"

"He's the man who killed Lee Hauck."

"Lee . . ." His indrawn breath was sharp and loud. "What the hell are you doing, Maris?"

"Did you know that the body of Lee Hauck's baby was never found?"

"But they convicted him of both murders —"

"On the basis of his confession, apparently."

"I don't understand the connection," he said.

"The child's body was never found. The Haucks don't even know if it was a boy or a girl."

"Holy shit. Did you talk to John about this?"

"Yes. He told me to go to hell and leave his family alone while I was doing it." She took a deep breath. "It's my only lead, Keir. And only Eniston knows the answers."

"Is he in Huntsville?"

"I think so," she said. "Can you get me in?"

"You might have to pose as a reporter or something."

"I'll go as Grandma Moses if I have to. Uh . . . Keir? This isn't going to get you in trouble, is it?"

138

"Heck, no. John isn't petty."

"Thanks," she said. "I appreciate it."

"We exist only to serve."

"Keir . . ." There were a lot of things she might have said. Another person might have made a pretty speech or something. But all she could think of was "thank you," and that seemed completely inadequate. "Cyndi and I are in town. Would you like to meet us for dinner somewhere?"

"Let me guess," he said. "Burger Wonder?"

"Only the best for our benefactor."

"How about your friend?"

"For our friend, we order onion rings."

He was silent for a moment. When he finally spoke, there was a warmth in his voice that went through Maris's veins like music. "I'll be there in twenty minutes."

Twelve

Maris took a deep breath before walking into the waiting room of the Eastham Unit of the Institutional Division of the Texas Department of Criminal Justice. Drew Eniston's home for thirty-four years. This was a starkly utilitarian chamber, with green-painted cinderblock walls and a worn tile floor. A host of molded plastic chairs hugged the walls, poised on thin metal legs as though ready to make their break at the first opportunity. They held women and kids, mostly black, mostly poor, all looking tired and beaten-down as though they'd been sitting there forever.

A Plexiglas window pierced the far wall, a speaker and a button mounted beside it. Maris pushed the button. A man's face swam into view in the glass, and a moment later the speaker squawked into life.

"State your name and business, please."

"Maris Guthrie, from Senator Hauck's office," she said, holding up the letter Keir had given her. "I'm here to see Drew Eniston."

He picked up a clipboard and peered at it. "Right. Go to the door on your right, Ms. Guthrie."

She obeyed, wading through a wave of who-is-she-to-just-walk-in resentment from the other women.

The door snicked open as she reached it, sucking her into the inner sanctum. Here, it was not America. There were no rules save prison rules, and those were based upon restraint, not freedom. Maris gave herself up to them, turning off her sense of dignity as best she could while a very large, very intimidating matron took possession of her purse and searched her for weapons.

"Do you find weapons often?" Maris asked.

"Honey, I find everything."

"But don't people realize they're going to be searched if they go into a prison?"

The woman laughed. "This ain't the cream of society, you know. The high-class criminals don't end up here. They go down to the minimum-security country club where they can play tennis."

"They ought to bring some of these teen offenders down here and show them the place," Maris said.

"Oh, honey, that ain't going to work. Those kids are too *smart* to get caught, don't you know?" The matron gave another deep belly laugh.

Finally, apparently satisfied with Maris's harmlessness, the matron turned her over to a uniformed guard, who then conveyed her through a maze of barred rooms, barred doors, bars, bars and more bars. It was like marching into the belly of some monstrous metal beast, and she couldn't shake the feeling that it was a one-way trip.

Her destination was a tiny box of a room with a window at one end. A shelf was built into the wall below the window, making a desk of sorts, and a telephone hung on the wall beside it.

"Oh." Maris said, surprised. "I'm not going to be in the room with him."

"No." He pointed to the chair. "Go ahead and sit down. He'll be out in a minute."

Maris was so nervous she was hardly aware of the guard leaving. Leaning forward, she peered into the room beyond the glass. It was much like the one she occupied, bare of any furniture save the chair, and there was a single door at the far end.

The door opened, and she sat back hurriedly. Two men came into the other room, but Maris registered only one: Drew Eniston. He was tall and whipcord-lean, his movements fraught with tightly leashed tension. An angry man.

The guard leaned against the far wall, out of immediate earshot but close enough to threaten privacy. Eniston ignored him and sat down across from Maris.

She found herself holding her breath, both repelled and fascinated by the man. He hadn't aged well. The dark hair she remembered from the photograph was gone, replaced by a thinning cap of steel gray, and his lean face was etched with discontent. Creases bracketed a wide slash of a mouth, echoed by twin grooves between his brows.

It was the face of a hard man. A man who had killed. *What must it be like,* Maris wondered, *to step across that threshold?* And threshold it was; once a man became a murderer, there was no going back.

He picked up the phone, motioning for her to do the same. She obeyed.

"Who are you?" he asked. His voice was harsh, impatient. "And what the hell does Ballard Hauck want with me?"

Ballard Hauck? "Ballard Hauck didn't send me. I got in here courtesy of John Hauck."

142

"The boy senator?"

"He's fifty-two years old," Maris pointed out.

"Still needs someone to wipe his nose for him. I pity the state if he ever becomes governor. Now," Eniston growled. "What the hell do you want?"

"Most people would have asked my name."

"I don't give a shit who you are. I just want to know what you're doing here."

Maris knew she ought to be offended. But he was too outrageous for that. She lifted her chin. If he didn't give a shit, then she wasn't going to give a shit either. "Didn't they tell you I was doing a biography on the Haucks?"

"Yeah. But that's bull. There's only one version of Hauck history allowed, and that's Ballard Hauck's."

"Ballard Hauck is no longer dictating history, Mr. Eniston. He's a vegetable."

"No shit?" Eniston grinned, a knife-edge flash of teeth. "That's *great*."

Maris raised her brows. "You hate him that much?"

"Lady, I'd step over a rattlesnake to squash Ballard Hauck," he said. "He is . . . was a royal bastard."

"He had more reason to hate *you*."

"He was a bastard before I killed his daughter."

Those words hit Maris like a wave of ice water. Then she looked into his eyes and saw mingled speculation and challenge there. He was trying to shake her up. Testing to see if she could take it. She lifted her chin. *My daughter is dying. I can take anything but that.*

"Okay," she said. "Ballard Hauck's a bastard. But I came here to talk about Lee's murder."

"The newspapers said more than I ever could,"

143

Eniston said. "Why don't you go to them for your story?"

"I don't believe everything I read in the papers," she countered. "Do you?"

"Sure. Why not?"

Maris found that she was clutching the telephone with a grip that made her joints ache. He was getting to her. Slowly, she forced herself to relax. "You were convicted of two murders, Mr. Eniston."

"That's right. Two consecutive life terms. Most of my fan mail, however, tells me it should have been the chair."

"Are any of those notes printed in nice, block letters?" she asked.

He snorted. "What asylum did you escape from, lady?"

"You don't give a shit. Remember?"

"Yeah."

Taking a deep breath, she looked straight into his strange, yellow-streaked eyes. "The body of Lee Hauck's baby was never found."

"That didn't stop them from convicting me."

"You confessed, didn't you?"

He laughed. "Do you believe everything you hear?"

"Was the child a boy or a girl?"

"That's none of your goddamned business."

"Yes, it is."

"It fucking well isn't!" he shouted.

Maris held the phone a few inches away from her ear. "Yes, it is!" she shouted back.

He hung up. Shoving his chair back, he got to his feet and walked away.

"You come back here!" Maris cried, beating on

the glass with her fist. "Don't you *dare* walk away from me! God damn you to hell, Drew Eniston!"

He didn't even turn around. A moment later the door closed behind him and his guard.

Maris leaned her head against the cool glass. "You sorry son of a bitch," she muttered, fighting an onrush of tears. "I wish they *had* given you the chair!"

Still fuming over the interview, Maris stalked down the walk toward Keir's condominium. Keir opened the door as she neared, putting his finger over his lips to caution quiet.

"Is Cyndi sleeping?" Maris whispered.

"She's fine. But we had a busy day, so I talked her into lying down for a while. Kids are all the same, aren't they? Never like to go to bed no matter how tired they are." His gaze shifted to a point behind Maris. "I used to flutter over Gary like a mother hen, begging him to rest. He fought me all the way down the line. Then came the time he didn't fight me anymore, and went to bed like a good little boy. And that's when I really got scared."

Maris didn't answer. Couldn't answer, torn as she was between gratitude for having met someone who truly understood what she was going through, and the desire to hide those feelings. Admit them, examine them, and they became real. Too, too real.

Keir studied her for a moment, then stepped back to let her in. Maris found herself in a comfortably furnished living room. If there had been some knickknacks or pictures, it might almost have looked like a home.

"How did it go?" Keir asked.

"He told me to stick it in my ear." She threw her

145

purse on the nearest chair and shrugged out of her jacket.

"Pretty bad, huh?"

"He's an SOB."

Keir put his hands on her shoulders. "How about a glass of wine?"

"Thanks. Dry and red, if you have it."

"I'll look. Go sit down."

Maris picked the recliner nearest the fire. Settling into it, she flipped up the footrest and watched Keir as he opened a cabinet near the fireplace, revealing a tiny, compact bar.

He opened and closed doors and drawers, obviously unfamiliar with the contents. It reminded Maris that this wasn't his place. He was the sort of man who seemed at home almost anywhere. *Or maybe I should have said nowhere.* Sometimes they were pretty much the same.

"How did you find this place?" she asked.

"Courtesy of the friend of a friend of John's friend the realtor. Some engineer on assignment in the Middle East rents his condo out to professional types."

"Do you have a place in Austin?"

"I pay rent on an apartment there." He found a bottle of wine, then held it up to read the label. "But I mostly live out of my suitcase."

"In John Hauck's service."

"Ooooh, let me pull my forelock," he said, grunting as he wrestled with the opener.

"The Haucks *are* kind of feudal, you know."

"C'mon, Maris! They plug Daddy Hauck into the wide-screen TV during football season. You call that feudal?"

146

She found herself smiling. "Do you like working for John?"

"I like the job."

"A very careful answer."

"I'm a careful man." With a sigh of exasperation, he set the bottle down, still unopened, and glared down at the implement in his hand. "A corkscrew I can handle. But this thing's got me."

She extracted herself from the recliner and joined him at the cabinet. "Will your ego let me take a look at that?"

"My ego will only suffer if it doesn't get a drink." His voice fairly throbbed with relief.

"No wonder it didn't work," she said a moment later. "This kind of opener doesn't stick into the cork. You slide the prongs down on either side and then just, ah!" With a deft twist of the wrist, she extracted the cork. "See?"

"Now I do. Damned if I did before."

He poured two glasses of dark ruby wine and handed her one. "What about you, Maris? Do you like what you do?"

"Mmmm, that's good," she said, taking a sip of wine. "I guess I do really like it. But most of my stuff went up in the fire." Shrugging to feign an indifference she didn't feel, she added, "It was a nice fantasy while it lasted. I think I had a shot of making it, but now. . . ."

"Why can't you start over?"

"Money. If Cyndi gets this transplant, I'm going to be adding a couple of hundred thousand dollars to my tab, which is already beyond human understanding. No, I think I'll be out looking for a full-time job."

"You can't give up your dream," Keir said.

Dream. She had no dream. It had been leached out of her by a capsized boat and an illness Man didn't know how to fight. Tears stung the inside of her eyelids, and she turned away, not wanting Keir to see.

"Maris," he said.

His hands fell on her shoulders, trying to turn her back around. She didn't want to face him, not now. "Don't," she said. "Don't touch me. Please." Her voice broke on the last word. To her fury, the tears started to flow.

The pressure of his grip eased, but his hands remained on her shoulders.

"Why can't you accept comfort?" he asked. "Is it me? Am I just doing this all wrong?"

"It isn't you. It's me."

"Why?"

She shook her head.

His fingers tightened. "Why?"

"Maybe . . ." She took a deep, shuddering breath. "Sometimes I feel like I'm a glass that's been broken and fitted back together. But somebody forgot to use glue. So I hold on to myself just as tight as I can, 'cause if I don't, I'm going to go flying apart in a thousand pieces."

"I'll keep that from happening," he said softly. "Just let me in a little, Maris. Let me help you. Let me *care*."

She shook her head again. Keeping his hands on her shoulders as though afraid she might bolt, Keir came around to face her. His eyes were on a level with hers, and the raw, naked emotion in them scared her silly. From their first conversation, he had

148

stepped over her boundaries, and he had continued to do it ever since. Pushing her limits. Making her feel.

"I can't do this," she said.

"It isn't hard, once you get used to it."

"Maybe you should think about the fact that everyone who has cared for me is either dead or desperately ill."

He stared at her in surprise. "Was that a joke?"

"If so, it wasn't a very funny one, was it?"

"Not very."

Maris's nerves were singing like fine-tuned violin strings. "Maybe you ought to take it seriously."

"I do."

They were so nearly the same height that all he had to do was lean forward. *I always had to stand on tiptoes to kiss Paul,* Maris thought. Then her senses kicked in, and all she thought about was being kissed. By Keir. Not Paul. Keir.

He drew back and looked into her eyes. "Again?"

"Yeah."

Taking her wineglass, he set it and his own aside. Then he pulled her closer, heat against heat. That first kiss had been experimental, a bit cautious, but this second one was something else entirely. Maris sank deep, deep, deep. For the first time in a very long while, she felt truly alive.

She had no right. With a convulsive movement, she pulled away.

"Look at me," he said.

She was too vulnerable right now, that vulnerability laid bare by his need, and hers.

"Look at me," he said again.

There was no choice. Opening her eyes, Maris let

him have it all. He let out his breath in a long sigh. A moment later she felt his hands drop away from her shoulders. She started to turn away.

"Where do you think you're going?" he asked.

She swung back around, startled. "I thought—"

"You thought I couldn't take it," he said.

"I'm not sure *I* can take it."

"Maris." He wrapped her in his arms again, holding her tight, holding her close. "All I want is for you to lean on me a little."

"I think you want a bit more than just that," Maris said.

He smiled. "I can hardly hide that fact, seeing how close we're standing." Then the humor vanished from his face. "Yes, I want you. I want a place in your life."

"I have no life."

"Only if you let it be that way."

"If Cyndi dies—"

"If Cyndi dies, you'll have a choice. You can let yourself die with her, or you can find a way to build something else for yourself."

She tried to turn her face away, but he cupped her chin in his hand and forced her to look at him. When he spoke again, his voice was tight with emotion. "Maris . . ."

"Don't."

With a sharp exhalation, he let her go. Then he picked up the wineglasses in one hand and grasped her arm with the other. "Come on, sit down." He set her on the sofa and handed her a glass, then sat down beside her. "Why are you afraid to let yourself feel?"

"Why do you ask?"

150

"Because I've got a lot at stake here, and it's obvious that if I don't fight for it, no one else will."

Again, he surprised her. She'd thought of this relationship as a new and fragile thing, easily set aside. But maybe it wasn't. Maybe it had gone far beyond that without her realizing what was happening.

She set the wineglass down on the coffee table. "I've been pretty blind, haven't I?"

"You've had a lot on your mind."

"I've been selfish," she said. "Look, Keir, this is all very new and strange to me. I was very much in love with Paul . . . my husband. When he died, I felt that something in me died with him." She laughed, a bitter sound. "Maybe it did. Maybe that's why we're having this conversation."

He chopped the air with his hand. "If it had, we wouldn't be here at all. How did he die?"

"A boating accident. We capsized, and his foot got tangled in the lines. He drowned." Maris held her hands up in front of her, not even caring that they were shaking badly. "I tried so hard . . . I was holding him when he died. His life came bubbling through my hands, and I couldn't stop it."

Her heart was pounding madly, and she pressed one fist against her chest to ease the pain. "Most of the time I just missed him. But since Cyndi got sick, there are times that I've been furious at him for leaving me to face this alone."

"Maris—".

"Great, isn't it? The poor guy is dead, and all I can do is blame him for not being here with me." Tears threatened, and she had to stop for a moment to get herself under control. "It was my fault for not being more independent during our marriage. You

151

see, Paul was a brilliant man, a math professor at Washington University. I was nineteen when we married, and I just sort of laid my life in his hands. When he died, I was kicked out into the world. And I wasn't prepared."

"It wouldn't have mattered, either way."

"Why not?"

"Nothing can prepare you for your child having cancer, Maris. You just endure it. For all you know, Paul might have broken under it, and you'd have been carrying *him,* too."

Maybe it was the implied criticism of Paul that annoyed her, maybe something else. "Paul was Cyndi's father. He had an emotional investment in her, and in me. You don't. And things are going to be getting real grim. If I let you into my life, if I let myself care, you might pull out at a time when I won't be able to handle it."

With a smooth, uncoiling motion, he leaped to his feet and strode across the room. "Goddamn you," he hissed. "Is that what you think of me?"

"You don't see it at all, do you?" Adrenaline coursed through her, and she welcomed it; anger was easier to deal with just now. "I trusted *life*. I assumed that I would grow old with the man I loved, that I would be able to watch my child grow up, get married, have children of her own. All that was taken away. Now you want me to trust again, and I tell you there's no security in trust. The moment you need it the most, it disappears. I've learned to stand alone."

"Great. Fine. Good. But being strong doesn't exempt a person from needing comfort. Don't you

152

want to have someone hold you when you cry, to feel the warmth of another human being during those tough times?"

"Yes." It was a whisper. "I want those things."

"And I'm willing to give them to you."

She searched inside herself. Reached deep, deep, deep, looking for the courage to accept what he offered.

And came up empty. "I can't," she said. "I'm doing good just to deal with friendship, and you want things I just don't have the capacity to give right now. I'm sorry."

"This is the spot where I become noble and tell you that friendship will be enough?" He raked his hand through his hair. "Come on, Maris. I'm human. I can't pretend not to want more than to be your buddy."

"You're pushing."

"Damn straight."

"Is this what you're going to do to the voters? Cram your chosen candidate down their throats?"

His eyes narrowed. "Talk about *pushing!*"

The phone shrilled, startling them both. Keir hesitated, his gaze still locked with hers, then turned and snatched the receiver out of its cradle.

"Andreis!" he snarled. Then his face changed. "Yeah, Hugh. No kidding? Have you talked to them already? Maris is here now. I'll talk to her, then get back to you. Are you at the station? Okay, I'll give you a call."

Maris couldn't breathe. "What is it?"

"Sit down."

"I don't—"

"Sit down!"

153

She sat. He sat down beside her, and she realized his anger had been replaced by concern.

"Hugh's gotten a response to the interview." he said.

"You mean . . ." Her voice was an absurd little squeak. Maris cleared her throat and tried again. "Someone has called with information?"

"More than that."

She picked up her wine, but her hand was shaking so badly she put the glass down again. "Someone has come forward . . . claiming to be my mother?"

"Yeah," he said. "Three someones."

"Three?"

"Three."

"What do I do now?" she asked. "Three!"

"Hugh said he'd be happy to arrange interviews for you. I suggest a neutral place."

"Neutral" meaning anywhere but Gavilan. "Where do you suggest?" she asked.

"Here or the station." Running his thumbnail along his jaw, he added, "Here would be best."

She cocked her head to one side and studied him. He'd taken over again. Running her campaign. "Why?" she asked.

"Do you want Hugh hovering over your interviews?"

"And here, you can be the one hovering. How about it, Keir? What do you want from all this except to get John Hauck into the governor's mansion?"

"How about my soul, Maris? Would you believe me if I said I'd lost it somewhere along the Great Political Way, and I was hoping you'd help me get it back?"

154

She stared at him, wishing she could see into his mind. If what he'd said was true, it was a brutally stark admission. "I don't know," she said. "I'm getting to the point where I don't know anything about myself, let alone anyone else."

"Do you have to *know?* Can't you have a little faith?"

"I left my faith behind a long time ago," she said. "Now all I have are doctors and medical procedures, and a marble slab in the cemetery."

He picked up the phone. "I'll tell Hugh to arrange for you to do it at the station."

Thirteen

The imitation leather of the chair was hot beneath Maris's legs. She shifted them, wishing she'd picked a different spot for these interviews. Back-to-back meetings, three long, long hours in Hugh Carideo's cluttered horror of an office.

"Talk about horror," she said, glancing at her watch. "The third and final round is coming up."

She sighed, shifting her legs yet again. The first two applicants for motherhood had been a waste of time. She'd been so nervous beforehand, but apprehension had quickly changed to boredom. The first woman hadn't even had sense enough to memorize what had been in the newspapers. Her story, while inventive, didn't match up anywhere. The second woman had been worse, for she'd burst into tears the moment she'd gotten into the room and had tried — albeit unsuccessfully — to clasp Maris to her bosom.

Maris could hear the echo of their voices in her mind. Different voices, saying different things. Different lies. Now she was going to have to endure the ordeal a third time.

The door opened, and Hugh Carideo's broad face appeared in the entrance. "You doing okay, darlin'?"

"Just having a ball," she said. "Where did those two come from, anyway?"

"You're going to get a lot of this, darlin'. Can't help it, not with five thousand dollars on the block. Better sharpen your claws. Some are going to be real slick; some are going to do their homework a whole lot better than those two."

"Is Cyndi doing okay?"

"Sure. Keir came by a few minutes ago to take her to Burger Wonder."

Annoyance pooled in Maris's stomach. She hadn't invited Keir today, but, unable or unwilling to take the hint, he'd shown up anyway. All he had to do was dangle the bait—Burger Wonder—and he was right back in the thick of things.

"You're looking kind of peeved, darlin'." Hugh said.

"I just don't like the idea of anyone taking my daughter out without my permission."

"She called *him*."

"She did?" Realizing that her mouth was open, she shut it hastily.

Hugh chuckled. "I've been around a long time, darlin', and I've seen a lot of this world and the people in it. And if you ask me, Cyndi's hungry for a father."

Before Maris had a chance to reply to that astonishing observation, Hugh gave a grunt and whispered, "Guard your girdle, darlin'. Number three is coming down the hall."

"And only fifteen minutes late," Maris whispered back.

Hugh pushed the door wider, ushering a woman into the room ahead of him. "Maris, this is Mrs. Ella Florian."

157

"Sorry I'm late," the woman said. "Got caught in traffic down at the Galleria." The words were shot out with a machine-gun-rapid delivery.

"That's okay," Maris said.

Ella Florian nodded, as though to say, "Of course it's okay." Maris found her rather intimidating. Everything about her had a certain aggressiveness, from the forward-jutting shelf of her bosom to the hard brown eyes that might have belonged to an old-time gunfighter. Her dark hair was an obvious dye job, making it hard to place her age. She might have been anywhere from fifty to sixty.

Whatever her age, the woman had seen plenty of life, and not the easy side of it. A real tough cookie, Paul would have said. Needing the psychological advantage of height, Maris peeled herself off the imitation leather seat and stood up.

"Won't you sit down, Mrs. Florian?" she asked, indicating the armchair on the other side of the desk.

"Thanks. I worked late last night, and I'm beat." The woman fitted herself into the chair, her slow, languorous movements at odds with the rapid-fire delivery of words.

"Where do you work?" Maris asked.

"I'm a bartender at the Nogales Lounge. You know it?" Without giving Maris a chance to answer, she continued, "No, you wouldn't. The Nogales ain't your kind of place."

Maris's gaze strayed to Hugh, who was standing behind Ella. He mouthed, "Watch it with this one!"

As if I needed a hint. Aloud, Maris said, "Thank you for coming, Mrs. Florian. There are a lot of things I'd like—"

"Is this going to stay?" Ella asked. She jabbed her

thumb over her shoulder at Hugh, who flinched as though she'd pointed a gun at him.

"No, he isn't," Maris said.

With obvious reluctance, Hugh backed out of the room, closing the door behind him.

Ella plopped her black patent-leather purse on her lap and opened it. "Mind if I smoke?"

"Sorry, but I do."

The purse closed with a *snick*. "So, where do we go from here?"

"I guess you tell me your story," Maris said.

Ella rubbed her fingertips along her bottom lip, a gesture that might have been prompted by nervousness, or might as easily have been an itch. The woman gave off nothing Maris could read.

"Okay, I'll tell you," Ella said. "But I don't want it going farther than the two of us. I'm not going to have your reporter friend sniffing in my business."

"I'm not going to go running to the press," Maris said. "Anything else will have to be left to my discretion."

Ella stared at her, her gaze boring deep. Maris returned the stare levelly.

Finally, Ella nodded. Folding her hands on her purse, she took a deep breath and began her story. It was delivered in her curt, rapid way, the words shooting out like hard little pebbles. "Thirty-four years ago, I was a sixteen-year-old kid, scared and pregnant. My dad kicked me out of the house when I started to show. Back then, there weren't any places that would take in pregnant teenagers. I slept in churches, sometimes spending a night or two with friends. I begged or stole food. When I went into labor, I crawled into an alley and had that baby all alone. I guess I just freaked, not knowing what to

159

do, not knowing how I was going to take care of her."

It was a very sad story, if true, but Maris was chilled by the flat, unemotional way it had been told. "Are you sure it was a girl?"

Ella gave a short bark of laughter. "I was pretty green, but not *that* green, or I wouldn't have been in that situation in the first place."

"Right. Go on, please."

"There isn't much to tell. I rested for a while, then put the baby in a cardboard box and left her beneath a trailer in a nearby trailer park."

Oh, my God! Maris thought. Her pulse roared in her ears. She hadn't told the press about the cardboard box. It might be a lucky guess. But then, maybe not. *Could it be this easy?* "Was the baby wrapped in anything?"

"Wrapped?" Ella cocked her head to one side. "You mean like a blanket?"

"Whatever."

"Well . . ." Again that gesture, the fingertips rubbing across her bottom lip. "I think I wrapped her in something; it's what you do with babies, ain't it? But it must have been something I scrounged in that alley, and I don't remember what."

Maris sighed. Could the woman really have forgotten a colorful Mexican blanket? Maybe. Maybe a scared and hurting sixteen-year-old girl, frantic to do something with her baby, had grabbed anything she could find and paid no attention to it. Maybe, maybe, maybe. Too many questions, not enough answers.

Maris studied the other woman's face, searching for something of herself in those features. It was the eyes that made her shiver involuntarily; they were as

160

hard as stone, no emotion there at all. Was this a woman who had come to meet her long-lost daughter?

Was this, Maris added silently, the woman who had sent her those messages? Who had called her "bitch"?

"I saw in the paper that you were staying with the Haucks," Ella said. "What's it like in that big, expensive mansion?"

"Big and expensive," Maris said.

"They say that John Hauck's going to be governor."

"Mrs. Florian, let's get back to—"

"Do they know you were born the day their daughter died?"

"The Haucks are not the subject of this interview."

"Interview? What is this, a job I'm applying for?" Ella gave a harsh bark of laughter. "Okay, then, what's the pay?"

"What are you talking about?" Maris asked, her insides going cold.

"You didn't ask me here because you wanted to fall into my arms and be a good daughter, did you? You're looking for a donor, plain and simple. Well, I might be that donor. I saw your face when I told my story. You think I might be, too." Jerking her purse open, Ella took out a cigarette and lit it. "You'd like to haul me right down to a doctor and get me tested, wouldn't you?"

"Yes," Maris said, meeting the challenge. "Will you go?"

Ella's eyes seemed to float in a curtain of smoke. "For a price."

"What price?"

"The five thousand dollars."

"The reward is for information leading to my biological mother," Maris said. "Payable *after* she is found and tested."

"So, change the rules, then. You want something from me, you pay me beforehand."

"It's a simple blood test, Mrs. Florian. A few minutes of your time, that's all."

The older woman smiled, revealing large, square teeth. "But it's my time and my blood, ain't it?"

Maris shuddered, part of her hoping this woman was not really her mother. If so, it was her worst fears realized. She'd almost rather be related to Drew Eniston. God, what a choice in genetics!

She put her hands flat on the desk and leaned forward. "Mrs. Florian, a little girl's life is at stake. A little girl who just might be your granddaughter."

"I got grandkids spread all over Texas. I think I can live without one more." Ella rose to her feet. "It's all very simple: you pay me five thousand dollars, I go get tested."

"And if you test negative?"

"Then you're shit out of luck."

Maris's hands itched with the desire to grab the woman by the scruff of the neck and toss her out. But she didn't dare. The one thing she could do, however, was to buy herself enough time to check Ella Florian out.

"I . . . don't have control of the funds, Mrs. Florian. I'll have to talk to the people who are administering it."

"You mean the Haucks," Ella said. "Talk good, and remember that they have deep pockets." She gave Maris another of those chilling smiles. "You got a number where I can call you?"

"Yes." Maris scribbled Cyndi's private number on

162

the back of one of Hugh Carideo's business cards. "Call me, or call Hugh and he'll get a message to me."

"Two days," Ella said. "I'll get back to you in two days."

"Give me your number." Maris was afraid that she wouldn't see the woman again once she walked out of here. "I'll call *you*."

"I don't have a phone." Ella walked out, the heels of her shoes making staccato beats on the carpet.

For a moment, Maris could only stand and shake. She wished she'd never started this. She wished she'd never laid eyes on Ella Florian. And most of all, she hoped that Cyndi's life would not hinge on that woman's sense of decency.

"Look on the bright side," she said aloud. "You weren't raised by her. Now, *that* would have been a truly horrifying experience. And . . ." she broke off, suddenly remembering something Ella Florian had said.

"I've got grandkids all over Texas," she'd said. Excitement rolled through Maris. It was time to contact a private detective. Maybe, just maybe, she wouldn't have to rely on Ella at all. It would be a great pleasure to tell the Wicked Witch of the West to stick it in her ear.

"Hot damn," Maris said, rubbing her palms together. "We got us a plan."

Maris sat cross-legged on Cyndi's bed, putting a second coat of nail polish on the child's toenails. "I really wish you'd let me use a different color. Blue just isn't the thing."

"Oh, it's the thing. It just isn't *your* thing," Cyndi said. She pointed the remote at the TV, holding it so

163

as to protect her still-wet nails. "It's been two days since you talked to that Mrs. Florian. She said she'd call in two days, didn't she? Then, why hasn't she called?"

"Maybe she got scared that I'd find out she was lying."

"You called her an ogress, Mom. Would she chicken out just because you might tell her what a naughty girl she was?"

Maris shook her head, unable to imagine Ella Florian being afraid of anything or anyone. "It's not quite a bust yet. After all, it's only ten o'clock. She might call yet tonight."

She concentrated on what she was doing, wishing she could stop thinking about Ella Florian. But she hadn't, any more than she'd been able to the past two days. Until now, Maris hadn't realized just how desperate she was. As Paul would have said, no matter what her politics, Ella might be Cyndi's ticket out. So might Drew Eniston—a small chance, but one Maris couldn't ignore. It was a hell of a world when Cyndi's best chance for survival lay in a killer and a con woman.

"Did you and Keir have a fight?"

Maris blinked, startled by the sudden change of subject. "What makes you say that?"

"It's *so* obvious. I mean, other than calling to say he'd found a good private investigator for you to use, he hasn't called or come by."

"Maybe he's just had something better to do."

Cyndi snorted. "Not unless you *made* him find something better to do. He likes you a lot."

"Did he say that?"

"No, I can tell," Cyndi said. "He's okay, Mom."

Maris didn't want to think about Keir, okay or

164

not. "What time is your appointment at the hospital next week?"

"As if you'd forget." Cyndi's voice fairly dripped with sarcasm. "You just want to change the subject."

"You're right, O wise one. I do want to change the subject."

"If I'm so wise, then why wasn't I able to talk them into giving me an afternoon appointment? They always like to give you chemo in the morning so you can puke the whole day."

"Would you rather puke all night?"

"At least the TV's worth watching at night."

Time for a reality check, Maris thought. She'd let external things blunt her focus on what was truly important here. And that was this brave, frightened child. Keir, the Haucks, Ella Florian and Drew Eniston were all minor in the scheme of things. The only truly important thing was getting Cyndi well, whether with this new chemotherapy or by finding a donor. Nothing else mattered. Nothing else was *going* to matter.

Forcing a smile, Maris capped the bottle of polish, then reached over to tug the brim of the baseball cap down over Cyndi's eyes. "We've got a week before you start the chemo. Let's make the most of it. How would you like to go to NASA tomorrow?"

"Yeah! Can we ask Keir?"

"I'm sure Keir has to work," Maris said.

Cyndi cocked her head to one side. "Maybe he'd rather make up with you."

"Cyndi—"

"I bet he's a good kisser. He looks like a good kisser."

"I wouldn't know," Maris lied. Memory washed through her, visceral heat trapped in flesh.

165

"His smile is pretty nice, too. Does squinchy things to my insides."

Mine, too. "You're too young for squinchy things," Maris said.

"So you know what I mean, huh?"

Maris sighed. Paul used to say that they had bred a monster, and that the human race was in for a shock in a few years. Well, he was right. Only his timing was off; the world was in trouble right *now.*

"Wow, look at that!" Cyndi cried, pointing to the TV.

Maris glanced over her shoulder in time to see a giant worm burst upward out of the sand, then fall forward and spew a host of snake-headed tentacles that slithered and hissed menacingly. She turned back to Cyndi. "God, child, what are you watching?"

"*Tremors.* See the blond guy? That's Kevin Bacon. Isn't he gorgeous?"

Maris turned around again just in time to see Kevin Bacon rush up to the camera and scream, "Fuck youuuuuu!'

While Maris groped for an appropriate response to that, Cyndi rushed into the breach. "Now, Mom, don't get upset. That's the only time he says that word. The rest of the time, they stick to less, ah . . ."

"Profane," Maris supplied. "I gather you've seen this show before?"

"Well, yes. You know how the movie channel schedules these things to run at least once a day. Really, Mom, it's a great movie. Remember how much you liked *The Blob* with Steve McQueen? This is even better. And after a while, you don't even notice the cussing."

"Oh," Maris said. Since it was obviously way too late to police this particular issue, she decided she might as well sit back and enjoy the movie. She *had* enjoyed *The Blob*.

"Okay?" Cyndi said.

"Okay." Maris slid off the bed. "How 'bout I sneak down to the kitchen and see if they've got something to snack on?"

"Rocky Road ice cream. Rosalia told me this afternoon."

"Okay, I'll be back in a minute." Maris padded out into the hall.

She was glad that Cyndi seemed to have forgotten the issue of Keir. But *she* couldn't. Keir was a bothersome subject, because of her own feelings for him, but even more, because of Cyndi's. It was obvious the kid adored him. Keir was charming and attractive, and undoubtedly a kind man in his own way. But the operative word was "manipulative." Maybe Hugh was right; maybe Cyndi was hungry for a father. But that just made her easy pickings for someone like Keir. And if he decided to move on to some new, more challenging endeavor, what would that do to Cyndi?

How do I protect her? How do I show her what's real and what's not, when I don't know myself?

The stairway was dark, lit only by the small lamp on the table in the foyer. Maris found the switch for the chandelier and flicked it on. Nothing happened. She tried it again. Down, up, and down again. Then, shrugging, she headed down the stairs, keeping her hand on the bannister for support.

The oak treads were hard and cool, even through her socks, and the polished rail felt like silk beneath her palm. It took three full-time maids to keep

167

Gavilan spotless. They started at the top and worked down, then went back up and started over again. In addition to the three maids, there was Dolores Munoz and Alejo, ever-present guardians whose only purpose in life seemed to be smoothing the wrinkles out of the Haucks' existence. Strange that they were so sensitive to their privacy being invaded, Maris thought, when the most intimate aspects of their lives were witnessed every day. Maybe servants didn't count.

Suddenly her feet shot out from under her, so fast that her hand was torn from the bannister. She bounced on her rear, her arms windmilling frantically as she tried to grab hold of the rail again. Her fingers scraped wood, but lost it again.

She bounced once more, striking her head hard on the edge of a stair. Sparks flew across her vision. She was aware of hitting wood again, the rolling downward, arms and legs spinning, thumping, uncontrollable, unable to stop her.

Darkness held out velvet arms toward her. She rolled right into it, and was swallowed.

Fourteen

Maris woke to pain pounding a steady rhythm in her head. Voices swam around her, muffled as though her ears were stuffed with cotton. Someone was holding her hand. She didn't need to open her eyes to know it was Cyndi.

"Are you all right, Mom?" There were tears in Cyndi's voice.

"I . . . think so. My head is pounding." It took some effort, but she managed to get her eyes open.

The Haucks were lined up beside the sofa, all staring down at her. Sophie, John, Robyn and Garrick—Maris wouldn't have been surprised if Ballard's wheelchair hadn't been queued up with the rest of the family. It was like waking up at your own funeral to see the mourners gathered 'round your coffin.

"Don't try to move, Mom. I think you've got a concussion again."

"I don't have time for a concussion." Maris tried to get up, but the moment she lifted her head, she was engulfed by a wave of sick dizziness. With a groan, she let her head fall back onto the pillow.

She must have drifted off for a while, for when she opened her eyes again, a strange man was bending over her. He had white hair and a bristly white mustache, and his eyes were very kind behind his glasses.

"Tell me you're not the Angel Gabriel," she said.

He smiled. "I'm Dr. Houseman, from the next estate. Garrick called me when they found you. Now let me take a look at you."

After feeling her head with gentle, expert fingers, he took out a penlight and flashed it into her eyes. "Garrick told me they found you lying unconscious at the bottom of the stairs. Did you fall?"

"Yes. I . . . guess I slipped. It was stupid, running around with only my socks on. My feet just went out from under me on that slick wood, and the next thing I knew, I was bouncing downhill."

The light went away. "There's no fracture, I'm glad to say, but you've got yourself a mild concussion and a beauty of a knob on your head. You're a lucky woman."

Maris reached up to touch the spot that was the center of the pain. "Ouch! You call this lucky?"

"You could have broken your neck."

"True," she said. "But it's hard to be grateful when my head is pounding like a bass drum."

"That will pass, but you've got several pulled muscles and some deep bruises. I'll see that you get something for the pain, and that someone checks on you periodically through the night. If you're not comfortable with that, I can arrange for you to go to the hospital—"

"No thanks," Maris said. "I've seen enough of hospitals to last my lifetime and yours."

"I expect you have," he said softly. "What kind of cancer does Cyndi have?"

"Leukemia."

170

"Ah, yes, now I remember the newspaper stories. My deepest hopes for her recovery." He closed his medical bag and straightened. "Your daughter is very worried about you."

"Thanks, I know." Maris let her eyes drift closed.

"Maris?"

"Yes, Dr. Houseman?"

"You might let Cyndi take care of you a bit. A person gets tired of being dependent, and of caregiving. A switch in roles might do you both some good."

She opened her eyes and looked at him. "Do you think she needs that?"

"Actually, I think *you* do. You've had the harder job. No," he said, raising his hands to stop Maris's protest. "I didn't say it isn't terrible for Cyndi to have leukemia. But to be a parent, and to have to watch . . . that is truly devastating."

A tear slid out of Maris's right eye and ran down into the hair at her temple. She could have kissed Dr. Houseman for pretending he didn't see it.

There was a soft knock at the door, then Cyndi called, "Dr. Houseman?"

"Come in, Cyndi. Your mother's fine."

She hurried into the room and sank down on the few spare inches of cushion at the edge of the sofa. "How are you doing, Mom?"

"I'm a little sore, but okay." Maris studied her daughter's face, noting the shadowed eyes that reflected both concern and fatigue.

"Is there anything I can do for you?" Cyndi asked.

"Well . . ." Maris wanted to say no. She wanted to keep Cyndi with her, conserving the little energy she had left. But then she looked past the shadows

171

and fatigue, and saw the eager hope in her daughter's eyes. Cyndi needed to be needed. It was one of the hardest things she'd ever had to do, but Maris forced herself to say, "I could really use a glass of water, hon. Would you mind getting one for me?"

"Sure, Mom." She got to her feet and trotted from the room.

Dr. Houseman caught Maris's gaze and winked. Then he shrugged into his jacket and strode out. Maris was left with a very warm feeling inside.

She drifted off again. Vaguely, she was aware of the sofa shifting under another person's weight.

"Mom, I've got your water," Cyndi said.

Maris bore the pain of lifting her head enough to take a few swallows. "Thanks, sweetheart."

There was a rap at the door, then John and Garrick came into the room. Garrick stood back several feet, looking ill at ease. John, however, knelt beside the sofa and took Maris's hand in both of his. "Dr. Houseman tells us you're going to be fine, Maris. I can't tell you how happy I was to hear that, and how distressed that you were hurt in my home. If there is any way I can make it up to you, I want you to tell me."

"You don't have to make it up to me," Maris said. "I was careless, and the accident was my fault. Or we could credit it to plain bad luck."

"Better start hoping for some good luck for a change," Garrick said. "Even a cat only has nine lives. You're using yours up fast."

"Tell me about it." She closed her eyes, not having the energy to deal with more conversation, and let herself slide away again.

* * *

Maris floated upward toward awareness. For a moment she lay still, assessing herself. Her head still hurt, but not as badly as it had before. But she felt strangely fuzzy, as though all her edges were blurred.

The bedside lamp was on, but turned down so low that it didn't reach the edges of the room. She raised her head enough to see that the windows were dark. It was still night, then.

That small movement exhausted her, and she lay back and closed her eyes. She heard the door open and close softly, but didn't have the ambition to force herself to look up again.

A large, warm hand clasped hers. "Maris, are you awake?"

Keir's voice. That smooth, smoky baritone rolled over her, through her, opening her eyes. He was sitting in a chair beside the bed, and seemed as though he had been for some time. Worry made him look ten years older.

Maris's tongue seemed to be stuck to the roof of her mouth, and it took her a moment to free it. "What . . . time is it?"

"A little after seven," he said.

"Are . . . you sure?" Seven o'clock made no sense; it had been nearly ten-thirty when she'd gone downstairs for ice cream. She tried to focus her thoughts on the problem, but the threads kept slipping away from her.

As though reading her mind, Keir said, "It's seven o'clock *Friday.*"

"I . . . I slept a night and a whole day?"

"You've been awake several times, even had a conversation of sorts with Cyndi. Don't you remember any of that?"

"No," Maris whispered. Fear cut through the fog that enveloped her. Something was wrong. She pushed at the mattress with strengthless arms. "Help me sit up," she gasped.

Keir levered her upright, then wedged several pillows behind her and eased her back onto the support. She hated that he had to do most of the work. But she was sitting up, and that was the first step. Her body whispered to her traitorously, urging her to close her eyes. *Sleep, Maris. You're too tired for this. Just go to sleep.*

She fought it, fought it hard. And began to win. Her mind wasn't working on all cylinders, but at least she could hold a coherent thought.

"Something's wrong," she said. "I shouldn't have slept that long. Talk to me, Keir. Don't let me go back to sleep."

"Okay. First, let me see your eyes." Reaching over, he switched the bedside lamp on high. Maris had to squeeze her eyes shut against the sudden increase of light. Closing her eyes, even for that small time, was dangerous, and she could feel the need to sleep pulling her down.

"Maris!"

Keir's voice jarred her back to awareness. "Thanks," she said.

Taking her chin in his hand, he tilted her face upward. "Pupils are the same size," he muttered, frowning. "Hell, who am I kidding? I'm no doctor. I don't have the vaguest idea what could be causing this." With an explosive sigh, he raked his hand through his hair. "Didn't you get a concussion before, during the fire?"

She nodded. "But I didn't have this kind of trouble then."

"Maybe there's some kind of cumulative effect if the injuries are too close together. Did you tell the doctor about the first one?"

"No. I . . . wasn't exactly thinking straight."

"Well, someone else should have been. Damn!" He swung his fist into the open palm of his other hand. There was a knock at the door, and he strode across the room to open it.

Mrs. Munoz stood framed in the doorway, a glass of water in her hand. "I didn't know you were here, Mr. Andreis."

"I just got in a couple of minutes ago."

"So good of you to come see our patient," the housekeeper said. "But I'm afraid she has been sleeping more than not. Perhaps tomorrow would be a better time."

"I'm awake," Maris said.

The glass Mrs. Munoz was holding tilted, almost, but not quite, letting water spill over the top. "I'm glad to see it, Señora Durant," the older woman said. "Your daughter was becoming worried."

"Where is she?"

"Downstairs in the kitchen with Rosalia."

Keir closed the door with a sharp, impatient gesture. "Who treated Maris last night, Mrs. Munoz?" he asked. "How can I get hold of him?"

"Dr. Houseman?" Mrs. Munoz moved farther into the room. "He will not be at home. Every Friday, he goes to Houston to play bridge with some friends."

Maris focused on the glass of water, suddenly conscious of a raging thirst. "Is that for me?" she asked.

"Yes," the housekeeper said, moving toward the

175

bedside table. "And it is also time for your medicine." Setting the glass down, she picked up a plastic medicine bottle and opened it.

Keir drew his breath in sharply, and Maris turned her head to look at him. He was staring at Mrs. Munoz, and his face wore the expression of a man who had just had a sudden, devastating revelation.

"Let me see those pills," he said.

Mrs. Munoz looked up, her surprise obvious. "The pills?"

Keir held out his hand. Slowly, the housekeeper reached out and placed the pill bottle in his palm. He shook two out and examined them. "What are these?" he asked.

"I don't know," Mrs. Munoz said. "Dr. Houseman gave them to Señora Hauck, who gave them to Señor Garrick to give to me. My instructions were to give her two every four hours."

"Maris?" Keir swung around to the bed. "Did Dr. Houseman tell you what he was going to give you?"

Maris peered at the small, pinkish ovals. "Something for the pain was all he said. Why? What's the matter?"

"I don't know. But you're not taking any more of these until I get hold of Dr. Houseman. Mrs. Munoz, go ask Señora Hauck to come up here, please."

Maris watched Mrs. Munoz's mouth tighten. That "please" hadn't taken the command, nor had it been intended to. And it was obvious that the older woman didn't much like taking orders from anyone but the Haucks. Then she turned and walked out, silently as always.

Maris shifted position. The headache was start-

176

ing again. Not bad, more like a feeling of pressure at the back of her skull. Still, it made it hard for her to think. And there was something important she was supposed to remember. Friday . . . Friday. . . . Her pulse jagged into high gear. "Keir, have you or Hugh heard anything from Ella Florian?"

"No. Sorry, Maris."

"Did you—"

"I turned everything over to the detective like you wanted," he said. "But we don't have to deal with that now. There's—"

"Has he found anything?"

Keir sighed. "There's no Ella Florian working at the Nogales Bar. It's a topless place, by the way, even the bartenders. There's no record of any Ella Florian anywhere. It's obvious the name is false, and there's simply nowhere to go with it."

"Oh." Maris let her breath out slowly. Ella—whatever her name was—had lied. What else had she lied about? The woman herself had been crass and greedy, her edges so sharp that she could cut you just by passing, but the story had been almost perfect. Until now, Maris hadn't realized just how much hope she'd put into it, and how disappointed she'd be if it turned out false.

"We've got to find her," she said.

"Maris, if she were what she seemed, she would have called."

"A lot of things could have happened. It's only been two days."

"Three," Keir said. "You lost a day, remember?"

She rolled her head from side to side on the pillow. "I can't let her go!"

"Take it easy—"

"I can't."

177

"Okay, Maris. Okay." Bending over her, he pressed her back down. "I'll help you every way I can, okay?"

She nodded. That brief burst of effort exhausted her, however, so she found herself drifting off with no way to stop it.

"Maris, you're closing your eyes," Keir said.

His voice was a lifeline, and she clung to it. Slowly, her vision focused. "I'm trying."

"I know. I guess I'd better keep you talking . . . and on a safe subject. Why don't you ask me why I took so long to come?"

"This is a safe subject?"

"You'd prefer the weather?"

She heaved a sigh, knowing this battle was lost before it started. Even if she wanted to fight it. "Okay, why did it take so long for you to come?"

"Because I didn't know until Cyndi called me late this afternoon. She said she didn't care if we did have a fight; she wanted me here, and that was that. Tell me, did you take her to assertiveness training?"

"I'm afraid it comes naturally," Maris said. She pushed herself up higher on the pillows. "Why did you come at all? We didn't exactly part on good terms."

"I came because I care what happens to you. And that is more important than the stupid argument we had."

Yes, she thought, *it is.* "Truce?" she asked.

"Truce."

Maris smiled. It was a bit fuzzy, as smiles went, but it worked. "Cyndi thinks you must be a good kisser."

"What did you say?"

178

"I denied all knowledge of it."

"What do you say now?"

"I say . . ." Her eyelids strayed downward, and she forced them open again. "I say she was right. You've had a lot of practice."

"I was motivated. By a—oh, there you are, Mrs. Hauck."

Maris turned in time to see Sophie come into the room. The old woman's hair was combed into its usual smooth white cap, her black and white print dress impeccably designed and tailored. In this light, her eyes looked like chips of polished jet.

"How are you feeling this evening, Maris?" she asked.

"A little better," Maris said.

"I'm glad to hear it." Sophie swung around to Keir. "Mrs. Munoz tells me you think there might be a problem with Maris's medication?"

"Something's not right with her," he said. "I don't want her taking any more until I check with the doctor." He held out the pill bottle. "Did Dr. Houseman tell you what these are?"

The old woman took the bottle and tipped its contents out into her palm. She looked down at the pills, then up at Keir, and her bewilderment was obvious. "But this isn't the medication Dr. Houseman gave me."

"What the hell it is, then?" Keir looked as though he was ready to explode.

"I believe it's Xanax," Sophie said. Taking a deep breath, she added, "My Xanax. It's an antianxiety drug."

"Shit," Keir said.

Astonishment shook Maris farther out of her fog. She tried to speak, but nothing came out. She cleared her throat and tried again. "What . . . what did it do to me?"

"I don't know," Sophie said, her voice wavering for the first time. Slowly, like a slow-motion film of a building being demolished, her serene expression crumbled. "I don't know what happened, Maris, I really don't. When Dr. Houseman gave me the medicine, I put it in the pocket of my robe. It was at least a half hour before I took it out again to give it to Garrick. I might unknowingly have had some Xanax in my pocket . . . I take it at night, you know, a few minutes before going to bed." She went to the bed and took Maris's hand in both of hers. "I'm sorry, terribly, terribly sorry."

Maris recognized the genuineness of the old woman's distress. But she could spare no more than an acknowledging nod, for she had more important things to think about. Namely, the drug that was coursing through her system. *I want it out of me!* Unfortunately, her body couldn't quite accommodate the urgings of her mind.

But then she noticed that Keir was already taking care of it; snatching the phone off the hook, he called Hauck Community Hospital and told the Emergency Room to expect her and why.

"But shouldn't we try to locate Dr. Houseman first?" Sophie asked.

"I'm not waiting another second," Keir said. "That stuff has been in Maris's system nearly twenty-four hours. She needs to be where she can get proper treatment."

"But this could get out to the press," Sophie said.

So, Maris thought, Sophie Hauck, one senator's

wife, another senator's mother, was back at work for her family's interests.

"I don't care," Maris said.

"But think of the publicity, my dear," Sophie protested. "After what you've been through, I'd think you would want to avoid any possibility of it."

Keir looked up, pinning the old woman with a glare that would have daunted a steamroller. And then he said something Maris would treasure until the day she died.

"Screw the publicity," he snarled.

Fifteen

Maris could feel the roll of the deck under her, hear the snap of the sail as it belled out in the wind. Excitement rippled through her as the tiller kicked joyously against her palm. The sea and sky looked like a watercolor painting, azure and blue and the white, wind-whipped clouds. And Paul etched against the canvas, his brown hair sifting upon the breeze.

She looked up at her husband and found him staring at her, a smile tugging at his mouth. She knew what he was thinking. Later, they'd make love, sex and the sea and the driving wind all mingled together. She loved him so much, so terribly much.

"If you keep looking at me like that, I'm going to have to drop anchor right here," he called.

"Do it," she replied, feeling the familiar, sweet heaviness between her thighs.

Please, no! I don't want to be here!

But she was. No matter how much she fought the dream, it was always the same. She was going to have to watch Paul die. Again.

Paul's smile turned to a startled shout as the boat heeled over onto its side, hurling him onto the sail.

Water closed over Maris's head, pulling her deep amid the bubbles of her own passage. Above her, she could see the shadow of the boat. It hung over her head, seeming to encompass all the world.

"Maris!"

She kicked frantically for the dark winged shape of the boat. Paul needed her. Maybe this time she could save him. But the water seemed to drag at her flailing limbs, holding her back. Keeping her away from Paul. *Even if you save him, you won't be able to keep him.* She struggled even harder, rejecting that. Because Paul and Cyndi were inextricably entwined, and giving him up meant giving her up as well. Death might take them from her, but she wasn't going to give them up.

"Maris!"

Strange, it didn't sound like Paul's voice. Even so, it was familiar. It drew her, pulling her away from the boat, away from Paul.

"Maris, wake up!"

That's right, I'm asleep.

And then she wasn't. Instead of the sea and sky, she found herself looking up at a white-painted ceiling. For a moment, she didn't know where she was.

Then her brain lurched into gear. She was in Hauck Community Hospital. Keir had brought her here.

He moved into her field of view, his face seamed with concern. "Are you all right?"

She nodded, but she was shaking so badly the bed was moving with it.

"The hell you are," Keir said.

He took her hands in his, but she pulled away. "Please, don't touch me," she whispered. When he let her go, she wrapped her arms around herself and

183

curled onto her side, huddling around her misery.

"Where's Cyndi?" she whispered.

"She's at Gavilan. Don't worry about her, she's fine. Jesus Christ, Maris, think about your own business for a second, will you? What were you dreaming about?"

"Paul."

"That wasn't a warm and cozy dream about a man you love."

"No." She closed her eyes. "It was about his death. I dream about it . . . occasionally."

"Frequently?"

"Any is too much."

He exhaled sharply. "Did you go for grief counseling after he died?"

"Yes. It helped for a while. But the nightmares came back after Cyndi got sick." With an effort, Maris controlled the shudders. "When they bring Paul up . . . drowned, he's got Cyndi's face. I don't need a psychiatrist to tell me what that means. The only people I have in the world are my mom and Cyndi. Mom is old and frail, and going downhill fast, and Cyndi . . ." She took several breaths to calm herself. "There's nothing I can do about Mom. But Cyndi's my *child*."

"I know, Maris. But a counselor might help you learn to live with it, maybe even turn it into a positive force in your life."

"Do you have any children?"

"No."

Maris levered herself to a sitting position. "Then, you don't understand. The death of a child is the most devastating thing that can happen to a person. You don't accept it, ever. You don't get over it, ever. See, parents aren't *supposed* to outlive their children.

184

When a child dies, the natural order of things is shattered. If I lose Cyndi, I lose it all. There won't be enough left of me to bother with."

To her surprise, Keir didn't try to argue. He leaned down and took her in his arms. It was an undemanding embrace, a mere offering of human comfort. And right now, she *needed* that. She let herself relax, listening to the slow, regular beat of his heart against her ear.

After a moment, she pulled away. "I must be . . . . What do I look like?"

He flipped the overhead light on, then took a mirror off a nearby shelf and handed it to her. She didn't like what she saw. There was a butterfly bandage across her right eyebrow, and the skin around her eye was a lovely shade of purple. Her hair stuck up every which way.

Shuddering, she laid the mirror aside. "Bela Lugosi's got nothing on me."

"I've seen worse."

"Where? At the freak show?"

Keir laughed. "Now I *know* you're feeling better."

"What was that stuff I was taking?" she asked.

"Do you remember anything from last night?"

"Most of it is pretty fuzzy," she said. "I do remember Sophie saying I was taking *her* medicine by mistake."

"It's called Xanax. Wait a sec, I took some notes when the doctor was telling me about it." He took a piece of paper from his pocket. "Here, and I quote: 'Xanax is an antianxiety drug used to treat short-term anxiety caused by trauma or stress.' He also said it's quite toxic. But you've thrown off the effects well, and he's planning to send you home in the morning."

185

"Toxic," she repeated. "You mean like poisonous?"

"In high doses."

"How high a dose was I taking?"

"High."

I could have died. "I could have died?"

"Well . . ."

"Tell me, Keir."

"Let's say strychnine is rated six on a scale of toxicity. Xanax would check in at five."

Maris met his gaze steadily, although her heart was jumping around like crazy. "You saved my life."

"Cyndi saved your life. She called me and *ordered* me to come over. Anyone with half a grain of sense—and that obviously doesn't include Mrs. Munoz—would have seen something was wrong."

"Mrs. Hauck—"

"Mrs. Hauck never bothered to goddamn check." He checked his watch, then thrust his notes back into his pocket. "Sorry, Maris, but I've got to go. I'm supposed to catch a plane in forty-five minutes."

"You're going away?"

He shrugged. "Business. One of the less attractive aspects of it, but necessary. I'll be gone a week, maybe ten days." With a grin that would have done Satan himself justice, he added, "Will you miss me?"

Maris did her best to match that smile. "Cyndi will."

"Touché," he said with a laugh. "Have you always been this feisty?"

Surprise washed over her. No, she hadn't always been feisty. Goal-oriented, certainly, but always willing to accommodate. The need to save her daughter had forced her to be pushy, to ask questions and demand answers. With Paul gone, she had to. In that process, sweet and compliant Maris Durant had been

186

shattered, reformed into a much different woman. Harder. More aggressive.

Was it better or worse? Who knew? Who cared? Whatever the case, she wasn't going to let herself be beaten. Not by Ella Florian, and not by Drew Eniston.

"Maris?"

Her gazed focused on Keir. "What?"

"Whew! For a minute there, I thought you'd gone into a coma or something."

"I'm going to go see Drew Eniston again."

He gaped at her. "After what happened last time?"

"Yes."

"Maris, you're just setting yourself up for more heartbreak. He's not going to help you."

"That kind of heartbreak I can take," she said. "Last time I let him manipulate me. I played right into his hands. This time is going to be different. I'm going to get some answers from him."

"What if he refuses?"

"Then, I'll keep going back. I'll annoy him until he gives up."

Keir laughed. "I believe you would."

"Believe it. I've got no scruples, no ego to be stroked, no limits." She grinned, feeling nothing but pure, unadulterated malice. "And whatever else he can do or say, *he can't run away from me.*"

Two days later, Maris sat in the tiny visiting room at Huntsville Prison, tapping her foot impatiently. It had been an hour wait so far, and she knew Eniston was doing it deliberately. Putting her at a disadvantage. *Only if you let him!*

"Get out here, you sorry so-and-so," she muttered.

187

As if on cue, the door in the other room opened. Drew Eniston came in, his gaze fastening on her immediately. His guard motioned him into the chair, then flipped him a pack of cigarettes and some matches.

Eniston lit up, watching Maris through the smoke. Again, the look in his strange, yellow-streaked eyes was both curious and challenging. When Maris picked up the phone, he just sat and studied her, not making a move toward his own phone until she tapped on the glass.

"What happened to your face?" he asked.

"I fell down some stairs," she said. "Didn't you know that smoking's bad for your health?"

"So's jail. Why did you come back?"

"Not for your company, that's for sure," Maris retorted. "Why did you come out to talk to me?"

"Because you had the balls to tell me to go to hell."

Maris felt as though she'd entered a boxing ring, not a conversation. "I don't want any of your crap today, Eniston."

"But if you want to interview me, you're going to have to take my crap, aren't you?"

"I'm not here to interview you," she said. "I have a story to tell you, and all I'm asking is that you hear me out before saying anything."

Eniston let smoke dribble out of his nose. "Is it a story about the Haucks? If so, you can save your breath."

"It's my story," Maris said.

"Okay, *Ms*. Durant. Shoot."

The last word was flung out forcefully, and Maris knew he was trying to fluster her. At another time, she might have been. But not now. "I'm adopted. My

188

daughter has leukemia, and the only hope for her survival is finding a bone marrow donor."

"And that means finding your biological family."

"Oh, you know about that?"

"We're allowed to read as much as we want. It's living we're not supposed to do."

"I've tried everything I know to find them, but it's been a dead end so far."

"So why are you bothering me?" Eniston asked.

Taking a deep breath, she leaned close to the glass. "Because I was born in Houston, Texas, May 23, 1958."

Something flashed in Eniston's eyes, but was so quickly suppressed that she couldn't interpret it.

"So?" he drawled.

"Oh, come on! If you were me, wouldn't you be here?"

He leaned back in his chair, his cigarette clamped between his lips. He looked downright disinterested. Maris was infuriated by his lack of response, and determined to probe until she got something from him.

"When I found out that I was born on the same day Lee was murdered," she said, deliberately choosing the harshest word, "I thought there might be a connection. And when I read that the body of the baby was never found—"

"Lots of bodies don't get found in the bayou," he said. "Go back to St. Louis, Ms. Durant. You're not only barking up the wrong tree, you're in the wrong damn forest. All you're going to find messing in this business is a bunch of grief."

Anger did a slow roll in her chest. "How so?"

"Wait until the senator learns you've used his name to get in to talk to *me*."

"He's not going to do squat," Maris said. "I'm

189

staying at his mother's house. They're putting me up while I—"

"What?" His elbows came down on the shelf before him as he shoved his face close to the glass. "You're living at Gavilan?"

"Yes."

"Those goddamned Haucks! Prancing around with their fancy ways, using their money and their goddamned good-ole-boy influence to fuck up other people's lives!"

Maris gaped at him, astonished at what she had unleashed. "What are—"

"I'd like to kill every one of them!" His fingers curved, as though he were ready to start squeezing someone's neck. "I'd like to go in there like fucking Rambo—Don't fucking touch me!" he shouted as the guard clamped his hands on his shoulders.

"Take it easy, Drew, or I'll have to take you back to your cell." The guard's voice came clearly over the phone.

Eniston relaxed. Outwardly at least; a vein in his forehead pulsed a steady, rapid rhythm, and the tendons in his forearms stood out like wires. After a moment, the guard let him go.

During it all, the murderer's gaze never left Maris. There, she'd said it. Murderer. Remembering how his face had looked when he talked about killing the Haucks, she believed him capable of it. She shivered beneath those strange eyes that were hot with rage. Whatever had prompted this blazing hatred of the Haucks, thirty-four years hadn't cooled it at all.

When he spoke again, it was in a soft, deadly voice that sent a frisson of alarm up her spine. "Did they get you an interview on the teevee?" he said, spitting the words out as though they tasted bad.

190

"Yes," Maris said.

"I get it. That prick John needed the publicity. I can see the headlines now. 'Senator John Hauck Takes Widow and Sick Child Into His Home. Vows To Find A Donor!' "

"Something like that," Maris said. "He also got Cyndi into the pediatric cancer program at M.D. Anderson. Which, by the way, I'd tried to get her in myself and failed."

"So." Eniston lit another cigarette, inhaled deeply. "You use him, he uses you."

"Something like that. Why do you hate them so much?"

"They fucked up my life."

"I thought," Maris said, "you did that yourself."

"Yeah."

Feeling rather like a ship that had crested one tidal wave only to find another looming ahead, Maris asked, "Was Lee's baby a boy or a girl?"

His eyes flickered briefly. "Girl."

"Did she have a name?"

"Didn't need one."

"You kept that baby's sex a secret all these years," Maris said. "Why?"

"Because the Haucks wanted to know."

"You killed their daughter. Isn't that punishment enough?"

He showed the edges of his teeth in a smile. "Not for my life."

"You have your life. From what I could tell, you were lucky not to have gotten the chair."

"I would have preferred the chair. I *asked* them to give me the chair. Being in prison is worse than dying." He said it coldly, calmly, as though it were true. Maybe it was.

191

"Eniston . . ." Maris leaned forward, wanting to look into his eyes when he answered her next question. "Did you kill that baby?"

He met her gaze levelly. "Yeah."

Maris was stunned by the flat admission. This must be how the police officers had felt all those years ago, she thought. They, too, had looked into this man's eyes, heard his words, and been chilled by the lack of conscience in him. He had held that tiny life in those big, corded hands of his, and he had tossed it into the water of the bayou. Or said he did.

He held her gaze for a long, quiet moment, and Maris felt the hairs rise up on the back of her neck. It was incomprehensible that a human being could do what he claimed to have done, and yet even more incomprehensible that one could lie about it.

"Why should I believe you?" she asked.

"What's the matter? Are you afraid life isn't going to turn out in true fairytale style?"

Her temper flared. "If this were a fairy-tale, Eniston, I wouldn't have to spend my time talking to a murderer."

"I thought you didn't believe me."

"For a man to kill a helpless infant —"

"Nits grow into lice." His voice was matter-of-fact, his face tight and cruel.

Maris could only stare into those cold, cold eyes of his. For a moment, she wondered if he was human at all.

He rose to his feet. "Like I said, Ms. Durant, you're barking up the wrong tree. Let me give you a bit of advice: shed the Haucks now, before they cost you too much. You might think you're getting what you want out of them, but believe me, you're not. As far as users go, they're world class. Born and bred, and with the name and money to get away with it."

Who is he to give advice? she thought. *Who is he to* judge? "There's nothing they can take from me that I wouldn't willingly give for my daughter. Goodbye, Eniston. It's been . . . interesting."

She hung up and turned away. A sharp rap on the glass brought her back around. Eniston gestured for her to come back and pick up the phone again. Reluctantly, she obeyed.

"That fall you had—was it at Gavilan?" he asked.

"Yes."

He stared at her for a long time, a speculative look in his eyes. Maris found herself unable to look away. She was caught, snared by his danger and strangeness, fascinated by the very lack of conscience that had made him a killer.

Then he looked away, breaking the spell. "Goodbye, Ms. Durant," he said. "Remember me in your dreams."

"I've got other dreams," she said, hanging up for good.

Sixteen

The next morning, Maris woke feeling as though she hadn't slept at all. Despite her words to Drew Eniston, he had stalked her dreams all night, the yellow streaks in his killer's eyes whirling like the spokes of a bicycle wheel. Somehow, he had touched something deep inside her.

"Yeah, right," she muttered. "The same fascination the fly feels for the spider."

With a groan, she sat up and swung her legs over the side of the bed. There didn't seem to be a spot on her body that wasn't either bruised or strained.

The door to the adjoining room opened, and Cyndi peered in. "Hey, Mom. You doing okay?"

"Yeah, hon. Just moving slow, that's all." Opening her arms wide, she said, "Come here and give me a hug."

Cyndi walked into her arms. They held each other tight for a long time, and Maris felt her own tension slowly ease. Pushing Cyndi to arm's length, she ran her palm over the golden peach fuzz on the child's head.

"It's almost long enough to comb," Maris said.

"Almost long enough to be a crew-cut, you mean. Maybe I should spike it. Look, it's almost time for

194

breakfast. If you don't get a move on, Mrs. Munoz is going to come fetch us."

"Anything but Mrs. Munoz." Maris headed for the bathroom.

The family was already in the dining room when Maris and Cyndi made it downstairs. Garrick was there, staring sullenly at the cozy picture of his mother and big brother's usual morning tête-à-tête. Maris didn't understand why he kept coming; maybe he couldn't stop punishing himself any more than Sophie could help ignoring him.

"Good morning, ladies," John called. "Maris, you look so much better this morning."

"He likes your shiner," Garrick said. "He's always been partial to yellow and purple."

"That is enough, Garrick." Sophie pinned him with the same look Maris had seen her use on the servants. "Cyndi, Maris, please sit down. Ballard is impatient for his food."

As Maris took her place at the table, she glanced at the old man. His eyes were vacant, like opaque glass, and his big, knobby hands lay relaxed on the arms of the wheelchair. At one time, he'd ruled the roost. *Patrón*. She'd looked up the word in a Spanish/English dictionary, and there had been a whole string of terms to describe it: protector, landlord, owner, *master*. And that was what Ballard Hauck had been. Master of his home, his family, his world. And his world still turned to his wishes, despite the fact that he was nothing but a helpless, senile old man.

It was sick and obsessive—and destructive. One look at Robyn, who was sitting beside her father, poised to serve, told Maris that. And there was Garrick, forty-four-year-old ne'er-do-well, scowling at

195

his plate like a reprimanded child. The Grande Dame, the Politician, the Bad Boy, and the Invisible Woman, all gathered together to preserve a myth.

Suddenly Ballard began smacking his lips, and avidity came into his eyes. Rosalia had come with the food.

Maris inhaled deeply. *Ahhh,* she thought, *Rosalia's fresh, hot biscuits*. Made, she knew, for Cyndi. The Durants may not have made many points with the Haucks, but the cook had a real soft spot for Cyndi.

The maid laid the trays on the table and served coffee and juice, then left, closing the door silently behind her. Before Maris had a chance to do more than stir sugar into her coffee, Alejo came into the room.

"Señor John, there is a phone call for you."

"They just can't let a man have his breakfast," John said, rolling his eyes.

" 'They' know you're going to be governor," Sophie said.

"I hope they're right." There was no doubt in John's face, however, or in his eyes as he shoved his chair back and got to his feet. Taking his coffee with him, he followed Alejo out.

"With all the excitement, Maris, we haven't had much time to talk lately," Sophie said. "How is your search coming along?"

"Not all that well, Mrs. Hauck. There have been a few leads, but they seem to have been dead ends."

"I'm sorry. I had high hopes that you would find your birth mother soon."

"So did I," Maris said. *Damn you, Ella Florian!* "But I'm not giving up, and we still have the drive going to register new donors. A couple of hundred people have volunteered to be tested already, and that's just here in Houston. We don't know how many we'll get from other cities."

"What are the odds?" Garrick asked.

One in twenty thousand. Aloud, however, Maris said, "Oh, pretty good, if we get enough people tested. Hugh Carideo wants to do another interview on me sometime soon, so that should bring more people."

"I'd like to be tested," Robyn said.

There was such incredulity on Sophie's face that Maris nearly laughed. The old woman couldn't have been more surprised than if the table had gotten up to do a jig. "Do you have any idea what it means, Robyn?"

Robyn nodded. "It's only a simple blood test, Mother. If I do happen to match, then they'll draw marrow from the back of my pelvic bones with a syringe. There's a slight risk from the anesthesia, and a bit of soreness. That's all."

"What sort of risk?" Sophie asked.

Robyn fumbled with her knife. "There's always a risk from general anesthesia, Mother. It's very slight."

The spoked lines around Sophie's mouth deepened. She glanced at Maris, obviously expecting her to refuse Robyn's offer.

Maris wasn't about to. For the first time since she'd met this family, Robyn was doing something *Robyn* wanted to do. And there was another reason. Maybe Robyn was that one in twenty thousand. Maybe she would match. Even if the risks were higher than what they were, Maris would let Robyn take the risk. Selfish reasons, unselfish reasons, and both good enough for Maris.

Turning to Robyn, she said, "I think it's great. It means a lot to Cyndi and me. If you'd like, I'll take you to M.D. Anderson with me Thursday when I take Cyndi for treatment."

"Thank you." Robyn returned to tending her father, taking bites of her own food in between spoon-feeding him. She had the air of a woman who had just gained the peak of her own personal mountain.

Maris buttered a biscuit and took a bite, savoring the taste of it along with that of Robyn's kindness. Maybe the woman wasn't invisible at all, merely outnumbered and outgunned.

John came back in, looking thoughtful and harried at the same time.

"Is something the matter, dear?" Sophie asked.

"Just annoyances, Mother." Instead of sitting back down, he crossed the room and opened the far door. "Rosalia! Lina! More coffee, please, and a cup. And make me some fresh eggs. These are cold."

"Robyn wants to be tested as a possible donor," Sophie said.

He glanced at his sister. "Won't work, Robyn. I've already been tested, and the results were so far off as to be laughable. The doctor said not to bother bringing in the rest of the family."

"Oh," Robyn said. Reaching over, she dabbed at her father's mouth with her napkin. "I guess there's no point in going, then, is there?"

They did it to her again, Maris thought, watching the faint glow of triumph fade from Robyn's face. Between Sophie and John, Robyn didn't stand a chance. It wasn't even anything she could fight; John's calm, logical reason left nothing to argue.

The maid came in, the coffeepot in one hand and

198

a cup in the other. "The eggs will be ready in a moment, Señor Hauck," she said, sliding the cup into his saucer.

"Fine. Just give me some coffee."

He reached for a biscuit, jostling her with his elbow just as she began to pour. Coffee splashed out onto the tablecloth. The maid muttered an apology and dabbed at the spill with a napkin.

John shoved her hand away. "Leave it," he snapped.

Maris was surprised by his curt reaction, and it was obvious that everyone else was, too. Whatever the Haucks did to one another, they treated the servants with perfect courtesy.

The maid took a step backward, clutching the napkin against her chest. "I . . . I'm sorry, Señor Hauck. I did not mean to offend."

"It's all right, Lina," Sophie said. "Go see if Rosalia needs help in the kitchen."

The old woman waited until the girl was gone, then folded her hands on the table. "What's the matter, John?"

He let his breath out in a long sigh. "Drew Eniston escaped from prison this morning."

"What? How . . . Dear God, John!" Sophie half-rose from her chair, stretching one hand toward her eldest son.

He ignored her. It was Garrick who got up and eased his mother back into her seat, Garrick who put his arm around her shoulders to comfort her.

Sophie began to calm down, regaining control with a visible effort. After a moment, she leaned forward, out of the circle of Garrick's arm. "Tell me what happened," she said.

"Eniston faked a heart attack and got himself

taken to the infirmary," John said. "They were stupid, and he knew it, played it perfectly. He'd been a model prisoner for thirty-four years. Now he was a sick old man, no threat at all. They left him alone in the infirmary. Thought he was asleep." His fist crashed down on the table with a violence that made the silverware bounce into the air. "They left him alone. Walked away and left him *alone!* When they got back to check on him, he was gone. He'd unscrewed the ceiling light and slipped up through the ceiling. Got out in the laundry truck."

"Why?" Garrick asked. "After all these years, why now?"

Maris's throat had gone tight with dread. *It's my fault. I must have triggered him somehow.* "I did it."

They all turned to stare at her incredulously. All but John. His face was so expressionless that Maris knew he'd already been told about her visit. *Okay,* she thought. *It's time to take the heat for it.*

"I went to see him yesterday," she said. "That must have been what set him off."

Sophie gasped. "But . . . why?"

Under the table, Maris felt Cyndi's hand creep into hers. She clasped it tightly, drawing courage from her daughter. "I wanted to ask him if he really had killed Lee's baby."

All color drained from the old woman's face. Garrick put his arm around her shoulders again, and this time she leaned against him.

"You've got balls, I'll give you that," he said.

John leaned forward, his palms flat on the table. "What did he say?"

"He said yes."

"Oh, my God!" Sophie began to cry quietly, her

200

face buried against Garrick's shoulder. "Lee," she sobbed. "Lee."

"Did Keir know about this?" John asked, too quietly.

"No. I did it all on my own," Maris lied, then turned to Sophie. "Mrs. Hauck, I'm sorry if this brings up painful memories. But with the coincidence in dates and the fact that the baby's body was never found—"

"I told you to leave it alone." John's voice was calm, his blue-gray eyes hot with anger.

"I had to know," Maris said.

"You had no right to push your way into our business. You had no right to use my name to get you into that prison . . ." Each point was punctuated with a flat-handed slap on the table. "You had no right—"

"No, I had no right. I also had no choice." Maris shoved her chair back and got to her feet, drawing Cyndi up with her. "We'll be leaving as soon as I get our bags packed. I'm grateful for everything you and your family have done for us, and I give you my sincerest apology for any pain I might have caused you by my actions."

"Sit down, Maris," Sophie said.

John chopped the air with the edge of his hand. "Stay out of it, Mother. This is between me and Maris."

"No, it is not." She and John glared at each other in a tense clash of wills.

To Maris's surprise, John was the first to look away. Sophie gave a taut little nod of satisfaction before turning back to Maris. "Sit down, Maris. Please."

Maris obeyed.

Sophie clasped her hands on the table. *"I* understand. In your place, I would have done precisely the same thing."

Truly astonished, Maris could only say, "You would?"

"I have children, too."

Tears stung Maris's eyes. Understanding was the last thing she would have expected from this woman. In those times that Sophie seemed cold and uncaring, she would remember this. "Thank you," she whispered.

"Now, let's stop this talk of leaving. You and Cyndi are welcome in my home"—she glanced at John, slightly stressing the "my" as she did—"and I hope you won't allow this minor incident to make you feel otherwise."

"Minor incident?" John yelped. "Mother, the man is a killer! He swore he'd get back at us, do you remember?"

"Come on, John," Garrick said. "The man is old, and on the run. He's got other things to think about besides a thirty-four-year-old grudge."

"Does he?" John glanced at Maris, his gaze burning with anger and contempt. "We'll find out, won't we?"

Thanks to me. Guilt was a hard knot in Maris's chest. She didn't think Eniston would be stupid enough to show up here, where he was bound to be expected. But she couldn't be sure. With Eniston, she couldn't be sure of anything.

"Maris, you're the one who talked to him," Garrick said. "What do you think he'll do?"

She spread her hands helplessly. "I only had a couple of minutes with the man."

"If you'd had a year, you still wouldn't know,"

Sophie said. "After he—" Her voice faltered for a moment, then steadied. "They had him evaluated by a number of psychiatrists, and they got nothing from him. I don't think anyone can know that man."

Lee had, Maris thought. *And he killed her.*

"They'll catch him," Robyn said. "They always catch escapees sooner or later."

Maris took a deep breath, remembering the cold, calculating shrewdness in the killer's eyes. She had the feeling it was going to take a lot to catch Drew Eniston.

"Well, I'm not going to sit here like a damned decoy waiting for it," John said, shoving his chair back. "I'm getting some security down here."

"What about the police?" Garrick asked.

"The Department of Public Safety is looking for him, the Texas Rangers are looking for him, and an APB has been sent out in every city in East Texas. But I want my own people here—people I can trust not to go to the media. I've put a lid on this thing, and I'm going to do my damndest to keep it there."

"It's free publicity, isn't it?" Garrick asked, with a smile a shark would have envied. "I would've thought you'd jump at the chance to get your name in the paper for something other than voting against social programs." He snapped his fingers. "Hey, I got it! You get Eniston to take a pot-shot at you, get you in the shoulder or something, and you can go in front of the cameras and look like a martyr. How about it?"

"Shut up, Garrick," John said. "Just shut up."

Garrick only smiled wider. "Dredging up Lee's murder can only help you. Times have changed, Senator. These days, no one's gonna care whether Lee was shacking up or not—"

Sophie slapped him. The sound of it was loud in the shocked silence of the room. Robyn half-rose, then sank slowly back into her seat.

Garrick's face turned scarlet, then white. The mark of his mother's palm was clearly visible against the pallor of his skin. He got to his feet and walked out, slamming the door behind him.

Sophie turned back to John, her face astonishingly calm. As if hitting Garrick hadn't mattered—hadn't even registered. "Ignore him, dear," she said. "Now, about Drew Eniston—"

"I know what to do about Eniston," he said, as calmly as she. He pointed at Maris. "I'll take your word that you won't talk about this to your buddies in the media."

Maris would have liked to slap that pointing hand away. Instead, she inclined her head in agreement.

"Thank you." He stalked out of the room, slamming the door nearly as hard as Garrick had.

"Will it all come out again?" Robyn asked. "About Lee, I mean?"

"I . . . hope not," Sophie said.

Ballard made a grating sound deep in his throat, like a rusty wheel grinding into motion. "Lee?" he asked. "Lee?"

"Lee isn't here, darling," the old woman said, bending over him solicitously. "Would you like a nice, warm bath before getting dressed this morning?"

But the light in his eyes had died. A drop of spittle trembled on his bottom lip, then fell onto his chest.

Sophie didn't seem to notice. "Robyn, take your father to his room and get him settled. I . . . wouldn't worry about reading to him this morning; I think we're going to be having a very busy day."

"It's like something out of *Rambo*," Cyndi said from her perch on the sill of Maris's window. "All those guys and guns just because of one man."

Maris moved to stand beside her. For two days now, Gavilan had been crawling with blue-uniformed security people. Walkie-talkies in hand, they patrolled the grounds. They'd even blocked off the private road, turning away all unauthorized traffic.

"Do you think that man is going to come here?" Cyndi asked.

"Senator Hauck seems to think so."

Cyndi turned her head enough to give Maris a speculative look out of the corner of her eye. "Do you like him?"

"The senator?"

"Come on, Mom, I'm serious."

"Sorry, hon." Maris sighed. "No, I don't like Drew Eniston. He's a very scary man. I hope they catch him and put him back where he belongs."

Cyndi pressed her nose against the windowpane, making a butterfly pattern of fog on the glass. "If he comes here, they're going to shoot him, aren't they?"

Maris recoiled from the question. Not that she hadn't been pondering it; for two days she'd done little else but think about Drew Eniston. They weren't comfortable thoughts. Did he intend to come to Gavilan? Maybe. Was revenge his motivation, or did he *want* to get himself killed? If so, it was obvious that the Haucks were willing to accommodate him.

Reaching out, she ran her fingertips across Cyndi's dusting of golden hair. "Are you scared?"

"A little."

"Me, too. What do you say we get ourselves a motel room close to the hospital."

"But Mrs. Hauck said we could stay. And Senator Hauck even apologized for yelling at you and hoped bygones could be bygones."

"I know, honey, and it was very nice of them both. But—"

"But I'm sick and it isn't good for me to be upset," Cyndi said.

There was a knock at the door. A man's knock, Maris thought, firm and aggressive. When she opened the door, she found John Hauck and another man standing in the hall. The stranger held a large cardboard box.

"May we come in?" John asked.

Maris stepped back, out of the doorway. The stranger, a small, quick-moving man in his forties, strode past her with his burden. He laid the box down on the bed, then turned around to look at Maris. His blue business suit was crisp and expensive-looking, his face sharp-featured and clever. Maris caught a glimpse of a wine-colored birthmark on the left side of his neck.

"Maris, this is Bobby Peterus, owner of Peterus Security. He's come down to handle Gavilan's protection himself," John said.

"Hello," Maris said, reaching to shake hands.

"Pleasure." His handshake was brief and firm. "That box—" Peterus jerked his head toward the bed—"came to you from the St. Louis *Post/Dispatch*. We opened it this morning—"

"I thought it was addressed to me."

"We're opening all packages coming into this house, Mrs. Durant."

206

"I suppose there *is* a chance that Eniston might send a bomb addressed to me, via the St. Louis *Post/Dispatch,* in the hope that the Haucks would blow up with me."

"You never know."

Fifteen-love, Maris thought. Turning on her heel, she went to the bed and peered into the box. It was another shipment of letters from Carl Hansson, envelopes of all varied sizes and colors from all over the U.S. They had all been opened. *Is there one from her?*

She turned back to Peterus. "Was it necessary that you read my private mail?"

"Now, don't get upset, Maris," John said. "I ordered them to open all our mail, too. Even Garrick's. And if anyone ought to worry about what we might see in his mail, it's Garrick. I think he still gets hate mail from his two ex-wives. Last year, one of them sent a twenty-pound box of manure with a very explicit description of what to do with it."

Peterus laughed. "No kidding? Which one was that?"

"Meg. You might remember her; she graduated from Hauck City Academy in '67. Her maiden name was Sarovich."

"Year before me," Peterus said. "Pretty, but dumb."

John laughed. "That she was. Smart enough to dump Garrick, though."

"Senator—" Maris began.

"I know, I know." He cleared his throat. "Cyndi, would you do us a favor and go downstairs to the kitchen for a minute? Rosalia has some ice cream for you."

"Mom?"

Maris nodded. "Go on, hon."

With obvious reluctance, Cyndi left. Maris crossed her arms over her chest and faced the two men squarely despite the fact that her stomach was jumping with nervousness.

"Bobby, show it to her," John said.

The security man pulled an envelope out of his pocket and held it out to her. It was addressed in bold, block letters.

A sense of violation swept through her, sharp and powerful, but she didn't know if it was because of the letter or their reading of it. "You had no right to read that," she said, without reaching for it.

"How many have you gotten before this?" Peterus asked.

"A few." She turned her back on the men, not wanting them to see her face. This was her own personal ugliness, the stain of not being wanted even now.

"Read it, Maris," John said, offering it to her over her shoulder. "I think you should know what it says."

She snatched it from him. Even before she opened it, she knew it was going to be worse than the others. "Bitch," it said. "I told you not to come. I told you not to stay. Now you're going to be sorry. You and your little girl."

For a moment she stood, unable to speak, while the paper rattled in her shaking hands. Her pulse roared in her ears. "You and your little girl." Cyndi. *Cyndi*.

"He's trying to flush you out, make you run," Peterus said.

"He?" Maris repeated. "Who are you talking about?"

"Eniston."

She stared at him in astonishment. "You think Eniston sent this?"

"Sure," the security man said.

"But the other letters . . . he was in prison when those were sent."

Peterus shrugged. "So he had someone else send them for him. Cons do it all the time."

"But why?" Maris asked.

"Because of the date," John said. "He must have seen your ad."

Suddenly, she got it. "You think Eniston is after *me?*" she yelped.

The two men glanced at each other; then John nodded. "He did escape from prison the day after you visited him, didn't he? For thirty-four years, he's been a good boy. You were the trigger."

"But . . . it doesn't make any sense!"

"Hell, it doesn't have to make sense," Peterus said. "Did it make sense for him to kill his lover and his kid?"

Maris shook her head. Not a whole lot was making sense these days, least of all Drew Eniston. "I guess it's best that we find another place to live—"

"No," John said.

Startled, she studied his expression closely. But The Politician was firmly in place, and she might have been looking at a campaign poster. Smooth. Polished. Flat.

"Gavilan is the safest place for you and Cyndi," he said.

"I could take my daughter back to St. Louis."

He nodded. "Yes, you could. And he could follow you there. Even if he didn't, are you willing to take

Cyndi out of Dr. Guaymus's pediatric cancer program?"

Maris looked down. "No. You know I can't."

"Yes," he said. "I know. Forget this idea of leaving, Maris. It's counterproductive. Focus your attention on getting Cyndi well, and let me and Bobby here worry about Drew Eniston."

He might be wrong. She wanted him to be wrong. But, remembering the intensity of Eniston's hatred, the man's lean, corded hands, the eyes that were frightening and compelling at once, Maris knew she didn't dare take the chance. Not with Cyndi. There was nothing she could do but nod, accepting the senator's protection.

"Good," he said. "Bobby, what do you want her to do?"

"Just keep your eyes and ears open, Mrs. Durant," Peterus said. "Here in the house, you're safe. Anytime you leave, you'll be taking a guard with you. That means the garden, the store, the hospital. Anywhere. You do otherwise, we can't protect you."

Maris realized that she was trembling. Slowly, she forced herself to relax. "How long will I have to do this?"

"As long as it takes," John said.

"If he comes here . . ." She took a deep breath. "Do you intend to kill him?"

"Of course not," John said in that smooth, precise voice of his. "Eniston's the killer, not us."

The two men left, Peterus talking into his radio as he walked. Maris returned to the window.

Suddenly the sun didn't seem quite so bright, the grass quite so green. She closed her eyes, trying to understand Eniston. Trying to *feel* him. Was he out there now, watching, waiting? Did he hate her? Did he want to kill her, just as he'd killed Lee? Did he want to hurt Cyndi?

Why not? He's already killed one child. And because of that, she was going to be looking over her shoulder, waiting for the blow to fall. Wherever she went, whatever she did, she would be aware of him. Her own personal Fury.

"Damn you," she said. "Damn you, damn you!"

Eniston had escaped from his prison, and in doing so, had put her in one of his making.

Seventeen

Wednesday afternoon was beautiful, bright and sunny and in the seventies. Maris sat in a lawn chair on the patio, enjoying the warmth and the scent of daffodils on the gentle breeze. She was also trying to ignore the presence of the very tall, very wide security guard who stood nearby. No Jolly Giant here; with that sour, jowly face and protuberant eyes, he looked like a surprised bloodhound. His name tag said Odell—first or last, she had no idea.

Sophie came out, pushing Ballard and his wheelchair before her. "It's such a lovely day that Ballard and I decided to join you."

Maris was barely startled by the phrasing. She was getting used to the family treating Ballard as though he were still the *patrón* instead of a near-vegetable. It was almost as if they were expecting him to snap out of it some day, and things had better be to his liking when he did. And then the natural follow-up to that thought: Or else. He must have been one hell of a hard man.

Sophie parked Ballard nearby and settled into the chair beside Maris's. Wisps of the old man's hair lifted on the breeze.

"On days like this, I almost feel young again," Sophie said. Reaching over, she adjusted the blanket over her husband's knees. "I think this garden is my favorite place on this earth. Ballard and I were married here on this spot. All the Haucks get married in this garden."

"Even Garrick?" Somehow, Maris couldn't imagine the Black Sheep dutifully fulfilling the family ritual. Elopement was more his style.

"Garrick has always been an exception to almost everything," Sophie said, as though reading her thoughts. "John, however, had a lovely June wedding here."

"I didn't know John was married."

The old woman's expression hardened. "Oh, it ended in divorce as so many do these days. The girl just didn't understand how much time and effort it takes to be successful in politics. I had hoped he would marry again, since he had no children by the first wife, but he seems content with his career."

Maris's curiosity was roused now, and she took advantage of the old woman's rare burst of openness. "What about Garrick? Does he have children?"

"Four. One by his first, two by his second, and one by the third. The children live with their mothers in other states. I fear Garrick is too unsettled for marriage."

"That never stopped anyone from doing it," Maris said.

"That is all too true," Sophie said. "I always regret that Robyn never married. I don't know why. There were plenty of suitable young men who would have been proud to marry into the Hauck family."

Oh, brother! Maris thought. "Maybe she wanted a man who would have been proud to marry *her.*"

213

Sophie looked at her blankly. Maris sighed; perhaps the old woman had failed to see Robyn as a real person for so long that she simply didn't know how to do otherwise.

There was a long, awkward silence. Just as Maris was considering going back into the house, Sophie said, "What do you think of the garden, Maris?"

"It's beautiful."

It was no mere social politeness. Someone had had the sense to let things grow naturally, instead of trimming everything into balls, boxes and cones. White gravel paths curved around freshly mulched flowerbeds. Daffodils swung in the breeze, butter yellow trumpets rising proudly from masses of crocus and pansies. Green spears of iris and gladioli were beginning to poke up through the ground, promise of glory in the coming months.

The far end of the garden broadened into a thick planting of pine and maple and pin oak. Even without summer foliage, the heavy interlacing of branches protected the wood's green-dappled dimness. A flicker of movement beneath the trees caught Maris's attention. It might have been a squirrel, or a bird, but she'd gotten the impression of something larger. A deer? No, not in the afternoon.

She glanced at Odell, who was still at his post at the corner of the patio. He, too, was watching the woods, and was obviously alert, also obviously not alarmed. *You're spooking yourself, Maris! Seeing ghoulies and ghosties and bumps in the night, and all with the name of Eniston.*

Sensible words, but they didn't help much. Maris couldn't seem to shake the feeling of being watched. Given a choice among her, Sophie or Ballard, which would Eniston pick to kill?

214

"How far back do the trees go?" Maris asked.

Sophie smiled, apparently unaware of her guest's unease. "Oh, quite far, actually. Beyond the trees is a small lake which we own, of course."

"How can they guard all that?" Maris asked. The trees suddenly seemed full of movement now, shadowy Enistons lurking everywhere.

"There's an electrified fence a couple of hundred yards into the trees," Peterus said from behind Maris, bringing her around with a start.

"You shouldn't sneak up on people like that!" she gasped.

"I wasn't sneaking. I just walk quiet." He handed her a cordless phone. "Call for you, Mrs. Durant. Dr. Guaymus's office. Just flick that button there, and you'll be on the line."

Maris obeyed, fumbling a little in haste. "Hello?"

"Mrs. Durant, this is Miss Gregory, Dr. Guaymus's nurse. We're going to have to reschedule Cyndi's appointment."

"Why?"

"There was a delay at the lab, and we just received the results of Cyndi's blood work. There are a couple of things Dr. Guaymus would like to check further before beginning treatment."

"What things?" Alarm beat a tattoo in Maris's chest.

"The doctor will have to speak to you about that."

They always let the doctor give the bad news. Had something shown up that would keep Cyndi from getting further treatment? *Oh, God, please don't let that happen!* "Would you get Dr. Guaymus on the phone for me?"

"I'm sorry, but he's not in right now," the nurse said. "I'll have him call you as soon as he returns."

Not trusting herself to say anything else, Maris broke the connection. She didn't think she had the strength to cope with another setback now. If Cyndi couldn't have this chemotherapy. . . . She drew in her breath harshly.

It wasn't until the phone shrilled that she realized she was still holding her thumb on the disconnect button. Automatically, she raised the receiver to her ear.

"Hello?"

"*Ms*. Durant."

Eniston. That harsh, impatient voice was as unforgettable as the man's killer's eyes. Her heart kicked into high gear. She snapped her fingers to get Peterus's attention, then pointed to the phone. The security man nodded and started whispering into his walkie-talkie.

"Who is this?" Maris asked. Stupidly, because she couldn't think of anything else to say.

"You know who it is," Eniston growled. "Are you alone?"

"Yes, I'm alone." She glanced at Peterus, who motioned for her to go on. "What do you want?"

"I've got to talk to you."

"I'm listening."

"Privately."

Maris felt her shoulders hunch, forced herself to relax. "What's it about?"

"You don't trust me?"

John's deep, fluid voice came on the line. "Forget it, Eniston. Maris isn't going to fall for that line. My sister did, and she's dead."

"If it ain't the boy senator, himself. Still meddling in other people's business?"

"This *is* my business," John said. There was a hot

216

tenseness to his tone that showed Eniston's barb had scored. "It has always been my business."

"Butt out," Eniston snarled. "This is between me and Ms. Durant."

"Why don't you turn yourself in?" John asked. "I'll be happy to mediate with the police for you."

"Put myself in your hands, huh?"

Peterus made a grab for the phone, but Maris fended him off.

"Look, Eniston," John said. "You're going to get caught, you know. If you turn yourself in, you'll make things a whole lot easier for yourself."

The killer's laugh was ugly. "I don't care if I get caught, Senator. As long as I get my business taken care of first."

"Is that a threat?"

"Yeah. *Ms.* Durant, I'll be seeing to you later."

The line went dead. The memory of that promise fluttered in Maris's mind like great, dark wings. Menacing. He'd seemed so sure of himself, so utterly sure he could get to her. She let the phone drop from fingers that had gone numb with terror.

Peterus snatched the receiver and held it to his ear. "Damn!" With an irritated gesture, he slapped the antenna down on his radio. "Sorry, folks, we're going to have to move this party inside."

"That was . . . *him?*" Sophie asked. "What did he want?"

It took Maris a moment to get her voice working. "He said he wanted to talk to me privately," she said. "Maybe I should have tried to find out more—"

"He wasn't going to tell you jack shit over the phone," Peterus snapped. "Pardon my French, but it's the God's-honest truth. That's one sick fella,

217

Mrs. Durant. The minute he sweet-talked you out from under our protection, you'd be dead."

"It's starting again," Sophie whispered.

Maris swung around to find the old woman hovering over her husband, as though to protect him from anything the world might offer. If Eniston were standing right here, aiming a gun at the old man, Sophie would take the bullet. Even now, when Ballard might call death a gift if he had the power to speak. *Obsessive loyalty, obsessive love,* Maris thought. *Too bad she hadn't spent some of it on Garrick and Robyn, who might appreciate it more.*

Who am I to judge? Sophie'd had her share of hell; maybe this was the best she could do. "Mrs. Hauck, would you like some help getting the chair inside?"

"Thank you, I would."

As Maris helped push the old man toward the house, she couldn't keep from glancing back at the trees once more. A bird was singing madly. The woods seemed so dim and deep and quiet. Secretive. The bird stopped singing in mid-note, almost as though someone had grabbed it by the throat.

She shuddered.

"Are you all right, Maris?" Sophie asked. "I felt you shiver."

"I'm fine," she lied. "A goose just walked over my grave, I guess."

Now what possessed me to say that? Of all the inappropriate things . . . No, it was all too appropriate. It was just that there had been too many graves lately. Too damn many.

Maris tossed and turned until long after midnight, afraid of what hovered in wakefulness, dreading what lurked in her sleep. Even the hushed dimness of her room didn't make her feel secure.

Since Eniston's call earlier today, the atmosphere in the house had been tense and strained. That phone call had turned the possibility of danger into something very real, very frightening.

"Why do I let that crazy SOB get to me?" she asked the quiet room. With a sigh, she flung the covers aside and got up. "Time to try a glass of warm milk." And maybe the reality of Rosalia's nice, bright kitchen would banish her fears.

The late-night quiet was broken only by the soft footsteps of the guards outside. And although the foyer light was off, the brazen glow from the outside floods lay in windowpane rectangles upon the floor. Maris padded through them on the way to the kitchen, her robe turning red to dark and red again as she passed from light to shadow.

Someone was in the kitchen already; Maris could hear the soft clink of glass on glass. She hesitated, not wanting company, then pushed the door open and went in.

This was Rosalia's domain, a huge, high-ceilinged room crammed with dark oak cabinets and copper-bottomed pots. A bank of stainless-steel stoves and sinks held one wall, and an enormous built-in refrigerator the other, all reflected in the beige ceramic tile of the floor.

Robyn sat alone at the big kitchen table, frozen in the act of pouring bourbon into a tumbler. Guilt, shame, the shattering knowledge that the secret was out — her face told it all.

Caught in the act, Maris thought. *So that's how she's learned to cope with her life. Or lack of one.* It was obvious Robyn expected a sermon or recriminations; if Sophie had been here, that was exactly what she would have gotten. Maris wasn't about to play mother. Friend, maybe.

Maris filled a mug with milk and warmed it in the microwave. Silently, she took it to the table and sat down opposite Robyn.

"I . . . was having trouble getting to sleep," Robyn said.

"Me, too."

Robyn wrapped her hands around the tumbler as though to warm herself. "I know what you're thinking. Why don't you say it?"

"Since you asked, I will," Maris said. "Why don't you get out of here while you've still got some life left?"

"Oh! I . . . I . . ."

"Thought I was going to take you to task for drinking?"

Robyn nodded.

"Why should I?" Maris asked. "You're smart enough to know what you're doing to yourself. I think you even know why. What I don't understand is why you stick around."

"Mother and Daddy need me." With a sigh, Robyn looked away. "No, that's a lie. They don't need me; I need them. The world frightens me. If I'd gotten out more, met more people, maybe I might have more . . . courage."

"It's not too late to start," Maris said, as gently as she could.

"It's been too late for a long time." Her face reflecting mingled defiance and shame, Robyn finished the liquor in her glass and poured another before getting up to put the bottle away. Then she left, carrying the drink with her.

"I might not have been happy a hundred percent of the time," Maris said, raising her mug in a mocking toast. "But at least I've *lived*."

But all hope of finding serenity was gone. Maris poured the milk into the sink and headed back upstairs.

There was even less comfort in her room. The corners were velvety with shadow, and the white bedsheets shone wraithlike and cold in the dimness. The thick curtains suddenly seemed too confining. She opened them, letting the welcome glow of the floodlights into the room. *Like a kid afraid of the dark.*

"So what?" she muttered in defiance. "Plenty of people are scared of the dark."

She got into bed and pulled the covers up to her chin, lying flat on her back while she waited for her body heat to warm the sheets. This was the time of night when she missed Paul the most. He'd always get into bed before her, making a nice, warm nest for her to enter. She'd climb in, nestle against his body, and soon. . . .

Tears leaked out from the corners of her eyes and dampened the hair at her temples. She wanted to be held. She wanted to feel someone's arms around her. Just for a few minutes, it would be nice to lean on someone, to cry without fear, to be comforted. That need was an ache inside her that grew and grew until she turned on her side, curling around it.

"Paul," she whispered. "Paul."

Could she ever let him go enough to love another man? If Keir had been in this bed with her, holding her, how would she feel? What could she give him? Sex, yes — the reactions of her body told her she was capable of that. But she wanted more from a man and more from life.

She hadn't called Keir to tell him about Eniston's escape, knowing he'd come back, hell or high water. He'd be supportive and protective and nurturing. Great stuff, on the surface. But it made demands on the person being supported and protected and nurtured. She should be *worthy*. She should be willing to give him something equally valuable in return. And that she couldn't do. It took every bit of her strength just to get from one day to the next without cracking.

"I'm sorry," she muttered. "I wish—"

Something dark moved across her window. She stilled, like a mouse hearing the soft, deadly glide of the owl's wings. Had it been a cloud moving across the moon? Her throat tightened. There was a new moon tonight.

Slowly, she pushed the covers down and slid her feet to the floor. There was no movement outside the window now, no sign of that dark shape. Maybe she'd imagined it. Maybe it really *had* been an owl.

Except that the feeling she'd had all afternoon had intensified, giving the lie to her rationalizations. Goose bumps rose all along her arms.

Close the curtain.

She took a step toward the window. This was crazy! The house was surrounded with armed guards, the grounds were lit up like Christmas, and there was nothing outside the window but a postage stamp of a balcony.

Close the curtain.

The urge was primordial, powerful. Shut out the darkness, shut out all the things that lived in the night. An instinct only children remember. The half-seen, half-imagined monsters that flee the light, flee the moms and dads who come to look in closets and

222

under the beds, then return to terrify when the lights go out again. The child lying awake, afraid to look, afraid not to.

Close the curtain.

Maris ran to the window, fumbling behind the curtain for the cord. "Come on," she muttered.

Drew Eniston appeared on the other side of the glass. Maris froze. He stared at her, the light slanting across his face to illuminate his cold killer's eyes.

"Open the window," he mouthed.

Maris could only stare. He'd come for her. With all the guards, the lights, the guns, he'd come.

"Open the window," he mouthed again, pointing to the lock.

Still facing him, she took a step backward. He grasped the window frame, rattling it.

She took another step backward, then another. Shock made her teeth chatter, her skin feel cold. The world narrowed into a tight little corridor, Eniston on one end, herself at the other. And it was not nearly long enough. His yellow-streaked eyes bored into hers, commanding obedience. She stared back, unwilling to obey, unable to run.

He rattled the window once more. Suddenly, without warning, he punched his fist through the window. Shards of glass flew inward, glittering like jewels in the light. Then he reached in and twisted the lock open. The window slid upward.

A wash of cool air swept into the room, releasing Maris from her strange stasis. *He's coming in.* She took a step toward Cyndi's room, then stopped. There wasn't a lock on the adjoining door. If she went in there, he'd surely come after her.

Whirling, she darted for the other door. For a moment, she thought she might even make it. Then his

223

hand closed on the neck of her pajamas, dragging her backward.

She drew air in with a sharp gasp. Before she could let it out again, Eniston's hand clamped over her mouth with cruel force.

He jerked her around to face him. "Quit fighting me," he hissed. "It isn't going to do you any good."

"Mom?" Cyndi called from the next room. "I heard glass breaking. Is everything okay?"

Her voice came closer. Maris strained against Eniston's hold, shaking her head frantically. *Go back! Don't come in here!*

The knob turned; the door swung inward. Cyndi stood in the opening, her nightgown billowing around her. Eniston turned his head to look at her, his upper lip lifting in a snarl.

Cyndi screamed.

The sound of her daughter's terror sent Maris over the edge. The veneer of civilization fell away, leaving only instinct. It was the same instinct that sent a mother bird darting into the hawk's path, the mother bear roaring into the face of the hunter's gun to protect her young. Beyond reason, beyond fear, she turned on Eniston. Kicking, gouging at his eyes, snapping like an animal at his restraining hand, she fought him with a savagery that surprised even her. She wrenched her mouth free.

"Run!" she shrieked at Cyndi.

But the child stood motionless, her mouth opening wide as she screamed again.

"God damn it," Eniston panted. "Hold still!"

Feeling his hand groping toward her throat, Maris ducked her head and drove her fist into his face with a strength she didn't know she had.

He staggered backward, dragging her with him.

Wrapped in each other's arms like dance partners, they bounced hard against the wall, rebounded, then slammed into the nightstand, bringing it down with a crash. The brass lamp rolled under Eniston's feet, bringing them both down. Maris landed on top, her elbow sinking deep into his gut. He let go. As he sucked for air, she rolled to her knees and scrambled away.

The outer door swung open, and light cleaved a path through the center of the room. Maris froze, pinned like a butterfly by the brightness. A man's shadow bisected the light. A tall, wide-shouldered man, his hair a platinum aureole around his head.

For one heart-stopping moment, Maris thought it was Ballard Hauck, risen like Lazarus from his wheelchair. Then reason kicked in.

"Senator!" she cried. "It's Eniston! Look out!"

She saw John raise his hand. Light knifed blue-steel reflections on something in his hand.

And she was in the line of fire.

"It ends here, Eniston," John said in a chillingly calm, quiet voice.

Maris saw his finger tighten on the trigger. With a cry, she threw herself to one side just as incandescence flared to life in John's hand.

Her ears ringing, Maris lunged to her feet and flung herself at Cyndi, sweeping her into her arms and into the other room with one motion. She fell then, landing hard on her hip and elbow, but with Cyndi safely cushioned in her arms.

Footsteps sounded behind her, hard and fast. Maris swiveled around, shielding Cyndi from the doorway. The flesh of her back twitched with the expectation of a blow. A moment later, however, she heard the crash of breaking glass.

"Eniston! God damn you to hell!" John's cry was a roar of anger and frustration. "Stop him, somebody! Don't let him get away!"

The night was suddenly filled with gunshots and shouts of alarm from the guards outside.

John raced into Cyndi's room, going down on one knee beside Maris. "Are you all right?" he panted.

Maris nodded, her gaze on the gun in his hand.

"Okay. Stay here. Someone will be up in a minute." He swiped at his forehead with the back of his hand, then jumped to his feet and dashed out of the room.

The sounds of the chase were loud. Maris thought of Eniston. Running, slipping into the shadows to catch his breath, then running again, one step ahead of the baying pursuit.

"Are they going to catch him?" Cyndi whispered.

"I . . . don't know," Maris said, holding her closer. Would they get him? Was tonight his night to die? Did she want him to die? A shiver went up her spine with icy fingers. Yes, she thought. If his dying meant that she and Cyndi could live, then she wanted him dead.

The noise moved into the woods at the back of the house, and grew steadily fainter. Finally, it stopped. *They've lost him,* Maris thought.

Cyndi buried her face against Maris's chest and began to cry. Feeling frightened and fierce at the same time, Maris stroked her daughter's heaving back. "Shhh, honey. Don't cry. He's gone now."

Bobby Peterus appeared in the doorway, a rifle held in the crook of one arm. His gaze moved around the room, checking doors and windows, then coming to rest on Maris and Cyndi.

"Are either of you hurt?" he asked.

226

"Only a few scrapes and bruises," Maris said.

"Let me through!" Sophie's imperious voice came from behind him. He moved out of the way, but returned to the doorway as soon as the old woman passed.

She bent over Maris. Her composure was intact, but her eyes were hot with what looked like outrage. That was something Maris had no trouble understanding; by coming right in the house after her, Eniston had violated the capsule of safety she'd thought protected her. For Sophie, who until now had held complete control over the world of Gavilan, the sense of violation must be awful.

"Are you hurt?" Sophie asked.

Maris shook her head. "A couple of new bruises is all."

Cyndi was still crying, but softer now, her sobs interspersed with hiccuping gasps. Sophie patted her back. A bit awkwardly, Maris thought, but with the intent of kindness.

"You're safe now, Cyndi. The man is gone," Sophie said. "And Mr. Peterus assures me he won't be back to bother us again." She glanced up at the security man, her jutting nose and black eyes giving her the fierce look of a hawk. "Isn't that right, Mr. Peterus?"

"Yes, ma'am."

Maris managed to sit up and keep Cyndi in her arms at the same time. She was surprised to find that she was shaking, constant, visible tremors.

"Mom?" Cyndi whispered.

"It's just reaction, hon. I'm okay."

"You are not okay." Sophie stripped the blanket off Cyndi's bed and draped it around Maris's shoulders. "You're both going to spend the night in the room next to mine. And Mr. Peterus is going to make sure your sleep is not interrupted."

"Yes, ma'am," he said again.

Maris would have spent the night in the barn—anywhere but in her own room. She could still *feel* Eniston there. Her flesh remembered the harsh grip of his hands, the way the calluses on his palms scraped across her skin as he groped for her throat.

Her teeth chattering, she pulled the blanket tighter around her shoulders, enclosing Cyndi in it with her. A symbolic gesture of enfolding her child close, keeping her safe. Symbolic, but meaningless.

"Here, let me help you up," Peterus said. With his free hand, he gripped Maris by the arm.

She got to her feet, using more of his help than she would have liked. Cyndi came back into her embrace. *We're propping each other up,* Maris thought. *What will I do if she's gone? How will I stand alone?*

Peterus looked from Maris to Sophie and back again. "Well, Mrs. Durant, it seems you got a taste of the real Drew Eniston," he said.

"That I did." Goose bumps raced up her arms, memory of fear.

"Do you believe us now? About him being after you?"

She nodded, rubbing her arms. "I . . . just don't understand why."

"Step on a rattlesnake, he'll bite you. Give him a chance to get away, though, and he'll leave you alone. A scorpion now, he'll go out of his way to sting you. Why? Because that's his nature."

"What's your point, Mr. Peterus?" Sophie asked.

"My point, ma'am, is knowing what kind of animal you're dealing with. Eniston's just like the scorpion. He kills because it's his nature to kill."

228

"It doesn't make sense," Maris said. "The man took such a risk coming here like this—"

"You heard him yourself. He doesn't care if he gets caught, and I'm not sure he cares if he gets himself killed. You don't understand a man like that. You don't talk to him; you don't reach him. If Lee Hauck couldn't reach him, or that baby of theirs, nothing on this earth will."

"So what do you do?"

He sighed. "The same thing you do to a scorpion. You make sure it doesn't sting you, any way you can."

"Kill it?"

"Whatever it takes," he said. "Look, Mrs. Durant. Leave Eniston to us. We know what to do with him."

Maris wasn't reassured. She'd felt safe here in the cocoon of Gavilan, surrounded by the men, the guns, the walkie-talkies, the floodlit yard. Eniston had walked right through them, proving that safety was only an illusion.

"Leave Eniston to us," Peterus had said. "We know what to do . . ." *Trust us.*

It wasn't enough. Until Eniston was stopped, it wasn't going to be enough.

Eighteen

Maris lay curled protectively around Cyndi, listening to the child's soft, even breathing. The room was dark and quiet, the bed warm from their mingled body heat.

Outside, the night seethed with tension.

This bed, this room, this warm, encompassing quiet held only the illusion of safety. Tonight, she had faced a killer. She had seen her own death in his eyes, and Cyndi's, and that memory would be with her forever. Even now she could feel him. Terror had imprinted him in her blood, bones and mind.

And still, even now, there was an insidious fascination with the man, a need to know *why* he'd done it. Any reason, even a crazy man's, was better than none at all.

She tried to forget Eniston, tried to force herself to sleep. Both were futile. So she lay motionless, watching the pale rectangle of the window behind the curtain. Waiting, against all logic, for a flitting shadow to cross that floodlit area.

Anger coiled, slow and hot, within her. Anger for the change this night had wrought in her. Yesterday, she had been a civilized person, living by civilized rules. Even her fight for her daughter's life had been civilized, played out by medicine's precise order.

But now she had been forced to enter Eniston's world. Had she been able to, she would have killed him tonight, for to do otherwise would have been to die. She wanted to live. For the first time since Paul's death, she realized just how much.

Gradually, the harsh artificial light outside softened into dawn. A bird began to sing in the cottonwood. It was a comforting sound—the normal world, not Eniston's.

The bird song suddenly seemed very far away. Sleep wrapped cocooning arms around her, and she sank into it eagerly.

And woke, some time later, to an empty bed.

"Cyndi?" Panic made her pulse leap. "Cyndi, where are you?"

There was no answer. *She probably went down the hall to the bathroom.* But logic had no place here. Maris scrambled out of bed and pulled her robe on, belting it on her way down the hall.

The bathroom was empty. Although Maris couldn't imagine Cyndi going into Sophie's room for anything, she opened the old woman's door a crack and peered in, just in case. Sophie was alone, sleeping on her back with that Hauck nose jutting into the air. Proud even in sleep, Maris thought.

"May I help you, señora?"

The housekeeper's soft voice came from directly behind Maris, bringing her around with a gasp.

"Oh, Mrs. Munoz, you startled me!"

"I am sorry, señora. May I help you?"

"I was looking for my daughter. Have you seen her?"

"Yes, she is downstairs in the dining room. Rosalia has put coffee and juice out on the buffet."

231

Mrs. Munoz reached past her to close the door. The gesture was seemingly casual, but Maris saw it for what it was: a rebuke for invading Sophie's privacy.

"Can you tell me what time it is?" Maris asked.

"Ten minutes to eight," Mrs. Munoz said without glancing at her watch. "I was just about to wake Señora Hauck for breakfast."

"They're going to have breakfast at the usual time?" Maris asked in surprise. "Even after last night?"

"Of course. Excuse me, Señora Durant." The housekeeper went into Sophie's room, closing the door behind her.

"Of *course*," Maris muttered. "Nothing happened that could possibly upset The Schedule."

Turning on her heel, she headed downstairs. The door to the dining room was closed, but she could hear Cyndi laughing. Maris's heart turned over in her chest at the sound of her daughter's joy. *Joy, after last night.* Cyndi was the strong one.

A man's laugh echoed the child's, the deeper, darker tones a musical contrast to hers. There was no mistaking that voice.

"Keir," Maris said, astonished by the depth of the joy that flooded through her. Until now, she hadn't known how badly she'd wanted him here.

Strange, how the feelings had crept up on her. When she'd met Paul, attraction had been lightning-swift. Love at first sight. But she'd been nineteen years old, ripe for love, ripe for everything, and she'd flung herself into the relationship eagerly.

With a sigh, she opened the door and went in. Cyndi, still wearing her nightgown and robe, was sitting at the table with her feet tucked beneath her.

232

The light from the chandelier glinted off her peach fuzz hair, turning it into a golden halo around her head.

Beside her was Keir. His suit was scruffy and travel-worn, and he nursed his coffee cup like a man who needed caffeine badly. He looked up as she came in, his face taut-drawn beneath a prickling of day-old whiskers.

"When did you get in?" Maris asked.

"About a half-hour ago. I hopped a flight as soon as I got John's message." He got up and walked toward her.

Half-afraid that he was going to embrace her — and half-afraid he wouldn't — Maris crossed her arms in an involuntary gesture of withdrawal.

He stopped. "Are you all right?" His voice was as intense as his eyes.

"I'm fine," she said. "Just a little bruised."

"I meant here," he said, tapping his chest.

"So did I."

He studied her for a long time, then nodded and went back to his seat. "Come have a cup of coffee. Cyndi was just filling me in on what happened last night. Let's see, Cyndi, where were we?" he asked with a casualness that might have fooled someone if his eyes hadn't been raging dark with emotion. "I think you'd gotten to the part where Eniston leaped through the window."

"Cyndi wasn't even there when he came in," Maris protested. "And he *climbed* through the window."

"C'mon, Mom, let me tell it!"

Maris rolled her eyes. "All right. But keep the melodrama to a minimum, huh?"

"Sure." Cyndi turned back to Keir. "Now, where was I? Oh, yeah. The murderer leaps in through the window and grabs Mom. She screams. I go running in, and find her wrapped in his arms, his hand over her mouth. That's when *I* scream. And then he turns . . . he looks at me with these crazy eyes—"

"Cyndi," Maris warned.

"And then Mom hauls off and socks him in the eye. You should have seen the look on his face; he was more surprised than I was."

Keir slowly turned his head to look at Maris. "You socked Drew Eniston in the eye?"

"I—"

"Right in the eye," Cyndi said, with unmistakable relish. "Pow! Then they go bouncing off the walls and stuff, and she knocks him down—"

"We *fell*," Maris interjected, desperate to keep some accuracy in the account.

"—and then Mr. Hauck comes in shooting—"

"Shooting?" Keir came up out of his chair.

"Yeah," Cyndi said. "That's when Mom grabbed me and ran into my room. People started yelling and shooting all over the place, but the guy got away anyhow."

Keir sank back into his seat. After a moment, he pointed to the chair across the table from his. "Sit down, Maris."

"Just let me get some coffee."

She dawdled as long as possible, stirring an extra teaspoon of sugar into her coffee just to take up time. Finally, there was nothing to do but sit down and face Keir.

"Cyndi," he said. "Why don't you run upstairs and get dressed?"

"Why don't you just say you want to talk to Mom alone?"

"I want to talk to your mom alone."

234

"Okay." Cyndi slid out of her chair, giving Maris a sly wink as she passed behind Keir on her way out of the room.

Maris grimaced. Things were so simple for kids. Love, hate, living—dying—all were drawn in black and white. Cinderella and her prince lived happily ever after. Well, Disney didn't do real life. Fairy-tale heroines might have to deal with wicked stepmothers, maybe even a dragon or two, but they didn't have leukemia. And they didn't die.

"Drink your coffee before it gets cold," Keir said.

Maris looked up, surprised by the gentleness in his voice.

"You should see the look on your face," he said. "Did you expect me to ream you out for not calling me?"

"Yes."

"Would it do me any good?"

"If you wanted to make me feel guilty, yes, it would."

"You don't need my help to feel guilty."

"I guess not." She took a sip of coffee, then set the cup aside. It was too cold, too sweet, and too late to be of any comfort to her.

"I must admit that I was pretty pissed at first," he said. "I was in meetings long past midnight last night. When I got back to my hotel, dog-tired, I find a message waiting for me. And what does it say? It says that you're in danger and I should get back to Gavilan ASAP."

"I thought you weren't going to ream me out."

He continued as if she hadn't spoken. "So I haul ass down here. When I get here, I'm stopped by a bunch of real nervous guys with real big guns. If Alejo hadn't come down to vouch for me, I'd still be

235

sitting out there looking down twenty gun barrels."

"And you say you don't want me to feel guilty?"

"Hell, yes, I want you to feel guilty," he hissed. "I want you to feel *something* toward me besides polite disinterest."

"You're starting to breathe hard," she said.

"So I am." With obvious effort, he got himself under control. But he wrapped his hands around his coffee mug, as though wishing it were her neck. "Let's talk about something else."

"Okay," she agreed, not believing for a moment that he was finished with her. "How about the weather?"

"How about why Drew Eniston broke into your room when he had a whole houseful of Haucks to choose from?"

Maris would rather have talked about their relationship. "Well . . . ah, the security people think he's after me."

"Why do they think that?" he asked. Coolly, calmly, his hands squeezing, squeezing the mug.

"I . . . since I first put that ad in the Texas papers, I've been getting some nasty letters."

Keir remained silent, but Maris could feel waves of recrimination rolling across the table at her. Feeling compelled to defend herself, she said, "There wasn't any reason to mention them—"

"No reason at all."

"There wasn't! Until the last one, they'd been . . . crank letters. Nasty and ugly, but not threatening."

Keir's voice had gone soft, his eyes hard. "And the last one?"

"The last one was threatening, both to me and Cyndi. The security guys think Eniston sent them, and that he escaped to make good on his threats."

She swallowed hard, not wanting to continue. But she owed this to Keir. "The writer said he knew who I was, and that I wasn't wanted when I was born, and wasn't wanted now. I didn't tell anyone about it, even Cyndi. I was . . . ashamed."

"Jesus Christ, Maris!"

"Jesus Christ, nothing! Can you imagine being told one day that you weren't who you thought you were? That your mother had given birth to you, then stuck you in a cardboard box and just dumped you somewhere? *Cats* take better care of their young than that! And then when you tried to find out who you were, someone makes a special effort just to remind you that you weren't wanted, weren't *ever* wanted?"

"Maris —"

"Let me finish!" She pressed her fist against her chest. "I was ashamed because I thought it was my mother writing those letters."

"Why?"

"Who else would give a damn?" Her voice was strained, forced through a throat gone tight with unshed tears. "The letters called me 'bitch,' Keir. All I wanted was a chance to save my daughter, and *she* called me 'bitch.' "

"You keep saying 'she.' Are you disagreeing with the theory that Drew Eniston wrote those letters?"

Maris rolled her napkin into a tight spike. "I just assumed it was my birth mother . . . hate mail seemed like such a *feminine* thing. But it must have been Eniston, 'cause he broke into my room last night. Not Ballard's, not John's. Mine." Her mouth was sour with the taste of remembered terror. "I looked into his eyes and asked him if he really had killed that baby. He said yes. As cool as you please. I wasn't sure I believed him then, but I do now. I've

237

never met another human being who was so cold, so completely without conscience. He's capable of anything."

Keir let go of the mug so abruptly that coffee spilled out over the rim, then surged to his feet and started pacing the room. "Jesus Christ, Maris. Je-sus Christ!"

The door creaked, and Maris turned to see John Hauck come into the room. "Good morning, Senator," she said.

"Good morning." He was dressed and combed and smoothly handsome — his usual photogenic self. So different from the man who had burst into her room last night, gun in hand.

Talk about melodrama! Maris thought. Hugh Carideo would have loved it. The senator bravely risking his own life to defend his home and family from the crazed killer. They might even make a TV movie out of it some day. But it was a much-too-Garrick thing to say, so she didn't.

John closed the door softly behind him. "Hello, Keir," he said. "Security told me you'd come. Did you talk to the people in Washington?"

"Yes. They were interested, very interested," Keir said. "The first order of business, of course, must be the governorship. Once we've got that, they'll be willing to talk in real terms about the next step."

"Good," John said. "That's exactly what I wanted. A couple of years from now, they'll come looking for *me*."

Confused, Maris looked from him to Keir and back again. She'd assumed Keir was going to Austin. But *Washington?* What the heck were they talking about? Then she got it. Ohhh, Johnny, she got it good!

"You're talking about the presidency!" she blurted. "If you're elected governor, you're planning to leapfrog from that into the presidential elections."

The senator went to the buffet and poured himself a cup of coffee. "That's the way these things work, Maris. One must always look at the big picture, you know." He turned around, a coffee cup cradled in his hands. "I always do. And that is why I value Keir's abilities enough to forgive him for putting your wishes above mine. This time."

"He didn't —"

"I did," Keir said. "It was totally my decision, John."

Maris shook her head. "It wasn't. I talked him into it."

"How touching," John said, carrying his coffee over to the table. "You don't have to rush to his defense, Maris. I already said I forgave him. He's the best campaign manager I've ever had, and I'm not about to lose him over something like this. In the future, however, I'll have to be sure not to ask anything of him that conflicts with Maris's welfare."

"What do you mean by that?" There was a hard edge to Keir's voice, and to his jawline.

"You're here, aren't you? Tending to Maris's business instead of in Washington taking care of mine?"

"Hell, John, you sent for me!"

"No, I didn't."

Maris watched confusion spread across Keir's face, softening the set of his jaw. "You didn't?"

"Why would I?" John asked. "I have security people to take care of . . . incidents like the one last night. Much as you would like, I'd hardly pull you out of Washington to hold Maris's hand for her."

239

"Well, why the hell did you send me that message, then?" Keir demanded.

"Message?" John asked, holding his cup suspended between the table and his mouth. "What message?"

"The one saying Maris was in danger and that I was supposed to get back to Gavilan ASAP."

"I . . . oh, that message." Setting his coffee aside, John reached up to run his fingers through his hair. "I guess I was in kind of a haze last night. I plain forgot calling you."

"You're doing better than I am," Maris said. "I'm *still* in a haze."

John smiled, all traces of ill humor fleeing. "Well, Keir, now's your chance. Swoop in while she's too confused to say no."

"Maris, how about going out with me tonight?" Keir asked.

"Where?"

"Does it matter?"

"What about Eniston?" she asked.

Keir didn't even crack a smile. "He's not invited. Cyndi is, though."

"Fool," John muttered, *sotto voce*.

Keir smiled. "The best way to a mother's heart is through her children, Senator."

Maris wanted to be reassured, wanted to do anything but sit here and watch the windows for flitting shadows. And yes, she wanted to be with Keir. A first step toward life from a woman who had newly discovered how badly she wanted to live.

"If you stay here twenty-four hours a day, he'll know where you are twenty-four hours a day," Keir said. "He doesn't even have to do anything; your own fear will punish you."

240

She drew in her breath sharply, seeing the truth in what he'd said, but still afraid.

"Besides," he said. "Those nice men with the guns can make sure he doesn't follow us."

"Seriously, Keir," the senator said. "The security people will have a stroke at the very thought. How about a nice, quiet evening here at the house? We can send someone out to rent a couple of tapes, get Rosalia to make some popcorn, and pretend it's family night at the movies."

Maris repressed a shudder. Spend the night watching TV with Ballard Hauck? Oh, brother! She glanced at Keir, saw that he was nearly as excited about it as she was. Caught by a surge of recklessness, she said, "I'd rather go out."

"Maris—" John began.

"No, Keir's right. I can't just sit here, even if I wanted to." She pushed a lock of hair back from her face with the back of her hand. "I mean, I've got a call in to Cyndi's doctor to find out when we're going to schedule her chemotherapy. When he says go, we go. If Eniston's determined enough to follow me tonight to murder me in a movie theater, then he's determined enough to get me at the hospital."

"Your logic is impeccable," John said with a sigh. "I guess I'll have to be the one to give Mr. Peterus the bad news."

He stood up, surprising Maris by laying his hand on her shoulder. "Last night, Maris, I failed to keep you safe. I apologize."

"There was nothing you could have done."

"Maybe not." His fingers tightened. "But I failed nonetheless. You have no choice but to take certain risks, I understand that. But that's outside Gavilan. This is *my* home. If I have to put a security guard in

241

every room, I'll make it safe. As God is my witness, if Drew Eniston steps foot in this house again, it will be the last thing he does on this earth."

Scarlett couldn't have said it better herself, Maris thought. It was corny, but there was nothing laughable about it; there was a deadly seriousness about John's face and voice that charged the statement with a grim sort of grandeur. She believed him. But she also remembered Eniston saying, "I don't care if I get caught as long as I get my business taken care of first."

"Senator, I don't expect — " she began.

"I give you my personal guarantee." He chopped the air with the edge of his hand. "You will be safe as long as you're under this roof."

"That's a heck of a guarantee, Senator," she said.

He nodded. "You can trust it."

"I can bet my life on it, you mean."

"Yes," he agreed. "That, too."

Nineteen

Maris knelt on the floor in the family room, contemplating the Backgammon board. She was wearing the only dress she'd had time to buy since the fire, a cherry red knit that made her feel like a five-foot-ten target. She was also losing the game.

"I should never have taught you how to play this," she said.

"Well, you did, and now you're stuck. Hey, look at that," Cyndi said as the dice came to rest. "Double fives. You look great tonight, Mom. Keir's going to go nuts."

"Plu-eease." Maris picked up the dice and rolled them slowly around in her hand. "Are you sure you don't want to go with us?"

"Positive."

"Keir invited you, you know."

"I know. Jeez, Mom, I don't want to go out on your date, okay?"

"It's not exactly a date," Maris said.

"It will be if you don't bring your kid along."

Maris sighed. Yes, it would be a date. It was hard to admit, even to herself, how intimidating that was. She hadn't had a date since Paul. Not since he'd died, since she'd *met* him. Fifteen years. Keir stirred things in her she'd thought Paul had taken with him. Somehow, without quite knowing it, she had moved beyond her husband's death.

And what about the dream? That, indeed, was a real kicker of a question. But dream or no, here she was, wearing a dress that felt too short, too tight, and much too red. She should never have let Cyndi talk her into buying it.

The phone rang, startling her. She turned to look at it, her fingers twitching with the desire to pick it up. But she couldn't; all calls were being screened by security.

"Mrs. Durant?" Bobby Peterus called from the doorway. "Call for you. Dr. Guaymus."

Dread clenched cold fingers in her throat. It must have shown in her face, for Peterus said, "It's okay. We checked it out."

Maris climbed to her feet. He'd read her emotion, but misinterpreted its cause. Fortunately, the phone was on the table beside the sofa; it gave her an excuse to sit down without giving away how shaky her legs were.

She waited until Peterus left, then lifted the receiver to her ear. "Hello, Dr. Guaymus."

"Good evening, Mrs. Durant." His voice was a clear, high tenor, heavily accented. "How is Cyndi today?"

"She's beating me at Backgammon." *Please don't tell me she can't have the chemo!*

He chuckled. "She is a pistol, our Cyndi. Now, first I want to reassure you that there is no reason to be alarmed. I canceled the appointment because I received a call yesterday from the National Marrow Donor Program in St. Paul."

"Yes?" Her whole being was focused on the man

at the other end of the line. Willing him to say it.

"We have a possible match."

Everything around her was preternaturally distinct; she could smell the scent of lemon polish on the table beside her, hear the clock ticking on the mantel, feel her breath moving in a warm column through her chest. In, out. In, out. Cyndi got up, pantomimed a drink, then pointed to the bar. Maris nodded, watching as her daughter walked across the room. The fine golden hairs at the child's nape looked burnished in the light from overhead. Maris closed her eyes, feeling too small to contain what was inside her.

I might get to keep her.

"Are you still there, Mrs. Durant?" Dr. Guaymus asked.

"Yes," she said. "I'm here."

"A blood-donor center in Little Rock has come up with a fellow who may be able to help us. I stress the word *may*."

Maris's euphoria vanished. "Yes?"

"This person is not quite a perfect match. And the less perfect the match, the more chance of graft-versus-host disease. You see, the bone marrow manufactures many components of the immune system. If the adopted marrow 'sees' its new home as foreign, it will launch an attack on almost every tissue in the body. In many cases, this can be fatal."

"I understand," she said. "I've researched the subject." Enough to be scared, enough to be hopeful.

"The match is promising enough that we've asked the center in Little Rock to initiate further testing. If the tests prove that this particular antigen is not going to act aggressively in Cyndi's system, then the transplant will be possible."

245

She closed her eyes, trying to stop herself from hoping too much. But it couldn't be contained. Insidious, dangerous, wonderful, it spread through her like a hot, fragrant summer breeze.

"There has been no further progress on your search for your birth family?"

"No," she said. *Damn you, Ella Florian!* "How long before you'll know whether or not to do the transplant?"

"A few weeks. If the match is viable, the donor will be contacted and counseled to be certain he is willing to go through with the procedure. As you know, we'll be giving Cyndi massive doses of chemotherapy to destroy her diseased marrow, and we can't have our donor backing out at the last minute."

Maris closed her eyes for a moment, pulling her teetering emotions into order. "And what if the donor refuses?"

"Then, we go on with the other chemotherapy. Truly, Mrs. Durant, we have not exhausted our options."

She didn't realize she'd bitten the inside of her lip until the sweet, metallic tang of blood stung her tongue. Hope was even sweeter. "You're not just . . . soothing me?"

"Mrs. Durant, I do not soothe. I *cannot,* for that would be far more cruel than the truth. There are many, many times when I must tell parents, 'Take your child home, or to a hospice. Place him in God's hands and let him go.' If Cyndi's case warranted it, I would say the same to you."

Tears stung Maris's eyelids, even as hot bubbles of joy seared through her veins. There was a chance, a real chance! "Okay," she said.

"Good. I will call you as soon as I have more information. And of course, if you should hear something about your birth family, call me immediately."

"I will." She added a belated "thank you," but he'd already hung up.

Cyndi came back, perching on the arm of Maris's chair like a frail, graceful birdling. "What did Dr. Guaymus have to say, Mom?"

Maris had a split second to weigh her answer. Tell Cyndi/not tell Cyndi. *Don't. Make sure it's real first.* "He just wanted to tell me not to worry. They just wanted to do a little more testing before beginning the new chemotherapy."

"Oh, okay," Cyndi said. "Maybe I *will* be able to grow some hair."

"I think you're kinda cute the way you are."

Cyndi leaned over and made gagging noises. "I think I'm gonna be sick."

No, Maris thought. *You're going to be well. Please, God!* "Keir's going to be here soon," she said. "Maybe we ought to clean up that board."

"Come on, Mom, let me finish beating you," Cyndi said.

"All right, but you'll regret it." Maris sank down to her knees beside the board. Scooping up the dice, she rolled them around in her hand. "All of a sudden, I feel lucky."

"So do I," Keir said from the doorway.

Maris swung around to look at him. Black pleated slacks, sherry-colored shirt that exactly matched his eyes, black leather flight jacket—suddenly he didn't look medium anymore. Give him a couple of days' growth of beard and a pair of sunglasses, and he'd look dark and deliciously dangerous.

With a grin, he pulled a pair of mirrored shades out of his pocket and put them on. "What do you think of the new me?" he asked, striking a pose.

"Wow," Cyndi said.

"Wow," Maris echoed. "Where's the overwhelming musk-and-leather cologne to go with the outfit?"

"I'm allergic to cologne." He came into the room and walked slowly around Maris. "You look good. You look *real* good."

"You must like tall, skinny stringbeans, then."

"Darlin', with those legs, you're a long, lean racehorse of a woman."

She grimaced. "You sound just like Hugh Carideo."

"*I* told her the dress was a size too big," Cyndi said.

"Hmmmm." Keir took a step backward, evaluating. "Next time, listen to the kid."

Maris couldn't help but laugh. "Let's go. Unless, of course, you've changed your mind about Saturday night at the Haucks'?"

"That dress deserves a better fate, and so do I. Cyndi, I want you to know that I'm making this next statement with complete insincerity: You're welcome to come along."

"No, thanks," Cyndi said. "Rosalia's going to let me help her make chocolate-chip cookies."

"Okay, hon." Maris bent to kiss her. "Try not to eat them all in one sitting, huh?"

"*Tremors* is on the tube again tonight." There was a look of complete guilelessness on Cyndi's face. "Do you think the Haucks will like it?"

Maris hesitated, torn between social duty and irreverence. This, however, was a poor time for resisting temptation. The thought of Ballard parked in front of a screen full of giant, underground worm-monsters was just too hard to resist. "I think *Trem-*

ors will be an enriching life experience for them all," she said. "You should recommend it."

"I will."

Keir took his sunglasses off and put them away. With a courtly bow, he extended his arm. Maris took it, enjoying the feel of leather beneath her hand, and let him lead her from the room. She was beginning to like dark and deliciously dangerous.

"I've seen *Tremors*," he said.

"Ballard hasn't."

His mouth twitched. "I almost wish I could stay and see the expressions on their faces." When Maris opened her mouth to speak, he held up his hand. "I said 'almost.' "

He led her outside, hustling her down the steps and into his car as though all the demons of Hell were chasing them.

When he slid behind the wheel, Maris asked, "Was that part of the security procedure?"

"Yup. I practically had to mortgage my soul to keep Peterus from stashing one of his guys in the backseat."

"Where are we going?"

"The safest place in East Texas," he said. "Trust me, you'll see soon enough."

Maris watched his profile as he put the car in gear and headed down the drive. Trust him? Yes, she did. It was the burgeoning hope inside her she didn't trust. Hope had deserted her too many times before, leaving her stranded.

Keir slowed down as he passed the ranks of armed guards, then made the turn onto the road and accelerated.

"It's been interesting," he said. "Before I was allowed to remove you from the house, I was given a crash course in how to protect against terrorist attack."

"Terrorist attack?"

"A slight exaggeration. But they wanted to be very sure we aren't followed."

Maris glanced out the rear window. The road behind them shot arrow-straight to the horizon, empty of any other vehicles. "What kind of special skills are we talking about here. After all, it's as flat as a pancake out here. You'd spot another car instantly."

"Here," Keir said. "But what if you were on a Houston freeway? It's easiest to hide in a crowd. But all in all, the only *real* dumb thing I can see doing would be borrowing John's Mercedes. Talk about a target!"

"It occurred to me that I looked like a big, red target in this dress."

He didn't say anything, just reached over and took her hand. His clasp was gentle, almost brotherly, and yet warmth seeped from his hand to hers. He wanted her. She knew it; he knew she knew it. All she had to do was say the word. It ought to make her feel awkward, but all she felt was a stirring of anticipation.

It's been too long since I've felt like this, much too long. There were so many things she'd forgotten. How to be alive, for one. How to be a woman again. Not a mother, not a care-giver, just a woman.

"You're in a strange mood tonight," Keir said.

"Strange like how?"

He glanced at her, his eyes catching the light as they passed beneath a streetlamp. "There's joy in you. It shows on your face."

"I talked to Dr. Guaymus," she said. "They may have found a donor."

His hand tightened. "That's *great, * Maris!"

"It's not a perfect match. They've got more tests to run before we'll know if the transplant will be possible."

"But there's a chance."

"Yes," she said. "There's a chance."

"Are you afraid to hope?"

As always, his perception disturbed her. She almost fell into the old habit of shutting her feelings away from the rest of the world, but the warmth of Keir's hand stopped her. "Yes, I'm afraid," she said. "If this match turns out to be viable, I'm the one who will make the final decision on the transplant. What if it doesn't work? Cyndi will die, probably very quickly. Will I have thrown away the possibility of a year with her, maybe more? How will I know what's *right?*"

" 'Right' stopped when Cyndi got leukemia."

"Why do the choices always have to be bad and worse? Why . . ." She paused, appalled by the pain in her voice, then forced herself to go on. "Why can't I ever choose between good and bad, black and white?"

"I don't know. But we'll get through it."

"We?"

"I'm with you all the way. If you want me to be." He lifted her hand to his mouth. "Maybe even if you don't."

His lips were warm against her palm, stirring things that ached even as they beckoned her. If she had been braver, she would have touched him, said something, anything to tell him it was all right. Instead, she pulled her hand away.

"You're a hard nut to crack," he said.

"Cyndi's illness takes up my whole life."

251

"It helps to share the pain, Maris."

"I'm doing the best I can." She closed her hand into a fist, holding the warmth against her skin. "Actually, I've come a long way."

"I guess you have." He heaved a sigh. "It's hard for me, this taking it slow. I'm a charge-ahead kind of guy, and when I see something I want, I go after it."

"You must be masochistic. A woman with a gravely ill child, medical bills beyond human understanding—"

"I want it all. You, Cyndi, the whole Durant package. It satisfies something in my soul."

She looked away from him, seeing and yet not seeing the landscape outside. Life. It was right there in front of her, ready for the taking. She ought to say something. But the words wouldn't come, and after a couple of minutes went by, it seemed to be too late.

Soon they entered the outskirts of Hauck, but this was an unfamiliar section of the city. Modest frame houses lined the streets, some in good repair, some not. A few blocks farther on was a grocery store that looked as though it hadn't been remodeled since the fifties.

"Here we are," Keir said, taking a right on the street beyond the grocery store.

"Here" was a long, low cinderblock building that squatted in the rear of a gravel parking lot. A neon sign blinked "Smokey Pete's" in lurid green and blue letters, and even at this distance Maris could hear the blare of country-western music from inside.

"This is the safest place in East Texas?" she asked.

"Not only do they hire off-duty cops to keep things quiet inside, but look." He pointed down the street.

252

She spotted two squad cars parked across the street, one facing east, one facing west.

"They're out there every Saturday night," Keir said. "They wait to pick off the drunks as they drive out of the parking lot. The fines are a huge source of revenue for the city."

"You've got to be out of your mind."

"You tell me: Is an escaped murderer going to walk past a couple of squad cars, then past two uniformed cops just to get into a bar? No. He turns away in a hurry, and goes someplace safer."

Maris could only laugh. "Makes sense to me."

"Good."

The nightclub—or dance hall, as Maris would have called it—was a single enormous room. On the right was a long stretch of a bar lined with stools. A good third of the place was dance floor, the rest occupied by a sea of tables and chairs. Smoke and music hung thickly in the air. Dancers were just as thick on the dance floor, moving like a single organism in the Two-Step. Maris surveyed the crowd, noting the preponderance of western hats. Keir was fine in his jeans and leather, but the cherry red dress seemed like a beacon screaming "outsider."

"I feel a little out of place," she shouted above the music.

He grinned. "With those legs? Are you kidding? I'll be lucky to get you out of here without having to fight some yahoo for possession." Taking her by the hand, he led her to the bar.

After acquiring two sweating bottles of Lone Star, he blazed a path through the crowd to a tiny, sticky-topped table at the far side of the room. Maris sank a little cautiously into the chair he held out for her.

"Is this the 'real' Hauck?" she asked.

253

"This is one aspect of it," he said, setting the beer down in front of her. "Gavilan is another. But these are the folks who work at the chemical plant outside town, or commute to the refineries in Texas City. Real people."

He pulled his chair beside hers and sat down. The music swirled around them, an almost palpable force. She took a swallow of beer. *Not bad,* she thought. The Lone Star seemed a part of the place, as though it had absorbed the smoke and steel guitars.

She was content to sip her beer in silence. Keir must have sensed her mood, for he merely draped his arm over the back of her chair and let her have her time. Slowly, she began to relax.

"Tell me about yourself," she said.

"You mean my background?" He shrugged. "Boringly middle-class, I'm afraid. My mother is a high-school history teacher, my dad a civil engineer. I'm the oldest of four. First me, then Gary, then my sister Anne and brother Eric. Nothing extraordinary about any of us."

"Except that your brother died of cancer."

"Yeah. His death affected us all differently. My parents clung even more tightly to their safe, suburban lifestyle. But I had this monumental epiphany. You know, life is too short to live it for someone else's dreams and all that. So instead of becoming an engineer like my parents wanted, I went into politics."

"Have you ever been married?"

"Nope. I got close a few years ago. It didn't work out. Half my fault, half hers, I guess. Anyway, with working sixty to seventy hours a week, I don't bother much with the social whirl."

"Shall I feel honored that you made an exception for me?"

"You," he said, "have been the exception to every rule I ever made in my life."

"So that's it for Keir Andreis?" she asked. "No sordid secrets, no shadowy figures in your past?"

He spread his hands. "Sorry. I told you I was basically a very boring guy."

"Dark and dangerous," she murmured.

"Huh?"

"That's what you looked like tonight in your leather jacket and shades. Dark and dangerous."

He snorted. "Give me a computer printout of voter demographics, and I'm a real killer."

"Do you like what you do?"

"Sometimes."

"Do you like doing it for John Hauck?"

"Sometimes." He raised his beer and took a drink. "But it's not a matter of like or dislike. Sure, John can be a pain in the ass sometimes. But he isn't the first pain in the ass I've worked for, nor will he be the last. He's paying me to do a job for him, and as long as I'm taking his money, I'm going to do the best job I possibly can."

"Uh-huh."

"Uh-huh, yourself. Now I see where Cyndi gets it. Come on, Maris. This is a dream of a job. The governor's mansion is up for grabs, and John's the most electable man in the state."

"Product recognition."

"Ouch," he said. "You make it sound pretty ugly. But yeah, I work to make John appeal to the most people on the most issues; that's what gets a man elected. And if he wins, I can write my own ticket in this business."

255

"Ambition, huh?"

"There's nothing wrong with ambition."

She crossed her arms over her chest. "I think John Hauck would make a lousy governor. And an even lousier president."

"Why?"

"Because an elected official is supposed to serve the people. I don't think John even *sees* the people. Hey, I'm not talking about the other highbrows in his private country club. I mean these people," she said, indicating the crowd around them. "People who go without health insurance because they have to choose that or food, people who live so close to the edge that a simple brake job for their car can put them out on the street."

"Maris—"

"What about the man who's running against him? What's he like?"

"Tim McPherson?" Keir cocked his head to one side. "Tim is a smart man, an idealist. Some of his ideas are very interesting, and ought to be explored some day. But the bottom line is that he simply doesn't have the connections, charisma or resources to get elected."

"And John does."

"John does."

There was a long moment of silence. Maris didn't know why she'd initiated this discussion. But now that she'd begun, she couldn't stop worrying at it. "The senator says you're good at what you do," she said at last.

"I hope so."

"Are you good enough to take someone like Tim McPherson and teach him how to get the connections, the resources and the charisma to be elected?"

Keir drew his breath in sharply, his face showing his surprise. "I . . . might be. Why?"

"Oh, I was just wondering."

"I don't think you ever 'just wonder.' What's your point?"

She shrugged; he'd asked for it, she might as well give it to him straight. "Keir, you're bright, you're capable, and you're a hell of a nice guy. I'm having trouble imagining you working seventy hours a week to elect a man who is wrong for the job, and I think you are, too."

"What I am is having trouble keeping my hands off you," he said. His breath stirred the hair at her temple.

An ache settled deep in her body. It was a bittersweet sort of ache, memory/anticipation/desire/loss all rolled in together. Too much, too soon. Or maybe too late. "You're distracting me," she said, striving to keep her voice even. "I think I was making a point . . . even though I can't recall it now."

"Then, let's dance," he said.

Pulling her up from her chair, he led her to the dance floor and deftly inserted them into the crowd of dancers. It was a slow dance. At first she was awkward in his arms; Paul had been taller, the fit of their bodies different.

"Sorry," she said. "I'm a little rusty at this."

"Relax," he murmured, his hand stroking slowly down her back. "It's only a dance."

Not to her, it wasn't. She was awash in sensation and memories, a slipstream of past, present, Paul and Keir. Of their own volition, her arms went around his neck. Their bodies came into full contact, swells and hollows accommodating very nicely. The fit was suddenly very good.

257

"Wow," he said.

A cowboy and his partner went by. The man's head was bent, his Stetson creating a little corner of intimacy, both hands planted firmly on his lady's blue-jeaned rear.

Keir watched the pair move away, then smiled into Maris's eyes. Slowly, his hands slid down her back.

She smiled back. "Try it, and you'll be singing soprano."

"I thought we could get, you know, more fully into the ambiance of the place." The movement of his hands stopped. "But perhaps another time."

"Perhaps."

"When?"

"Keir—"

"I'm kidding." His smile faded. "No, I'm not."

The dance ended. Maris pulled her hands from around his neck and stepped back. "I need to find the rest room." What she really needed was respite from herself; she'd been much too close to telling him yes. Now. Tonight, before she started to think again.

"Over there, in the far corner. Come on, I'll walk you."

She shook her head. "Why don't you get us some more beer? I'll meet you back at the table."

"Okay." He hesitated, as though he wanted to say something else, then turned away.

Most of the crowd seemed to be moving toward the rest rooms. Maris sighed, thinking that there was bound to be a line, especially at the women's, then allowed herself to be caught up in the current of bodies.

Then, off to the left near the stage, she caught a

glimpse of a man. A whipcord-lean man, his hair thin and streaked with gray. His back was to her, but she could see his hand moving with short, sharp motions as he spoke to another man.

It couldn't be.

Run and hide. But where? If he could find her here, he could find her anywhere.

Something—it wasn't a decision, a plan, or anything resembling conscious thought—pulled her toward him. She was acutely conscious of being taller than almost all the women and many of the men. *All he has to do is turn around.*

If he could find her here, he could find her anywhere. If he could kill her here, in front of all these people, then there was no safety for her, ever.

She drifted through the crowd, untouched by the roar of conversation. People jostled her; a couple of men called out to her. She hardly noticed. Her being was focused on the sinewy arms and long, fast-moving hands of the man sitting near the stage.

The man's companion looked up as she approached. His face registered surprise, then speculation, and he leaned forward to say something to the other.

"Drew Eniston," Maris said, too loudly.

He swiveled around to stare at her. Her breath went out in an explosive gasp. He was lean and leather-hard, his narrowed eyes set in a network of sun wrinkles. But he wasn't Drew Eniston. He looked her up and down. Twice. "Hello, Red. Lookin' for some company?"

The room whirled around her. She'd been so sure, so damned sure, that for a moment she had trouble adjusting to this new reality. "I . . . I'm sorry. I thought you were someone else."

259

"Oh?" His gaze went to her legs again. "Too bad. Will I do as a substitute?"

"No. I . . . sorry, I'd better be going."

As she hurried away, she heard a plaintive, "Well, shee-it! Ain't it a shame?"

She headed back to her own table. Keir was waiting, staring thoughtfully at the bottle in front of him. He looked up as she sank into her chair with a sigh.

"What's up?" he asked. "You look as though you've seen a ghost."

"Almost," she said, reaching for her beer. "Almost."

Twenty

It was nearly midnight when Keir pulled up to the barrier at the end of Gavilan's driveway. Three security guards flanked the car, and one leaned down to shine his flashlight into the interior.

"Okay, go on in," he said, stepping back and motioning one of his men to open the barricade.

Keir eased onto the driveway. Ahead, the house sat in a pool of floodlight, its white-painted walls almost seeming to glow from within.

"I guess John went to the banquet over Peterus's objections," Keir said.

Maris saw that John's Mercedes was parked in front of the house, its dark metal hide gleaming in the floodlight. "What banquet?"

"One of Ballard's cronies organized a fund-raising banquet for John's campaign."

"Probably at a hundred dollars a plate," she said.

Keir shot her a look. "More like a thousand."

"No wonder he risked his life to go."

"Maris, the thousand was only hors d'oeuvres with this crowd. Once the dessert is eaten, the speeches speeched, the *real* exchanging begins. And not just money. Favors get swapped, promises made, influence traded."

261

"What kind of favors?"

"Any kind you can think of."

"No wonder you like going to these things."

He grinned. "I've got nothing to attract the kind of favors you're talking about."

"Youth and beauty won't do?"

"Nope. It's all power, Maris. No matter how much they have, they always want more. Support the candidate, gain his goodwill. Or at least that's the assumption."

"Is it wrong?"

"Usually not." He parked behind the Mercedes, leaning over to peer up at the house. "I see they got your window fixed. Are you going to move back into that room?"

"I'm bunking with Cyndi right now. Two security guards are stationed in my room in case Eniston tries to get in again. Actually, we've got security men stationed everywhere but in the toilet bowl, and I'm half-afraid to look there."

Keir glanced up at the house again. "So that light means Cyndi's waiting up for you."

"And I'm going to get grilled like a teenager coming home after curfew."

"Hey, I *feel* like a teenager." He ran his fingertips along the curve of her cheek. "Wanna neck in the backseat for a while?"

A guard walked past Maris's side of the car. He glanced in the window briefly, shifted his shotgun from one arm to the other, then moved on.

"Hell," Keir muttered. "Talk about killing a mood."

"I think we're making them nervous."

"They're certainly making *me* nervous."

"Well, I'd better be going in."

Keir looked at her, and there was such need in his eyes that her hand stilled on the buckle of the seat belt. Recklessness washed through her as he slid across the seat to her. *To hell with the security guard,* she thought, wrapping her arms around Keir's neck.

He kissed her, and she let herself sink deep. Maybe it was the music, the beer, the slow, smooth dancing or the scare she'd gotten — or maybe, just Keir. Whichever, she wanted this moment.

"We're fogging up the windows," she murmured against his mouth.

"You're fogging up my *brain,*" he said. "No, don't go away yet. Give me a minute longer, huh?"

Someone tapped on the window behind her. Keir released her abruptly, muttering something dire under his breath. Maris turned to see John Hauck peering into the car.

"Sorry, Keir," the senator called through the window. "I didn't know you were, ah, occupied. Security said you'd come in, and I didn't want you to leave before I had a chance to talk to you."

Someone else might have been embarrassed at intruding on what was obviously a *very* private *tête à tête*. But not John. Not only was he unembarrassed, he even opened the car door and leaned in. Maris glanced at the look on Keir's face, then quickly turned away, too close to laughter to risk it.

"Do you know who came to the banquet?" John asked, his face alight with excitement. "Grant and Alva Franklin."

263

"But the Franklins have been supporting McPherson," Keir said.

"Well, they've decided they want to back a winner. And since McPherson obviously isn't going to be one, they've come over to me."

"That's great, John."

"I want you to get back to Austin tomorrow to meet with the Franklins and get this thing nailed down."

"Well—"

"It'll only take you two, three days," John cut in smoothly. "I think Maris can do without you that long. Right, Maris?"

"Right, Senator," she said. "Whatever you say."

He didn't seem to hear the sarcasm in her voice. "See, Keir? Now, how about it? What's the plan?"

"This opens up a whole series of doors for us," Keir said. "I've got to think it over before adjusting our game plan around it. But I'd say the loss of the Franklins is the coup de grace for McPherson."

"God, but I feel great! It's in the palm of my hand, Keir. It's mine. The whole fortune cookie." John's eyes caught the light oddly as he held out his hand, palm up, then slowly closed it into a fist.

Maris drew in her breath sharply. The gesture had been greedy, possessive, a blatant claim to the election. And Keir was going to give it to him. She didn't want to see any more.

"Excuse me," she said. "I'd better be going."

John stepped back to let her out of the car. She hurried up the stairs, wanting only to get away. But she could hear Keir coming up behind her, his footsteps fast and determined on the concrete.

"Maris—"

264

"You go ahead and take care of your business," she said.

"Not without saying good night."

"Good night."

She opened the door. Before she could go in, however, he pulled the door closed again.

"I *am* thinking about what we talked about earlier," he said.

The tension went out of her. She glanced over his shoulder at John, who was leaning against the side of the car, his back to them. "I—"

"Senator!"

Peterus's shout came from the left. Maris turned to see the security man come hurrying around the far corner of the house.

"What's the matter, Bobby?" John pushed away from the side of the car and walked toward the other man.

"What the hell are you doing out here like this?" Peterus yelled. "Why don't you just paint a goddamn bull's-eye in the middle of your back!"

"There's nothing to—"

"Get in the house, damn it!"

John got officious. "Now look here—"

Something arced down from above, trailing fire like a comet. It crashed through the rear windshield of Keir's car.

"Look out!" Keir shouted.

He slung Maris down onto the porch just as fire exploded in the vehicle, blowing glass in every direction. A torrent of flame belched from the car's windows. Maris flung her arms up over her face as heat and smoke blasted across her skin. It was too much. She scrambled on hands and knees to the door, reaching up to fumble blindly with the doorknob.

"He's on the roof!" Peterus shouted. "Shoot him! Shoot him now!"

There was a fusillade of shots, half-drowned by the hungry animal-roar of the fire.

"Jesus! He's got another one!" Peterus screamed. "Get down, everybody!"

There was too much smoke for Maris to see the missile itself. But then a sun burst into life on the pavement between the cars, blossoming into a vast, incandescent billow of flame. As the explosion rolled up the steps toward her, she got the door open. Something hit her between the shoulder blades, sending her sprawling awkwardly on the hard floor. The foyer table hurtled over onto its side, then screeched along the tile in a welter of sparks and broken glass.

Then Maris saw Keir slide past her, the back of his leather jacket scorched and smoking.

"Keir!" She scrambled after him, yanking him out of a pool of sparks and bits of flaming upholstery. "Are you all right? Keir!"

He rolled over and opened his eyes. Maris let her breath out, only now realizing that she'd been holding it.

"Are you all right?" she asked again.

He felt his hair, ran his hands down his chest and stomach as though to make sure everything was indeed there. "Yeah. You?"

Maris nodded. Suddenly she found herself sitting down. Tatters of pantyhose hung from her outstretched legs, and she noticed that both knees were skinned.

Keir sat up and put his arms around her, holding her so tightly it hurt. They clung together, silent and still.

The roar of the fire was punctuated by shouts and the occasional report of a gun. Through the open doorway, she could see that the night had turned into a flickering orange hell.

"He's getting away," she said through chattering teeth.

"Maybe not. Maybe—"

"He's getting away." She knew it. Mind and soul, she *knew* it. She'd been a fool tonight. If that man had been Eniston, he would have killed her there. What would he care about witnesses? He'd been forged by prison, hate, and the killings he'd already done. A man with nothing to lose. Implacable as . . . death. A laugh bubbled up in her throat. She pressed both hands over her mouth to keep it in, but it escaped, seeping out from between her fingers.

"Take it easy," Keir murmured. "Don't cry. It's over. It's all right now."

"I'm not crying."

"No," Keir said. "You're not crying."

She blinked, and was surprised to find the glare from the fire fractured into tiny points by drops of moisture that clung to her eyelashes. She reached up, catching one on her fingertip. It tasted of salt.

"But I'm not crying," she said again.

Silently, Keir pulled his shirttail out and wiped her face, transferring wet soot to the fabric. She pushed his hand away.

They both flinched as a man appeared in the doorway, almost seeming to materialize out of the roiling smoke. It was Peterus, gun out and ready, his eyes looking strangely pale in the mask of soot that covered his face.

His gaze swept the area. Foyer, stairway, hallway, then back again. For what? Maris thought. If Eniston were here, they'd already be dead.

"You okay?" Peterus asked.

When Keir nodded, the security man turned to the door and called, "Okay, John. Come on in."

For a moment, the senator's body was an angular silhouette in the doorway, his salt-and-pepper hair backlit by the fire behind him. Then he moved farther into the house, limping slightly. Other than the limp, some soot and grass stains and a scrape on the point of his chin, he seemed to be unscathed.

"Are you all right?" Maris asked.

"Yes, I just sprained my ankle diving for cover." John went down on one knee in front of Maris. "You two seem to have gotten pretty well cooked."

Keir fingered his singed eyebrows. "Just toasted a little. Although for a second I thought we were going to be charcoal for sure."

"Good thing you had sense enough to get into the house," Peterus said.

Luck was all it was, Maris thought, remembering those few heart-stopping moments when she'd fumbled at the doorknob.

Peterus came to stand over them, his chin thrust forward aggressively. "Now," he said. "When I tell you to get in the house, I mean *get in the house.*"

"Yes, sir!" John saluted, a half-serious and half-mocking gesture.

"Did Eniston get away?" Keir asked.

268

Peterus nodded, a short, sharp jerk of the head that showed how frustrated he was. "I think the son of a bitch has got wings. He was on the roof, big as you please, and the next moment he was gone. Pretty damn spry for a man his age."

"He's fifty-four years old," Maris said. Remembering Eniston's long, big-knuckled hands, the sinewy forearms with their roping of tendons, she added, "And as tough and mean as all of us put together."

Peterus's radio squawked. He spoke into it briefly, listened as it chattered back, then turned to John. "Senator, we've had your family and Mrs. Durant's little girl in protective custody upstairs. Your mother is raising seven kinds of hell—"

"By all means, let my mother out of her room," John said.

A few moments later, Sophie hove into view, the skirt of her robe flapping around her legs as she ran down the stairs. Her white hair was a wild halo around her head, and her face nearly matched it in color.

"John!" she cried. "John!"

He went forward to meet her, and she enveloped him in arms and tears and frantic maternal concern, like some elemental force come to protect its hatchling.

"I thought I'd lost you," she sobbed. "I looked out and saw the car burning, and I thought you were in it!"

"I wasn't anywhere near it, Mother," he said, patting her hands before taking them from around his neck. "I got a few bruises, and a real big scare, and that's all."

"You might have been killed." She reached up to touch his face almost wonderingly. "Oh, my son . . ."

Maris didn't hear the rest, for Robyn had appeared at the top of the stairs, holding Cyndi tightly against her side.

"Mom!" Cyndi shrieked, wriggling out of the woman's grasp.

Maris managed to get to her feet just as Cyndi plowed into her. The child was crying hysterically, and her lack of control steadied Maris.

"Shhh, baby. Everything's all right," she murmured, bending to lift Cyndi into her arms.

The child clung tightly. Maris stroked her back, feeling the bird-fragile ribs beneath the skin, the knobbed line of the spine, and closed her eyes against a sudden rush of panic. *What if I'm not going to be able to be there for her?*

Each family clustered together—Maris and Cyndi, John and his mother and sister—as though that could hold the world at bay. Maris looked around for Keir. He stood off to one side, alone, watching her. She drew her breath in sharply. Something needed to be taken care of. Now, before anything else happened.

Still holding Cyndi, she walked slowly to Keir. "Will you do something for me?" she asked.

"Whatever you want."

She took a deep breath, feeling Cyndi's back shudder beneath her hands. God, she wanted to spare her daughter this! But she couldn't; Cyndi needed to know. "If anything happens to me, will you see that Cyndi gets the treatment she needs?"

If Eniston kills me. She could see the thought

echoed in Keir's eyes. It hung in the air between them, invisible, yet all too real. Maris saw him recoil in automatic rejection.

"Maris—"

"I have no one else."

He turned his head, the sweat on his forehead catching the orange glow of the light for a moment. Then he nodded. "You have my word," he said. "I'll see to it."

"Do you hear that, Cyndi?"

The child looked up, her face a mess of tears and soot. And defiance. "I don't need to hear that. Nothing's going to happen to you. I won't *let* anything happen to you!"

"Cyndi, I asked you a question."

"I heard, okay?" Cyndi cried. "I heard!" Then her face crumpled, and she buried it against Maris's shoulder again.

"Shhhh, baby," Maris crooned. "Shhh. I love you. No matter what happens, I will always love you."

It was the only truth she knew anymore, the only reassurance she could give. And as she felt Cyndi's thin body shuddering in her arms, she knew it wasn't enough.

Later, they all sat in the family room, drinking tea. Robyn had even gotten her father out of bed to wheel him in. No one spoke much, but evidently no one wanted to be alone, either.

Maris sat on the sofa, cradling Cyndi across her lap. The child had fallen asleep. Keir, looking wrung out and agitated at the same time, sat at the opposite end of the sofa, his legs stretched out on

271

the coffee table in front of him. He hadn't spoken a word in the hour they'd been here.

Maris looked over at Sophie. The old woman stood beside her husband's wheelchair, her fingertips resting on his shoulder. Her hair was back in its neat white cap, her tightly belted robe molding the square, strong lines of her body. She had regained her air of cool dignity, but there was a shadow of fear in her eyes — the fear of losing a child. Maris knew it well.

The old woman turned to look at John. "I would like to speak to your friend Mr. Peterus," she said.

"He's very busy right now, Mother."

"Now, John."

He raked his hand through his hair, obviously weighing refusal. Then he shrugged and went to talk to the guard who was stationed in the hallway outside.

The Matriarch is back, Maris thought. *And there's going to be hell to pay.*

Peterus came back a few minutes later, his expression harried and grim. A look passed between him and John, and the security man's face got even grimmer.

"Any sign of him, Bobby?" the senator asked.

"No. My guess is he climbed one of the trees near the back fence, walked out along an overhanging limb, then dropped down inside. He knocked one of my men unconscious to get access to the roof."

"I'm not interested in excuses, Mr. Peterus," Sophie said, moving to stand in front of him. "When I hire someone to do a job, I expect that job to be done. This . . . murderer has gotten through your men twice now."

"Mrs. Hauck, you have to be realistic," the security man said. "There are bugs in every operation. It takes a while to find them all."

"I'm not paying you for bugs, young man. I'm paying you to make sure my family is safe in my own home. And that you haven't done."

Peterus glanced at John, evidently expecting some backup. He didn't get it; the senator was at the bar, pouring himself a drink.

The security man licked his lips. "Look, Mrs. Hauck. This guy Eniston is slick. We've been doing our best, considering the size and openness of this estate."

"Excuse me." The voice was male and unfamiliar, and came from the hallway outside.

Maris turned to see a wiry, dark man standing in the doorway. He was impeccably dressed — gray suit, tie, polished black dress shoes. His dark hair was cut short, and he had the flat black eyes of a cruising shark.

He strode farther into the room, flipping his badge up for everyone to see. "Lieutenant Morales, Department of Public Safety. I'm coordinating the search for Drew Eniston."

"Thank you for coming so quickly, Lieutenant," John said. "But isn't Eniston's case being handled by a fellow by the name of Ter . . . Ter . . ."

"Terrell, sir," Morales said. "Lieutenant Terrell has been reassigned."

Leaving Morales with a veritable political hot-potato, Maris guessed. The heads were beginning to roll.

273

"Why haven't you caught that . . . madman?" Sophie demanded.

The lieutenant's sleek, dark head turned toward the old woman. "This is his turf, Mrs. Hauck. He's smart, keeps moving around too fast for us to pin him down. But we'll catch him, in the end."

"When? After he's murdered us in our beds?"

"Now, Mother, let's not go off half-cocked here." John came out from behind the bar, drink in hand.

She ignored him. "How long do we have to live in terror? Can't anyone *do* something about that man?"

"Yeah," Peterus said. "Something with a .38."

"Excuse me," Morales said, breasting the flow like an experienced swimmer. "I'd like to ask a few questions about what happened here tonight."

"What do you think happened?" Sophie cried. "Didn't you see those cars out front?"

"Yes," he said, taking a notebook out of his pocket, "I saw the cars. Now, who wants to go first?"

John stepped forward. "Look, Lieutenant. My parents, sister and Mrs. Durant's daughter were all upstairs asleep when the attack was made. Is there any reason to keep them here?"

"I suppose not, Senator," the policeman said. Maris saw that he was clearly reluctant to agree, but even more reluctant to anger the probable future governor of Texas.

"I have no intention of leaving this room," Sophie said.

"Well, I've got to get Cyndi to bed," Maris said. For once, she was glad of the Haucks' influence; Cyndi was completely exhausted, and this night

274

looked as though it might go on forever. She shifted Cyndi to a different position and started to get up.

"I'll take her upstairs for you," Robyn said. "If you don't mind."

Maris's first impulse was to hold her daughter tighter. Then she looked more closely at Robyn's face, saw the diffidence and hope there, and reconsidered. "Of course I don't mind," she said.

Gently, Robyn slid her arms beneath the sleeping child. "Would you like for me to stay with her until you come up? In case . . . she has a dream or something?"

"Thanks," Maris said. "I appreciate it."

She released Cyndi into the other woman's arms. The child murmured something, then nestled her cheek into the curve of Robyn's neck. *Such a trusting little gesture,* Maris thought. She saw Robyn react to it, her expression softening, her arms closing more fully around the girl.

Maris was caught by the sudden, powerful memories motherhood had imprinted in her flesh: the heart-twisting pull of her newborn daughter's mouth on her breast for the first time, the scent of powder, the slick smoothness of soapy baby-skin as they took a bath together.

At least I have that, she thought. *Robyn missed it all.*

She looked into the other woman's eyes, glad to give her this moment. Robyn straightened, cradling Cyndi in her arms, and left the room.

"Now, Senator, suppose you fill me in on what happened tonight?" the lieutenant asked.

"It's all my fault," John said. "I went outside,

275

even engaged Maris and Keir in conversation. Then, when Bobby tried to tell us all to get into the house, we ignored him. Hell, with me and Maris both standing out there like that, Eniston probably thought he'd died and gone to heaven."

He waited for a moment for the policeman's pen to stop. "I saw the Molotov cocktail—that's what they're called, isn't it? Yes? Well, I saw it come down from the roof. I even had time to see a shadowy figure clambering around up there before all hell broke loose."

"Two firebombs were thrown?"

"Yes."

"Are you sure it was Eniston?"

"Of course it was Eniston," Sophie snapped. "Who else could it be?"

"Please, Mother," John said. "The lieutenant is only trying to do his job."

Morales's shark gaze went from John to Sophie and back again. "Thank you, Senator."

"As far as being sure it was Eniston, well, he'd already threatened to burn the house down around our ears."

Maris jerked in surprise. "Oh?" she asked. "When did he do that?"

"A couple of days ago."

"He called you?" Morales asked.

"Yes. Several times. We've sent a copy of the log to you, as well as a list of the phones he's called from. But even Caller ID hasn't helped much; he uses pay phones, and doesn't stay on for more than a minute or so."

"A man's going to learn *something* useful in thirty-four years in prison," Keir said. "But I can't say I understand his actions tonight; there have got to be easier ways of blowing people up than climbing around on a slippery tile roof to toss a couple of firebombs."

"The man is insane, obviously," John said. "Maybe he was just playing some sick cat-and-mouse game with us, making us suffer for a while before making his *real* move."

The notion should have been absurd. But not with Eniston. Remembering the man's strange, yellow-flecked eyes, the intensity, the hatred that drove him, Maris knew Eniston was beyond her understanding. Perhaps there *were* no measures of human behavior that applied to him. Was he insane, or was he evil?

"Mrs. Durant?"

The policeman's question startled her back to awareness, and she saw that everyone was staring at her. "I'm sorry, Lieutenant. Did you ask me a question?"

"*You're* the one who asked the question," John said. "You asked, 'Is he insane, or is he evil?' "

"I . . . wasn't aware I'd spoken aloud." She tried to pretend it didn't matter. "I was just woolgathering. Go on—"

"Does it matter?" John asked.

"Does what matter?"

"Whether he's insane, or merely evil?" John's gaze bored into hers, as though he were trying to see straight into her mind. "Does that change anything? Did it matter to Lee or to that baby he tossed in Buffalo Bayou?"

Morales cleared his throat, returning them to the concrete business of question-and-answer. Maris

277

found it a relief. "I saw this, I heard that." Facts, solid and comforting.

But a nagging little imp kept thrusting its face into the corners of her mind. *Insane or evil?* it whispered to her. Or, as Senator Hauck had phrased it, *insane or merely evil?*

Merely evil.

Did it matter? To Lee, to the baby, to Maris Durant? She didn't know. But it ought to matter to *someone*.

Twenty-one

Maris leaned over the back of the sofa, reading the phone log over Lieutenant Morales's shoulder. Eniston had called a lot. So many times, in fact, that the security people had stopped writing "Eniston" and merely noted an "E."

She glanced at Keir, who was sitting at the lieutenant's right. He'd been uncharacteristically quiet since Morales had opened the phone log. It might have been dismay, anger, concern or all three; his face showed nothing of what was going on inside his head.

"What are these numbers in the margin?" Morales asked.

"Those are numbers the Caller ID identified," Peterus said. "They're listed under their exchanges. We had them traced to public phones in Alvin, Pearland, Angleton and Rosharon. Never twice from the same phone. Seems Eniston likes to move around."

"Well, he *is* a fugitive," Maris said. "Did you expect him to have an office with an answering machine?"

"No," Peterus drawled, "but I sure hoped he'd screw up. And that's not an unreasonable hope,

Mrs. Durant. Most criminals are pretty stupid. That's why they're in prison in the first place."

"What do you say about that, Lieutenant Morales?" Keir asked. "Is the D.P.S. working on the assumption that Drew Eniston is stupid?"

Morales looked up at him. "That would be a serious tactical mistake, Mr. Andreis."

"If Eniston were smart," Peterus said, "he wouldn't keep coming around here, where he's gonna get his tail—" He broke off abruptly, his birthmark flushing brick red.

"Where he's going to get his tail shot off?" Morales asked.

"Not at all," John said, so smoothly it didn't seem like an interruption. "What Bobby was going to say was that Eniston was going to get his tail slapped right back into jail. Isn't that right, Bobby?"

"Yeah."

Maris glanced at Sophie, who was fussing with the blanket covering Ballard's wasted legs. Poor Sophie; would it take another death for her to lay her ghosts to rest?

Morales tapped the log with his pen. "Eniston called one, two, three . . . six times yesterday, and four times today," he said. "What went on? Did anyone talk to this guy?"

"I did," John said. "He wouldn't talk to anyone else."

"What did he have to say?" the lieutenant asked.

John shrugged. "Oh, mostly he just ranted and raved, screaming about how we ruined his life, et cetera, et cetera. And then he got into threats."

"What kind of threats?"

"Hell, Lieutenant, he wants to kill everyone in this house. My name figured high on the list, as well as 'that bitch Durant.' "

Bitch, Maris thought. *Bitch.*

Sophie gasped. "Dear God!"

"God," John said, "has nothing to do with it."

"What about Garrick?" Keir asked. "Have you taken any measures to protect him?"

Morales smiled. "Garrick Hauck is in California at the moment."

"Oh? Business or pleasure?" John asked.

"You didn't know he was gone?" Morales's eyebrows went up.

"Garrick is a grown man, Lieutenant. He doesn't check in with us." Sophie reached out to smooth her husband's sparse yellow-white hair. "Such a horrible, horrible situation. If only Ballard weren't . . . ill. He always knew what to do."

A spot of red appeared on each of John's cheekbones. He strode to her and put his hands on her shoulders. "And so do I, Mother. Remember when Daddy had his stroke? At the hospital, when we were waiting to hear if he was going to live or die, you turned to me and said, 'John, you're the head of the family now. The destiny of the Haucks is in your hands.' " He sighed. "I was so proud, so terribly proud to know you trusted me so much."

Tears welled into the old woman's eyes, dimming them. For a moment, she looked very old, very tired. Then she let her head drop forward until her forehead was resting on John's chest.

"I just miss him so," she said. "He was such a strong man. All our years together, I knew that all of us were safe in his hands. Nothing ever frightened him; nothing ever stopped him, once he'd set his mind to something."

"No," he murmured. "Nothing ever did." He held her for a moment, then took her by the shoulders and gently pushed her out to arm's length. "Now, why don't you take him back to his room? I'll send Alejo to get him settled back in bed. And then I want *you* to go get some rest. You're going to worry yourself into exhaustion, and that's exactly what Eniston wants. Trust me, Mother. I've got everything under control."

Sophie nodded. "You're right, dear."

"Of course I am."

The wheelchair squeaked faintly as Sophie pushed her husband toward the door. His head bobbed with the movement of the chair.

John went to the bar and got himself another drink. Then he sat down in the chair opposite Morales. "Now we can talk openly," he said.

Morales nodded.

"Eniston made a lot of threats," John said. "As I told you before, one was to burn this house down around our ears. But he also threatened me personally."

"What did he say?" the policeman asked.

"He said he was going to make me pay for what Daddy did to him all those years ago."

"Oh?" Morales looked up from his notebook. "And what was that?"

"Eniston blames Daddy for getting him put into prison." John's voice turned bitter. "Of course, Eniston doesn't see his own part in it. Two killings, and he blames someone else for the punishment he rightly deserved. And the threats weren't the

282

worst," John continued. "Of course, he called me every name in the book—and some that weren't. I can handle that." His lips curved in a rueful smile. "After all, if I couldn't take a bit of name-calling, I'd be in the wrong profession. But when he started calling my sister a slut—"

"Robyn?" Maris asked in confusion.

"No. Lee. It was Lee he called a slut, and a lot of other things, too." John's expression changed, becoming more a baring of teeth than a smile. *That's* what I don't want Mother to hear. She went through hell back then, knowing Lee was living openly with Eniston, having his illegitimate child, going against everything she'd been raised to believe. And Daddy—Daddy cut her off without a cent. My sister gave up *everything* for that bastard, and he paid her back with three bullets in the chest. And now he has the nerve to call her a slut. . . ."

He braced his hands on his knees, his breath coming in long gasps. His face was bloodless, almost gray, and for a moment Maris was afraid he was going to have a stroke.

"Are you all right?" she asked, leaning forward to grasp his wrist.

He took a deep breath, then another. After a moment, the color came back into his face. "I'm okay. It's just . . . having to sit there and listen to it. . . ." Suddenly he reached over, clamping his hand over the one she'd laid on his wrist. His fingers were long, strong. Hurting. "I couldn't save Lee, but I promised to keep you safe, Maris, and I intend to do just that."

"Senator, Cyndi's illness taught me that there's

no such thing as safety. I could live in a padded room without windows or doors, no sharp edges or risks — and still manage to die."

"I can't accept that."

She tugged at the hand he was holding. Almost as an afterthought, he let her go. The huge room suddenly seemed too small, the air too warm. The past seemed to press close, and it was full of ghosts. *Hauck ghosts. Not mine.*

"Well, folks, I'm done in." The senator slapped his palms down on his knees, then rose from the sofa. "It's nearly three AM. I've got a hell of a long day tomorrow. If the lieutenant has everything he needs . . . ?"

There was a pause; then Morales snapped the logbook shut and stood up. "I've got everything I need for now."

"Good," John said. "Thank you for coming out tonight, Lieutenant Morales. Let me walk you out."

The senator paused in the doorway and glanced over his shoulder at Keir. "I want you to do over the latest draft of that speech I'm giving at the rally next week. Something about it bothers me, but I can't quite put my finger on it."

"Sure, John. Do you have a copy here?"

"No, but you can pick one up at the Houston campaign office on your way to Austin tomorrow. Bobby, will you see that one of your men drives Keir home?"

"Sure."

He led Morales out, to be followed a moment later by Peterus. Keir put his arm around Maris's shoulders and pulled her close.

284

"I wish I could stay. I wish—"

"Shhh." She put her hand over his mouth. "You might wish for things you'll regret."

"I'll take the chance."

"I'm not sure I can let you take the chance." She let her hand fall away from his lips. "Other people have futures, dreams—I've got nightmares that I don't know how to stop. Demons aren't easy to exorcise. Surely you know that by now."

He tapped his forehead. "Here, I know it. Here"—he tapped his chest—"*I* want to be in your dreams, not Paul."

"That dream isn't about Paul," she said. "It's about death. That's why he has Cyndi's face at the end."

"Maybe you should try to change it, then."

She sat forward, away from his arm, then got to her feet. The concept of change was too abstract for her now. Too much had happened tonight; she couldn't think, couldn't feel, and didn't much care.

"I've got to go," she said.

"Maris—"

"Just leave it, okay? For tonight, just leave it." Without waiting for an answer, she turned and walked away.

She tried not to dream The Dream. But it haunted her sleep, following her through all the highways and byways her mind took to escape it. Inevitably, it caught her, sinking its hooks into her and sucking her, protesting, into . . .

The tiller bucked in her hands as the boat sliced through the water. Wind in her hair, wind in her face, as intimate and warm as a man's hands on her skin.

And Paul up in the bow, balancing with unconscious grace against the roll of the deck. His brown hair and tanned skin counterbalanced the almost surreal aqua of sea and sky—earth, as opposed to water and air.

The wind rose suddenly, and she knew the time was coming. If she could only warn him about the rope, it might not happen the same way.

Keeping her right hand on the tiller, she cupped the left around her mouth. "Paul, watch the lines," she shouted. The wind tore the words from her mouth and flung them away.

Smiling, Paul turned to look at her. "I love you, Maris."

"Watch out! Don't go near the line!" she shrieked. Still he didn't react. *Why can't he hear me when I can hear him so clearly?*

Then came the all-too-familiar jolt, the violent plunge into water. Surrounded by the bubbles of her own passage, she fought to reach the boat.

"Are you all right?" she shouted as she broke through to the surface.

"I'm fine, just fine and dandy." Eniston's voice, Eniston's face on the man beside the boat.

This isn't the same dream!

Maybe not. Still, she was compelled to go through the same motions: trying to loosen the line binding his ankle, trying to lift the mast out of the water, trying to hold him up . . . long enough. And failing. Screaming, screaming as his head slipped beneath the surface.

You don't care! It's not Paul.

286

But when his life came bubbling up between her hands, she tried to hold it as desperately as she'd tried to hold Paul's so many months ago. She still cried when his limp body was pulled up and dropped facedown beside her on the deck of the rescue ship.

Utterly terrified, she stared at the back of his head, at the seal brown hair that drizzled streams of water onto the deck. In a moment, they were going to turn him over. And when they did, he was going to be wearing Cyndi's face.

"Don't!" she cried, her voice high and tinny. No one heard her; no one paid any attention.

Two pairs of hands moved into her field of view, grasped the dead man and heaved him over onto his back. This time, he wasn't wearing Cyndi's face.

He was wearing her own.

Maris found herself sitting up in bed, panting as though she'd actually done everything she'd dreamed. Around her was the solid, everyday reality of the room. It should have been comforting. The line between reality and fantasy had blurred, however, and the room was peopled with ghosts. *Her* ghosts, this time. She much preferred to deal with the Haucks'.

"God," she groaned, scrubbing her face with her hands. "Not now. I can't handle this now."

Slowly, she regained her composure. Realizing that dawn had come and gone, she leaned over and turned the bedside clock so that she could see its face.

"Ten minutes to nine," she said, sliding prone again. Evidently there wasn't going to be breakfast as usual today. In a way, it was comforting to know there was *something* that could interrupt the Haucks' rigid schedule. But the change hinted that the tightly woven fabric of the family was beginning to fray. And once that began, where would it end?

Someone knocked softly at the door. "Mrs. Durant?"

A man's voice. Maris flung the covers aside and reached for her robe. When she answered the door, she found a uniformed security guard standing outside.

"Yes?" she asked, a bit breathless.

"There's a call for you. A woman. She wouldn't identify herself, but Mr. Peterus thought you'd want to take it anyway."

"Yes, I would." She closed the door and hurried to the phone on the nightstand. When she put the receiver to her ear, the line sounded open, as though someone were listening in on an extension. Someone probably was, she thought with a grimace. "I've got it," she said, louder than was necessary.

There was a click. Maris waited a moment longer, then said, "This is Maris Durant."

"Remember me?" the caller asked.

There was no mistaking that machine-gun-swift delivery. *Ella Florian.* Instantly, Maris's attention narrowed to a tight focus. "Yes, I do."

"Good. I need to talk to you, pronto."

"You could come here—"

A snort. "Take Route 6 to Julain. About a mile past the exit is a roadside diner called Lola's Barbecue Beef. It's off the road a ways, so you've got

288

to watch for it. Meet me there at ten. Alone. I see anybody with you, following you or whatever, I'm gone."

"Wait a minute—"

"Shut up and let me finish." There was a pause, then the sound of a lighter being snapped. "You were found in a trailer park off Old Spanish Trail. You were wrapped in a striped Mexican blanket."

Maris drew a breath in, held it. *She knows! That's exactly how it was!*

"Now, do you want to talk to me, or don't you?" Ella asked.

"Yes."

"I thought you might. You like what I just told you? Well, I got better things for you. Much, much better. You won'te be sorry you came, believe me."

"But I—"

The phone went dead.

"—I'm not familiar with the area. Don't worry if I'm a little late," Maris finished. "Shit!" Letting the phone drop, she scrambled for her clothes.

Just before leaving, she peeked into Cyndi's room. Robyn was still there, lying atop the covers beside the child. She'd hardly moved since last night. Maris hadn't had the heart to disturb her then, and didn't now. She left a note on the bathroom mirror, saying she'd be back by afternoon, then hurried downstairs.

She found Alejo on the porch, scraping scorched paint off the front door.

"Good morning, señora," he said. "You are well today?"

"I'm fine, thanks for asking. Is my car back from the body shop yet?"

"*Si*. I brought it back yesterday. You are going out?" When she nodded, he wiped the scraper clean with a rag. "I will bring the car around to the door."

"I really don't mind—" she began, but he'd already walked away.

She stood on the porch, fairly dancing with impatience. A moment later, Alejo drove up in her Regal. The car looked better than it had in years. Evidently someone had tinkered with the engine a bit; it sounded as smooth as a cat's purr.

"Hey," she said, trotting around to the driver's door. "It looks great, Alejo. They did a beautiful job on it."

"Thank you, señora."

He looked as though he wanted to say more, but Maris was in too much of a hurry to wait. "I'll be back in a couple of hours," she said, opening the door for him and taking his place behind the wheel as soon as he vacated it. "Will you tell Mrs. Hauck for me?"

"*Si*. But, señora—"

"I hope my maps are still in the glove box," she said, leaning over to check. "Thank God, there they are. Okay, it's off to the races. See you!"

One of the security guards made noises about waiting for Peterus, but Maris rolled down her window and asked, "Do you see Drew Eniston in the car with me?"

"No, ma'am, but—"

"But nothing. I'm in a hurry, and you're holding me up." She tightened her hands on the wheel, ready to drive right through the barrier.

He shrugged, waving her through. Maris did take the precaution of checking the road behind her periodically to see if anyone was following her, but other than a couple of farm tractors and one station wagon filled window-to-window with kids, she was alone.

She took advantage of a red light in Hauck to find Julain on the map. "Let's see . . . I pick up Route 6 off of 288 and go east. Then we've got one, two . . . ah, looks like six or seven miles until the Julain exit. Okay, I got it."

The light turned green. Traffic moved slowly, and she barely managed to squeeze through before the light turned red again. As soon as she made the turn, she found the road blocked by an overturned flatbed truck. Lumber lay scattered everywhere.

"No, damn it!" she cried, banging her palms down on the steering wheel.

Slapping the gear shift into reverse, she backed down the street to the intersection. A moment later she turned again, onto the first road that seemed to run in the right direction.

Her watch read 9:31.

She soon left the city behind. The road arrowed straight through fields of foot-high corn stalks, acre after acre of them as far as she could see. She passed several intersecting streets, but none seemed promising.

"Please," she muttered. "Don't let me be lost."

A mile or so farther on, she spotted a battered, hand-painted sign that said, "Mike's Garage." Below it was an equally battered cinder-block building. She pulled in, stopping in front of the open service bay. A man in mechanic's overalls came out, wiping his hands on a rag. He was short and middle-aged, his pants riding low beneath his paunch. His name badge read "Mike."

"Can I help you, ma'am?"

"God, I hope so," she said. "I'm trying to get to 288."

"Well, ma'am, the best thing to do is go back that way about three miles. When you git to Conifer Road, turn right. The next light, take a left. That'll be Busbee Road. Take that for about three or four miles, then—"

"Hold it!" Maris fought the panic welling up inside her. "I'm trying to get to a place called Lola's Barbecue Beef. It's on Highway 6. Is there another way besides backtracking? I'm in an awful hurry."

"Why, sure, I know Lola's. You take this here road down to Abbeyville Road, then turn left. Follow that another say, seven miles, and you'll hit Highway 6 just west of where you want to be."

"Thanks."

She waved goodbye as she pulled out. His directions proved to be accurate, and except for the couple of minutes it took her to navigate past a flock of sanitation trucks, she had little trouble finding Highway 6. Her watch read 10:01 when she pulled off the road near the restaurant.

Lola's Barbecue Beef was a long, low frame structure, set a hundred yards off the highway on a rutted, overgrown gravel track. Lola had given up the barbecue business a long time ago; the paint was long gone, the boards weathered to a dusky gray. The corrugated roof was more rust than not, and the windows looked like gaping, hungry mouths ringed with broken-glass fangs. Weeds sprouted man-high around it.

There was no car, and no sign of Ella Florian. Maris put the Regal in park and got out, her tennis shoes crunching on the gravel. She walked around the building, wary of ticks in the tall grass.

"Ella?" she called. "Ella?"

A shadow passed over her, and she looked up to see the graceful, deadly shape of a hawk high overhead. Cruising. She went back to the car and leaned against the fender to wait.

10:03.

10:04, 10:05, 10:06.

10:10. Maris pushed off the fender and started to pace. Maybe Ella had had a flat tire. Maybe she'd had car trouble, or gotten stuck behind an accident.

Maybe she wasn't coming.

"Don't do this to me, damn it!" she muttered, turning to look at the old restaurant. The empty windows stared back at her silently.

"Surely not," she said.

Surely not, but she couldn't leave without at least taking a look inside. "God knows what's in there," she muttered. "Rats as big as pumas, probably."

Gingerly, she reached through the tatters of rusted screen that was all that was left of the storm door. Hinges squealed shrilly as she pushed the inner door open.

The interior was cool, the sunlight lying in bright squares on the cracked linoleum floor. The former restaurant had been one long room, with a set of doors in the far wall showing where the kitchen and rest room were located. Wallpaper hung in brown shreds from the walls, and fat, black spiders sat contentedly in the corners. Other than scattered trash and a few broken chairs, the room was empty.

The floor felt fragile beneath her feet, so she stayed away from the center of the room as she made her way toward the doors at the other side. She passed one of the windows, dust motes drifting around her like specks of captive sunlight.

The first door led to what had once been the bathroom. Now it was a dim cavern, peopled with crickets and festooned with spiderwebs. The toilet was tilted, half-submerged in rotten plywood like a ship going down beneath the waves.

Something scuttled toward her foot, and she shut the door hurriedly. The kitchen was better than the bathroom, but not much. Mouse droppings lay everywhere. Among them ran swift-darting roaches, decendents of those who had come to partake of Lola's barbecue.

But no Ella.

"Damn you, anyway," Maris said to the empty room.

As she turned to go, something big and brown dropped from the ceiling onto her head. She shrieked, pawing frantically at her hair.

"Get off!" she cried, envisioning scorpions and tarantulas and Black Widow spiders. *"Get off!"*

She shook her head violently, and the creature flew out of her hair and hit the floor with a thump. Maris leaped backward, coming up against a wall with enough force to send her down to her hands and knees.

Her attacker lay on its back, waving its legs wildly as it struggled to turn over. It was no tarantula, but a tree roach as long as her thumb. It stared at her balefully, legs and antennae going like crazy. Maris would almost rather have had the tarantula.

"Okay, I've had enough," she said, climbing shakily to her feet.

She retreated, keeping a sharp lookout at the ceiling until she got outside. Disappointment lay like wet ashes in her chest. Why had Ella dragged her all the way out here like this? Was it some sick kind of joke? Well, she wasn't going to fall for it again.

Dusting her hands off on the back of her jeans, she made her way back to the car. The hawk passed overhead again, the clear, high *skree* of its call floating down on the air. Its shadow slid swiftly along the ground ahead of Maris, its shape distorting as it passed over the bumps and gullies of old tire tracks. Reaching the road, it turned and came toward her again.

Maris sidestepped it. It veered after her, as though the bird were tracking her. Goose bumps rose on her skin as the shadow passed over her. The hawk called again, and she shaded her eyes to look up at it. The bird floated effortlessly upon the air, as graceful as a sword. Then it folded its wings and plummeted toward the ground, to rise a moment later with something squirming in its talons.

Survival of the fittest. Kill-or-be-killed, eat-or-be-eaten. The law of the jungle. Eniston's law.

Shuddering, Maris got into the Regal and started it, only looking back once as she made her way

295

back to the main road. The restaurant lay behind her, sagging and forlorn, as tattered as her spirits.

"Well, this was a waste of a morning," she said, gunning the car into a tight U-turn.

She hoped they weren't having barbecue for lunch.

Twenty-two

Maris leaned her shoulder against the frame of the big double door that separated the family room from the garden. Dinner had been fried chicken, mashed potatoes and gravy, and peas, — and sat in her stomach like a lump of concrete. Courtesy of Ella Florian. Even now, half a day after being stood up at the restaurant, Maris was still depressed and angry.

"Damn her," she whispered, hugging herself hard. She'd been saying that a lot, as far as Ella Florian was concerned.

Hearing a noise behind her, she turned to see that the others had come into the room. Robyn pushed Ballard's wheelchair into position in front of the TV, while John and Sophie strolled arm-in-arm to the sofa.

Cyndi came in, her red baseball cap a crayon-bright note amid the gentle earth tones of the room. Maris held out her arm, and the child came to nestle close against her side. *God, I love her!* Maris thought, reaching up to run her fingertips along the peach fuzz at her daughter's nape.

I might get to keep her! The thought ran like laughter through her mind, washing away some of the stain left by Ella Florian's betrayal.

"Look at that moon," Cyndi said. "It's a great night for vampires."

Maris smiled. "I think you've been watching too many monster movies."

"You can't watch too many monster movies." Cyndi shifted position to look at Robyn. "Is it time, Robyn?"

"Yes, dear, it's time."

"All *right!*"

"Time for what?" Maris asked.

Robyn came to stand beside Cyndi. "I told her I'd let her play with my collection of model horses once supper was over." She reached out as though to stroke the child's cheek, then dropped her hand to her side. "That is, if you don't mind."

"Of course I don't mind. Cyndi loves horses."

Cyndi nodded enthusiastically, causing the bill of her hat to slide down over her nose. Pushing it back into place, she said, "I started taking riding lessons a couple of months before I got sick. It was cool. Mom says I can take them again when we get our own place."

"You mean when you get well," Sophie said.

There was a moment of silence, then Cyndi said, "I'm strong enough now, Mrs. Hauck. Kids with cancer can do stuff, you know."

"Oh, I see," Sophie said, although it was obvious she didn't.

Maris's throat ached as she watched her daughter take Robyn's hand and lead her from the room. Despite the disparity of ages, it seemed that Cyndi had taken Robyn under her wing. Good. Maybe the child would teach the woman something about joy and the courage to risk living. No one could do it better.

Evidently Sophie had been watching, too, for she said, "Cyndi's a very special little girl."

"I know," Maris said softly.

"Sometimes I feel badly that Robyn never had any children."

Only sometimes? As Keir would say, Je-sus, God!

"Robyn told me many times that she didn't want children, Mother," John said.

"I suppose so." Sophie sighed. "At least she's had her father. It's been a great relief for me to put his care in her hands; I'm not as strong as I used to be, and Ballard did so hate the idea of being tended by strangers."

Maris glanced at the old man. His indigo eyes were focused on the blank TV screen, one corner of his mouth drooping downward pitifully. A poor substitute for children, she thought, and a damned poor substitute for a life. With a shudder, she turned back to the window.

"Where did you go in such a rush this morning, Maris?" John asked. "Security told me you got a phone call, then ran out of here as though the Hounds of Hell were nipping at your heels."

She took a moment to compose her face, then turned around. "Oh, I just had to meet someone about the marrow donor thing."

"Oh? I thought Hugh Carideo was screening those calls for you."

"This was a woman I'd met before. She wanted to talk to me again, without the press hanging over our shoulders."

His eyebrows went up. "Oh? Why is that? Has she asked you for money, by any chance?"

"She wanted five thousand dollars up front before she'd go in for testing."

"You didn't give it to her, did you?" Sophie demanded.

"I'm not quite that gullible." *Close, but not quite.*

"Nevertheless, you considered it," John said. "Why?"

"She knew too many details, even where I was found and what kind of blanket I was wrapped in. When she asked me to meet her, she gave the impression she had even more specific things to tell me."

John sat back, propping his elbows on the chair arms and steepling his fingers in front of his face. "And did she?"

"She didn't even show."

"Ah, I see." He rose to his feet and came over to lay his hand on her shoulder. "I'm sorry. I know it was a blow to have your hopes raised, and then lost again."

"Yeah."

He gave her shoulder a squeeze before turning away. "Well, I'm going to tuck myself away in my office and get some phone calls made."

"Oh, I thought you were finished for the day," Sophie said.

"Mother, this election is going to be a twenty-four-hour-a-day job."

"Then, hire more people, darling. Keir—"

"Mother, Keir is one of the best campaign managers in the business, but there are things only I can do. Other people may write my speeches, but I've still got to give them. I've got to attend the rallies, shake the hands and kiss the babies."

"Oh, John." Sophie's mouth was wreathed with spoked lines of disapproval. "Won't you be in danger going into crowds with this madman running around loose?"

300

"Shall I let him ruin my chances of being elected? No, Mother. I can't run my life around Drew Eniston any more than Maris can. Besides, I have confidence that he'll be caught soon. Everything's going to come together just fine, you'll see."

"Yes, dear." Her face radiating fond maternal pride, Sophie reached up to place her hand on his cheek. "My soon-to-be Governor Hauck."

He took her hand, kissed it, then strode from the room. As the old woman went to tend Ballard, Maris realized she'd never seen John touch his father.

Who, by the way, was still staring at the blank television screen. Maris was acutely embarrassed for him.

"So," she said, "what shall we watch?"

"Ballard loves sports," Sophie said. "Perhaps we can find a basketball game for him."

"Uh, sure," Maris said, reaching for the TV listing. *Heck, if it doesn't bother her, why should it bother me? It sure doesn't bother Ballard. We ought to just let the old guy keep watching the blank screen, and save the electricity.*

She dropped the schedule hastily when a man shouted outside, sharp and sudden, to be answered by more shouts and then the sound of running feet. Maris ran to the window and peered out into the moonlit night.

Two security guards rushed past, headed toward the garage. Maris could see more men out there, and a slew of nervously darting flashlight beams.

"What is it?" Sophie asked.

"I don't know." Maris shifted to the other side of the window, trying to see better. "There's something on the ground out there. I wonder . . . Hey, I think someone's been hurt!" She whirled away

301

from the window and headed for the back door.

"Maris, wait!" Sophie cried. "Let the men handle it!"

Maris ignored her. The air was cool and damp, and felt as if it were coating the inside of her lungs as she hurried toward the knot of people standing beside the garage. No one seemed to be doing anything for the person lying on the ground.

Peterus broke away from the group to block her path. "Get back in the house, Mrs. Durant."

"Someone's hurt!"

"We've already called for an ambulance."

"I might be able to do something," she panted. "I'm trained in CPR, got my certification when Cyndi got sick."

"Mrs. Durant —"

Brushing past him, she went down on one knee beside the still form.

It was Ella Florian. Maris stared for one shocked moment, then got down to business. There was no need to wonder what was wrong; the gaping hole in the woman's upper chest told the whole story. Although there was surprisingly little blood coming from the wound itself, Ella's clothes were soaked with it.

"There's nothing you can do for her," Peterus said, putting his hand on Maris's shoulder. "Come on, get back to the house."

She shook him off. "She's still breathing! Ella, can you hear me?"

"You know her?" Peterus demanded. "How the hell —"

Without looking away from the injured woman, Maris silenced him with a sharp gesture. "Ella, just try to hang on. An ambulance is coming; you'll have help very soon."

Ella's eyes fluttered open, and there was death in them. Maris had been a visitor to enough cancer wards to recognize it.

"I came . . . talk to you . . . tell you . . . Ah, it hurts!" Ella's voice was just a breath of sound.

"Shhh," Maris said. "Save your strength. We can talk later."

Ella closed her eyes, opened them again. Her next breath was a rattling wheeze. "Zios," she whispered.

Maris bent closer, taking the woman's hand in hers. Suddenly Ella's grip tightened convulsively. Her mouth worked, forming words but making little sound. Maris bent close.

"Zios," Ella whispered. "R'member . . . Zios. He . . . killed her, too. Don't tell . . . any. . . . Don't . . . tell . . ."

Her head fell back limply. Maris lunged forward, frantically feeling for a pulse in the folds of flesh of the older woman' s neck. Nothing.

"Oh, my God!" Maris muttered. "Oh, my God."

She started compression then, reciting her instructions under her breath. "Heels of the hands at the tip of the breastbone, then press. One and two and three . . . Peterus, do you know how to give artificial respiration?"

"It's been years—"

"Time to remember. When I say switch, you breathe into her one time. Then we check her for response."

"Damn. Okay." He sank to his knees and tilted Ella's head back, watching Maris for instructions.

"Four," she said, compressing. "And five. Go!"

He puffed into the older woman's mouth, then sat up again.

"Any response?" Maris asked.

"No."

Maris began compression again. One. Two. *Dear God, please make it work. This might be my mother.* Four. Five. "Switch!"

Peterus obeyed. There was still no response.

Compression again. "Switch!"

Breathe. No response. Compression, no response. Breathe again, compression again.

No response.

Breathe, compress, breathe, compress. Sirens screaming in the distance, coming fast. Not fast enough.

"Come on, Ella," Maris panted. "Come *on.*"

The woman's skin was bluish, the well-padded torso beneath Maris's hands strangely slack, as though something important had left it. Maris shook her head, denying it as she started another round of compression.

"Give it up, Mrs. Durant," Peterus said. "She's dead."

"Switch!"

"Shit," he said, even as he bent to obey.

The sirens were closer now, but Maris only dimly registered them. All her attention was on Ella, on bringing her back. "One and two and three and four and five . . . Switch!"

Someone pulled her away; someone else's hands took the place of hers on the dead woman's chest. Men crowded around, their skin looking like Ella's in the garish, flashing lights.

"Let's get her in the truck," one man said, his voice rising above the well-organized babble.

"Hank, Joe, ready . . . lift!"

Ella was slid onto a stretcher, then rolled quickly toward the open back of the ambulance. A moment later the vehicle was screaming off into the night from whence it had come.

"Is she going to make it?" someone asked.

"She's already made it," Peterus said. "To the goddamn Pearly Gates."

Maris turned away, knowing he was right and hating him for it. She nearly ran into John Hauck. The senator stood immobile, his hands at his sides, and his face was as white as the moon above him. Even his eyes seemed to be bleached of color, stark beneath the dark slash of his brows. For a moment, Maris thought he was going to faint.

"Senator?" she asked, putting one hand on his arm. "Are you all right?"

His Adam's apple went up, then down as he swallowed hard. "What . . . who was she?"

"I knew her as Ella Florian." Maris took a deep breath, trying to shake the weight of the life that had slipped through her fingers. "She's the woman I was supposed to meet earlier today."

"Is she dead?"

"I don't know. Are you sure you're okay, Senator? You look awful pale."

His breath went out with a rush. "It's the blood. I . . . don't handle it well, I'm afraid." He looked down at his sleeve, then back up at her, his eyes as pale and chill as the moonlight. "And you're covered with it."

"Oh." She took her hand off his arm, leaving a dark palm print on the white fabric. "Sorry."

He turned on his heel and walked back to the house, his back held unnaturally straight. To keep

305

from folding, Maris thought. She knew that trick well.

Slowly, she turned her hands palm upward. They were covered with Ella Florian's blood; more of it soaked into the sleeves of her sweatshirt. Another life had just passed through her hands.

"Mrs. Durant, are you all right?" Peterus asked.

Maris looked up in surprise; he was standing right in front of her, and she hadn't even seen him coming. "Yeah, I'm fine."

"You'd better go in and wash your hands." His voice was gentle.

"Yes," she said. "I should."

Cyndi had finally fallen asleep, clutching a model of a Palomino stallion—a gift from Robyn. Maris stroked the child's forehead and the smooth curve of her skull, wishing she could erase the past half-hour from both their minds. Cyndi was as tough as they come, but seeing her mother walk in, blood up to her elbows, had been beyond tough.

I was supposed to protect her. That was my job— protecting her from all the ugliness of the world.

"I'm sorry, baby," she whispered.

She straightened and went into her own room, leaving the adjoining door ajar so that she could hear if Cyndi woke up. For a moment she stood at the window, looking down at the bright ribbon of concrete driveway, then went to the telephone and dialed Keir's Austin number. It rang once, twice; then an answering machine picked up.

"You've reached Keir Andreis," the recorded voice said. "If you'll leave your name and number, I'll get back to you as soon as possible."

He even sounds good on tape, Maris thought as

306

she waited for the beep. When it came, she said simply, "Call Maris," then pressed the disconnect button. She held the receiver to her ear a second longer, and was rewarded with a double click.

"Damn eavesdroppers," she muttered.

A faint knock pulled her away from the nightstand. She opened the door to the unwelcome sight of Mrs. Munoz standing in the hall. The housekeeper was as unflappable as always, but there was a tightness to her mouth that showed a wealth of things going on beneath the mask.

"Señora, Señor John wishes to speak to you."

Maris went to the door to Cyndi's room and peeked in. The child was still sleeping, the curve of her cheek reflecting a touch of the nightlight. "Okay," Maris said, stepping out into the hall. "Where is he?"

"He is in his office. If you will come with me, señora, I will take you there."

Maris was glad of the escort; John Hauck's private office was located in the rear of the east wing, a section of the house she hadn't been in before. After delivering her to the door, Mrs. Munoz turned and walked away.

"And goodbye to you, too," Maris muttered under her breath. "Holy cow!"

Taking a deep breath, she knocked on the office door.

"Is that you, Maris?" the senator called.

"Yes."

"Come on in."

It was like walking into an entirely different world. A male world, full of dark, heavy paneling, dark, heavy furniture, bookcases jammed with law books. The rug beneath her feet was thick and Persian, probably worth more than most people earn in a year. The senator was seated behind an enormous stretch of mahogany desk top. He looked rich and powerful and very much in charge, all emotion hidden beneath The Politician.

Maris turned in a slow circle to take in the rest of the room. In keeping with the masculine ambiance, there were a number of trophies on the walls. Deer, bighorn sheep, the snarling head of a bear, an absolutely hideous boar—all had fallen to some Hauck sportsman.

John, following the direction of her gaze, smiled and said, "My father and grandfather were both avid hunters."

"Are you?"

He shook his head. "I've always failed to see the challenge in shooting some poor, dumb animal. That was one of my father's biggest disappointments, that neither of his sons cared for the hunt." With a smile, he added, "Not that Garrick wouldn't cheerfully blow the bejesus out of something, but he just didn't have the discipline for learning the skill."

"And you can't stand the sight of blood."

"Right." He smoothed his already smooth hair. "Ella Florian was pronounced dead on arrival at the hospital. I'm sorry, Maris. I know you tried very hard to save her."

Maris found herself wiping her palms on her pants. Hastily, she thrust her hands in her pockets. Talk about having a thing about blood! She had washed, over and over, but she could still feel Ella's blood on her skin.

"How is Cyndi taking all this?" John asked.

"As well as can be expected," Maris said. "Look, Senator—"

"I know, I know; you want to get back to your daughter. I'll get straight to the point. Lieutenant Morales is on his way over to question us about what happened tonight. Have you thought about what you're going to tell them?"

"I'd planned to tell the truth, actually."

"I didn't mean to suggest otherwise. But there are certain things about the Florian woman's death that would be very upsetting to my mother, and I'd like you to be careful what you say in front of her."

"Senator, a woman was just murdered on your mother's property. What could be more upsetting than that?"

He reached into his pocket and pulled out a scarf made of white, gauzy fabric. It was patterned with the terra-cotta stain of dried blood. "One of Bobby's men found this in the gully at the western side of the estate. We think it belongs . . . belonged to Ella Florian."

"What does that have to do with your mother?"

"Did you happen to notice how similar the two women are in build? At a distance, and with this scarf over her hair, Ella Florian could be mistaken for my mother."

Maris took a deep breath, let it out again in a sigh. "You mean you think Eniston did it."

"Do you know any other murderers running around?"

"He just lurked around, looking for a target, and just sort of . . . potted that poor old woman, thinking she was your mother?"

John folded the scarf and put it back in his pocket. "Maris, Eniston proved long ago that he doesn't care whether his victims are seventy or seven . . . or seven minutes old. Let's face it. The guy is

309

completely uncorked. What sane man would do *any* of the things he's done?"

"Then, why didn't they put him in a mental hospital instead of prison?"

"Because he was judged sane, able to distinguish right from wrong, able to understand trial proceedings. He never pretended not to understand that what he did was wrong. He just didn't give a damn. And he doesn't give a damn now. You, me, Mother, Ella Florian, or even that little girl of yours—he'd kill any of us in a heartbeat."

Maris thought of her dreams of Eniston, the image of those killer's eyes staring, staring, the yellow flecks turning like the spokes of a Ferris wheel. . . . With a shudder, she banished it.

"Anyway," he continued, "I think you realize now that Mother isn't as strong as she seems, at least emotionally. This thing with Eniston has her on the verge of a nervous breakdown. You can understand why I don't want her to know that this woman died in her stead."

"I understand. Why don't you talk her into taking one of those pills of hers and going upstairs to bed?"

"I tried," he said. "She told me in no uncertain terms that she was in for the duration."

"I'll be careful what I say in her hearing. Now, I'd better be getting back to Cyndi," she said, turning away.

"Oh, Maris," he called.

She stopped, turned back to look at him. "Yes, Senator?"

"Bobby Peterus happened to mention that the Florian woman spoke to you." His hands rested on the desk top, the heat from his palms fogging the polished surface. "Did she say . . . anything that

310

would help you in your search?"

"She said she came here to talk to me, and then she said it hurt." Poor Ella. Whatever she had been, whatever she had done, she hadn't deserved *that*.

"Is that all she said?"

"Don't tell," Ella had whispered, struggling to hold on to life long enough to get the words out. Until Maris found out more about "Zios"—whoever or whatever that was—she intended to obey the dying woman's last words.

Looking John square in the eye, Maris said, "Yes, Senator. That's all she said."

Twenty-three

'Most men eddy about
Here and there—eat and drink,
Chatter and love and hate,
Gather and squawk, are raised
Aloft, are hurled in the dust
Striving blindly, achieving
Nothing; and then they die—
Perish;—and no one asks
Who or what they have been.'

*Matthew Arnold,
"Rugby Chapel"
New Poems (1867)

Maris stood at the living room window and
watched the last police car move down the driveway.
It was just dawn, pale lemon light spilling across the
world. *Poor Ella. She'll never see another sunrise.*
Maris felt as though she'd been beaten on a riverside

312

rock, squeezed out and hung out to dry.

"Thanks for nothing," she muttered under her breath.

She could hear John and Sophie conversing softly behind her, but she was too tired to deal with them, too tired to go over Ella Florian's death any longer. Morales had questioned them all for hours, mind-numbing layers of questions for which no one had the answers.

Privately, Maris had told the lieutenant about Zios. She'd watched his face for a reaction, but he hardly seemed to register it at all. He wrote it down dutifully, then went on to other things. Whatever Zios meant, it was something personal to Ella.

"Have the police gone, Maris?" Sophie asked.

"Yes." Her gaze shifted, focusing instead on the old woman's reflection in the glass. Sophie sat in the Queen Anne wing chair beside the fireplace, her big, knobby hands clasped in her lap. She hadn't moved in three hours.

"Now I know how the other half lives," John said. "If I were a criminal, I'd confess just so I could go to bed."

"You'd think they suspected one of *us* of killing that poor woman," Sophie said.

"Of course they don't think that, Mother. But suspicion's the nature of the beast; surgeons do surgery, preachers preach, and detectives suspect. Hell, Keir's the only one of us who has an alibi. That is," he amended, "if he can prove he was really in Austin yesterday."

Maris gave a start; she'd made two more calls to Keir at his Austin home, but had gotten only the answering machine. It bothered her, bothered her a lot.

313

For the first time in a very long while, she actually *felt* like leaning on someone, and now he was unavailable.

"I wish someone would shoot Drew Eniston," Sophie said in a perfectly calm voice. "I wish they'd kill him like the mad dog he is, and I could go on with my life."

Startled, Maris swung around to face the old woman. Sophie's face was composed as always; but her hands were clasped a little too tightly, and her gaze darted around the room as though hoping to find salvation written upon the walls.

"Mrs. Hauck—"

"That's how I feel, Maris. Thirty-four years ago, Eniston killed my daughter and all but tore this family apart. Now he's doing it again, and making a horrible, evil game of it. I want it to stop."

"We all do, Mother," John said.

The touch of impatience in his voice caught Maris's attention. He and Robyn shared the sofa, their positions so different as to be striking. John sprawled out over half the sofa, his arms flung wide. Robyn had curled herself in the opposite corner, her legs tucked beneath her, her arms crossed tightly over her chest.

And yet there was something similar in their expressions; both had a taut, shadowed look about the eyes, the look of people who'd just had their world turned upside down and inside out. John managed to hide most of it, but Robyn wasn't handling it well. Her lips were bloodless, pressed so tightly together that Maris could see the outlines of her teeth through them. No, Robyn wasn't handling it well.

Maris turned back to the window. She breathed

314

hard on the glass, fogging the image of the people behind her. A tow truck went by, yellow lights revolving slowly. She leaned forward, trying to see better.

"What is it, Maris?" John asked.

"A tow truck just went by."

"The police are impounding that rental car they found just west of the estate," he said. "The rental agreement read Ellen Smith, but I think we're going to find that the fingerprints match Ella Florian's."

Maris lifted one shoulder, dropped it again. Whatever her name—Ellen Smith, Ella Florian—the woman was dead. "So she came to see me, had a flat tire, and decided to walk it. And Eniston shot her."

"I think it's the most probable explanation."

Eniston, Eniston, Eniston. His actions simply made no sense. First Lee, then her baby, then Ella, then Zios. Four lives, and for what? Was the man a pure psychopath, completely beyond normal understanding, or was there an answer buried somewhere in this mess?

Hearing the door open behind her, Maris turned to see Bobby Peterus come into the room. He looked like hell. There were dark purple smudges beneath his eyes, and every line in his face seemed to have grown deeper in the past few hours. *Having a person die in front of you tends to do things like that,* she thought, too bitterly.

"You asked to see me, Mrs. Hauck?" Peterus asked.

Sophie laid her arms along the arms of the wing chair. That proud Hauck nose lifted and aimed itself at Peterus. "Yes, I did," she said. "You have until noon today to remove yourself, your men and all your equipment from my property."

315

"Mother!" John shot up off the sofa.

"No, John. I should have done this days ago."

Peterus shrugged. "Don't worry about it, Senator."

"I *have* to worry about it," John snapped. "I've got a house and people to protect—"

"I asked the police to help us. Detective Morales has agreed to station three men here to take care of security."

John wheeled in a circle, flinging his arms out dramatically. "Three? Come on, Mother. If twenty of Bobby's men couldn't keep this place secure, how are three going to do the job?"

"They couldn't do worse," the old woman said.

"Mother—"

"I've made my decision, John. Mr. Peterus goes."

"He stays."

"Don't use that tone of voice with me, young man."

"I am not your little boy!" John shouted. Veins stood out on his forehead.

"And I am not one of your employees, to take orders without question."

Maris looked from one to the other, following the argument as though it were a tennis match. And argument it was; Sophie was tight-lipped and furious, and John looked like a man who had expected to get his way and been handed a very nasty surprise.

Robyn sat up. "Mother, I don't think—"

"Hush, Robyn. This is between me and your brother."

"Now, Mother," John said, holding his hands up in a conciliatory gesture. "Why don't you go upstairs and get some sleep, and we can discuss this when we're all feeling better?"

"I feel fine, thank you."

The senator's jaw tightened, and for a moment he looked just like his mother as they faced off. Maris noticed that his fists were clenched.

And that was when she realized what had happened here: bit by bit, the carefully maintained structure of this family was unraveling. And all courtesy of Drew Eniston. If he'd planned this, he couldn't have done it better.

A month ago, the Haucks wouldn't have changed their breakfast time for an earthquake. Now Mama and Favorite Son were squaring off in a bitter argument *in front of outsiders*.

"You don't know what you're doing here," John said, too softly. "Daddy—"

"Your father had no patience with failure."

"He had no patience with anything."

"He got results. If he hadn't become ill, he would have been governor of this state."

John's voice got low and deadly. "Well, he didn't get there, did he? *I'm* the one who's going to be governor. *I'm* the one who's going to get results!"

Now that the dam was broken, the Haucks were getting it all out in one knock-down-drag-out-all-those-long-buried-emotions argument. Great. But Maris didn't want to be a witness to it. The emotions were too jagged, too powerful, and she had problems of her own. She walked out.

And nearly ran down Mrs. Munoz, who was making a show of dusting the baseboards in the hall. The housekeeper straightened.

"Good morning, Mrs. Munoz," Maris said.

"Good morning, Señora Durant," the older woman replied with perfect aplomb.

317

Maris admired her poise. She and the housekeeper stared at each other, neither moving while John and Sophie's angry voices swirled around them.

Maybe it was fatigue, maybe the flat insolence of the housekeeper's gaze, but Maris just *had* to needle her. "Don't you have maids to do that sort of thing?" she asked.

Mrs. Munoz's black eyes didn't waver a millimeter. "They did not wish to come in today, señora. The murder, you know, it frightens them."

"What about you? Aren't you frightened?"

"This is my home, señora."

The housekeeper turned and walked away. Maris stared after her, then shrugged and continued on toward the back of the house. She had to get outside; as big as this place was, the walls were beginning to close in on her.

"Mrs. Durant!" Peterus called from behind her.

She stopped and waited for him to catch up. He looked as tired as she felt, and might be out of a job to boot. In a sudden burst of sympathy, she said, "I was going to get some fresh air on the patio. Want to come?"

"Sure."

As they walked toward the rear of the house, Maris felt strangely at ease with him. Maybe sharing Ella's death had built a rapport between them. It was welcome.

Outside, it was warm but very breezy, the wind driving the clouds pell-mell across the sky. Maris's hair whipped around her face, blinding her, and she dragged it back into a ponytail with her hands.

"Do you think you'll have a job when it's all

318

over?" Maris thrust her thumb toward the house.

"Nah," he said. "The old woman's going to win. She was riding high, fast and furious."

"I'm sorry," Maris said.

He shrugged. "It was a losing proposition from the start. No one can keep this place secure. Oh, they can build a wall with razor wire on top, put bars on all the windows, and maybe, *maybe* keep someone like Drew Eniston out. But hell, then all the guy has to do is get his hands on a rifle with a scope. Bang, bang, you're dead."

Maris shuddered. "Do *you* think he killed that woman? Just shot her down, thinking she was Sophie Hauck?"

"I don't know. I'm just glad to be out of it." He glanced at her from the corner of his eye. "You did okay out there last night. Better than I did, although it hurts my ego to say it."

"She still died."

"Not your fault. It was that .44 that killed her. That's a big mother of a slug, Mrs. Durant."

"Maris," she said absently, staring at the expanse of ground over which Ella had crawled last night. Something nagged at her, something important. "Will you show me the gully where the scarf was found?"

"Sure, but we can only look; the cops have been busy with their little yellow ribbons."

"Looking is fine."

The breeze plucked at their clothing as they walked across the lawn. A trail of crushed and uprooted grass marked Ella's path, punctuated by dark, ominous stains. The woman had crawled, stopped to rest, crawled again, her lifeblood pouring out of her

319

with every movement.

"She fought hard," Peterus said.

"Yeah." *Ella fought hard to live, fought hard to tell me that one word, "Zios." She lost her life, and I don't have a clue as to what "Zios" means.* Maris wrapped her arms around herself. "Cold out here, isn't it?"

It wasn't cold. But Peterus glanced at her, understanding in his eyes. He moved on. The footing roughened as they left the formal lawn behind. Here, a finger of the woods poked out, shielding the view of the street.

"The gully's just up ahead," Peterus said.

It was more a shallow ditch than a gully, its walls festooned with weeds and honeysuckle. A section of vines had been stripped away, apparently as Ella had clawed her way upward through them. Dried blood was dark against the green of the leaves.

"She fell into the gully there." Peterus pointed to the opposite side of the ditch, where the vegetation was crushed.

"Where exactly was she shot?" Maris asked.

"I don't know. If the cops know, they're not saying."

Peterus led her toward the road, where the gully became shallower. He leaped over it, holding his hand out to help her after him. A stretch of freshly painted white rail fence separated the property from the road.

"There's where the rental car was found," he said. "Looks like she had a flat, and decided to take the shorter route across the lawn."

A nearby section of ground about four-foot-square was enclosed by yellow plastic ribbon strung

320

on stakes. Peterus led her toward it, talking fast and easy like a good tour guide. "See how much blood is on the ground here? She fell here, and lay here for some time before she started crawling toward the house."

"How long do you think it took her?"

He spread his hands. "Too long."

Maris opened her mouth, then closed it again. "I don't know why no one heard the shot."

"Remember, it was garbage day. Refuse trucks were roaring up and down the road all afternoon, loud as hell."

"Oh, right. I forgot all about that."

Frowning, Maris scuffed at the spiky leaves of a dandelion with her foot. A cloud shadow passed over her, bringing on a shiver. She watched the dark shape rush fleetly over the ground, changing to accommodate the contours of rocks and grass. It dipped into the gully, then slid up the opposite bank and rushed to lose itself among the trees.

Maris stood still, caught by a memory that had burst like a bottle-rocket into her mind. Déjà vu, deep and visceral, from the day before, when another shadow had moved swiftly over the ground, its shape distorting as it passed over the rutted driveway of the abandoned restaurant. Her memory followed, picking out details she hadn't realized she'd registered. Most of the ruts were old. But there were some where the heavy matting of weeds had been compressed. There had been more than one set, although she couldn't quite remember how many. But that meant more than one car.

Ella had been there. Something or someone had either drawn or frightened her away. *Did I lead Enis-*

ton to her? Did he follow me, and somehow figure out our meeting place from my route? Maris drew a deep breath, remembering the gas station attendant who had given her directions. Had she been chatty to someone else, someone who managed to get there before her?

God, this is so confusing! And then, almost against her will, *I wish Keir were here!*

She felt so alone. Alone and scared, and feeling that the police weren't going to get to the bottom of this until it was too late. Who was next? Eniston could be hiding in the woods just over there, a gun trained on her heart. Was he squinting down the sight now? Even at this moment, was his finger tightening on the trigger? Would she hear the shot, or only feel it?

Like a lamb to the slaughter. Bang, bang, you're dead.

Maris rejected it savagely. She'd fought every battle that could be won, and some that couldn't. Eniston wasn't going to beat her. At least, not easily, and not without paying a price for it.

Zios. Ella had held Death himself at bay long enough to whisper that word. It was time to find out what it meant.

"Let's go," she said to Peterus. "I've seen enough."

They took a different path back to the house, neither wanting to follow Ella's silent, poignant trail. Peterus opened the door for Maris, but didn't follow her in.

As she turned to go, he said, "At least she didn't die in that ditch. Alone."

"Yeah," Maris said, closing the door. *She came to die in my arms, and I forgot to pray for her.*

322

The lower floor was deserted, everyone apparently having gone to bed. Maris, aching from lack of sleep, wished she could do the same. But her mind kept chanting "Zios, Zios," and she knew she wasn't going to get rid of it until she did something about it.

She trotted upstairs to Cyndi's room. The child was asleep, one arm out of the covers, the hand palm upward, fingers in a relaxed curve. The model horse had fallen out of her grasp and lay a few centimeters beyond her fingertips. Maris sighed, beset with sudden memories of dimpled baby hands, warm against her lips as she kissed them. Then her gaze caught the red Cardinal's cap on the nightstand. The white lettering caught the light, almost seeming to wink at her.

"I love you, baby," she murmured, turning away.

She hurried to Robyn's room and knocked softly at the door. A moment later it opened.

"I didn't wake you, did I?" Maris asked.

"No. Is something wrong?" Robyn opened the door wider.

"No, nothing's wrong. I just wanted to ask a favor of you. I've got to go to Houston for a couple of hours—"

"Now? "

"Now. Would you mind watching Cyndi for me?" Maris took a deep breath. "I'd take her with me, but if Eniston is watching the house and follows me . . . I want her to be safe."

Robyn nodded, her fatigue-shadowed eyes like bruises against her pale skin. "Don't worry. I'll keep her safe."

"I'll be back by noon, no later."

"Take your time. Cyndi and I will have loads of fun."

Great," Maris said. "I just checked on her, and she's still asleep. If she doesn't find me in my room—"

"I'll go up and lie down with her so she won't be alarmed."

Impulsively, Maris reached out and clasped the older woman's hand. "Thanks, Robyn."

"No problem."

Echoes of Cyndi, Maris thought as she loped toward the stairway. She could feel Robyn watching her.

Twenty-four

"How are you doing over here?" Fancie Foster asked in her warm-honey drawl.

Maris looked up. The librarian was wearing a jade green and black dress and matching knee-length jacket, and looked gorgeous. All that bounteous beauty made Maris feel like a scarecrow.

Then she noticed the stack of books half-buried between the woman's arm and generous bosom. "Oh, no!"

The bosom jiggled with laughter. "You look like you've seen a snake."

"Fancie, I'd rather it be a snake. I had no idea there was so much material to go through."

"Honey, we haven't even *gotten* to the hard stuff, yet. You come in here with a single word to research, and not knowing whether it's a person, place or thing, and you're lucky I don't set the whole library right in your lap."

"I know, I know."

"I sure hope you find what you're looking for. If it were a more accessible subject, we'd have no problem a'tall. Whoops, there's somebody at my desk. Holler if you need anything."

She hurried away, ample hips swaying. Maris sighed. She hadn't finished the first stack, and now she had another to go through. So much information, none of which was useful to her.

She had referenced and cross-referenced "Zios," to no avail. Fancie had been great, steering her from the microfiche to the encyclopedias, to phone books, to magazines and back to the microfiche. Oh, there were pages and pages in the phone book—four in Houston alone—of people named Zios, Zeos, Zees and Zeus. If Maris had a spare day or two, she might even have time to call them all.

"And then what do I say?" she muttered. "Do I ask 'Are you or anyone you know named Ella or Ellen? Oh, and by the way—do you happen to know a murderer named Drew Eniston?'"

She pressed the heels of her hands against her eyes. It was nearly ten-thirty. She had been awake for twenty-eight hours, and there was a week's worth of work sitting on the table in front of her. She forced herself to look down at her scanty notes. Was Zios a person's first or last name, or was it a place? The writing blurred, and she closed her eyes. "God, I need a break." She pushed away from the table and headed for the front of the library. A storm was brewing outside, the brooding sky tinted even darker by the smoked-glass windows. Papers skittered like mad butterflies across the parking lot.

Fancie was at the desk, her plump fingers darting over the computer keyboard with impressive speed. She paused to look up at Maris. "Need something, honey?"

"May I use your phone for a minute?"

"Sure. Just come around here and sit in that green chair so you can reach it." She turned back to her keyboard. "Looks like we're going to get some weather. Weatherman says a line of thunderstorms is moving into the area, dumping a whole lot of water. It's going to be a slam-doozey of a day."

Maris nodded absently as she dialed Gavilan's number. Three rings, four. Then someone picked up.

"Gavilan." John's smooth tones were unmistakable.

"Senator? It's Maris. Is everything okay out there?"

"Just fine. Quiet as a . . ." he checked himself, then continued, "as a church service. Cyndi's doing fine. She and Robyn are up in the attic, digging out generations of Hauck toys, but I can send Alejo up—"

"No, don't bother," she said. "Just give her my love when she comes down."

"I will. By the way, she said to tell you to bring either pizza or Burger Wonder hamburgers home for lunch."

That kid. Tired as she was, Maris couldn't help but smile. "Tell her it'll be pizza."

"Morales called to say the fingerprints in the rental car matched the murdered woman's. One thing's for certain, she isn't Ella Florian."

"Has anyone . . . claimed her?"

"They can't contact relatives until they know who she is, and that might never happen, especially since there was no match in the FBI fingerprint files."

"Has Keir called?" she asked.

"Keir?" he repeated. "Wait a second, let me ask. Bobby!" His voice became muffled, probably by his hand over the mouthpiece. "Have there been any calls for Mrs. Durant? Okay, I'll tell her."

A moment later his voice came through clearly

again. "No, Keir hasn't called. He may not have gotten your message; last I heard, he was headed out to kibitz a rally for my opponent. If it's important, I'll see if I can track him down—"

"It's not that important," she said. "If he does happen to call, would you just tell him I've been trying to reach him?"

"You've got it."

"Thanks."

"You be careful," he said. "We've got half the law enforcement people in East Texas looking hard for Eniston, but he's given them all the slip. He's found himself a real good hidey-hole somewhere. When are you planning to get back?"

"Sometime around noon," she said.

"Okay. We'll be watching out for you."

"Thanks."

She hung up. Leaning her elbows on the desk, she propped her chin in her hands and stared out at the storm. Big, fat drops were beginning to fall, patterning the dusty ground with dark splotches.

"Hey, wake up," Fancie called.

"Sorry," she mumbled. "I was a million miles away."

The librarian got to her feet, reaching to pick up an armload of just-returned books. "I've been thinking," she said. "This Zios being so hard to find and all . . . well, I've been wondering about it. Are you sure it's contemporary?"

"Contemporary?" Maris echoed, astonishment slashing through her tired brain. God, she'd been blind! Blind and deaf and stupid! What had been the connection throughout this whole thing? Not Eniston, not Ella—not people at all, but a date. May 23, 1958.

328

"I just wondered about it, since we had so much trouble — "

"Yes! " Maris cried, sending the startled librarian back a step. "Thank you! I'll need the newspaper files for May, 1958."

Fancie blushed like a teenager. "I guess you like the idea, then. You go sit down, and I'll get them for you."

Maris went through the May 23, 1958 paper. She read it top to bottom and end to end, but there was no Zios anywhere. Ditto with May 24. Completely frustrated, she leaned her forehead against the cool glass of the microfiche reader.

"Going to fight me all the way, aren't you?" she muttered.

Taking a deep breath, she got back to work. May 25 turned out to be a bust, and so was May 26. But on May 27, she hit pay dirt. It was a brief story, buried far back in the newspaper:

Local woman found dead, death ruled accidental. The body of Serafina Zios, age 47, was found lying facedown in a flooded ditch in a remote section of Deer Park. She was apparently the victim of a hit and run. Police estimate the time of death to have been sometime Tuesday morning. Zios, of the 900 block of Navigation, was a midwife serving the Mexican community. She is survived by her husband, Jesus, daughter Ella, and son Roberto.

Ella. Ella *Zios*.

Maris could hear Ella in her mind, that faint, labored voice with the note of death in it. "He killed her, too," she'd said, struggling to stay alive long enough to give her warning. "He killed her, too." Serafina Zios had died one day after Lee Hauck had been shot to death. Serafina Zios had been a midwife; Lee Hauck had just given birth.

"Oh, God!" Maris whispered. "Oh, God!"

Whirling away from the microfiche, Maris ran to the table that was still high-piled with reference books. She dug out an atlas from the stack and flipped through it until she found a map of Houston. Memory pinpointed the location of the apartment where Lee Hauck had died. Now all she had to do was find the 900 block of Navigation.

And there it was. Maris sank down hard in the nearest chair. Serafina had lived not three blocks from Lee and Drew's apartment.

He killed her, too.

Moving like a sleepwalker, Maris got up and walked back to the microfiche. Still, she had to see it. Her hand trembled as she scrolled back to the front page of the May 26 *Houston Chronicle*. The headline read, SOCIALITE'S LOVER ARRESTED FOR MURDER.

Drew Eniston was arrested Monday afternoon and charged with first-degree murder in the brutal slaying of Leonora (Lee) Hauck, daughter of Senator Ballard Hauck. Mr. Eniston will be held . . .

Maris closed her eyes. Monday afternoon. Drew Eniston had been in jail at the time of Serafina's death.

There were too many possibilities. Too many uncertainties. Ella had been dying, her words disjointed.

"Maybe I heard wrong," Maris said. "Maybe I put it together wrong."

But maybe wasn't good enough. Ella's last mark upon this world had been that trail of blood, a battle fought only to get those words spoken. Everything had just been turned upside down, the line between

330

bad guys and good guys blurred, the very structure of safety and danger shattering.

And Gavilan was right in the middle of it. Maris surged to her feet, ignoring the scattering of papers behind her, and ran to the librarian's desk.

Fancie looked up, her eyes widening. "Is something wrong, honey?"

Maris grabbed the phone and pulled it closer, stabbing at the numbers with her finger. She counted nine rings before it was picked up.

"Hello?"

The woman's voice was blurred and frantic-sounding, and Maris didn't recognize it. "Who is this?" she demanded. "Isn't this the Hauck residence?"

"Maris? Oh, thank God you called!"

"Mrs. Hauck?" Terror beat frantically in Maris's chest. *That* was Sophie Hauck? "What's happened? What's wrong?"

"Eniston . . . Eniston . . ." The old woman broke down completely.

Maris struggled with her own fear to keep her voice calm. "Mrs. Hauck, settle down. Take a deep breath—"

"I can't," Sophie sobbed. "He broke in . . . I tried to stop him, but he . . . knocked me down. . . . He went upstairs and he . . . Oh, I don't know how to . . ."

"What happened?" Maris screamed.

"He . . . took . . . Cyndi."

Maris whirled, dropping the phone and snatching her keys from her pocket in one motion.

"Maris? Maris!" Fancie cried.

Maris hit the door at a run, flinging it open as she pelted out into the rain. Water splashed up as she ran through puddles, wetting her jeans to the knees.

A moment later she was in the Regal, slamming it into gear. She gunned it out of the parking lot, nearly causing an accident as she hurtled out into the street.

He's got my daughter.

She made an illegal U-turn, scattering oncoming traffic. Horns blared angrily, but she was already moving around the next corner.

The freeway was a couple of hundred yards ahead. She took the ramp much too fast. The Regal slued crazily, but held the road. Once on the freeway, she stomped the accelerator pedal to the floor and held it there as she weaved recklessly through the traffic.

Terror rode with her, a presence that gripped her soul with black carrion hands. She drove in a haze, her hands and feet controlling the car while her mind tormented itself with images that were too terrible to be seen, too terrible to ignore.

Is he hurting her?

Will I ever see her again, or will I bury an empty coffin like Sophie did?

Maris felt her breath burning in her chest and realized she'd been holding it. Her hands gripped the wheel so hard, her knuckles looked as if they might burst through the skin.

"I'm coming, baby," she said.

The storm grew steadily worse. As she exited the highway onto South County Road, visibility was down to a few hundred yards. The city of Hauck, which lay straight ahead, was lost in a slate blue cloak of rain. Thunder was an almost physical force, the nearly constant noise thrumming along her nerves. Wind tore at the Regal and sent the rain slashing almost horizontally across the road.

The only awareness Maris had of Hauck was the

332

red eye of a stoplight that seemed to stare accusingly at her as she passed beneath it. Then she was on her way down Aberdeen Road, the last stretch. The road was awash, but she just kept the car centered between the double border of white picket fence.

One mile, two, three, four. . . . She slowed down, watching for the turn-off to Gavilan. The sign was down, hanging along one side of the arch. Ahead, the house lay like a huge tortoise in the rain, shedding water from its gleaming, red-tiled back. There wasn't a single light on; the storm must have knocked out the electricity.

She parked in front. Rain thundered on the hot hood, sending a plume of steam up to be shredded by the wind. Flinging the door open, Maris ran up the steps toward the house.

Sophie opened the door as she approached. She seemed to have regained a measure of control; but her eyes were red and swollen from crying, and she reached out to Maris with a tentative, groping gesture.

"Have they found Cyndi?" Maris gasped.

Sophie shook her head.

Maris's breath went out in a rush, and she put her hand on the door frame for support.

"They'll find her," the old woman said. "He's not going to get away with this; they went after him moments after he ran out of here. Come inside—"

"I'm going after her." Maris straightened abruptly and fumbled in her pockets for her keys. "Which way did they go?"

Sophie's tightened. "Running after them is not going to do any good, Maris. It's been nearly an hour now."

"But—"

"John said to tell you to stay put. He promised to call every half-hour to update you on how the search is going. And look at the weather out there! You're not going to help Cyndi by getting yourself drowned in a ditch somewhere."

Maris tried to shrug loose, but the old woman just held on tighter. "Maris, listen to me! The electricity is out, but the phones are still working. John said you'll do more good coordinating calls than driving aimlessly around."

Maris's breath went out in a long sigh. It was logical and sensible, and she hated it. "You're right." *Damn it.*

"Of course I'm right. Fortunately, we still have gas, and I just put the teapot on to boil. Why don't you come into the kitchen and let me make you a nice, hot cup of tea?"

Maris let the old woman lead her into the kitchen. Rosalia's domain. But Rosalia and her bright, accented chatter were gone, leaving it merely a room. The big window framed the roiling clouds outside. A trio of fat candles sat in the center of the table, dripping wax onto the polished wood.

"Rosalia, like the maids, did not come in today," Sophie said. The teapot was just beginning to hiss. "Although I'm all but useless in the kitchen, I *can* at least boil water." She urged Maris down onto a chair, then bustled over to the stove.

She talked the entire time she dealt with mugs and tea bags, sugar and honey and lemon wedges. The stream of bright, chirpy chatter was so completely unsuited to the woman and the situation that Maris's shoulders hunched under the burden of hearing it.

Finally, Sophie brought a pair of steaming mugs and set them down at the table. "I don't know whether you take sugar or not, but I put it in anyway," she said. "It will give you a boost. If you'd like something to eat, I might be able—"

"No," Maris said through clenched teeth. "Thank you."

"Well, how about—"

"No, Mrs. Hauck."

The old woman's gaze dropped to the mug in front of her. "Strange, to be doing something so quiet and domestic, when all the world seems to be running out of control."

"Yeah, strange." Frustration at her own helplessness made Maris's fingers twitch. It would be so much easier to jump in the car and look for Cyndi, even uselessly. At least it would be *something.*

She looked for the phone and found it on the wall beside the refrigerator. Why didn't it ring? How long was she supposed to sit here, while . . . She didn't have the courage to think about what might be going on.

"Tell me how it happened, Mrs. Hauck," she said.

"I had just finished dressing," the old woman said. The candle flames were reflected in her dark eyes. "I opened my door, ready to come downstairs and get something to eat, when I heard a loud crash from the attic. Since Robyn and Cyndi had been rummaging around in there for at least an hour, I didn't think anything of it. Then someone screamed. I . . . I'm not sure if it was Cyndi or Robyn. But I'll never forget . . ." Closing her eyes, she pressed her lips tight for a moment. "I rushed out into the hall just as that . . . man ran by, Cyndi in his arms. I tried to grab her, but he knocked me down and raced away. The policemen tried to stop him, but they couldn't

335

shoot, not with the child in his arms like that. Oh, Maris, I'm so sorry!"

Through the roaring in her ears, Maris thought she heard her daughter's voice. Calling for her. *Help me, Mom!* Her breath came fast and hot, as though she'd been running.

"Don't," Sophie said. "You can't panic. Not now."

Maris closed her eyes, striving for control. After a moment, she nodded. "Okay. I'm okay."

But she wasn't. Shivers rippled through her, a quivering layer around a core of solid fear. She wrapped her hands around the mug, trying to absorb its heat.

Her mind reeled, frantically searching for an anchor in the midst of chaos. And finding none. Lee Hauck dead, Serafina and Ella Zios dead, an infant dead. Two killed by Eniston's hand, by his own admission. Then what of Serafina, who had died at a time when he *could not* have killed her? And what about Ella? "He killed her, too," Ella had said. Maris was sure she'd meant Serafina. Had it been merely a dying woman's delirium?

Lee Hauck and child. Serafina Zios and child. Two mother/daughter teams. And what now? Was it to be Maris and Cyndi Durant? *Not Cyndi, please. Anything but Cyndi!*

"I can't stand this!" Maris jumped to her feet, sending the mug crashing down onto the floor. Porcelain and tea splattered.

"You have to stand it," Sophie said. "For Cyndi's sake."

Fists clenched, Maris stalked to the window. The storm was moving north, toward Houston. But another was marching on its heels, turning the southern sky an ominous blue-black. A webwork of

336

lightning sketched fire across the swollen underbelly of the clouds. But even Nature couldn't match the storm raging inside her. To have Cyndi back safe, she'd do anything. Anything.

She closed her eyes. Behind her, she could hear the clink of pottery as Sophie picked up the broken mug. "Mrs. Hauck," she asked, "why did he take my daughter?"

The clinking stopped. "Why did he take mine?" the old woman whispered.

Maris turned around to find the old woman kneeling on the floor, staring blindly at the handful of broken porcelain she held. Blood dotted her fingers where she'd held the jagged glass too tightly.

Maris drew her breath in a sharp sigh. For the first time, she realized how deeply Sophie was suffering. Her daughter's murder was as clear and painful today as it had been then. The old woman was holding on by her fingernails, and losing ground. Drew Eniston couldn't have hurt her more if he'd held a gun to her head and pulled the trigger.

Maris knelt beside Sophie. "Mrs. Hauck—"

"I'm sorry, Maris. I, of all people, know what you're feeling right now, and I meant to be strong for you."

Gently, Maris lifted the broken glass from the old woman's hand. No amount of strength was enough to bear something like this, or to help someone else bear it. And there were no words of comfort, for her or for Sophie.

"Hello, ladies," John said from the doorway.

"John!" Sophie cried, scrambling up from the floor to hurl herself into his arms. "Oh, my son! I've been so frightened! I needed you . . . *we* needed you!"

337

"Yes, Mother." He held her loosely, almost impersonally, staring over her head at Maris. The flickering candlelight picked out the silver threads in his hair.

"Is there any news?" Maris asked. "Have they found Cyndi?"

"No," he said. "They haven't. But I—"

The phone rang, the shrill, imperative sound seeming to echo through the kitchen. Maris was on her feet and moving before she'd quite realized what she was doing.

"I'll get it," John said, intercepting her adroitly. Lifting the receiver to his ear, he said, "John Hauck. Oh, hello, Keir. Did you just get back in town? No, Maris still isn't back. I haven't heard from her all morning."

Maris gaped at him, completely dumfounded. Then anger swept her shock away, and she stepped forward, intending to snatch the phone out of his hands.

That was when she saw the gun.

Twenty-five

Almost casually, John aimed the gun at her.

To Maris, it looked like a very big gun. She stared at the muzzle, afraid to move, afraid to speak, afraid even to breathe, while John continued his conversation with Keir as though nothing out of the ordinary had happened.

"Yes, I told her you called earlier, and I told her it was important. I don't know where she is now. If I do hear from her, I'll tell her you called again. And now I'd better—What?" He fell silent, listening intently. A flush spread over his cheeks. "I'm sorry you feel that way. This is going to have a negative impact on your career, you know. How? I'll tell you how." His voice rose to a shout. "Because I'm going to see to it. When I'm finished with you, you'll be lucky to get a job shoveling manure!"

He slammed the phone down. "He quit! He's walking out of the campaign, says it's a matter of principle. He doesn't think I'm the right man for the job. God *damn* him to hell!"

At another time Maris might have been glad. Now there was only room for fear.

For a moment the senator stood still, breathing heavily, then turned his full attention on her again.

His eyes had turned flat and ugly, and she felt her knees start to shake.

"Why don't you have a seat?" he said.

"John, what are you doing?" Sophie's words were staccato and harsh, as though they'd been driven out of her by a physical blow.

"What does it look like, Mother?" he asked. "Sit down, Maris."

"I'd rather stand."

The muzzle of the gun moved slightly, centering on her chest. "It wasn't a request."

Maris sat.

"John, put that gun down this instant!" Sophie cried. She clutched at his arm, almost losing her balance when he shoved her away.

"Didn't Daddy ever tell you not to touch a man who's holding a gun? Go get yourself a cup of tea, Mother. I have a story to tell you."

The old woman backed away from him. Her square, sturdy frame looked shrunken and fragile, as though all vitality had been sucked out of her. She settled in the seat beside Maris, looking neither to the right nor left, only at John.

A lot of things were falling into place in Maris's mind, settling like the madly whirling flakes of a Christmas snow scene.

"Drew Eniston took Cyndi to *save* her," she said. "From you."

John grimaced. "That bastard. He must have been hidden somewhere close, 'cause he broke in not ten minutes after Peterus and his men left."

"Your mother gave them until noon."

"I didn't."

"You were going to get rid of the policemen, too, weren't you?" she asked.

He smiled. "Of course. I found an errand for Mrs. Munoz and Alejo, too. So don't worry, we have complete privacy."

Maris couldn't take her gaze off the gun. She'd looked down the barrel of a gun once before. A gun held by this man. At that time, she'd thought he'd come to shoot at Eniston. But he hadn't. He'd been shooting at her. If she hadn't moved. . . . "What kind of gun is that, Senator?" she asked.

"It's a .44 caliber. I doubt you're interested in the manufacturer."

"No," she agreed. "The police might be, though."

"I don't understand," Sophie said.

"Of course not, Mother. You never did." John's gaze flicked back to Maris. "So Ella *did* tell you."

"She didn't say who. She only gave me pieces of it, and the name Zios."

"What is going on?" Sophie half-rose to her feet. "What are you talking about?"

Maris saw John's gun hand twitch nervously. For one horrified moment she thought he was going to shoot his mother. Slowly, so as not to startle him, she grasped Sophie's wrist and urged her into her seat. "Mrs. Hauck, he killed Ella Florian. Or rather, Ella Zios."

"Who . . . my son . . . my son *killed* that woman?"

"Yes, I killed her," he said in a voice as quiet and chilling as death itself. "I shot her with this gun. Bang, right in the chest."

"Don't," Maris said. "Send her away. She doesn't need to hear this."

"Yes, she does. She's a star player in it."

Sophie shook her head. "No . . ."

"Yes." He came forward, facing the two women

341

like a lawyer arguing his case before a jury. "You see, she killed my sister."

Anger sparked in Maris's chest, ran along her veins in a hot tide. "Come on, Senator. Leave the political game-playing alone for a minute. Why don't you take responsibility—"

"Yes, let's talk about responsibility. This woman"—he pointed at Sophie—"only knew how to love one person. And that was Ballard Hauck. Blindly, slavishly, she loved him. He wanted to be governor. She wanted to be *Mrs. Governor*. And she didn't give a damn who had to pay the price for that dream."

"What's wrong with a woman loving her husband?" Sophie cried. "What's wrong with helping him realize his dream? Ballard should have been governor. He had the talent, the brains, the integrity—"

"Integrity!" John shouted. "He was a bastard. A sleazy, slimy, son-of-a bitch—"

Sophie slapped him. He drew back, his teeth bared like an animal's. Then he leaned forward and slashed the back of his hand across her cheek. His face mottled with ugly color, he drew his arm back again.

"Don't," Maris said, striving to keep her voice calm. "She's your mother, Senator."

His eyes were still wild, but he lowered his arm. "Why do you still defend him, Mother? When are you going to see him for what he is?"

"I *know* what he is, John. A good man, a great man—"

"God!" he cried, raking his left hand through his hair. "How can you go through life being so blind and deaf that you can't even see what's going on in your own house? What do you think Daddy was doing while you were going to teas and speaking at women's clubs to garner support for wonderful Senator Hauck? Well, I'll tell you what he was doing. He was here, fucking your children."

"I don't know what you're talking about," Sophie said.

"Then, let me say it again. Daddy. Was. Fucking. Your. Children. I think that ought to be clear enough, even to you, Mother."

He leaned close, his eyes boring into Sophie's. "He started in on Lee when she was eleven. Why do you think she took up with Eniston? He was nothing, came from nothing and was never going to be other than nothing. But she loved him. Why? Because he took Daddy up by the lapels and told him he'd rip his balls off if he came near her again."

Sophie shook her head, denying it all.

John bore in closer. "Daddy started in on me when I was ten. Yes, Mother. Me. His son. He didn't care what he screwed as long as it was young and scared."

"It couldn't have happened," Sophie whispered. "Lee would have told me—"

"You thought Daddy was a god! You never looked beyond him to see the frightened eyes of your children. The one time Lee tried to tell you—sugar-coating it like we've sugar-coated all the bad news for our dear, emotionally fragile mother—you patted her on the head and told her Daddy was just being affectionate."

He pushed away from the table and began pacing again. "Thirty-four years ago, there was no such thing as child abuse. No one listened to a kid. No one believed the word of a child over the parents. And who was going to believe anything bad about the handsome, powerful Senator Hauck? Surely not

343

you, Mother. God, I think you'd have held us down for him if that would have made him happy."

Sophie shook her head. Tears ran unheeded down her cheeks, spotting the front of her pale blue dress.

"You let him have us, Mother," John said. "You turned your back and let that bastard have us. And you know something else? The older he got, the younger he liked them."

"I don't believe it," the old woman gasped.

"Believe it," Robyn said from the doorway.

As they all turned to look at her, she stepped forward into the room. She looked terribly young in the candlelight, and terribly beautiful. Her indigo eyes were black against the extreme pallor of her face. "He started on me when I was six."

"Six . . ." Sophie closed her eyes. "Garrick, too?"

"You don't think he'd stop with three, do you?" John asked. "Remember what you've always told us? Daddy never, ever left a job unfinished."

Maris wrapped her arms around herself, drawing in, wishing she could push the ugliness away. So much destruction caused by one man. The *patrón*. Head of the family, the protector . . . and even now, the family was dancing to his tune. Tearing themselves apart because he was no longer able to do it.

"Why did you kill that woman?" Sophie whispered.

"Ella Zios?" John asked. He smiled. "Tell her, Maris. I know you've figured that much out."

"Ella Zios was the daughter of Serafina Zios," Maris said. "Serafina was the midwife who delivered Lee's baby."

He nodded. "Right on the money. That's how low my sister had fallen, letting some Mexican deliver her child."

344

"You killed Serafina, too," Maris said. "Drew Eniston was in jail when she died."

"Of course I killed her. She knew I shot Lee."

Sophie moaned, an inarticulate cry of pain. "Please, God, not this. Anything but this!"

"Oh, Mother, spare us the dramatics," he drawled.

"You knew?" The old woman turned to Robyn. "You knew all along?"

"He came in that night with his clothes all bloody," Robyn said. "I helped him put everything in the washer."

"All these years . . . You . . . you never said a word. That man spent thirty-four years in prison for something he didn't do."

Robyn bent her head, putting her eyes in shadow. "That night, he stopped Daddy from . . . hurting me. He frightened Daddy into promising not to touch me again. For that, I'd have left ten men in prison."

"Oh, dear God." Sophie buried her face in her hands.

Understanding speared through Maris's brain, bright as the lightning outside. Lee, her baby, Serafina and Ella—so many lives, so much pain. And John standing there, secure in his handsome armor, polishing it to a shine that repelled all life's dirt and ugliness. Well, it wasn't going to work.

"Oh, Robyn!" she said. "So you made him your hero? You protected him all these years for it? Think about it now, without the judgments of the child you were. He did it for himself, not for you."

"What?" Robyn's head jerked up.

Maris gave it to her straight and hard. "If he'd really been protecting you, he would have killed *Ballard*."

345

"Bravo, Maris." John was still smiling, but there was a ruddy stain above each cheekbone. He shoved away from the doorjamb. "You're right. Daddy wanted Lee back under his thumb. He started putting pressure on her by getting Eniston fired from his job, having them thrown out of one apartment after another. Then he threatened to have the baby taken away from her as soon as it was born."

He took a deep breath. "When Lee found out he'd already taken steps to do so, she decided to go to the newspapers and tell her story. She asked me to do the same, hoping that if both of us talked, *someone* would believe us. Even if they didn't, the publicity would have destroyed my father's career. I think that would have made Lee happy, too. But it would have destroyed my career, too, and I couldn't let that happen."

"You killed her for *that?*" Robyn cried.

"Can you imagine what my chances would have been if the newspapers had gotten that story? God! The name of Hauck would have been shit, and my career over before I'd even been through college. You know what these good old boys are like. You can drink, fight, ball anything in skirts, but you've got to be *manly* about it. If they knew about me, they'd only be able to think about how my father had been screwing my ass. Then he'd have won. He would have managed to fuck up my adult life just like he'd fucked up my childhood."

"Ten years ago," Robyn said, "when Daddy had his stroke, you were the one who suggested I take care of him. I hate him. I hate the sight of him. But because you asked me to, I took care of him. I bathed him, fed him, changed his diapers . . ." She drew a breath that was half a sigh, half a sob. "All

346

those years. I did it for you, John. I did it for you."

He strode to her. Slowly, as though she were a bird that might fly from him, he reached up to stroke the back of his free hand along her cheek. "And I'm grateful for it," he said. "I didn't have to worry about him babbling what he knew to a stranger."

"Ballard *knew?*" Sophie gasped.

"Of course he knew, Mother. I told him. I went in to Robyn's room just as he was introducing her to the joys of sodomy, and I stopped him. I told him I'd just killed two women, and if he touched one of us kids again, I'd kill him, too."

He cocked his head to one side. "And what do you think he did about it, Mother? He started covering his ass—and mine, incidentally—by making sure Eniston got nailed. He didn't give a fuck about Lee dying. Just his career."

"A father protecting his son—" Sophie began.

"Stop it!" he shouted. "Just . . . stop it. All my life I've listened to you make excuses for him, watched you worship him. He wasn't worth it. Didn't you ever wonder why Eniston didn't get the electric chair for what he did? Don't you think that with all his influence, Daddy couldn't arrange to put him there?"

"I—"

"Sure he could," John continued. "The old bastard pulled every string there was to keep Eniston *out* of the electric chair. And why? Because he knew Eniston was like an ax hanging over my head. He didn't care if it ever fell, as long as he could enjoy me squirming beneath it."

His gaze turned inward. "I gave Lee a chance. I went to her that day, tried to talk her out of going to the press. But she was just like Daddy when it came to stubbornness. She'd made up her mind to break him, and by God, she was going to do it. I knew I had to stop her. I saw Eniston's gun lying on the nightstand, and something clicked off in me. It was like watching someone else's hand pick up the gun, someone else pointing it, someone else pulling the trigger."

"And did someone else kill Serafina Zios?" Maris asked. "Did someone else kill Ella?"

"*I* killed them," he said. "You know, Maris, for someone who's done so well until now, you're missing the obvious question. Why don't you ask *why* I had to kill Ella Zios after all this time?" Without waiting for a reply, he continued, "You see, she came to me a couple of weeks ago, demanding money. Blackmail."

"So you paid her with a bullet."

"That's cliche, Maris. I would have expected better from me. But yes, I shot her. It's the only good way of dealing with a blackmailer. Do you want to hear why she was doing it?"

"Do I have a choice?"

"No. When I killed Lee, I didn't know the midwife was in the other bedroom, tending the baby. When the woman heard the shots, she grabbed the baby and went down the fire escape. I didn't catch up to her until after she'd gotten rid of the baby. Ella happened to see her mother going into that trailer park and followed her. She saw Serafina put the box under the trailer, but didn't figure things out until you came back to Houston a few weeks ago."

Maris clasped her hands together to keep them from shaking.

"You see where I'm heading, don't you?" John asked.

"Yes." She knew he was toying with her, with them all. He'd killed one sister and ruined another's life for his own gain. The lousy. . . . "Talk about theatrics," she said, hoping her voice fully conveyed her contempt. "Why don't you say it and get it over with?"

"All right," he said. "I'll say it. You're Lee's daughter, come back to haunt me after thirty-four years."

"Lee's . . . daughter?" Sophie gasped.

"Why did you let me get away all those years ago?" Maris asked. "Why didn't you finish the job?"

"Do you think I wouldn't have if I'd been able? I held the midwife for a while to ask her some questions. Under . . . let's call it duress—"

"Come on, Senator. Call it torture," Maris snapped.

"Under *duress*." His eyes dared her to challenge it, the gun convinced her to remain silent. After a moment, he smiled. "Under duress, Serafina told me she'd left the baby in a spot where it was unlikely that anyone would find it. A newborn, lying out in the open. . . . Well, after three or four days, I figured the kid was dead. But I couldn't be sure. All these years, I've wondered, doubted, suffered."

He flung his arms wide. "Haven't I suffered enough? Thirty-four years of looking over my shoulder. . . . Everything is in my grasp, the culmination of my whole life's efforts. Tell me, is it fair to have that threatened? Is it fair for a man's life to be haunted the way mine has been? Is it fair to come back from a business trip to be told the greatest threat to my safety has just been issued an invitation to live in my mother's house?"

"John—" Sophie began.

"It's your fault!" he shouted. "Why did you have to listen to Keir? Why did you think I needed your goddamn help to get elected?" He took several deep breaths, regaining control with a visible effort. "In a way, I suppose it turned out for the best. I was able to keep my eye on things—"

"How convenient," Maris murmured.

"Now, everything is falling into place. Eniston is making it easy for me. As soon as I get things cleared up here, I can get my life back on track."

Get things cleared up. Maris stared at him, only now realizing how far over the edge he'd gone. There was no conscience there, nothing in his soul but ambition. No one was real except John Hauck. *Get things cleared up.* She was only an inconvenience, one that would be swept aside, and responsibility laid somewhere else. The senator was too powerful to be touched, too rich to be thwarted.

She didn't want to die. Not here, not now, not like this. In a desperate bid for time, she decided to play to John's self-absorption.

"It must have been quite a shock when Ella told you who I really am," she said.

"Ella?" he repeated. Then he grinned, a terrible parody of his campaign smile. "I knew long before she came along," he said. "I've known since your first ad in the Personals section. That's when I sent someone up to St. Louis to take care of the problem—"

"You burned my house!" *I almost lost Cyndi in that fire.* Anger did a hot dance in her guts. "A lot of things are starting to make sense now, Senator."

"Like the truck that ran you off the road on your way down here? Like the time you were given my mother's Xanax instead of Tylenol?"

350

"What about the Cadillac's brakes?" she asked.

"An impulsive act, born of opportunity. If I'd known more about cars, I would have gotten both the front *and* rear brakes. I should have paid more attention to Alejo's lectures on automobiles, eh?" His voice hardened. "You managed to survive it all. You're a very lucky woman, Maris."

"You lied," she said. "You lied about being tested, and you lied to keep Robyn from being tested, too."

"Of course I lied," he said. "I couldn't allow the kind of questions that would come up if my sister matched, could I?"

"My daughter needed . . ." Cold rage made Maris reckless. "You bastard!" she hissed.

He only smiled. "That's the pot calling the kettle black, isn't it?"

Lightning struck somewhere close, filling the kitchen with searing platinum light. Maris jumped to her feet, only to find herself staring into the muzzle of the gun.

"Go stand by the refrigerator," he said.

Thunder rolled, died. Rain began to fall on the tile roof with renewed force, filling the house with sound.

"The weather's getting worse," John said. "Is it a good day to die, Maris?"

"It's never a good day to die, Senator."

"Now I"—he tapped his chest—"would love to go out amid the thunder and lightning. Almost like applause, don't you think?"

"Are you planning to shoot me in front of two witnesses?" Maris asked, staring into the grim, dark eye of the gun. "Or are you planning to kill them, too?"

"These aren't witnesses, Maris. This is my mother and my sister. They're not going to tell on me." Smiling, he waggled the gun from side to side. "Look at Robyn. Lovely, isn't she? But she's afraid of men, of sex, of life. I'm the only thing standing between her and the world. Do you think she's going to be able to make it on her own? She'll protect me if only to protect herself."

He swung around to face Sophie. "And Mother. Dear, doting, ambitious Mother. Nothing is dearer to her than the Hauck name, nothing more important than getting a Hauck into the governor's mansion. Daddy failed her. But now the prize is being dangled again. Mother of the governor is almost as good, don't you think? If she was willing to give up her children for one, why shouldn't she give some stranger's bastard up for the other?"

Maris glanced at the old woman, seeking denial. But Sophie's gaze was turned inward, focused on something only she could see—something terrible enough to drain the Hauck pride from her shoulders. The flesh of her cheeks looked sunken, and even the strong lines of her jaw seemed blurred. Whatever she was thinking, it had nothing to do with saving Maris's life.

Maris turned to Robyn. The other woman returned her gaze, then slowly looked away.

John laughed. "You see, Maris?"

"Yes," she said. "I see."

"Lee might have been your mother, but you're no Hauck," John said. "We're conquerors. Get in our way, and we'll destroy you."

"Even your own sister?"

Before he could answer, Robyn turned around. There was moisture glistening on her cheeks. "That's how we are. The Haucks either destroy or are destroyed. There's no middle ground. We're

352

just born twisted, I guess. Even our love is sick."

"Oh, Robyn! Did *he* tell you that?" Maris asked. The look on Robyn's face confirmed her guess. "Well, he lied! You were born as pure and innocent as anyone else in the world. That was *taken* from you, first by your father when he abused you, and then by John when he made you carry the burden of his sins."

Robyn shook her head.

"An interesting theory," John said. "But wrong. Robyn, why don't you tell Maris who wrote those nasty little notes that upset her so?"

"I wrote them." Robyn's voice was flat and dead.

Maris could only stare.

"John didn't even know I did it. I . . . was frightened when I saw your ad in the newspaper. I wanted to discourage you."

"So there you go, Maris." The triumph on John's face was an insult. "You know, I'm downright grateful to Drew Eniston for escaping from prison at such a convenient time. He was the perfect patsy before, and he will be again. The ravening killer strikes again—God, it's so easy!"

He raised the gun and aimed it at her forehead.

I wonder if it will hurt, Maris thought. *Oh, Cyndi!*

"John, no!" Robyn shrieked, making a lunge for the revolver. "This isn't—"

John swung his arm in a short, vicious arc, catching her on the jaw with the barrel of the gun. She went down, hitting the back of her head on the hard tile floor. She didn't get back up. He looked down at her, his expression one of contempt and a strange sort of tenderness.

"In a way, I wish you had the guts to betray me,"

353

he said. "But I know better." His gaze shifted to Maris. "You tried hard to give her some backbone, but it was bound to fail."

"She tried to stop you, didn't she?" Maris asked.

"Only because she thought she was going to have to watch. But when presented with a *fait accompli,* she'll do exactly what she did when Lee died: let me protect her from the ugliness and the consequences so she can go on with her blind, comfortable little life. And so will my mother. Right, Mother?"

Sophie didn't respond, didn't even glance at the limp form sprawled at John's feet.

"Come on, Maris," John said. "It's time for you to go."

Twenty-six

"Don't even think about running," John said, grabbing Maris's wrist as she went past.

He twisted her arm behind her back and marched her toward the front of the house. She bit her lip against the pain, refusing to give him the satisfaction of hearing her cry out. Or cry.

When they reached the foyer, he paused, dragging her back against him. "So, Maris. Tell me what it feels like to know that bastard Eniston is your father?"

"A whole lot better than knowing you're my uncle," she spat.

He jerked her arm upward, and for a moment she thought he'd broken it. Gasping, she went up onto her tiptoes in an attempt to ease the pressure.

"You put up a good front," he said. "But deep down you're just like him. Poor white trash, trying hard to live off your betters. Neither of you had sense enough to know when to back off."

"You call yourself better?" she hissed. "You killed your own sister. Shot her down while she begged—"

He jammed the gun beneath her ear, and Maris froze, inside and out. *I take it back!* her mind shrieked, but she clamped her lips shut against the words.

"I'm not going to let you goad me into screwing this up," he said. "Much as I'd like to do it now" — the muzzle dug in a little deeper — "I can't. You see, the beauty of this is making Eniston take the rap — again. But since no one knows where he is, I'm going to have to take you somewhere out in the countryside. Hell, as long as I'm careful, I could probably kill twenty people and still get Eniston to take the blame."

He reached around her to open the front door. Using the gun as a prod, he urged her out onto the porch. Rain pummeled her with brutal force, and the wind slapped wet tendrils of hair against her face.

Her Regal was still parked at the bottom of the stairs, looking sad and disreputable beside the Cadillac.

"Get in," John shouted against the wind.

"Which one?"

"Yours." He dangled her keys in front of her. "You left them in the ignition. A very bad habit, Maris. Anyone could get them."

If she let him get in that car with her, she was dead.

She had to do something. But the muzzle of the gun pressed against her spine, deadly reminder of what would happen if she tried to run. *Die now, or die later,* the cynical part of her mind whispered. *At least it will be on your terms, not his.*

Terror rode her as she started down the stairs, testing the slippery concrete beneath her tennis shoes. There was some traction, not much, but more than John had in those expensive dress shoes. A bolt of lightning sizzled overhead, and a moment later a clap of thunder rolled through the air, so loud it was like a physical blow. John flinched. Maris flung herself forward and down, breaking his hold, and skidded painfully down the steps on her hands and knees.

Before she could recover, his hand clamped in her hair.

"Get up," he snarled.

For a moment she resisted his pull. Then she surged to her feet, driving her shoulder into his midsection as she came up. His leather-soled shoes slithered for a moment on the wet surface, then went out from under him. He fell heavily on the steps; the gun went in one direction, the keys in another.

There was one chance, and Maris took it. Scooping the keys up, she scrambled to her feet and dove for the Regal.

The engine sputtered, rolled, died. Her teeth chattered as she fought the upwelling panic. She tried again. Out of the corner of her eye, she saw John straighten, caught the reflection of lightning on metal.

The engine coughed to life, and she slammed the accelerator to the floor. The wheels spun for a moment on the wet concrete; then the car shot forward, its rear end slewing wildly as she made the turn onto the road.

The road was several inches deep with water, her only guide the fenceposts that sprouted like mushrooms from the flooded land. Rain slashed across her windshield much too fast for the wipers to deal with effectively. The storm closed in behind her, hiding Gavilan behind a watery veil.

A sign loomed in the drenched dimness just

ahead. It said "Hauck, Texas, 6 miles." Six miles to safety. And then John would be exposed like an insect beneath an overturned rock, squirming in the bright light of day.

Headlights glared suddenly in her rearview mirror. The sleek, dark shape of the Cadillac appeared, coming fast. It looked like a vast, metallic beast of prey, spewing water from beneath all four wheels.

"Go, go!" she cried to the Regal, straining forward as though to lend her energy to the car.

The Cadillac gained steadily. There was no way the Regal was going to be able to outrun the more powerful car. Maris weaved from side to side across the road, risking a plunge into the ditch in the hope of keeping him from coming up beside her.

Lightning stabbed down all around, turning the world into an incandescent Hell. And in the car behind her, the devil himself. She could see him now. The searing light cast strange, angular shadows beneath his brows and cheekbones, glinted off his bared teeth.

She jerked the steering wheel right, then left, aware that the Cadillac was only a few feet off her rear bumper. John stayed with her, those white, white teeth gleaming to match his car's expensive front grille.

"God, if you're up there, this is the time to show yourself," she said.

But no lightning bolt came to hit the Cadillac, no Hand of God to punish the guilty.

Her breath came with a rasp that was audible even through the noise of the storm. Terror clamped her hands on the steering wheel, giving her the strength to drive recklessly enough to keep the Cadillac to her rear.

A voice kept whispering, *"You're going to see your daughter again, you're going to see your daughter. . . ."*

It took her a while to realize the voice was her own. Right, left, weave, slide . . . she used every trick she could think of to keep John from reaching her. He might have rammed her, sending her off the road, but she knew he was thinking of the police and their forensic labs, and detectives scraping the Regal's paint from his fancy grille.

Something whined past her ear, and a hole appeared in the windshield. Moisture spattered into the car. God, that had been close! She nearly lost her grip on the steering wheel as panic clutched her chest with cold skeleton hands.

"You bastard!" she sobbed. "You goddamn bastard!"

He had nothing to lose, now that she was some distance from Gavilan. If he shot her, Drew Eniston would get the blame; if she killed herself trying to get away from him, well, so much the better. She could hear him now, holding a press conference, that smooth, well-modulated voice throbbing with regret as he told of his guest's unfortunate demise. Getting the sympathy vote.

"No," she said, wrapping her fingers more firmly on the steering wheel. "No."

She let the Regal drift to the right a few feet. John took swift advantage. As the Cadillac's grille came even with her car's rear fender, Maris suddenly wrenched the steering wheel to the left. The Cadillac veered away, almost going off the road, and a moment later was hidden by the driving rain.

"Another couple of miles," she said aloud, just be-

cause the sound of her own voice was comforting.
"A couple of minutes, just give me—"

She slammed on the brakes. A few hundred yards
ahead, a river was flowing across the road, deep
enough to form a current. Trapped. She was trapped.
Behind her, a faint gleam of headlights marked the
Cadillac's approach.

"God damn it!" she cried, beating her palms on
the steering wheel. "God damn it to hell!"

Then she spotted a gap in the fence a few yards
ahead. Beyond it squatted the boxy shape of a
switching station. She made a tight, sweeping turn
onto the drive, flinging up a graceful fantail of water, then backed up so she was facing the opposite
direction. The twin glaring orbs of the Cadillac's
headlights came swiftly nearer, the hunter homing
on the quarry's blood-scent.

"You want me, come get me," she said, slamming
the Regal into drive and hurling it forward, straight
toward her enemy.

The Cadillac shied away, nearly plowing into the
ditch on the left-hand side of the road. Maris caught
a glimpse of John's face as she zoomed past. He
shouted something at her, his hand a flashing white
blur in the dark interior of the car.

The gun, the gun! He's going to shoot!

Light blossomed at the end of the gun, almost immediately eclipsed by the brighter flare of lightning.
Maris heard only the thunder; but a second hole appeared in her windshield, and another smashed a
crater in the front of the stereo. Hot plastic stung
her hands and face.

She was headed straight into the teeth of the
storm. There seemed to be no demarcation between
earth and sky; both were slate gray and aboil with

wind. The steering wheel bucked in her hands as she fought to keep the car steady.

And behind her, headlights. So she drove into the whirl of wind and water, pushing the pace past all sense. But there was a madman after her, and only crazy recklessness was going to save her. Lightning danced among the clouds, a stitchery of fire. She flinched as a massive bolt stabbed at the earth, groping along the ground as though searching for prey. Transformers blew all along the road, arcing brilliant aqua sparks into the sky.

The headlights came closer and closer, filling her rearview mirror with blinding yellow light. Terror closed her throat, or she might have screamed.

As her hands moved the wheel, weaving the car right, then left, then right again, her brain skittered from panic to reason and back again. Finally, she no longer knew the boundaries between them. One thing was certain: no matter what happened to her today, he wasn't going to get away with it. He wasn't going to go free. *He wasn't going to have a chance to get his hands on Cyndi.*

She drifted to the left, allowing the Cadillac to ease up on her right fender, almost close enough to touch. Certainly close enough to shoot. John drove with his left hand, fighting the wind, his other hand holding the gun awkwardly across his body.

Instinct made her flinch to one side just as he fired. There was another yellow flash, and another, then the glass of her window shattered outward. Rain slashed across her face. Her breath sobbing in her throat, she wrenched the steering wheel hard to the right.

Metal shrieked, louder than the storm. The steering wheel tried to tear itself from her hands, but she hung on desperately, steering left, then right again. Again, metal squealed as the two cars scraped fenders.

The Cadillac fell away. Headlights and taillights swapped places in her rearview mirror as it spun out of control. A moment later, she saw it come to rest sideways across the road. Steam coiled up from beneath the hood.

Safe. He can't follow me. I'm safe!

Her hands started to shake. She was going to live. Almost giddy with reaction, she slung her hair back from her face with a toss of her head. "And now I'm going to town, Senator. It's time to pay the piper; I'm going to burn you."

Something big and white flew out of the storm in front of her. A horn blared. Reflexes took over, and she veered sharply to avoid a collision. It took her a moment to realize that the thing was a car, moving at top speed.

And there, a few hundred yards away, the Cadillac squatted across the road.

"No! Look out!" Maris jammed the brake pedal to the floor, as if to stop the other car. The Regal shuddered to a halt; the newcomer did not.

The white car plowed into the Cadillac with a force that sent chunks of metal flying into the air. Time seemed suspended, and the vehicles appeared to move in a terrible, slow-motion dance. They compressed, pleated, almost seeming to meld into one, then broke apart to spin almost lazily to opposite sides of the road.

"Oh, my God!" Maris gasped. She flung her door open and splashed through ankle-deep water toward the other cars.

The Cadillac was nearest. It had been hit on the

driver's side, and had crumpled inward around the point of impact. The inside of the starred and broken windshield looked as if someone had slung a bucket of red paint against the glass.

She approached cautiously, her body anticipating danger even though her mind told her nothing could have survived that crash. John lay across the torn and broken seat — at least part of him did. His legs were thrust beneath the steering wheel, his feet still resting on the pedals. But his lower torso looked as though it had been stretched and broken by a giant's hand. Blood and bone and pieces of things whose identity Maris didn't want to know floated upon the seat.

Only his eyes were recognizable. They stared back at her, unseeing, tiny flecks of blood dotting the whites.

Maris staggered backward. She tripped over something in the water, came down hard on her buttocks, then scrambled to her feet again. For a moment she stood panting, fighting the urge to vomit, and an even stronger urge to run. Rain beat down on her head and shoulders and ran in rivulets down her face. It tasted salty, however, so she knew some of it was tears.

Slowly, she turned to look at the other car. She couldn't even tell what kind it was; there was little there but a mass of twisted metal.

She had to force herself to walk forward. The water dragged at her feet; the storm muttered and spat overhead as though to warn her off. Steam poured out of what was left of the engine compartment. The windshield was gone, the frame bent into a sharp vee. And inside, a shape.

Maris's breath went out in a hiss. Had that figure

moved, or was it the effect of the steam and the rain? Adrenaline went through her with a rush, and she broke into a run.

The driver's face was all bloody, but the tumbled white hair told Maris who it was. There was no sign of life. Gently, she touched the old woman's cheek.

"Sophie?" she murmured. "Oh, Sophie."

She started to turn away, but a twitch of Sophie's eyelids froze her in place. The old woman's mouth opened, showing bloody stumps of broken teeth.

"John . . . ?" she asked.

"Dead," Maris said. "Don't try to talk. Just save your strength. I'm going to get help."

"No. Too late. Stay . . . with me."

"But you need an ambulance."

The old woman shook her head, a small gesture that was full of pain. Maris leaned closer, peering into the interior of the car. A moment later she drew back. Sophie was right; there was no need for an ambulance.

Maris took a deep breath, then reached in and put her hand on Sophie's shoulder. "I'll stay with you until the end," she said.

The old woman's gaze remained on her, trusting. Seconds ticked away, seeming like hours. Overhead, the storm was grumbling its way north. Rain was still falling, but it had gentled. It sluiced the blood from Sophie's face, falling away in pink streams to be lost in the crimson lake that filled the floor of the car.

"Maris—" the old woman began.

"Shhh. Save your strength."

"For what?" Almost, she smiled. "Talk to me. Too much silence in my life. Don't let me go out in the silence."

"I don't know what to talk about," Maris said

"This seems like a good time to pray, but I stopped believing in prayers when my husband died. I'm not sure I remember the words."

"Don't pray," Sophie said. "Forgive."

"Forgive John?"

"No. Me. I . . . made him."

"Sophie—"

"I made him. So stupid not to see what he'd become . . . what he'd always been. Ah!" She bared her teeth in a rictus of pain.

Gently, Maris smoothed the old woman's white hair. "Is that why you felt you had to do this? Oh, Sophie. This wasn't the way at all."

"Yes. John . . . killed Lee. My fault. Wanted too much for him . . . for me. I brought him into this world. So many lives, so much pain. . . . It was my job to stop him."

Maris shook her head, appalled at the price the old woman had been willing to pay. And why not? Today she'd learned that her beloved Ballard was no conquering hero, but a sordid, nasty pedophile. She'd learned that her favorite son was a murderer who had cold-bloodedly shot his own sister to death. Sophie's world had crumbled. She had put so much of her life into the two men who had betrayed her most that dying was the only option for her.

Tears stung Maris's eyes. Tears for the woman's pain, yes, but also for the two children she still didn't know how to love or to live for.

"Sophie, what do you want me to say to Robyn and Garrick—"

"Please!" The old woman strained forward, her eyes wide with pain and need. "Please. Forgive me."

Maris couldn't deny that need. "I forgive you."

Life fled Sophie's eyes.

"I'll say the words for you," Maris said. She closed the old woman's eyelids, then smoothed her white hair once more before straightening.

Some people might have said that justice had been served. But this justice tasted like vengeance, and bitter.

Twenty-seven

Dark clouds to the south heralded still more bad weather as Maris drove back to Gavilan. *I'm coming, Cyndi. As soon as I find out where you are, I'm coming.*

The house sat sullenly beneath the dripping branches of the big cottonwood tree. Maris parked the car and ran up the steps, praying the telephone still worked. The air inside the house was hushed and closed, an atmosphere that even the sound of the rain on the tile roof didn't quite penetrate. Maris broke that stillness, her wet shoes squeaking on the tiles as she hurried through the foyer toward the nearest phone.

Cyndi. Cyndi. Cyndi. It beat through her with her pulse, making her fingers shake as she punched Keir's number.

"Come on," she muttered. "Come on."

Three rings, four. Then Keir's answering machine came on. 'I can't come to the phone just now . . .'

Maris beat her fist on the edge of the table. "Damn it!"

The message droned on. Just as Maris was about to hang up, however, she heard Keir's recorded voice say, "Maris, Cyndi's safe. She's with me. We talked

367

Eniston into giving himself up, so we're taking him over to the police station now. I'll bring her down as soon as I can."

"Oh . . ." Maris's breath went out with a rush, and she had to close her eyes against a sudden deluge of tears. "Thank you, God!"

A faint noise brought her swinging around, heart pounding, to see Robyn standing in the doorway. She was wearing a neat navy blue suit and white blouse, with a red scarf that lay like a wound upon her breast. Her face revealed nothing of what was going on inside her.

Maris did not want to deal with another Hauck. But this one had tried to save her life, and Maris owed her. Not only for the act itself, but for having the courage to be the person she was *supposed* to be, not what the Haucks had made her. A lot of debts had been paid today; this was the last, and the easiest.

"Are my mother and brother dead?" Robyn asked.

Bland words, delivered without visible emotion. Maris gave the news the same way. "Yes, they're both dead. I'm sorry."

"Mother told me she was going to make sure he didn't hurt anyone else."

"That she did."

There was a long, awkward moment of silence. Then Maris gave her the only thing she could, knowing it wouldn't be enough. "She said to tell you she loved you."

"No, she didn't, but thank you for trying," Robyn said. "Have you called the police yet?"

"No, but I'm going to."

"Could we talk for a few minutes first? I have something very important to tell you."

368

Maris followed her into the living room. Robyn sat in the armchair nearest the sofa and gestured for Maris to take the seat opposite.

"I want to explain," Robyn said. "About the letters, I mean."

"It doesn't matter."

"Yes, it does. I did it because I was afraid. First, for John. Later, I did it because I was afraid of John. He started acting strange, just like before he'd killed Lee."

"Was it you who called Keir in D.C. and told him I was in danger?"

Robyn nodded. Her voice was as calm and steady as though she were talking about the weather. "All my life, I worshipped my big brother. I would have worshipped anyone who stopped Daddy from doing . . . what he'd been doing to me. When John said he'd no choice but to kill Lee, I believed him. When he said I was too damaged, too fragile to go out alone into the world, I believed him. When he said I was weak and malleable, I believed him. And I became all those things.

"It wasn't until you came that I began to realize I might not be as weak and malleable as I'd thought. John said you had to be stopped, that you would dig and dig until you destroyed this family."

"He wasn't so far off, was he?" Maris asked, surprised by the bitterness in her voice — and in her soul. Until now, she hadn't realized just how hard guilt was riding her.

"Yes, he was! If he hadn't killed Lee in the first place, if he hadn't let an innocent man pay the price, all our lives would have been different. We wouldn't have been walking a tightrope to preserve his secrets. And you would have known who you were."

And I would have grown up a Hauck, with old Pa-trón Ballard as my loving grandpa. "I've had a good life," she said.

"I envy you that," Robyn said. "Although if I'd had the courage, I wouldn't have let them convince me I was nothing."

"I'm sorry," Maris said. And was. True, Robyn had let herself be victimized. But she'd been so young when it began, and the woman had been built on the child's pain.

"When you and Cyndi came, everything changed," Robyn said. "I watched the two of you together, and saw how you loved each other, how you helped each other through the hard times, and how you relied on each other's strength. You *listened* to her. For the first time, I began to realize what I had missed. I wanted . . . I wanted . . ." Her gaze faltered.

"Say it."

"I wanted to be part of it, just a little. I didn't know how to go about it at all. Then the night of the firebombing, Cyndi took me by the hand and just sort of expected me to comfort her, and there it was. I was afraid you would push me out—believe me, my family never shared anything, not even love. But you let me stay."

Tears welled up in her eyes, then spilled over. She made no attempt to wipe them away. Maris half-rose, intending to put her arms around the other woman, but Robyn shook her head.

"The last note was written to scare you away," she said. "For your sake, and Cyndi's. I know it wasn't enough, and wrong, but it was as far as I could go against John at that point. I'm sorry if I hurt you."

"I forgive you," Maris said softly.

Robyn blotted her eyes with the back of her hand.

"Alejo came back a few minutes ago, and I sent him into town with some papers that had been in Daddy's private safe for thirty-four years. They contain evidence that John killed our sister. I also typed out my own statement and signed it, telling what I should have told long ago."

"Why?"

"I wanted to be sure everything was made right."

Made right. God, Maris thought, how could things be made right when so many people had died? "Robyn, your mother and brother died today. Don't you feel anything?"

Robyn got up and went to the window, putting her back to Maris. "I feel angry. I feel cheated. But mostly, I feel . . . relieved. It's over, the only way it could be over."

"No!" Maris cried. "It didn't have to be that way. Your mother didn't have to kill today. She didn't have to die."

"Yes, she did." Robyn whirled, letting her pain show for the first time. It was stark and powerful, and hit Maris hard. "You see, there was no such person as Sophie Hauck. There was only the senator's wife, or the senator's mother. When that was taken from her, dying was the only thing she could do. At least she did the world a favor and took John with her."

Maris opened her mouth, then slowly closed it again. It was a hell of an ugly truth, but impossible to deny. Maybe tomorrow she would be able to, but not today.

Reaching into her pocket, Robyn pulled out a piece of folded paper. "Here," she said, holding it out.

Maris took it, unfolded it slowly. It said, "Maris, I

371

want you to have this. It's little enough for what we have cost you." It was signed "Robyn Jean Hauck," and witnessed by Alejo Gomez. Stapled to the bottom was a check, written on a money market account, for . . . her mind skipped a beat. A half-million dollars. "Wh . . . what is this?"

"Daddy gave us each our own money when we turned twenty-five. Lee never got hers. I figure you're entitled to it."

"I can't take this."

"It will pay for Cyndi's transplant."

"So it will." Maris looked down at the check again, trying to assimilate all the zeros. "But—"

"Take it. At least one unselfish thing will be bought with Hauck money. Please, Maris."

"Since you put it that way, thanks."

"I phoned the Hauck National Bank to tell them what I was doing. They'll be glad to open an account for you today. I think you'll find that easier than going to another bank, at least for now."

"I don't suppose many banks are going to want to cash a check for five hundred thousand dollars," Maris said.

"Probably not." One corner of Robyn's mouth quirked upward.

"That's the first time I've heard you make a joke," Maris said.

"I think it's the first time I've tried to make a joke."

Maris studied the other woman closely. "Why this thing with the check and letters and phone calls? Why don't you just wait to tell your story to the police?"

"Because I'm leaving for good as soon as we're finished talking."

"Leaving?" Maris asked in astonishment. "Why? Where are you going?"

"Anywhere. Everywhere. It's time this bird left the nest, don't you think? All my life, it seems I've been hiding. First, from my father, then from myself. But there's still time. I'm only forty-two. I can learn to live, maybe even love. But not here." She cocked her head to one side. "I think you could also learn to do a little living yourself."

She means Keir. "After today," Maris said, "that no longer scares me."

"Good." Robyn touched her fingertips lightly to Maris's cheek. "Thank you for what you and Cyndi have given me. But now that everything's been taken care of, I really do have to go. Oh, will you do me a favor and wait a half-hour or so before you call the police?"

A terrible suspicion bloomed in Maris's mind, claiming it with icy fingers. She reached out, intending to ask the question. Then she let her hand drop to her side. It was not up to her to judge Robyn; Man had made too many judgments this day, and she was willing to let God have this one. Or maybe Robyn. In this case, maybe she had more right to it than God.

"I hope you find happiness," she said.

"So do I." Robyn backed slowly out of the room. "Goodbye, Maris. When I get to wherever it is I'm going, I'll be sure to get tested for compatibility. Under another name, of course. Oh, and tell Cyndi I'd like her to have my collection of model horses."

"If you get a chance, look us up someday," Maris said. The check lay heavily in her hand. "Under the name Durant."

"Or Andreis."

373

"Now that's a possibility," Maris said.

Lieutenant Morales leaned over the bed and took the pillow off Ballard Hauck's face. The old man lay on his back, his face gray-white, his eyes bulging.

"He was like this when you found him?" Morales asked.

"Yes. I felt for a pulse, but other than that, I didn't touch anything," Maris said.

Looking down at the corpse, she felt nothing for him. No sympathy, no remorse, nothing. He had gone through lives like a tornado—hurting, destroying, twisting his children into broken-backed parodies of what they might have been.

"What time was it when you found him, Mrs. Durant?" the lieutenant asked.

"Right before I called you," she said. "I'm not sure what time it was; my watch got broken during my scuffle with John, and with the electricity off, the house clocks weren't working."

"You called us at two-twenty," he said. "Does that sound right?"

"Lieutenant, I spent my day either looking down the barrel of a gun or being chased by a murderer. I feel like I've walked through Eternity. If you said it was midnight, I'd have to take your word for it."

A smile came into his eyes, softening the hard cast of his face. "Let's see . . ." he flipped back through his notes. "After the crash in which the senator and his mother were killed, you came back here. Why?"

"The road to town was still blocked by water, and this was the closest phone. Also, Robyn had tried to stop her brother. He hit her pretty hard, and I wanted to be sure she was all right."

"She only stayed long enough to give you a check for half a million dollars."

"And to say goodbye."

"Rather a lot of money, isn't it?"

Maris nodded. "Bone marrow transplants cost a lot of money. Robyn wanted to be sure Cyndi could have hers."

"Do you have any idea why she left so suddenly and, as you say, for good?"

"She told me she was tired of being a Hauck. I can't say I blame her."

"And you think Senator Hauck killed his father?"

"He didn't *say* he did, and I didn't see him do it. But he did say he intended to get things cleared up so he could go on with his life." This was the only gift she could give Robyn, who didn't expect it, and might not want it. "I got the impression the senator wanted to make a clean sweep. And if you asked me, Ballard Hauck ranked right up there on the list of things to be swept."

Morales blew his breath out sharply. "This is one hell of a story you've told me, Mrs. Durant. I've got to admit it; if it weren't for the papers Robyn Hauck sent to us—"

"I know. I'd have been locked up as a raving lunatic. No one bucks the Haucks."

"No one bucks the Haucks without evidence," he corrected. "We've got that now. We called Garrick Hauck, and he confirmed the sexual abuse situation. He said, and I quote: 'If John finally killed the old bastard, then someone should give him a fucking medal.' "

"That sounds like Garrick."

"Drew Eniston will have to go back to prison until

things get straightened out, but I've already sent copies of the evidence to the attorney general's office. I expect Eniston will be a free man before you know it."

"It's about time," Maris said.

"I guess it is." Morales glanced down at Ballard's corpse. "So the great Senator Hauck was a child molester, huh? You know, my father voted for him. Twice. Told me he thought Ballard Hauck was a fine man, a man's man—"

"The *patrón*," Maris said, without trying to hide the bitterness in her voice.

"Yeah." He picked the pillow up from the floor and dropped it back onto the dead face. "I've seen enough. Let's get some fresh air."

A horn honked outside. Morales went to the window and looked out. Smiling, he glanced over his shoulder at Maris. "There's a guy down there, and a kid in a red baseball cap—"

Maris was out of the room before she realized she was running. "Cyndi!" she shouted as she ran down the stairs.

The front door opened. Cyndi and Keir stood poised in the doorway, framed by the lowering sky. They were the embodiment of her future, all the new dreams she now dared to face. She was no longer afraid.

"Mom, are you all right? We were so worried—"

"Come here, baby." Maris held her arms out.

Cyndi rushed to her, holding tight and hard. Time stuttered and stood still as Maris wrapped her arms around her child. For this brief, precious moment, none of it mattered. John, Sophie, Ballard—all the ugliness that had passed through this house—paled in the sheer joy of holding Cyndi again.

"I was so scared," Cyndi sobbed. "They told me he tried to kill you!"

Maris tried to smile, felt her lips tremble. "Yeah, hon, he tried. But he's gone for good now. He can't hurt anybody again."

She smoothed her daughter's short, bright hair, no longer regretting that it would be lost again. That loss was a step forward; she had learned that it was only the steps backward that should be regretted.

Gently, she tilted her daughter's face upward. "We're going to pack our stuff and rent an apartment as close to the hospital as we can, okay? There's no reason for us to come back here again."

Cyndi nodded, then buried her face against Maris's chest again. The tension drained out of her.

Maris looked at Keir over her daughter's head. He looked calm and composed, but there were worlds of emotion in his eyes. This time, it didn't frighten her.

"Come here," she said.

He smiled. His arms came around her and Cyndi, enclosing them, and Maris leaned her head against his shoulder.

"Are you all right?" he murmured.

"Yes," she said. "Now I am."

Twenty-eight

Drew Eniston looked different in street clothes. No less intimidating, but different. He glanced around the prison waiting room, his yellow-flecked eyes still fierce, still uncompromising.

Maris tried to calm the nervous twitch of her stomach. She hadn't expected him to come out, hat in hand, ready to kiss his new-found daughter, but a *little* softening would have been nice. To be honest, even a glimmer of uncertainty on that hard, lean face would have helped her along.

When his gaze found her, she rose from the hard plastic chair and went to him. "Hi," she said.

"Hi. Thanks for the clothes."

"You're welcome. Are you ready to go?"

"Yeah." He walked outside with her, his back stiff and tense as though he expected someone to grab him and pull him back inside.

Maris led the way to the car, wishing she knew what to say to him, wishing she hadn't come alone. But there were things that needed to be said. Even if he told her to go to hell afterward, she needed to say them.

378

"The results of the testing came back this morning. Did they tell you?" she asked.

"Hell, no. They told me goodbye, and good luck, and don't show your face around here again."

"You're a perfect match."

He shrugged. "I heard you had another match."

"Not as good as you."

"So you want your pound of flesh?"

"A few ounces," she said. "But yes, I want them."

"You don't have to worry. I got no problem donating a little bone marrow. Hell, that's nothing compared to what the Haucks took from me."

"Thanks." Maris might have hugged another person. But this man, who had already saved Cyndi's life once, and now was willing to do so again, was unapproachable. She took a deep breath; this next subject was going to be even harder for her. "The tests also showed you're my father."

"I didn't need any goddamn laboratory to tell me that." He thrust his hands deep into his pockets. "Were you afraid maybe Ballard Hauck might have been your father?"

"The thought crossed my mind," she said. "It wasn't a pleasant one."

"That bastard never touched her once she took up with me. I'd have killed him, and he knew it."

Thank God. Thank God it wasn't Ballard, another visitation of hell upon his family.

"How's the kid?" he asked.

"Doing fine. She said to tell you hello. I want to . . ." Her throat tightened, and it took her a moment to find her voice again. "I want to thank you for what you did. You saved her life."

He shrugged, absently rubbing at an almost-healed bite mark on his hand. "When I saw John

379

Hauck hustle the security people out of there, I knew something was going down. That's when I grabbed the kid."

"Did Cyndi do that?" Maris asked, pointing to his hand.

"This?" He glanced down at the semicircle of red marks. "Yeah. Got me good. Three weeks, and it's only now going away. She's a tough kid."

"Tougher than both of us put together, if she could convince you to turn yourself in."

"I found out I was too old for running," he said.

"But not for blowing up cars, huh?"

He turned that almost frighteningly intense gaze on her. "I thought you'd gone into the house."

Or didn't care who you killed, as long as you got John. Maris had had enough of hate. A few short weeks with the Haucks had given her a lifetime worth of it. She didn't want any more.

"Why did you break into my room that night?" she asked.

"I just wanted to talk to you. The Haucks weren't going to let me talk to you on the phone, so I took the only way I had."

"You scared the crap out of me."

"Scared is better than dead, which is how John would have had you."

They walked in silence after that. Maris felt cold inside despite the warmth of the sun beating down on her shoulders. The Regal was just ahead, its crumpled passenger side a gut-ramming reminder of how close she'd come to dying.

"You're going to have to get in my door," she said. "The passenger door doesn't open."

"John Hauck did that?" Eniston asked.

"Yes."

He waited for her to unlock the driver's door, then slid across to the other side. Maris got in after him, buckled her belt, then looked expectantly at Eniston.

"What?" he asked.

"Fasten your seat belt."

He looked at her with those strange, unfathomable eyes, then slowly pulled his belt across and locked it in.

Maris started the car. "Where do you want me to take you?"

"The nearest motel will do." The window grated as he rolled it down. "So, Sophie Hauck killed her own son. I wish I'd been the one to take him out."

Frustration made Maris savage. Once, Lee had loved this man. It was obvious he had loved her in return. But thirty-four years had passed, and she was beginning to think that his emotions had shriveled until they'd become as hard and lean as the man himself.

But he was her father. She had to try.

She slammed the car into park and turned it off. "All those years, you let people think you killed Lee and your baby. You signed a *confession*."

"That doesn't matter now."

"But it does! It does because you looked me in the eye and told me you killed that baby. You said that, knowing I was your daughter."

Suddenly he slumped, his elbows resting on his knees, his hands lying limp between his legs. "John shot Lee with my gun; my prints were all over it. The cops came down on me like thunder and lightning, and I knew I was screwed. When Ballard offered me a way out of the electric chair, I took it."

"What way?"

"He said that if I confessed to the murders, he'd

381

pull strings to get me prison instead of execution. And then he said he knew who had taken you and where, and that he'd keep that secret if I cooperated. I had no choice. It was the only way I could protect you. And one thing about Ballard: he was a royal sonofabitch, but he always kept his word."

Ballard Hauck again, Maris thought. *Manipulating those strings, making people jump.* "I'm surprised someone didn't kill him long ago," she said, surprising even herself.

Eniston laughed, a harsh sound. "If I'd had half a chance—"

"Will you quit?" she shouted. "I'm sick of hearing how you were going to kill this guy and that guy. You haven't killed *anybody.* You're ten times better than Ballard or John, and you ought to be damned glad of it!"

His eyes narrowed. "You got—"

"Look, do you have a problem with me?" she asked.

"What do you mean?"

"I don't know how to deal with you. I don't know what you want. Yes, you say you're willing to donate marrow for Cyndi, and I'm grateful for it. But afterward, are you going to walk out of our lives again?"

"Why should I stick around?"

"Because . . . because I want you to." A couple of months ago, she wouldn't have been able to take the risk of opening her heart. But she was different now.

He stared at her for a moment, the yellow flecks in his eyes almost seeming to whirl. "You going to stay in Texas?"

"Yes."

"With that Andreis fellow?"

"Uh-huh.. He's taken a job managing Tim

382

McPherson's campaign. I'm moving my mother and my jewelry business down here. I've already found some stores interested in carrying my designs."

With a grunt, he looked away. Maris's hopes shriveled. Well, she'd tried. Love wasn't always accepted; that didn't mean it had no worth. She could treasure it, let it warm her life.

She reached for the ignition key. Eniston's hand shot out, anchoring hers in a grip that hurt.

"All these years, the only thing that kept me sane was knowing you were safe from that bastard. And then you had to come down here and stay right in his goddamn house. I had to get you out of there. Scare you out, if that's what it took. I should have known you'd be too goddamn stubborn to be frightened away."

"What are you trying to say?" she asked.

"I want you to remember who you are. You're just like me, and so is that kid of yours. Both of you faced me down, stared me right in the eye and told me to go to hell. You don't think you got that kind of courage from the *Haucks,* do you?"

"Does that mean you're going to stick around?"

"You've got a one-track mind, just like Lee." His breath went out in an explosive sigh. "What the hell do you want someone like me for? I got years of hard living, years of hate behind me, and nothing in my future."

"You do, if you've got the courage to take it. I'm willing, and Cyndi's willing. What about you? Want to give it a try?"

He held her gaze for a moment, then let go of her hand. "I'll . . . think about it."

Maris studied him. Hard, lean, hammered as tough as leather by the life the Haucks had forged

383

for him. He had some healing to do. They all did. Right now, he was giving her Cyndi's life; maybe some time in the future, he'd let her into his.

"Take your time," she said.

Some days, you took what you could get.